Nov 19, 2019

ON
WINGS
OF A
LION

By

Susan Wakeford Angard

Dear Chandra
A good read is like
A good friend... Best
Susan Wakeford Angard

Tudor House

Editorial and production management by Flying Pig Media with typesetting and cover design by Kerry Ellis.

A CIP record for this book is available from the Library of Congress Cataloging-in-Publication Data.

ISBN: 978 1 73389 840 9

To

David Turner Carnell

*My intrepid brother, Dave, you
are always in my heart.*

For
Ed and Carol Sacks,
your treasured friendship
is beyond compare.

CHAPTER ONE

ABADAN, IRAN
August 25, 1978

"It's no use!" yelled Hans.

"Strike it again!" Anthony Evans shouted, steadying a crowbar wedged against the rear door jam of the barricaded *Sohbe Emrooz* newspaper building. His helicopter pilot Hans raised an ax high and slammed it into a rear door bolted from the outside, a SAVAK trademark.

The ski mask clung to his sweltering face in the afternoon sun, heightening Anthony's rage and increasing his anxiety about stopping these bastards. Though he would not survive the day if he was caught interfering with the Shah's Secret Intelligence and National Security Organization—the SAVAK.

A bearded student paced behind him, wringing his prayer beads, muttering a prayer begging Allah to save his family trapped inside. His white shirt was bright against a pale, worried face, a face Anthony could smack for his arrogant behavior. He'd been stupid enough to pit his family against the secret police, risking their lives.

Anthony could not rewrite his own history, but *this* family's suffering had to end today.

Inside the building, someone moaned.

"Once more!" Anthony shouted.

Hans swung, the bolt finally cracking to pieces under the weight of the ax head.

Anthony kicked in the door, and the two men exploded into the building.

Looming presses stood silent in the vast room where once they hummed with the business of printing news. Huge metal-cased windows were blackened like hooded eyes. Flames licked up the far wall, the smoke building into a thick cloud along the ceiling. Blood pooled across the linoleum floor, a whimpering child tugged at the arm of his prostrate father, smears following him. His sobbing mother clutched her husband's ankles, trying to tow him away from the blaze, her palms slippery against bloody flesh. Her face dripped sweat. She seemed oblivious to the two men in ski masks.

Anthony lifted his mask. "We have no time, Madame! We must go."

"Your accent. You are an infidel?"

"I'm a friend." Anthony held out his hand. "The SAVAK will return to make certain you're dead. You can't help him anymore. Come!"

The bearded student rushed up, coughing. "Maman, these men will help us. They help many. Please! Get up."

Tears streaked her face. "My son, you are safe." She

shuddered with relief, and then she clutched Anthony's hand, letting him help her up.

"It's my fault, Maman," the youth cried. "I ordered the type changed. I added a story charging SAVAK agents with the Rex Cinema fire. We thought they did it. . . ."

"Your father told you it was not SAVAK, son, yet you brought this to our door."

". . . but then I found out about the Black Glove," her son spoke over her words. "It was them . . . but I felt tortured."

"So you brought these Black Glove terrorists to us as well."

"My friends burned to death—so many," he sobbed. "I—I'm—forgive me, Maman."

Hans eased the clinging child away from his father and bent over the bleeding newspaper owner. "He looks bad, mate." Hans leaned down and gathered the man into his arms and picked him up.

Anthony lifted the younger child in one arm, using his other sleeve to wipe tears, blood, and soot from the small boy's face.

The woman looked past her elder son, her gaze following Hans as he carried her husband out of the building.

Anthony grabbed the young man's arm. "Take your little brother!" he yelled. "Get in the van. NOW."

The student let go of his prayer beads, grabbed his little brother, and ran after Hans.

Anthony heard his pilot shout from outside, "Hurry! Black Glove Lincolns have turned up the road."

Anthony yanked down his ski mask. It would be a

miracle if they made it to the airfield. "Madam, we must go now."

She stood frozen. "My home . . ."

Something ignited in the room. Molten glass splintered, spraying the room in shards, and Anthony exhaled, impatient.

"I'll apologize later," he said and hefted the woman over his shoulder, fleeing moments before the roof caved in.

HOLLYWOOD, CALIFORNIA, 1978

The morning dawned clear and bright; it was about 80 degrees in the Hollywood Hills. Panting from exertion, Kathryn Whitney jogged up the driveway of her little rental off Mulholland Drive.

She was waiting for Brett's decision: Would the Boeing shoot in Iran be hers to direct or not?

God, she needed this one. She was broke. Two long years without a decent directing job, scuffling to make ends meet on pay from industrials and infomercials had barely covered her rent.

She bent over, hands on her knees, cooling down on her tree-lined street, reveling in the physical release she always felt with exercise. Stretching, she pushed away niggling reminders of her precarious situation if this shoot didn't come through.

Inside her kitchen she brewed a Kona blend, turned on the stereo to Billy Joel's "Just the Way You Are" and brushed past tall birch shelves that housed her father's used but cared-for books. She almost choked on her longing to have him back again. Her chest rose and fell in a shuddering cadence as she ran her fingers along the spines of art and archeology volumes she loved for their legends, laws, and ways of life contained within. Her father had stoked this appreciation, and the images had all come alive for her, inspiring her concept for Boeing. She knew it was a winner.

You always said thirty-three was your best year, Dad. Well, let's hope it is for me, too. She headed for the shower.

Afterward, towel-drying her hair, she inhaled the scent of star jasmine wafting into the bedroom through sliding glass doors to her garden, enjoying a moment of peace. She heard the deep sound of Brett's Maserati Quattro Porte roaring up the driveway and slipped on her terry robe. *This was it.* He was here in person with his decision. Her body ran hot then cold, not knowing what was coming. Her peace evaporated. *Calm down, relax.*

Through her kitchen window she saw him get out of his car holding a large manila envelope, then walk around her 1963 vintage Porsche Carrera, eyeing the dented rear fender. She couldn't keep her eyes off the envelope. Was her answer inside?

He looked to be in a calculating mood—she could tell by his purposeful stride.

She eased the look of anxiety from her face, tightened her terry robe, and opened the front door before he rang the bell.

At forty-six, Brett was still alarmingly attractive. He eased past her into her house as she held the screen door open, one hand jammed into the pocket of his leather jacket, his head tilted back slightly.

He removed his sunglasses, his gaze piercing her composure as though he were doing her a favor by being there. She would see.

He shot one more glowering look over his shoulder at her car. His look softened and a smile spread across his face. "Porsche is a mess. I'll get you a new paint job, huh?" He leaned forward and pecked her cheek.

Why all the charm? Was this a yes? Or was he softening the blow?

"Thought you weren't going to race anymore," he said.

"I'm not." It had been three years since she'd raced, and she didn't need him to remind her.

She gestured for him to come farther into the house.

"Good. I couldn't stand to scrape you off another wall." He sauntered into her living room. As he scanned her simple faded chintz and country pine furnishings—so different from the lavish, ultra-modern Brentwood estate they had shared—his face changed from compassionate to serious.

"It's planes now, isn't it, Kathryn? Wings?" His fingers skimmed over some trophies grouped on a shelf. He brushed his hand over the etched crystal award from the American Film Institute for Best Short Film she had won after graduating film school, when she worked nights and weekends on a shoestring budget.-

"That's right," she said. "Aircraft. Clouds. Peace. No out-of-control corkscrew turns. No unforeseen oil slicks."

"But you've recovered beautifully. Not a scar on you."

None that anyone can see, anyway.

He picked up a Clio she won for an IBM commercial when she had started a fledgling production company three years ago. "You sure you want to direct, Kathryn? It's a big risk."

She ignored his comment, her eyes set on the envelope tucked now under his arm. Why was he delaying things when her future was in that package?

He looked at her with an incisive stare. "Great work. The glory days as a film school prodigy."

Kathryn glanced away, uncomfortable as Brett stroked the Clio statuette. She felt his gaze on her and flipped her damp, messy hair over her shoulder, self-conscious of her state of déshabille. She took the statuette from him and crammed it back on the shelf.

His voice grew soft. "You were my top student, Kathryn. The best."

"Is that a problem for you, Brett? That I'm not a school girl anymore?" She pointed at the row of trophies, all gathering dust, like her career. "Those years are long gone."

"I know. You graduated and went on to bigger and better things." His smirk was so arrogant she longed to slap his face.

"Very funny." She took another trophy away from him and scooted it back onto the shelf, her hand a little shaky.

He walked away, ambling through her house, into the bedroom, bathroom, then into her kitchen where he poured himself a cup of coffee. What was he looking for, a hidden lover?

She trailed behind, feeling violated by his presence. *Oh, please come in and step all over my life!* Instead she said nothing, keeping the peace for the sake of the Boeing job. He had no rights as her ex-husband, but she tread lightly because he might soon be her boss.

He scanned her work-covered kitchen table, drawings and aerial shots she'd long admired from a *National Geographic* magazine. He looked up at her, his mood changing. "Come on, Kat," he whispered, reaching over, brushing tousled hair off her forehead. "You know you adored me."

She had worshipped the air he breathed. "*Adored* you. Past tense." But not since she'd caught him bagging a script girl on location, her hurt and rage driving her into disaster. She shoved the memory away and poured orange juice for them both.

"I don't believe you," he said. "You haven't been with anyone since we split."

He moved closer.

She moved away and tried to switch the focus back to business. "How would you know? Right now I'm honoring our divorce bargain. I bring your company a major job, then I get to direct the shoot. Boeing—profit, prestige, Super Bowl, big budget." She searched deep into his eyes. "That was the deal. Are you fighting me?"

"I don't want to fight you," he said, his look heated, the corner of his mouth tilting upward as he edged forward until she felt herself pressed against the refrigerator. "Don't you remember how good it was between us?"

She pushed him away. "We're not doing this, Brett."

He grabbed her upper arms, his hungry gaze deepening. "I want to make you feel something again."

"Stop it." Kathryn jerked away, appalled, pushing painful memories away, pushing him away. She lowered her gaze. "Haven't we hurt each other enough by now?"

"You left me." Brett pulled her to him.

She yanked back away from his arms. "Don't touch me, Brett. I went running and—"

"You're such a jock! You can't face your emotions so you play ball, race cars, fly planes—any fucking sport to avoid feeling, right?"

"Since when do you care what I feel?" She straightened.

"You use your body to cover your emotions—which isn't all bad with a body like yours."

"Cut to the chase, Brett. What's in the envelope?"

The fire in his eyes changed from desire to something she'd seen often: petulant anger.

He stepped back, folding his arms across his chest. "I've decided. Whitney Productions will do the Boeing shoot. But you're not going to Iran, Kathryn. I'm going to direct this one."

Kathryn's heart plummeted like an elevator out of control, crushing her dreams.

"What?" She shook her head. "What do you mean? I've brought a key job to your production house."

"Wake up, Kathryn. You're not cut out for this business." He shook his head. "This production is too big for you. It's in the Middle East, for Christ's sake."

Brett's words washed over her like a bad dream. "No."

"Women have no power in that country," he said. "You'd be lost in Iran."

"I'm good on location. We both know that. I'll be surrounded by crew, Peter, Buzz—professionals."

"The *hell* you will." He stood up, stalked across the kitchen. "I can't risk you. I can't. You're not putting my company's rep on the line."

Dear God, he was bumping her off the shoot. Somehow she'd felt this coming. Once more he drove the knife in.

"They hired *me!*" She had taken his bait, damn it.

"Irrational. This is too much for you. Remember the last time?"

He shoved the knife in deeper. It hurt. How dare he throw old wounds in her face?

"*We* are leaving Tuesday, Brett."

He towered over her. "No. You're not."

She stood silent, paralyzed. He seemed to grow larger as she shrank inside.

"You're out. You can't cut it." A tight-lipped sneer stretched his mouth, and she wanted to smash his face. But he held the power. It was his company.

"The client wants *me*, Brett," she said, calming down. "Wally Brandt thinks I can do it. His approval is what counts."

"No! *I'm* the boss, and you're history, Kathryn," he snarled. "Gone. Off this shoot." He went over and grabbed the manila envelope from the counter and shook it in her face. "Revisions from the ad agency." He ripped it in half. "Thought about giving you a shot, but not now."

"The all-powerful Brett Whitney once again welches on a deal!"

He snatched his keys off the counter and stormed toward the front door, then whirled around at her, the veinsp protruding on his neck. "I was going to give you a gift—a birthday fuck. But you're too uptight. Don't expect me to pick up the pieces for you, baby. Not letting you screw up this shoot like you did Purina. You're fired."

"You scumbag. Get out!"

He glared at her, as if about to say something else, but spun around and left, slamming the door behind him.

Kathryn fell back against the counter, shaken as she heard Brett start up the powerful Maserati engine and screech out of her driveway. She fumed as she pushed out through the French doors to her secluded patio, pacing, shoving away the turbulent emotions that could once again suck her under.

A handful of silky magnolia petals shuddered from a branch above her, floating to the swimming pool's surface, where she caught her reflection in the glistening water. *Brett always did know how to brighten her day. Now she was back at the starting line.*

Kathryn dropped her robe and dove into her cracked swimming pool. She swam laps, trying to rid herself of the images in her head, pushing away pain from the past. *You're such a jock, hiding from your emotions.*

Even when he wasn't there, Brett's angry words screamed inside her head. *You can't handle this! You're history.* She swam.

Through the water she pulled and stretched, and reaching the wall, she flipped around in a racing turn and sped back, counting laps, mentally calculating her time, kicking against the water, pulling long steady strokes, uniformly kicking.

Her marriage gone, her career in shambles, her one chance at a family lost at Laguna Seca Raceway. She felt the stab of pain again. She swam harder, drowning Brett's hurtful words, her tears mingling with chlorine water. Thirty laps, forty, fifty.

Kathryn hadn't known she was pregnant when she'd

entered that race, dismissing nausea as upset over the sham of her marriage. A fateful mistake. How could she ever get over the sorrow and guilt?

And now the only thing that could bring her back was to smash this horrible cycle of loss. She had to fight Brett on this. She reached the edge, did a flip turn, and pressed off the wall, powering back through the water again and again. Eventually her strokes smoothed out, and her panic and anger ebbed.

She swam another ten laps until her arms lost their power, and she slowed down. Her thoughts raced to find a way forward.

Arms shaking, Kathryn pulled herself out of the water and flopped onto the sun baked flagstones rimming the pool. She lay panting, droplets of water glistening on her eyelashes, the world before her a kaleidoscope of re-fracted rainbow light. She listened to the breeze whistling through a stand of pine trees nestled along the back fence and searched for the idea that would change this colossal disappointment into success.

Her eyes widened and she sat up. "There's only one thing to do." She looked up at the cloudless blue sky. *Nab Boeing's top dog and convince him he can't get what he wants without me.* A nervous giggle erupted from her. *What are my odds?* It didn't matter—there was nothing left to lose. She grabbed her towel and went inside, her jaw set firmly.

CHAPTER TWO

"You yanked me off the green," he bellowed over engine noise. "So this better be good."

Wally Brandt, senior vice president of advertising for Boeing Aircraft, was strapped into the seat of the twin-engine Cessna, clamping on his headset. He held his commanding frame with the poise of a retired Air Force colonel.

Kathryn shifted in her seat and wiped away external thoughts with an affirmation she was ready to win this challenge. She piloted the Cessna aircraft, gradually steadying the horizon level in the pressurized cabin. Her focus held on the altimeter and the angle of rise, the aircraft responding beautifully with the plane's rapid ascent.

"I'll do better than tell you. I'll show you," she said, glancing over at Wally and gulping down any misgivings she had about coercing him onto this flight. She was here to get her shoot back. No holds barred. *Nothing to lose.*

His brow pinched under a close-cropped haircut that reflected a time gone by; his dark eyes were unreadable.

The Cessna soared steeply through the morning marine layer over Marina Del Rey, then rolled out over the Pacific coast, bursting from heavy mist and looping into a vivid blue cloudless sky.

"I haven't had a such a thrill since I went up with Chuck Yeager, testing Boeing's F-14 fighter series," Wally teased, his mood capricious.

"Next time we'll take your Phenom 100 jet."

"You fly jets, too?" he asked with mock surprise.

"And helicopters." She grinned and pulled back on the speed, banking the plane into a gentle left turn inland and headed southeast.

"Who else knows about this little jaunt of ours, Ms. Whitney?"

She shrugged.

With a weighty look Wally said, "Something's on your mind, so out with it."

Kathryn turned her radio control volume down and said, "'All things want to fly.' That's the quote by Rainer Maria Rilke that leapt out at me a few weeks ago. From the beginning of time, man has wanted to fly. Massive winged figures both human and animal are depicted everywhere in ancient art and in the earliest temples and palaces."

Wally looked out the window at the orange groves. "Disneyland's down there."

"Let's say it's ancient Persia," she continued. "As Alexander the Great first saw it. The dazzling Palace of Darius, a sprawling ancient metropolis of splendor."

"I'm with you."

"We approach as if we're travelers. Our chopper swoops down over a procession of richly costumed extras, nobles paying homage to the king." She indicated the stream of tourists heading into the theme park.

"We circle." She banked left. "We see the winged lion of Persepolis, a symbol of power and majesty. Boeing theme music rises with full orchestration. James Earl Jones, the resonant voiceover, says, 'From the dawn of time, humanity desired to fly, believing it was possible even then.' Then we pull back."

"Powerful. I'm there."

"We rise, tight on the lion's face, the powerful wings. We hear swooshing wind, and, with the help of our special effects lab, the lion's stone wings move, come alive. There's a great roar and the ancient beast takes off—we're with him—flying over Persepolis from the lion's point of view."

She glanced at Wally's hard-set jaw and forged ahead.

"We cut to modern day aircraft. A Boeing jet streaks across the sky. The orchestra hits full crescendo."

Kathryn finished and sat back, steadying herself. She knew not to speak after a presentation, because the next person to speak was buying.

"Sensational!" he said. "It's a winner. I love it."

"Hang on, Wally. We're outta here before the FAA cops come." They both knew Disneyland had a restricted fly zone, so she banked west and headed out toward the ocean.

"Who's your DP?" he asked.

"Teddy Wright is the director of photography."

"Good, good. What about stills?"

"The best—Anthony Evans." She was on a roll. "We loved his stuff in *National Geographic*, the one on nomadic tribesman. You used him at White Sands Proving Grounds, didn't you?"

He sent her a sharp look. "That's top security clearance. How'd you know that?"

"I have my sources, too." She grinned.

His gaze was intense. "It'll not only be our Super Bowl spot, Kathryn, but if it's as good as you present it, I'm thinking a Boeing documentary for tight-fisted Washington R&D funding, training films, and . . ."

He was dreaming the dream. Now she had to close the deal.

"There's something else, Wally." She glanced over at him.

He watched her with that inscrutable Air Force colonel look. "What?"

"Before you hear it from our producer, I want you to know three years ago I decided to shoot a dog chow commercial *differently* than the agency and client wanted it. Foolishly, I felt I knew more. So I shot it my way. Everyone went ballistic, especially Brett."

"Dog chow . . . Purina?" He wasn't smiling. "I remember the uproar over that spot. Our advertising world is a small one, isn't it?"

She nodded. Her throat tightened. Once again, her career was about to be derailed by a sack of dog chow.

"That was you, huh?" Wally laughed, shaking his head. "Listen, honey, I liked your spot better before it was reshot. You were ahead of your time on that one."

Covering her incredulity, Kathryn marshaled her nerve. "You believe in me."

"Damn straight I do." He stared at her, as if to confirm. "My team watched your winning documentary at Sundance, as well as the AFI award short. I'm on AFI's board. And your car commercials are legendary. How many Clios?" He shook his head. "Ms. Whitney, your talent's no mystery. So yeah," he nodded, "I believe in you . . . or you'd never have this project."

Nervous, she laughed. "Well, you won't have heard this, but Brett fired me off this shoot. He wants to direct." She swiveled and leaned toward him. "But this is *my* vision. And I want this job."

He studied her. "Relax. You got the job. I'll fix it." A wry smile crossed his mouth. "But not without a challenge."

"I'm listening." She braced herself for what was coming.

"You've gotta bring that baby in two days early and two hundred fifty thousand under budget or you're toast. Got it?"

Was he kidding? No. She would have to be a tyrant on the shoot and watch every cent. "What would life be without another challenge?"

"This is between you and me, but those are the stakes. You in or out?"

Right. He was covering his decision and would be a hero if she followed through. She'd find a way. "I'm in."

They high-fived.

I'm going to Iran.

CHAPTER THREE

IRAN

Hundreds of miles from Tehran, the desert night was hot and dark. Arabian horses snorted and stomped, disturbed by an approaching sandstorm and the whomp of helicopter rotors somewhere nearby. The Mahvis, a death-listed family Anthony was smuggling out of Iran, huddled together in the back of the chopper. *One less family would be killed by Black Glove revolutionaries.*

Blasting through turbulence, Anthony's chopper bucked, teetered from side to side, and landed roughly, the skids crunching into coarse sand fewer than five miles from the Turkish border.

"They're here!" Anthony shouted over the noise. Lights from the helicopter probed eerily through the swirling sand.

Captain Hans' blond buzzed crew cut caught the greenish light. "Make it quick!" he yelled. "We gotta get out of this whirlwind."

Anthony climbed down, sheltering the Mahvi children under his coat, coaxing them from under the rotor's blast. A group of Kash'kai tribal horsemen waited not fifty yards away on a crag, easing Anthony's anxiety.

"Tabriz!" Anthony shouted over the din, relieved to see the dark robed figure waiting as planned. "Hurry!"

Tabriz fought to contain the terrified horses hobbled behind a boulder. His tribal headgear was pulled up over his mouth and chin, his robes plastered to his body. Tabriz hated the Black Glove as much as Anthony and Hans.

"Let's go!" Hans held his headphones over his ears. "Those fuckin' Air Force patrols will be on our arse in two minutes when they see we've veered off the radar screen!"

In seconds, the chopper blades gathered momentum again. The increased velocity spit sand and rocks everywhere.

With Anthony helping Mahvi and his family, they all ran toward the horsemen. The wife was crying; the baby she held wailed. Sasson, a boy of eight, pulled his four-year-old sister along, acting brave in front of Anthony. But the boy lost his grip, and the little girl sprawled in the dirt. The little girl shrieked, and the boy's eyes widened, filled with shame and horror. Anthony scooped her up and grabbed the boy's hand.

"Help me take your sister to safety, Sasson." Anthony let the boy tug him, hoping he felt brave again. Mahvi needed a confident son if they were to get across the border into Turkey.

"Quickly!" Tabriz waved, frantic.

They climbed behind a boulder, temporarily safe from the rising sand.

The girl clutched her arms around Anthony's neck. "I'm scared!" she wailed in Farsi.

Anthony hugged her. "Now let your brother take care of you. Promise you'll be a good girl, and Tabriz will let you ride his horse."

"I will," she said, her smile tentative.

"Good. Go!" He lifted up the little girl to the tribesman. "The coming sandstorm will give you cover. They're looking for the chopper anyway, not you."

Tabriz settled the child in the saddle and nodded, pulling a scarf securely around her head.

Mahvi grabbed Anthony's hand, his eyes wet. "*Mamnoon*—thank you. I will never be able to repay you for this."

"Stay well, Mahvi." Anthony patted his back. "It's enough. *Insha Allah*."

Tabriz, with all the Mahvis, melted into the night.

Anthony sprinted back to the chopper, his arm shielding his eyes, and climbed in.

The dials on the instrument panel glowed in the dim cabin.

Hans shouted, indicating his headset. "Aircraft will be on top of us in no time."

"Let's go."

As the engines gathered speed, the chopper wobbled, lifting unsteadily. The rotors cut through gathering sand. "Go, go, baby," Hans urged, his eyes riveted to the instrument panel gauges. "I love flyin' blind." Hans corrected the aircraft pitch. "Get ready. When we blast out of this soup, who knows who'll be waitin' for us!"

With increased power, the nose of the craft dipped.

The chopper shuddered, then pushed forward as if propelled by an unknown force.

Anthony buckled his harness, kicked out his door, and aimed his American-made M-16 outside, sand pelting his face. He hated the thought of having to use his weapon in this crazy way, but was confident the M-16 could hit a bull's-eye at a thousand yards if it didn't jam. Anthony adjusted the infrared tracking and searched for the aircraft they could barely hear approaching over the storm.

They broke out of the turbulence into Iranian radar range. Hans listened in on the radio chatter, monitoring communiqués. "Here." He nudged Anthony, handing over the other set of earphones.

A voice in Farsi pierced the static. "We have the unknown aircraft on radar tracking, Captain Aran. What are our orders?"

"We're in for it." Hans' jaw tightened. "Big guns. Aran. Black Glove.

"Get the hell out of here!" Anthony yelled back over cockpit noise, his nerves amped.

Hans veered off as flashes of tracer bullets whizzed past. "We'll never make it back. They've got us nailed."

Bullets ricocheted off the rotors like marbles pelting a tin roof. Anthony jumped back. He leaned out again, and recognizing a Black Glove aircraft, fired on it. His gun jammed.

"Damn!" Hans said, shoulders hunching. "Something cracked. Could be a fuel line." He checked the fuel gauge and scanned the other instruments.

"We have to land." Fear belted Anthony's gut.

"And quick. Where the hell do you suggest?"

"Change course—northeast to two hundred forty degrees," Anthony shouted. "Stay low. Get to the mountain! NOW!"

"You crazy? I can't land in there. It's pitch dark."

"When I tell you, veer off due east. Go!" Anthony spotted the two turbo-fan helicopters on their tail, searchlights still tracking them as they fired on their chopper. Anthony grabbed a new weapon, leaned out the open door with the M-25 sniper rifle, got one of them in his sights and fired, emptying half a magazine, hitting the side panel of the aircraft. The enemy chopper still came at them. He steadied himself to aim better. Bullets blasted their target. This time, he caught the engine. One Black Glove helicopter rolled, spinning wildly through the night, and hit the ground, exploding. Flames and smoke erupted into the sky, lighting up the surrounding terrain.

The dark plume camouflaged the second 'copter's lights long enough for Hans to change course, swinging out over the foothills, losing the rebel chopper and leaving the edges of the sand storm behind.

Anthony directed him along the route from memory. They flew northeast over the snow-tipped Sahand Mountains and swooped down onto a rocky plateau. There, an unexpected pasture bordered by scrub oak and poplars lay next to a winding stream.

"Look!" Anthony pointed in between a line of boulders. "Quickly, there's the spot."

Hans took the chopper in low, hovering above the ground, halogen lights illuminating a thirty-foot circle. "You gotta check for rocks. That grass looks deep."

Anthony jumped to the ground to make sure of the terrain then waved Hans in, waiting for the rotors to shut down.

Hans climbed out of the chopper shaking his head. "Mother Mary, I'm glad to be alive."

"Let's get this bird out of sight." Anthony took hold of a rudder.

Together they covered the chopper with military-issue camouflage netting Hans always carried for emergencies. Anthony caught his shuttering breath and let go. He hadn't realized how anxious he'd been. He wrapped his weapons in canvas and buried them close to a boulder he marked. Tabriz would get them later.

"How the hell'd you know this place?" Hans asked.

"I came here often with Tabriz as a boy. His lodge is in these mountains." And so were leopards—sleek, beautiful, deadly.

Anthony brushed sand from his sweaty face. He felt a clear wind whip his jacket. "Looks like we stay here till it's safe to go." He leaned against a rock still holding warmth from the day and faced the sky, listening to the sounds of egrets, an owl's wings flapping overhead, the distant screech of bats. The adrenalin he had lived on for weeks dissipated, with no sleep in the near future.

It drove him crazy, trying to figure out where he had slipped up. He rubbed his irritated eyes. Before last night they had made two trips each night. Now it was like they had left a trail of breadcrumbs.

"Come on," Hans said, holding out a blanket, his face ravaged by fatigue. "Let's get some rest. A few hours of sleep will do you good."

Han's loyalty to rescuing families from SAVAK never wavered. This loyalty was Hans's stance against tyranny and the butchers who'd gunned down his young wife last year at a human rights protest while she held their nine-month-old son in her arms. Hans, his Swedish-American pilot, had come to Anthony bitter and full of hate. Together they had put an end to those particular butchers, but now with the inception of the Black Glove terrorists, tyranny had a longer reach in Iran.

Rest? Anthony thought of so many lives with uncertain futures, children ripped from their homes, as he'd been. He scooted down to the cold ground, his own tragic childhood pulling at him. He sensed a haze of doom hovering over him.

Rolling onto his back, he gazed up at the starry Persian sky. A breeze carried the scent of rosemary and pine, desert cactus blooms and juniper. Crickets set a cadence, the nearby stream gurgled, frogs croaked to one another in a nighttime mating ritual. Tranquility surrounded him, yet he failed to shake his grim feelings.

His grandfather was fine in England. Raymond, his butler, and all the rest of Anthony's household servants were safe in Shiraz. His close friends, all fine. So far. And he was in no more danger than usual. Why a sense of doom? He gazed off into the night.

At the edge of the plateau a family of Marad red deer loped past. A mountain lion or perhaps a panther growled in the distance. Hans snored beside him, tame sounds after gunfire and exploding aircraft.

No more wrestling with unresolved questions.

He turned over to the sound of Hans' snoring. If Hans

could sleep on this lumpy ground, then he could. Anthony pulled the rough blanket over his head and then remembered: The American film crew had flown in from L.A. He was supposed to meet them at the airport in Tehran. Damn! He didn't even tell someone else to do it. But at the moment the film group's comfort did not top his list of priorities, and he allowed his eyes to close.

CHAPTER FOUR

As the Boeing 747 landed in Tehran, Kathryn opened her eyes, looking up from her first class seat in late afternoon sun. Excitement seized her and her anticipation grew. A different world, one she'd only dreamt and read about awaited beyond this plane that taxied to the gate. She could not wait to get out. They were already deodorizing the cabin.

Teddy, her cinematographer, with his stocky but agile build, slipped into the aisle seat across from her, shoving his Hemmingway felt hat over his clumpy light brown hair. His sleepless gray eyes were rimmed with red.

Peter Shuman, tall and lanky in faded jeans and a Grateful Dead T-shirt, already sat next to her right, smoothing his Fu-Manchu mustache and brushing his hair back from his shoulders, gathering it into a ponytail with a rubber band. Peter, a lean man of thirty-four, was a year older than Kathryn. *Her Ivy League hippie.* He had been her best friend since film school and now was a ruthless assistant director she had begged to have on this shoot. Peter never failed to get the job done right.

He shot her a look. "You could do something with yours, too, Kat. It's a mess."

She touched her tousled blonde hair and felt messy compared to the other passengers in the first class cabin. The men wore well-tailored sport coats or business suits. The ladies were dressed in smart pants suits and dresses. Her crew wore faded jeans and T-shirts; she was dressed in khakis and an olive drab anorak.

"I guess we're the Mötley Crüe," she smirked.

Teddy laughed.

"Film crew, whaddaya expect?" Peter shrugged. He passed her a hairbrush.

She gave her tresses a quick brush and twisted them all up under a red baseball cap.

Peter grabbed his camera case, duffel bag, and briefcase filled with their official documents. Urging Teddy off the aircraft would take some doing; he was obviously cranky. Kathryn guessed he wanted a drink but was cleaving to his best behavior for her sake.

"Don't worry, we're set. Anthony Evans, our photographer, is meeting us at the gate. He'll smooth out any red tape." Peter opened the folder and pulled out a full-page photo of a man on a polo pony swinging his mallet. He pointed at it. "From *Town & Country.*"

"I know, Peter. Evans is quite the polo player. So?" Kathryn looked away.

"Hey," Peter called out, still trying to get her attention,

"Look at this one, Evans on some princess' yacht. Look. This guy's for you, Kat. You need some fun."

"Right."

"Hey, I'm your only social outlet since the divorce, and I'm gay."

She had to laugh at the truth in Peter's words if not his bad timing.

"And he happens to be handsome and rich."

"You know that kind of social life *or* the men who lead them are not for me. Yeah, I've hired a world-class playboy to do my stills because he happens to be a world-class photographer. I don't care what he does on his time. It's *my* time that concerns me, and *my* dime. Don't make me worry about him."

"He's an artist."

"Right. A talented jerk who spends one month a year shooting pictures, and eleven sipping champagne from some cupcake's silver slipper."

"Well, why can't that cupcake be you?"

Kathryn shot him an incredulous look. The door to the 747 swooshed open. "Come on. Let's go." She felt wide awake.

A smile that hinted at matchmaker crossed Peter's generally serious mouth. He snapped his notebook shut.

They stepped off the airplane into dry, foreign-smelling air, with ancient earth and exotic spices mixed with diesel exhaust. A land surrounded by the towering Alborz Mountain Range. Kathryn breathed deeply, already searching for their contact, needing to get through customs and then catch another flight straight to Shiraz and Persepolis.

They trudged into the air terminal. It was crowded

with boisterous people in all manner of dress from western to acutely ethnic—djellabas, chador, vibrant tribal gear. Many were pilgrims, waiting to leave on their journey to Mecca. The seventy-day season of the *Hajj* would climax in November.

But these Muslims seemed ready to riot, shouting, waving documents in a fervor. Her anxiety heightened.

Peter pulled her toward Customs.

The terminal was a sad, dilapidated combination of slum and army barracks bordered by gray low-ceilinged walls and concrete floors. Armed teenage militia circled the perimeter, glaring at travelers. Their eyes darted here and there with suspicion, settling on anyone who dared make eye contact.

Kathryn cringed. She had expected some state of unrest from news articles in the *London Times* she read on the plane, but the atmosphere felt heated, a pot about to boil over.

"What's up, you guys? Did anyone on the plane mention there'd be trouble?"

"No," Peter said. "Just stay close, Kat."

Kathryn looked around expectantly. "Our famous photographer should be here to meet us."

"Don't see anyone holding a sign with our name on it, do you, Kat?" Teddy said.

"I'll ask at the information counter, wherever that is." She dodged in and out of travelers until she found a bulky, uniformed official scrutinizing customs lines, his shaggy mustache twitching as he watched, wary.

"Excuse me, sir, I'm meeting a representative from the Ministry of Culture. Where—"

"Get in line. Wait!"

"No, no. You don't understand. We're meeting an official to assist us through customs. We have clearance for our equipment from the U.S. State Department and—"

"You wait!" The man's shaggy eyebrows did nothing to hide his scowl. His neck bulged from his collar as he spoke, his stomach was pressing his shirt buttons and protruded over his belt, the fabric stretching like a hide being tanned.

Calmly Kathryn pulled her documents from her carry-on bag. "Perhaps you can help us. You see, it says Anthony Evans, from the department of . . ."

The man grabbed her papers. "This is no good." He stuffed them into his shirt.

Alarmed, Kathryn said, "Hey, I just asked a question."

"Go wait in line!"

"My papers, sir. I need them back, please." *What the hell was this imbecile up to?*

"Go!"

Peter sauntered up beside her. "What's going on, Kat?" Peter remained cool.

"This guy pinched my papers and won't give them back. For godssake, where's someone who knows something?"

"Calm down." Peter took her arm.

"Peter, let go! I need my passport." She gave the man a scathing look, not about to be victimized.

"We'll get in line," Peter said, "and get someone to handle this guy."

Peter tugged her toward the end of the line, but as she passed the man, she whirled around at Peter and crashed into the man with her papers sticking out from his shirt.

"Oh! Sir, I beg your pardon," she said to the red-faced man. "My mistake, I'm so sorry. . . ."

"Insolent bitch of Satan!" the sweaty man yelled.

Kathryn spun away, afraid he was going to clobber her. Her baseball cap flew off, bumping along the concrete.

The man gestured wildly, shouting in Farsi.

People around them turned and stared. Within seconds, armed militia surrounded her, the harsh sound of metal clicked against metal. Five Russian assault rifles were leveled at her head.

She closed her gaping mouth and managed to squeeze Peter's hand, looking into faces of the men holding the weapons. So young, their expressions filled with such hatred. Why?

"Come with me!" the official shouted at her.

Her gaze swerved to meet his. Cold fear struck her belly and cleared her mind. *Gotta do something.* She looked at Peter's shocked expression, upset with herself. "Call the ministry. Tell them to get us out of here." She gestured for Peter to move away before they grabbed him, too.

"Now!" said the official. He removed his dark glasses, a sly grin spreading over his wide mouth. He reached for a strand of her hair.

Kathryn brushed his hand aside and tucked away the strand, feeling his scrutiny scorch over her.

She was ushered into the airport commandant's office.

The balding man behind the desk wore a dark suit and had a wiry build. He fingered his thin goatee. She read the nameplate on his desk: DEVI SAED. He looked disgruntled at the intrusion, his dark eyes alert.

His expression changed from grim to speculative the moment he finished giving her a quick once over.

She felt her skin crawl.

"Commandant Saed, this woman has caused a grievance against an official of this country," the sweaty one puffed out.

"You, Taji," Saed sneered, "would be the official?"

"Yes, Excellency."

"Give me her papers." He held out his hand.

"She tried to take them from me!"

The commandant shook his head. "I'll handle this. You can go."

Taji shuffled his feet, looking Kathryn over, then narrowed his eyes at his superior and left.

Commandant Saed moved from behind his desk.

Kathryn stepped back, masking her revulsion with bravado. "How do you do? I'm Kathryn Whitney. I . . . and my associates are in Iran as guests of the minister of Culture and the Shah himself."

He stepped closer, ignoring her words. "It's a serious offense, tangling with an official in this country, especially for a woman." He closed the blinds on his office door and turned back to her. "Imprisonment in a Qasr cell would be dangerous for an infidel such as yourself, with your . . ." he moved toward her. "There is only one way to avoid such an ugly fate as prison."

"I'm certain we can clear up any misunderstanding, Commandant Saed!"

"Oh, I'm certain we can."

Inflamed with panic, Kathryn reached inside herself, grasping for the strength to get out of this. "This is a mistake." Her voice sounded strange to her own ears, stronger than she felt. "You understand? The Shah expects my colleagues and me to be treated with courtesy!"

He stepped even closer. "Certain people are on their high horse!" He shook a sinewy finger in her face. "Don't count too much on their authority."

Click!

The door opened and a young Iranian wearing a gray suit shoved inside the office. He appeared to be in his early twenties. He whisked over to the desk, his nimble body reverberating energy and strength. "Ah, dear lady! Here are you!" The young man's enthusiasm far exceeded his English, but she was so glad to see him she could have hugged him.

"I am Ali Zahedi from Ministry of Culture. Your car outside awaits. Sorry to be delay."

Kathryn shook with gratitude and relief. "I'm so happy to meet you."

Ali looked at her with kindness, then turned to the airport commandant and spoke rapidly in Farsi. He counted off a stack of rials, folding them into the man's hand.

Commandant Saed frowned and shook his head. Ali frowned back.

What was going on, some kind of barter? What a mess she had created with her lack of foresight. She needed to be a helluva lot more responsible for this production and its crew.

Saed squared his shoulders, unmoving.

Ali Zahedi pressed a few more bills into Saed's outstretched hand. They negotiated with more looks between them until the official nodded curtly and stuffed the wad of bills into his pockets.

With a wide grin and a slight bow, Ali said to her, "Ms. Whitney, please, I'm sorry this trouble you have." He took her papers from Saed and escorted her from the dismal office.

"Thank you for getting me out of there, Mr. Zahedi." Kathryn's gravelly voice croaked; she was so upset she could barely speak.

They made their way out of the terminal to a waiting area where Teddy and Peter stood. Teddy was white and rigid, Peter silent. Her own fear turned to anger. "What happened to Mr. Evans? He was supposed to meet our plane."

"Oh, it is all so unfortunate. Sir Anthony must go to serve the crown."

"His own or someone else's?" Kathryn asked.

Ali grinned. "But do not fear, I am here. We go tomorrow to Bank of Tehran for letter of credit." Ali motioned them to a waiting limousine.

"But you had to give that awful man money." Kathryn felt perturbed.

"Ah, yes. It insults him if no. Here, we call it *pishkesh*. It is normal."

Peter looked at Kathryn with a sly smile. "Slipping cash into the right hands."

Ali nodded. "It is something you must to remember."

"Yes." Kathryn stored that info. Remember to bring cash. There was much she did not understand about this country, so different from the many European and South American countries where she had previously been on location. She quelled all distracting anxiety; there was no leeway here for a screw-up. The side deal she'd made with Wally at Boeing was airtight: Either come in under budget or consider the production a failure.

"Hey, guys, you ready to fly into Shiraz now? We'll scout the location, make sure we've ordered the right equipment, get settled. Tomorrow we'll get in and out of the Bank of Tehran and the equipment rental early, be back on location, and start setup by noon."

"You sure, Kat?" Teddy squeezed her shoulder.

"We've got an invitation from Anthony," Peter said deadpan, "to join him for dinner at some embassy soirée."

"Oh, please!"

"Sightseeing?" Peter grinned.

Teddy shot Peter a look. "Then let's book it."

She turned to Ali. "Can you make this happen? Charter a Cessna to Shiraz right now?"

Ali bowed. "My pleasure." He disappeared into the terminal.

Kathryn wanted to move past this incident, play it down with Teddy and Peter. Obviously she had to learn a lot quickly about Iran's customs for this job to go smoothly. She shuddered; this episode had been a jab at her confidence. Determination took over.

She could care less about dinner with Mr. "Playboy" Evans. After all the arrangements made in advance in Los Angeles, Evans had nerve not showing up. This was his fault. If he even attempted to screw up her location schedule she would scale the snake alive before allowing it to devour her.

In the dark and quiet, the air was dense two hours before sunrise, Anthony's battered chopper landed back at the outskirts of the Mehrebad airstrip. They needed to get the chopper out of sight before there were too many questions. He glanced at Hans' haggard face, feeling his own fatigue and concern over their leaked flight plan weighing on him.

Three SAVAK cars came from behind a shed and circled their aircraft, bright lights pinning them like prey. *Damn.* Anthony's fatigue fled, his survival instincts heightened.

Hans shut down the engines, his face soon drained of color, his eyes squinting under the glare.

Anthony had hoped to be inconspicuous. "Don't. Don't give into it, Hans. Not now." Anthony saw the terror of SAVAK prison closing in on Hans' imagination and grabbed his shaking arm. "Get a grip—you're exhausted."

"The window, the window!" Hans hissed.

"The sandstorm blasted out the window. And I was too drunk to help you."

"Right."

Anthony jumped out of the chopper.

Hurried footsteps approached. "So it's you, Evans. In trouble again?"

Hearing the unpleasant but familiar voice of a SAVAK sergeant, Anthony whipped around. "I'm not in the best mood, Jamal. What do you want?"

"Out late again, I see."

"Flying in after the soirée at the Summer Palace," Anthony said.

Jamal, with his black gloves and mirthless grin, motioned for two of his men, flashlights in hand, to begin inspecting the chopper. They circled, shining their torches in every crevice. Then Jamal examined the desert tree limb Anthony had shoved through the bullet-shattered window.

"If it weren't for the frigging sandstorm I'd have slept a few hours in my own bed last night instead of a frozen desert!"

Jamal knelt behind the chopper, muscles in his thighs bunching. He yelled to his men to examine the undercarriage Hans had repaired with putty then smeared with mud and sand. Anthony prayed it had held together through the flight back. He waved his hand at the chopper. "Look at this damn mess. There's nothing unusual about a sandstorm in the desert, is there?"

"I'm not sure about that." Jamal turned and yelled to one of his men, "Grab the pilot, now."

Hans was yanked from the chopper and shoved against the metal frame under the rotors. The man brought back his arm, fist ready, and Hans flinched.

"That's enough!" Anthony shouted. He turned back to the sergeant. "Really, Jamal? A bit touchy late at night?"

"You push your luck, Evans. Photographer to the Shah. Pfft."

Hans climbed back into the chopper and closed the door.

"Jamal, it was so nice of you to stop and say hello." Anthony grabbed his camera gear from the cab. "But I must go."

"We'll be seeing you soon, Evans." Jamal leaned into the chopper. "And you, too, Hans Eber, you, too."

"Evil bastards," Hans muttered as they walked away.

Anthony watched them go, betting he'd see the ugly lot of them again soon. Screw them. He was on his own time now. And he must get to his destination before dawn.

CHAPTER FIVE

Alone in her room at the Hotel Persepolis in Shiraz, Kathryn Whitney yearned to see the great winged lion. She would begin pre-production for her Boeing shoot tomorrow, but by the time she had arrived in Shiraz late last evening the monument was closed. She paced, unable to sleep. The anticipation was killing her. Her lion was waiting for her, finally.

She dressed quickly in a white gauzy sundress and flats and slipped out of the room and down the wooden stairs off her balcony. She felt the cool stillness of the waning night and wrapped a silky shawl about her shoulders. She headed down the deserted road toward the monument, the aroma of juniper and desert sage brushing past her. *At last she was here.* Her heart beat faster.

In the distance the ruins were silhouetted against the pre-dawn Persian sky, soaring columns and massive capitals bathed in purple shadow. Spurred by childhood memories, Kathryn made her way closer still to the ancient sculpture.

Light from a guard shack caught her up short. Why had she worn a white dress? Deep in the lion's spell, she hadn't worried about guards. She heard them chatting in Farsi outside the hut and her heart thudded. But she couldn't turn away from her goal.

She spotted a broken chunk in the four-foot wall shielding the monument and crouched low, waiting until the guards turned away. She vaulted the wall, checking to see if she'd been spotted. Nothing moved, so she sprinted toward the citadel, perched high on a palisade of mythical rock.

The guards, by some miracle, had left open the gates; a second miracle kept them from seeing her breach the ramparts.

Awed and breathing hard from the run, she took it all in, from the tall stone figures to the endless vista of nothingness across the plain to the red clay dirt dusting her flats.

Hardly believing this was real, she glided through the ruins where the images of her many childhood dreams were brought into astounding reality. This trip was Kathryn's renewal, a rebirth of her withering career submerged for eight years in a dead marriage. At thirty-three, needing to begin again, she moved quietly forward.

At last she stood below the wide stone staircase lined with ten thousand carved immortal warriors, winged bulls, and other creatures, all with wings, stationed as they had been for 2,500 years. It was the perfect iconography to illustrate her concept for Boeing and the birth of flight.

Lost in reverie, she moved toward the lion she had come here to see. Reaching the massive creature, she looked up at its staggering height. She touched the rough surface, feeling the ancient stone, then grabbed hold and climbed toward a ledge beside the top of her beautiful lion. Even in the dusky pre-dawn light she knew instinctively where to put her feet and hands, as if she had done this a thousand times before.

Kathryn reached the top as an edge of light cast a magenta glow across the horizon. She breathed in the last of the night, her heart expanding with the joy of a fresh new day in this magnificent place. The magic of the hours in her father's library enveloped her—the nights enraptured by his stories of ancient Persepolis, her imaginary adventures riding on the wings of this lion.

Filled with new energy, Kathryn pressed her face to the stone lion and felt her father's presence alongside her. She heard his words whispered on the breeze, "I'm right beside you, kitten."

Bronze and silver light vibrated against the soaring columns, and every carved creature appeared to come to life. Kathryn pictured her father's smile and clung to the lion, choking on tears. "Daddy, I'm here at last. It's as beautiful as you described. I miss you . . ."

It was nearly dawn when Anthony Evans parked the dusty Range Rover, grabbed his camera equipment, and walked to the spot he had chosen below the monument. He paid the guards *pishkesh*, the usual bribe.

He hungered for creative expression, longed to show the richness of Persian history, the exotic splendor of its lands, and the astute intelligence and cosmopolitan culture he feared now faced extinction.

Here at Persepolis, the glamour of the posh polo club and elegantly dressed Iranians and Europeans in their haute couture clothes fell away, fading like colored tissue in the sunlight. Their beauty held little interest for him now. Much was at stake in these unpredictable days. He was keenly aware that this might be his last creative moment in his beloved Iran, brewing as the country was with impending religious revolution. Worse, activists and leaders, scientists and writers, musicians and thinkers were being slaughtered at will, and with all his energy, he could not fly enough secret night missions to save that many more.

He fixed both his Hasselblad and his Nikon to tripods, selected a 75-millimeter lens for his Hassey, clicked it into place, checked the light meter, and set the exposure. His cameras loaded, he was ready for the shots of the gigantic winged lion towering over the ruins, a symbol of the power and majesty of a time gone by. These images he'd shoot tonight would be the climax of his Persian suite of photographs headed for London.

Stillness surrounded the ruins, intensifying the aching void that swelled inside him until quiet despair filled the hollowing shell of his chest. He was described as a man of action: action taken to dispel these crushing bouts of anguish, haunting him vengefully over the years since his parents' murder.

A light breeze reclaimed his attention. Any moment the sun would rise and filter away his pain in revelation of the grandeur before him.

He leaned into his Hassey, and the winged lion came into view in the early morning stillness. As the sun heralded the new day in the sky, a young woman—a vision of radiance—suddenly appeared forty feet above him on the ledge next to the face of the great, ancient beast. He changed the lens for a closer view and was struck by her features, far more beautiful than those of the models he had photographed in Paris last month. He was seeing an astonishing figure draped in a white gauzy dress. Was she real?

With her eyes closed, she caressed the stone with a slender hand, as if it was beloved to her. Then her eyes opened, a smile trembled on her lips. Anthony's heart nearly stopped. The depth in her expression stirred him. Shards of light exploded into the sky and he went into action, clicking off shot after shot, his adrenalin flowing.

She leaned into the beast, nuzzling its head as if it were living. Tears glistened on her delicate face. Passion for this ancient symbol of Iran radiated from her. He saw strength and vulnerability, beauty and ferocity. No woman—no vision—had so powerfully affected him before. Her connection to his country's majesty echoed his own.

Capturing his vision on film, he was inspired, filled with certainty for the future of Iran, already changed by this sight. He wanted to know her, to be with her.

Then she stood up very straight, long hair sweeping her shoulders, her arms raised in an ecstatic gesture to the heavens.

He worked vigorously, changing cameras until the moment ended when the woman turned and fled.

Anthony pulled away from his Nikon. His pulse surged. She was gone. But she had been there. He leaned forward again, his nerves quickening, and searched through the lens. Only the enigmatic winged lion remained, and with a sharp sense of loss, he determined he would find her, this sensual yet ethereal being.

Shaken, he gathered up his equipment, slung his camera bag over his shoulders, and headed toward his Range Rover, barely able to contain his eagerness to search for her at the base of the winged lion, the icon they both clearly worshipped. Somehow he would find her.

CHAPTER SIX

With one hand braced against the gold-plated iron gate encircling Niavaran Palace in Tehran, Anthony Evans threw back his head, tilting a Baccarat snifter, swallowing amber cognac. His gaze fell on the soft-skinned young woman who clung to him with anticipation glowing in her dark eyes. Like the night, she was a woman to be savored. For now, all part of the role he played. She was here to be seen in society. He was here to be seen and uncover who had unmasked him.

Bright lights and fancy cars lined the palace courtyard wall, where princely villas studded the northern slopes of Tehran. It was an Iranian night of splendor for the elite of the Shah's court, all of whom held little interest for Anthony Evans. He had already photographed most of them earlier for a special issue of *Life* magazine. The ease of their lives glared in contrast to the misery of many in a country verging on revolution. But then who was he to speak of hardship? For him, this glittery night was a rare moment of pleasure in tense times, and he would take it, even while he sought to uncover his enemy's identity.

Excitement vibrated in the air around him. A balmy breeze tinged with jasmine and orange blossom scent stroked his skin. Yes, he'd lose himself for an hour in this sensuous night before he had to go.

The raw anxiety etched into his nerves slipped away with the fiery liquid and the supple brunette draped in pearls and lilac charmeuse silk, shimmering in the moonlight. Her slender arms slid beneath his black dinner jacket. Sounds of a Brazilian bossa nova floated from the ballroom terrace above the sheltering tree where Anthony moved with Alexandria to a rhythm more subtle than music.

"You're a fabulous dancer," she whispered.

"With you."

"Especially with me."

"Hmm." With an indecent smile he bent toward the beauty in his arms who warmed his body but not his frozen heart. An image came to him of a woman whose face was washed with sunbeams, and he felt a thaw. He quickly suppressed the memory, planning to revisit it later. He scanned beyond Alexandria into the circular courtyard where voices rose; two men were arguing.

Even though the taller man's back was turned, Anthony couldn't mistake the cut of his ornate Iranian military dress uniform. The man gestured flamboyantly as he spoke, like a seasoned politician. He was General Omar Houdin, governor of Tehran, a man always in the public eye these days. He was also a leader in the terrifying SAVAK. Barrel-chested Omar Houdin, a butcher with a demon's soul.

He paused, listening, but was unable to catch a word.

"Oh, don't stop, darling," sighed Alexandria.

He laughed softly, moving again, playing his lips against her slender neck.

The man engaged with Houdin was Pavriz Sabeti, head of SAVAK, the bald head to Houdin's silver movie star hair. A dangerous pair, he thought; as dangerous as it gets. Anthony pushed away his constant need to expunge treachery breeding within the palace walls and dropped the half-full snifter into the grass. His mouth took Alexandria's with as much fire as he felt inside.

"Yes, yes. Wicked." She gripped his back beneath the dinner jacket, raking her nails against the starched Egyptian cotton of his shirt. He laughed softly, nibbling her delicate earlobe. The two men he watched bid each other goodnight, and the lethal Houdin waited as Sabeti was chauffeured away in his Mercedes. Houdin moved toward the festivities.

At a change in tempo, Alexandria turned toward the music. She squeezed Anthony's arm. "Isn't that your cousin joining General Houdin?"

He hoped not. But as he craned for a better look, Sabeti's black Mercedes circled past the fountain, blocking his view, then curved toward Anthony's surveillance post.

Glaring headlights pinned him. He drew Alexandria away from the approaching car. It pulled up next to him. The tinted back window lowered, and Sabeti's bald pate gleamed in the moonlight. He smiled as if his position as leader of SAVAK were a private joke.

Anthony leaned, staggering for effect. "Pavriz, my friend, you can't be leaving us this early!"

"You appear to be in capable hands, Evans," said Sabeti, his gaze sliding toward Anthony's companion, eyes softening. "Alexandria, how lovely you look in the moonlight. See that our champion polo player gets home safely, won't you? There may be another demonstration tonight."

"I always do. Don't I, Anthony?" she said, possessively wrapping her arms through his.

"These radical Shiites are ruining our country," Sabeti said. He looked around as if the Shiite clerics might be listening, then composed himself. "I wouldn't want you to miss your match tomorrow, Evans," Sabeti said. "It isn't often I can win a polo bet."

Anthony drew Alexandria close. "We're leaving," he slurred, his arm draping over her shoulder.

"Perhaps not yet," said Sabeti. "I was asked to give you this on my way out." He handed Anthony an envelope with the Imperial Seal of the empress. "Pull yourself together, man. The empress wants to see you now, something about photographs for a London exhibition. Remember, it's an honor to be royal court photographer to the Shah of Iran. Goodnight, then."

Anthony nodded, dismissing the pompous remark, and gave a wobbly salute for effect. The car pulled forward and turned onto the boulevard. He opened the missive and read.

The luscious woman beside him leaned in and nipped his chin. "You're drunk again, my darling."

"So it seems." He smiled, sliding the note into his breast pocket, then leading Alexandria to a sleek limousine.

She pouted. "You're not coming over, are you?"

He shook his head, suppressing desire. "Tomorrow. I promise."

"How do you manage, darling? You're always so inebriated when I leave you."

He smiled mischievously. "The gods are with me."

She touched his lower lip with one long, manicured fingernail. "They had better be when you stagger in before the empress."

Anthony nodded to her driver. He opened the door to the limo, and she climbed in. She blew him a kiss. It would be so easy to blow off his obligations for once—if lives didn't depend on it.

He saw her car reach the road and disappear into the night, both relieved and sorry to see her go. Time to move to a different tune.

He made his way into the palace, careful to keep his drunken state evident to the guests. He seized a flute of champagne from a passing tray. A woman lifted her eyebrow at him. He blew her a kiss. She laughed and shook her head. With English blood and ties to the Iranian royal family, he could get away with behavior not openly tolerated of Iranian men, especially with Iranian women who did not belong to them.

Crossing the ballroom, Anthony headed for the staircase. He set the glass on the balustrade and climbed the stairs to Empress Farah Diba's private office chambers, far more sober than he'd pretended to be in the last few hours. He had a few reasons of his own to anticipate this meeting with the empress. He checked his watch. He couldn't stay long. People were depending on him.

Anthony waited. A chilling breeze whipped through half-opened filigree shutters lining the east wall of the palace chamber. He paced, then shook himself, breathing deeply in an effort to clear exhaustion from his sleep-deprived mind. This playboy charade was wearying.

"She will see you now."

He spun toward the familiar voice. "Oriana." He nodded to the personal secretary to the empress and followed. He entered the empress' private office suite and saw her standing across the room.

Dressed exquisitely as always, she was wearing a soft green silk ball gown, one he'd photographed on a Paris runway last month for *Vogue*, unmistakably Dior. Her ensemble was accented by a diamond and emerald crown matching her necklace and earrings. But her jewels gave off a luster missing from her smile. The sense of joyous spontaneity that had endeared her to everyone she met merely shadowed her. The empress offered her hand, which he respectfully kissed.

She smiled then nodded to her personal secretary, who placed a leather-bound portfolio of Anthony's photographs on the coffee table and withdrew from the room. He knew they would not be disturbed.

"Anthony, I only have a few minutes, but I had to see you were all right."

"Kind of you, with all that is in your care."

"How did you manage to escape SAVAK?" Her warm expression failed to mask her concern. Farah Diba gestured to a pair of French brocade sofas. They sat, facing each other, as they had so often over the years. "We feared last night was your final mission."

"We made it with only minor repairs to the helicopter," he said, recalling their narrow escape.

"The Behanian family?"

"Safe in Iraq." He leaned back against the sofa.

"I sent Habib to warn you last night at the French ambassador's dinner party."

Anthony leaned forward.

"He learned that your flight plans had been compromised. A cousin—a sometimes driver for SAVAK—let it slip."

"Can we use this cousin again for information?"

She shook her head. "Doubtful. The man knows the risk."

"How is SAVAK getting wind of these missions? Where is the leak coming from?"

"We don't know the source, but we're investigating." She swept to the window, looking out over the city. "It's intolerable what SAVAK has become," she said. "A monster. Some tiny infraction—words at a dinner party against some policy, a quote in print—then something is whispered, and in the dead of night entire families disappear, their fortunes vanish. We couldn't save the Devis and the Paziz families." With a murmur of regret, she turned to him only in profile. "You know I studied architecture in Paris with Dr. Paziz's daughter, Mahine. They were a lovely family." She looked away.

Anthony could feel her grief, much like his own. "You stood up for them, Highness."

"After SAVAK killed Mahine, I knew I had to find a

way to fight back." Slowly she turned to look at him. "You are my way."

"I can't do it without the information you provide, Majesty."

"Last night you were nowhere to be found." She looked toward the doorway. "I suppose I can thank my secretary's daughter for that."

"In no way have I meant to lead Alexandria on—"

"Please, Anthony," she said, her palm raised. "It was at my request that you keep Alexandria occupied until her father returns." She smiled. "I realize that when she's offered a diamond she wants to own the mine. I'll speak to her."

"If you please, no, Majesty. I believe that task is my responsibility." Although it was not one he looked forward to.

She sat down again and leaned toward him. "You're going away again tonight—another mission."

"Yes."

"The feckless international playboy, living for the most superficial pleasures of his class." They both smiled. "How ironic that so few will ever know the real you. So brave."

"There are half a dozen groups helping marked people flee Iran." He, though, could have no ties to them.

"Your contribution, however, is unique."

"My *tacit* agreement is that the British Foreign Office will look the other way."

"As long as you don't embarrass them and get caught." She turned away. "I'm protected by the monarchy and have little to lose in this venture. You, however . . ." she faced him. "It would be treason. I couldn't help you."

How well he knew. If he were caught ignoring foreign laws, no one could help him. "I've chosen my path."

But loyalty to Persia, his birth country, had never been a question. It was the same with England, his father's land. He had been torn between two countries since he was thirteen and had buried his murdered parents on his grandfather's estate. He remembered the English air that day had been cold and still as death.

"Very well then." She handed him an envelope. "The new death list. Do what you can—carefully, my friend."

He gave her a grim nod and slid it into his inside jacket pocket without looking at it. He'd do everything to help those on the list, but he couldn't yet face the names. He patted his coat pocket where the list seemed to burn into his chest and leaned forward.

The empress rose and crossed to the window again, her gaze reflective as if she looked within. And for a moment before she suppressed it, Anthony saw the fear and panic etched into her features.

"What is it, Majesty?"

The empress seemed to make up her mind. She looked searchingly at him. "Informers tell me there is a plot within the Black Glove to quietly extract the crown jewels from the bank and replace them with replicas." Her gaze followed his to the portrait of her on the wall.

"I can't believe it's come to this." His gaze moved over the portrait and the magnificent Coronation Crown, the heart of it a diamond of matchless splendor. It was the second largest diamond in the world, the famous Daria-I-Nour of 182 carats, the mate to the Star of India owned by the British.

"I know you were encouraged to take an interest in

jewels, Anthony. Your family vaults contained an extensive collection, so you understand—"

"My father once explained to me," Anthony said, "that priceless jewels financed the Iranian military before the oil boom—jewels housed in the great vaults of the Central Bank of Iran. I see how easy it would be in the current political climate to employ the crown jewels of Iran to finance a revolution."

"I refuse to take the chance," she said. "I'm removing the crown jewels from the Bank of Iran viewing cases."

"Beating them at their own game."

"I suggest you consider removing your Persian Glories. Surely traitors who would take the crown jewels couldn't resist your choice diamonds."

"Many dream of owning the Persian Glories, I know.

"Best you remove temptation from greedy hands." She stepped toward him, her lovely face expressing determination, her graceful fingers clenched into fists. "I must ask more of you—something more dangerous than your rescue missions. You must be more careful than ever, dear Anthony," she said. "No one must know."

And he'd foolishly thought the stakes were at their highest. "Go on."

"I need the crown jewels delivered to safety, a place you can secure for me and one to which I can have access in a moment's notice. Perhaps London. I would leave the location entirely in your hands."

He looked up at her, astonished. "Very well." Considering the situation, he chose the safest option. "My grandfather will contact you, if you agree."

Her face was solemn as her eyes looked keenly into his.

"Then the reports I've heard about the Shah's illness . . ."

"They are true. But we have the world's finest doctors and expect a complete recovery."

"Of course, Majesty. It must be so." Anthony realized then the Shah's illness had progressed. He must be too weak to counter this revolt or to stop this SAVAK splinter group, the Black Glove, from terrorizing the country. A threat to the Shah's safety was imminent. Soon would come the time for them to flee. It was plain Farah Diba no longer questioned the obvious. Besides, she might need quick bargaining resources at her immediate disposal. He knew her wisdom in retaining as much control as possible.

"The jewels must not fall into the wrong hands, and you understand why," she said.

He understood perfectly. These were the crown jewels of Persia, and she was asking him to smuggle them out of the country. To keep them safe. "There is no way, Majesty, I'll allow these traitors to put their filthy hands on the symbol of the Persian monarchy."

Her gaze warmed. "Thank you, Anthony."

He walked to the window, an idea forming. "Consider it done."

Moments later Anthony hurried to his car in the palace parking area. The night, though lit earlier by moonlight, had turned dark.

Even now at a remote airstrip, a hidden family, huddled in a cold shed, waited for him. Tonight he would use the Jet Ranger to fly them to freedom. The Cessna was a less conspicuous target, but the Ranger allowed him to hide in mountainous terrain. He'd chance it.

He was baffled about security leaks concerning his flight plans, especially with many missions to fly this week. How could he be more circumspect? With each trip he changed routes, changed aircraft. The destinations varied, yet someone knew. He'd find whoever it was.

He spotted his Ferrari between stuffier luxury sedans and shifted his concern, struck by the image of General Houdin earlier in an argument with Sabeti; his apprehension surged. It was the body language of those two that disturbed him. The head of Savak had appeared overpowered by Houdin. Granted, Houdin, governor of Tehran, was a feared member of SAVAK. But what influence could Houdin hold over Sabeti, its leader? No one except the Shah held such power.

A shadow fell over him.

"I see you let the lady leave without you, Evans. You're slipping."

Anthony spun to face General Houdin himself.

"Ladies require a more private venue than a palace ball for a rendezvous," Anthony slurred. He turned unsteadily toward Houdin's companion, his own darkly handsome cousin, Mirdad Ajani.

"Good evening, cousin," Mirdad said, adjusting the sleek lapels on his St. Laurent dinner jacket.

"Mirdad! Great to see you here." Anthony was furious seeing Mirdad so chummy with Houdin.

General Houdin gloated. A gold tooth winked from his wide mouth, giving him the appearance of a sixteenth-century pirate. Or was it the ill fit of his dress uniform? It looked to Anthony as if he were stuffed into it.

Anthony leered at him and leaned against the hood of his silver Ferrari. He took out a small French filter-tipped cigar, thinking that Houdin was about as refined as a wild boar and probably more deadly: bad company.

"If you're social climbing, Mirdad, you're in the wrong hands."

"Watch yourself, Evans." Houdin's voice was tight.

Mirdad looked stricken.

Anthony patted him on the back and pulled out a gold Cartier lighter from his inside pocket, tilting it toward Mirdad. "Can't let ambition get in the way of judgment." Anthony feigned a try at lighting the cigar, his anger growing.

Irritated, Houdin snatched the lighter from his hand and gave it to Mirdad.

Mirdad lit the cigar and said in his melodious voice, "Having a rough go of it tonight?"

"I've had better nights. But I'm not down yet!" Anthony shot his right arm up above his head, then lost his balance and stumbled against the general.

"*Merde!*" Houdin growled. "Stand up, man!"

Anthony smiled, exhaling Rémy Martin breath in the general's face. "Excuse me, old man," he mumbled.

With a tolerant expression, Mirdad took hold of Anthony and steadied him. "You'll be all right, but you can't drive in this condition."

"Oh, yes I can!" Anthony managed to open his car door and flop himself into the driver's seat. He turned the key in the ignition, revved the engine, and slammed the door. "I've never felt better!" he shouted over the grinding of the gearshift. The car swerved out of the long driveway and skidded onto the street. Anthony waved goodbye wildly as he made the turn.

The whine of Anthony's Ferrari engine had disappeared into the distance when Mirdad slipped into the back seat of Houdin's limo. Anthony was a fool, and disaster awaited him. But he dismissed his cousin because tonight Mirdad was here to cement his future.

"Well, Mirdad," General Houdin demanded. "Have you got it?

Mirdad smiled at his mentor, his strategy about to pay off.

"Of course," he said, taking an envelope from his inside coat pocket and handing it to the general.

Houdin scanned the document. "You made copies and left the original?"

"Naturally." Mirdad lowered the window. "Straight from Evans' safe."

General Houdin relaxed in the leather seat, lighting a cigar. "How clever of you, Mirdad, to discover your cousin, the bon vivant, in his role as savior to condemned traitors. Evans is someone I'll admit would never have awakened my suspicion. How did you unmask him?"

Mirdad leaned back against the plush leather seat, crossing his legs. "An accident, really. Late one night I followed him to the airport with an urgent message from the empress."

"I find it odd the man doesn't suspect you, Mirdad. Even you don't look that innocent. He must be blinded by filial love."

Mirdad's jaw tightened; his hands grew icy cold. "Blinded by guilt, General. Guilt for a thousand sins—sins which will never be forgiven."

"Whatever you say . . . I don't care. As long as we continue to use him."

The general handed over a plump envelope, which Mirdad stuffed into his breast pocket. Warmth once again flowed through his body. He didn't want to betray Anthony. He had loved him once. But years of rejection by his idolized cousin made Mirdad's perfidy a little easier.

"When our next task is completed," Houdin said, "I'll deposit the sum we agreed upon into your account."

"Thank you, sir."

Houdin waited a beat then said, "How is your lovely mother, Rena?"

Rena? Mirdad was puzzled at this concern Houdin had for his mother, the wife of a disgraced prime minister. "She is well, sir."

A smile appeared on Houdin's face, lighting up his usually cold eyes. "I look forward to seeing her," he said softly, then tugged at his tie, recomposing himself. "I'm on my way to meet Sabeti." He turned. "Next week you'll join me when I meet the head of SAVAK."

"Of course." SAVAK. Mirdad squirmed getting out of Houdin's car. He exhaled, rejecting a prick of apprehension regarding his future career. What if he could not continue to deliver as promised? SAVAK was a bloodthirsty group.

Alone in the bedroom of her modest home, Rena Ajani leaned back against her mahogany headboard. She had lived in this hovel for twenty-two years since her fall from grace. Her husband, a convicted murderer, had once been the prime minister of Iran, and everything she had ever wanted had been hers. It had all been torn away.

The aroma of savory spices from the meal she'd cooked earlier hung about the air, reminding her of meals years before in her father's home, a time when she felt safe, before she had lost her title, her wealth, and even her good looks. The time before she had met Omar Houdin.

She remembered their first meeting when she was seventeen, when Omar visited her father's home. He had been a twenty-two-year-old lieutenant, the driver for the illustrious prime minister of Iran—her now dead husband.

She had memorized Lieutenant Omar Houdin's gaze, his intense dark eyes filled with compelling desire. It was the beginning of their illicit affair. At her young age, never in her life had anyone looked at her quite like that, and to her embarrassment she could barely pull her gaze from his. Inordinately polite, he nonetheless seemed to study her and would laugh when he caught her making mischief on her sister Ilyia or other members of her household.

She had burned for his attentions, using any excuse she could to be around when he came to her house, but never openly acknowledging him except with some haughty gesture like having him carry in her packages after shopping, or insisting he hold a parasol over her in the sunny garden while she had tea with her father and the prime minister.

Omar Houdin, however, seemed to recognize her game, his full mouth curving slightly with her requests, a quiet fire smoldering behind his downcast eyes. She sensed he would ultimately rise to great power.

Alone at night she could not stop thinking about him. She wondered what he looked like without his clothes on. She wanted his large hands to roam her untouched body.

One afternoon when the hot sun slid behind a bank of clouds, Rena walked directly to the garden and found him waiting. She knew her father and the prime minister were there in the house, but she could no longer control her longing.

She guided Omar back into the sheltered arbor. When he professed his ardent affections, she recognized passion burning in his eyes and felt her own desire ignite. Unbuttoning her blouse, she uncovered her fully naked torso. "Touch me, Omar. Touch me now."

His large trembling hands held the weight of her breasts against his palms, his thumbs reveling in her hard nipples.

He moaned, looking as if he might fall over right there, straining.

She had been so excited herself, standing behind the tall hedge outside in daylight, that she then let him reach under her skirt, caressing her thighs, rubbing them gently but with a firm, steady stroke.

He lifted the hem higher and put his face against her panties, pressing his cheek against her, breathing in her scent, his breath hot. Slowly his fingers slipped under the silky hem, stroking her moistening curls, then into her slick, soft, woman's flesh.

He placed his tongue upon her there, flicking over her clitoris again and again, her body searing with electric spasms until she knew she would explode beneath his touch. She stood there, knees weak, her fingers entangled in his thick dark hair. She bit down on her lip, drawing blood, struggling to suffocate an endless shriek of ecstasy. But she did not dare alert her father and the prime minister inside the house sipping tea as she writhed beneath Omar's touch.

When this unexpected and mysterious moment had ended, she knew she had sampled something she could never again deny herself.

But she *had* denied herself this pleasure, the pleasure of Omar Houdin touching her again. Not for much longer. If she played this reunion right, everything she deserved would be hers. It all waited beyond a phone call.

She would entice Omar Houdin, leader of the Black Glove, back into her life.

Anthony was almost to Golestan airfield for his mission. The pressure was on, the death list was expanding rapidly, and the Jobrani family was out of time.

A car racing toward him nearly blinded him with flashing high-beam headlights. He slowed, recognizing his own Range Rover driven by Hans, his pilot. Hans pulled off the road.

What the hell had happened? Anthony got out and scanned the horizon to see if Hans had been followed. The Range Rover made a U-turn and pulled around in front of him.

Hans leapt out, his eyes searching the road. "SAVAK agents, three carloads of the buggers, swarming like black beetles into the flight office." Shaking, Hans wiped his brow on his shirtsleeve. "I didn't wait around to see what they were up to."

Anthony took hold of Hans' shoulders. "The Jobranis! Where are they?"

"They're in the car. They're okay."

"Right. Probably scared out of their wits by now."

Hans swiped his hand over his short hair. "The kids are crying, the grandmother's praying." Hans shook his head, clearly not dealing well with the situation.

"Can you take them to your place, Hans? This is the wrong hour to pursue our flight plans."

"Shit, Anthony, my landlord is a nosy old devil always poking around . . . I dunno."

"Hans."

"Okay, okay, I'll do it."

"I'll bring food for them as soon as I'm certain it's safe." Anthony turned to go. Another pair of oncoming headlights raced toward him: a black Lincoln, unmistakably SAVAK, followed closely by two more cars.

"Son of a bitch. Kill your lights and get out of here, Hans." Anthony kicked a tire, scuffing his polished evening shoes.

"Don't worry, we'll get 'em out later tonight for sure!" Hans yelled, jumping into the Range Rover, headlights off, skidding away.

Apprehension whirling inside, Anthony slid his knife from the car door pocket. Quickly, he bent to his right front tire, viciously jabbing into it. Hissing air escaped the tire. Gravel on the side of the road crunched under the weight of the black Lincoln pulling up in front of him. He pocketed the knife.

The two following cars wedged in behind his Ferrari as he stood up in the glare of headlights. Fighting a sinking feeling, Anthony staggered to the rear of his car. He lifted the trunk, peering inside for the tools and spare he'd need to change the tire. He heard the Lincoln car door slam.

"Good evening, Mr. Evans."

"Nothing good about it, Captain Aran!" A dark countenance he loathed came toward him. "Not with a bloody flat."

In the shadows, the SAVAK captain's grin did nothing to disguise his virulent nature. Bezad Aran was a man who derived pleasure from each heinous task he performed in the name of duty under orders from SAVAK's top echelon and secret leadership, the Black Glove.

Anthony figured Aran, their chief thug, was the man who had locked the Rex Cinema doors in Abadan yesterday while 400 students had screamed, burning to death. What had brought him out tonight?

"Having difficulty finding your way home tonight, Evans?" His smile faded. "You're way off course. Your home lies to the north, I recall."

"How the hell do I know?" Anthony stumbled against the car, leering at Captain Aran with an unfocused grin. "I'm blitzed." Anthony peered down the road to see if Hans was out of sight and cursed his careless gaze as Captain Aran's quick eyes narrowed suspiciously, turning to see what had drawn Anthony's attention.

Anthony belched loudly and slapped Captain Aran on the shoulder. "Well, I say, Aran, since you're already here, could your men give me a hand with the tire?"

Aran turned back to Anthony, irritably flexing the fingers on his gloved right hand. "You may be pampered by Sabeti, Evans, but at night on the streets, you're on your own." He gave Anthony a snarl and turned, gesturing to his men. "Let's go! We have work to do."

Anthony winced at the thought of what Aran's "work" might be. He tossed his dinner jacket in the car, rolled up his shirtsleeves, and went to change his demolished tire, both relief and fury coursing through his blood.

After his conversation with Houdin, Mirdad climbed into Anthony's borrowed limo, dismissing his concerns about SAVAK. He acknowledged Ali, the driver, with a nod.

At twenty-two, Ali Zahedi was the only member of Anthony's household Mirdad could tolerate. He was a bit of a Shiite zealot but a close friend whom Mirdad had watched grow from a boy to a young man. Ali had followed Mirdad incessantly over the years with questions, always asking questions. But Ali's probing queries highlighted his intelligence; he was a knowledge seeker, much like Mirdad.

"Good evening to you, Deputy Minister." Ali eased out onto the highway. It was after midnight, and the air had turned cold.

Mirdad pulled a cashmere throw across his lap and settled into his seat. The rolling *click, click* of Ali's prayer beads contrasted with the purring engine of the new Cadillac limo shipped to Iran courtesy of Anthony's international connections. The car smelled faintly of French perfume— Anthony's frolics.

Then Mirdad remembered the sardonic smile Anthony

had cast him as he was driven off. *For the sake of your infidel hide, cousin, don't get in my way. I'm about to make my fortune.*

He patted the envelope from Houdin, knowing his mother would be glad General Houdin still thought of her as lovely. Houdin always mentioned his mother, but why? Hadn't Houdin made inquiries only to be polite, respectful? But to say she was lovely? When had this dangerous man actually met his mother? She hardly ever ventured out. No matter, he would ask her later.

"Did you enjoy the ball and the decadent display of Pahlavi wealth, sir?" Ali said, interrupting his inner query.

Amused, Mirdad leaned back. "Such sudden formality, Ali. Has someone at last taken your etiquette tutelage in hand?"

"I must be polite since I wish to borrow more books from your magnificent library. Besides, I keep my distance from the depraved." He put on his driver's cap. "Home, sir?"

With a smile Mirdad said, "I seek further depravity: Madame Shala's. It's a night to celebrate."

Ali's head swerved toward Mirdad for a moment, eyes glowing contempt, a predictable reaction from a devout Shiite. "Humph. Fornication is against our Muslim laws," he said. "You endanger your body and your soul."

"My soul, perhaps, but my body will dwell in paradise in an hour's time."

Mirdad enjoyed mentally sparring with this pious student of history and the Koran. But Ali, caught up in his religion, faced a narrow future. He would follow strict laws of some crusty ayatollah, as would most Iranians.

With ties to Houdin, Mirdad would be safe from

mullahs and maybe even rich. A smile of hope crossed his lips. Houdin was a man to take seriously. The sly general secretly played the Shah's SAVAK against the revolutionary Shiites with his terrorist creation, the Black Glove, more ruthless than SAVAK. As such, Houdin had an activist, one might say, in every camp. Mirdad chuckled for a moment at this conspiracy until his own predicament roared into his thoughts, and he felt the Black Glove's fist tightening around his throat. He must tread a careful line and not embroil himself too deeply with Houdin. He must remain a minor player, making only enough money to lift him and his mother out of poverty.

Click, click, Ali's prayer beads again. Ali's eyes flashed at Mirdad in the rear view mirror as the nightscape whizzed by in a blur.

"Speak up, Ali! What's on your mind?"

"I saw you with that butcher, Houdin. Are you not concerned he'll turn on you? Best be on guard, Mirdad. SAVAK has long arms."

"Look to your militant Shiite rebels. They have high stakes in the escalating turmoil, discrediting the Shah's ability to govern."

"They are religious men!"

"They are men, nonetheless, who blame much of their rebellious dirty work on SAVAK."

Much of the plundering done by Houdin's Black Glove was blamed on SAVAK, too, blurring the distinction. And now Houdin was insistent Mirdad become part of SAVAK. But SAVAK belonged to the Shah. Mirdad had no love for the Shah or his coterie. They had brought down Mirdad's own father.

In the mirror, Ali's eyes flashed. "Before long, that general will insist you join SAVAK. Then what will you do?"

Was he a mind reader? "And how do you know so much about SAVAK, student?"

"I know it is scum, founded in 1957 as a national intelligence and security organization to gather information on foreign powers."

"And?"

"And the Israeli Mossad and the CIA originally trained SAVAK agents for international development."

Yes, and naturally the SAVAK cooperated with the CIA, collecting information on the Soviet Union, information the U.S. administration deemed vital. Mirdad shuddered with distaste, resolute. "We've all watched SAVAK grow malevolent. Becoming a member of SAVAK is one line I'll not cross, Ali."

"Maybe you're SAVAK already."

Mirdad looked up. "If I were, your goose would be cooked, you anarchist."

SAVAK was so powerful in Iran everyone from courtier to janitor had reason to fear them. Informers operated at every level and could be anyone from your banker to your best friend.

"How, Mirdad, did they get so much power? They override ministers, cancel visas, ban publication of books, interfere with the release of films, tamper with our mail . . ."

Ali banged on the steering wheel with each mention of SAVAK abuse.

"Only a few of its lesser tyrannies. You *have* studied." Mirdad leaned forward. "Slow down, and take the next right."

SAVAK had tightened security with the increasing political upheaval. Troops now guarded every main artery in and out of the city. "I'm told it's a safer route. You'll still come out on Jasmine Road."

Ali made the turn, and Mirdad sat back, considering. "Maybe *you're* with them?"

Ali gasped.

"The rewards could be great."

"Never!"

"Then keep your mouth shut. Don't mention SAVAK to anyone—ever. Once in their clutches there's nowhere to turn, a prisoner has no contact with the outside world."

"Enough!" Ali drove with his arms straight out on the wheel, speeding down the unlit road.

"If they take you, they torture you. Their methods are gruesome."

"I know this!"

They drove in silence, the topic dragging down their mood.

Mirdad imagined the horror of the Black Glove gaining power, insatiable with greed. *Think of it*: billions in gold, jewels, and funds stolen from companies and families who then disappeared. Everything confiscated would then be transferred to secret accounts around the world. *That* was a lot of wealth, and Mirdad would tap into it. Finally, he would realize dreams he'd clung to through years of deprivation. He straightened in his seat, shifting his focus. Almost there: pleasure-land.

Ali swerved onto Jasmine Road, then turned up a winding driveway. He pulled in front of a garish house trimmed in gold, then jammed on the brakes.

"You are in more danger than I, Deputy Minister, with the company you keep." Ali jumped out of the car and opened Mirdad's door. "Your depravity awaits." Ali swept his arm wide, his face turned down, not revealing further disapproval.

Mirdad tossed the cashmere throw to Ali. "I'll be a while. Get some sleep."

Ali nodded and climbed into the back seat.

Mirdad leaned in. "Soon your hand will not be enough to satisfy you, *Koocooloo*."

He walked up to the garish house with anticipation.

Inside Madame Shala's salon, Mirdad fumed, forced to wait on the red silk settee, his fingers drumming on the Victorian side table. Ten minutes had passed. True, he hadn't been there in over two months, but this was no way to treat an old customer. This slight he would remember.

His stormy mood brought thoughts of his cousin, Anthony, and resentment. He'd watched the bastard drive drunkenly from the palace ball tonight, evincing not a care in the world, treating Mirdad with a revolting sham of affection. Anthony didn't care what happened to him. When his parents died, Anthony had deserted him for England and never looked back.

Mirdad would never forget the day twenty-one years earlier . . ..

CHAPTER SEVEN

TEHRAN, APRIL 1957

It was Mirdad Ajani's twelfth birthday, and as the son of Iran's prime minister, he attended a school for élite Persian boys, all dressed in smart school uniforms: gray slacks, white shirts, blue blazers, and school ties, the laces on their blue and white oxfords neatly tied. Mirdad was trying to make this day his happiest birthday ever though his favorite person in the world, his cousin Anthony, was no longer at school with him. Nothing seemed right without his best friend.

It was after the noon meal, and the boys cheered the huge, tantalizing slices of Mirdad's cake they were receiving; it was decorated like a soccer field with goal posts and players. Thick fudge frosting dripped from their mouths and sticky fingers as they gobbled it up. Raymond, his father's chauffeur, had said Anthony had called from England to order the cake. Tomorrow would be Mirdad's official birthday party, and for this he was excited. Mirdad loved parties, especially when he was the star.

"Tell us, Mirdad," skinny Touraj asked, "are you really having elephant rides at your party tomorrow?"

". . . and American hot dogs?" asked plump little Jira.

He grinned at them and nodded. "Yes, there will be elephants to ride."

Jira leaped up with a joyful cry and overturned a jar containing frogs for the jumping contest, the escaped creatures hopping about the classroom. It was a hilarious sight for Mirdad, and the boys barely noticed when the teacher was called out of the classroom.

"Get 'em, Ali," shouted Mirdad, laughing.

"Help me, Touraj."

"Look, there they go!"

The boys laughed harder.

"I bet on the darkest one," said Ali.

"Five urals on the fat one," said Mirdad.

"Okay, five more on the spotted," said Touraj.

"No, let's get them." Plump Jira scurried after the hopping amphibians. "Quick, you guys, before the teacher gets back."

"Hey, Jira, you look like one of them," Mirdad teased. "Go, Jira. I'll wager five on you."

Mirdad was having fun, the first fun he'd had since the family tragedy nearly a month ago, when Aunt Ilyia and Uncle Richard had died in a plane crash, and Anthony had been taken away to the estate in England of Lord Charles, his grandfather. Mirdad had been devastated.

He wished Anthony were coming to his party, and his Aunt Ilyia and Uncle Richard as well. Sir Richard Evans had loved parties, loved introducing his wife when she was wearing the Persian Glories. He was the personification of what Mirdad wanted to be when he grew up. Flying jet planes with the Shah, riding sleek horses in polo matches, marrying the most beautiful woman in all of Persia. Aunt Ilyia never talked back to Richard in the inappropriate way Mirdad's mother used against his father, contradicting polite Persian society. Uncle Richard loved fast cars and trips to Paris, where he'd even let Mirdad and Anthony sneak in to see the Follies Bérgère and other risqué shows.

Mirdad wanted to be like Sir Richard Evans—except he didn't want to die young.

He would miss them all—especially Anthony, his idol.

With Anthony, Mirdad felt safe because the older boy looked out for him. Anthony was solid. Even when Mirdad was a pest or Anthony told him to shut up, Mirdad knew that in the next moment if anyone picked on him at school, Anthony would jump right in and defend him. *Why was he always the one to be picked on?* Because he bragged once in a while that his father was the boss of Iran? Well, next to the Shah, he was; his mother told him so. Anthony used to say he wanted attention, and perhaps that was true. When he was at home with his parents they seemed to argue a lot and were too busy to notice him much.

"Is Anthony coming to your party?" asked Jira, cupping a slick green frog in his hands.

Mirdad hadn't heard from Anthony, not a word. He squeezed his eyes, shutting back tears. *What if his cousin was gone forever?* He didn't want these thoughts. He didn't want his friendship with Anthony to be so important, but it was. "I think he's coming," he told Jira, and the boys cheered.

Today Mirdad had made his secret birthday wish peering down at twelve glowing candles on his cake. *Anthony, come home.* Mirdad would wish it into reality, and he cheered fervently with the others, "Anthony's coming to the party!"

The door to the classroom burst open, and the headmaster, furious, stood in the doorway. The laughter ceased abruptly. Tense silence replaced it. The startled boys sat frozen.

"Ajani. Mirdad Ajani, come here at once!"

Tentatively, Mirdad turned to face the headmaster, his thoughts racing to find the reason why he had been stingingly singled out in the classroom, but he could think of none.

"You are dishonored! Your family has been denounced. Your father, the *former* prime minister, has been stripped of his position. He is accused of murder—a traitor."

Mirdad found his voice. "Wh-what murder?"

"The murder of a high ranking British diplomat, his wife—members of your own family—and five members of his staff. He had their plane blown up. Seven people have died by his hand."

There was an intake of breath around the room as the other students looked at each other in disbelief.

The horror was happening again. Like the day he was told of the plane crash and someone had shouted, "Look! Look outside." Several boys had rushed to the window, all their attention drawn to the sight of a long black car flying British flags pulling up in front of the school. Mirdad had watched as Anthony was chaperoned out of the building, objecting loudly at being escorted to the limo. Someone had said, "There goes your cousin," and Mirdad's heart had contracted.

Now, he couldn't even comprehend what the headmaster was saying. His father was still prime minister of Iran, one of the most respected men in the nation. "My father is innocent."

The boys whispered among themselves. "Anthony Evans," said Touraj, staring straight at Mirdad to see his reaction, "his parents were the ones that were killed."

Mirdad shook his head. "No!"

"Mirdad's father killed them?" asked Jira, sounding confused.

"I can't believe it!" said another boy.

"Silence!" The headmaster pointed at Mirdad. "Your father murdered your aunt and uncle. Traitor, do you hear? A disgrace!" He crossed to Mirdad and ripped the school emblem from his jacket.

Mirdad clutched his chair, not able to catch his breath. The room closed in on him. He couldn't quite grasp it all. His mind told him it wasn't happening, but as he turned to his classmates, they were shouting at him—Touraj, Ali, Jira—all of them. This couldn't be happening. They had been having fun together!

"Traitor! Traitor! Murderer!" As if he, a child, had killed his beloved Uncle Richard and Aunt Ilyia.

Over their voices he heard the headmaster. "Leave this school! Never come back!"

The boys threw things at Mirdad: erasers, leftover food from their lunches, fruit, tomatoes, and all the remains of his delicious birthday cake—everything splattered on him.

"No! No, you are wrong!" he shouted back, but panic overtook him, and he pushed through the students surrounding him. He ran as fast as he could out of the building and through the gates. And kept running.

For hours Mirdad ran, desperate, unable to stop himself. Up and down filthy streets of wretched neighborhoods, gutters littered with rancid refuse, places he never knew existed. Could anyone actually live in this miserable foulness? He was completely disoriented. He was lost.

The sun disappeared behind the buildings as he ran in and out of deepening shadows. A strident noise alarmed him. A threatening black bird cawed, then ferociously pecked at a disintegrating animal carcass. What it once had been, Mirdad couldn't imagine.

Looking behind him, Mirdad stumbled and fell to the pavement, scraping his hands and knees, burying blacktop in his soft palms, blood oozing to the surface, stinging. He scrambled to get up and heard strange malevolent laughter echoing off high, crumbling walls. His pants torn, his knee bleeding, he blew on his palms, cooling the abrasion, then wiped his sweaty face on his sleeve. He looked about. Which way should he go? It was getting dark. He thought of Anthony's courage and quelled a whimper. Somewhere close by he heard an animal howl. He had to move.

From out of the darkness several bulky shapes drifted toward him, their faces covered in shadow. He was trapped in a narrow alley, unless he turned and ran back the way he came. But men were there, too. Then he heard one of them laughing, that same malevolent cackle, and other voices joined in.

"Such a tender, innocent boy. Have you ever seen such lovely eyes?"

Mirdad didn't know where to run.

"What a price he would fetch with Salim."

"Grab him!"

Suddenly there were shouts and curses coming from all around him, behind windows and doorways, his own thundering pulse pounding in his ears, drowning the noise around him as his terror rose. He had to make it home to see his mother on his birthday. From someplace within, fury took over in him, and he thought again of Anthony. What would he do? Impetuously, Mirdad grabbed an offensive garbage pail, spinning around and around. His startled assailants backed off, and in that split second he hurled the metal pail, splitting the pack wide enough for him to run through the opening. The shouts behind him sounded closer as he ran harder than he ever had in his life, up the sloping alley toward a street. He heard a car honking, honking, and through his panic he recognized his Uncle Richard's Bentley. But Uncle Richard was dead, killed by his father, they said. *Why?*

The Bentley screeched to a halt. There was his father's driver, Raymond, waving wildly. "Get in, Mirdad, get in the car!"

Mirdad stared, reeling with fright.

"Mirdad! Get in, boy!"

Mirdad clambered into the car and sagged against the soft leather seat, weak with relief.

Raymond sped away. "Blessed Allah! What happened to you? Where have you been? They told me at school you ran off."

Filled with shame and horror at what had happened at school and afterward, Mirdad could not answer. How could it be he wouldn't be going back to his school again with all his friends? But they were no longer his friends, were they?

He looked down at himself. He was a filthy, ragged mess with bloody knees and torn clothing, and he felt awful.

"Are you badly hurt?"

"No. No, it's a few scrapes," he said. "Thank you, Raymond. Thank you." Mirdad reached over the seat and hugged his friend. Raymond looked at him sadly, questions hanging in the air that out of courtesy Mirdad knew he would not ask.

"You must be brave, Mirdad." Raymond's face grew tight. "The SAVAK are at your house. They've come for your father."

Mirdad gasped. If only he could ride an elephant. He could make the beast crush these men who would take his father, bloody their bodies, and leave them to bake in the sun. Because his gentle, loving father would never be violent, he would never save himself.

Mirdad sank lower in the seat, wretched. He knew he'd never get to ride his birthday elephant.

Clutching the gilt arm of Madame Shala's settee, Mirdad fought a familiar, burning stomach pain brought on by these futile recollections. Anthony, the young lord, had gone to Eton, while Mirdad's privileged life was stripped away. This tore at him.

Yanking his thoughts away, Mirdad patted his pocket stuffed with rials. His thoughts again turned to the pleasure awaiting him. He needed to explode the rage inside, and only a particular whore would give him the release he craved.

"Good evening, Mirdad."

Madame Shala entered and he stood, more out of impatience than courtesy. She was a handsome woman of advanced age, maybe in her fifties. Her dark hair was swept in a coil of elaborate braids at the back of her head. She had a high forehead accentuated by a deep widow's peak. A woman who lived indoors, her skin was fine and pale. Her sharp amber gaze leveled on him, softening.

"Mirdad, how nice to see you again. It's been too long."

He made no move to respond.

"Please forgive me for keeping you waiting, dear friend."

"Think nothing of it, Madame." He smiled disarmingly. She knew too many secrets for him to lash out at her.

"The perfect choices await you. I personally made sure all is ready."

He started to pay her, but she refused. "No, no. A gift from General Houdin, who told us you deserve only the best."

"Does he know . . . ?" Mirdad nearly shrieked.

Madame Shala shook her head, her smile wise in the ways of the night. "Have no worries. He paid for a night of pleasure. The details he will never know."

Mirdad almost choked on relief, nodding.

"The general told us you richly deserve the best and has given you one he had planned to keep for himself. This girl is called Siri. She has recently come to us from

Estonia. She is young and pure. Unfortunately, she speaks no Farsi, but has no problem with English."

"She sounds delightful, Madame Shala. No drugs, I trust?" Mirdad couldn't stand to be with anyone on drugs; he wanted the woman's full attention, the excitement of their pleasure, pain, and surrender.

"No drugs, I assure you." She clapped her strong, aging hands, and a powerful African wearing billowing trousers and a jeweled dierette on his turban came to escort Mirdad upstairs to a private salon, then discreetly departed.

Mirdad opened the door and was pleased at Houdin's generosity when he saw Siri standing in the middle of the salon. She was a girl of about fifteen, looking small and fresh, wearing a pale pink silk halter top, barely covering her sweet breasts and matching silk harem pants. She nervously played with long blonde hair falling over her shoulder to her tiny waist. Her slender bare feet stood on the many layers of richly woven carpets cushioning the floor.

She looked particularly small surrounded by the huge tapestries on the walls and a large banquette partly tented in sheer, white gauze. Her smile was tremulous and utterly vulnerable. Mirdad knew why. She hadn't come to Iran by choice, but no doubt had been abducted from her home by one of Madame Shala's many "talent scouts."

He walked toward her, aware of the discomfort she must feel. So frightened . . . and he loved it. With his fiery mood he would not take his time with Siri.

"Yes, you will do nicely," he said. "Come here."

She obeyed.

He stroked her silky hair, then twisted a handful around his fingers, tugging her head back, kneading her young, full breasts, grinding his body into hers. In seconds, he was erect. "Undress me."

Siri awkwardly obeyed. Mirdad enjoyed her childish manner. The more difficult it was for her, the more aroused he became. Naked, he went to the banquette and lounged, drinking in her loveliness. Catching shock in her eyes as she took in the size of his jutting cock, he smiled. She had probably never seen one, but soon he would enlighten her with what he'd do with it.

"Off with your clothes."

Her filmy outfit fell off her body like petals from a flower.

"Walk about the room." He watched her legs and buttocks move. "Yes, yes. Caress your breasts for me. Oh, they're lovely. Now bend over, let me see. Yes, on your hands and knees. Crawl to me, little one."

Rage mounted in him with the memory of Anthony and lovely Alexandria together in the palace courtyard. "Come here," he growled.

Siri scurried to the bed.

He threw her back, spreading her legs. He chuckled when she tried to push away his hands. He grabbed her small wrists in one large hand, holding her arms above her head.

She cried out.

"Shut up!" he ordered.

With passion, Mirdad initiated Siri into his particular sexual specialties, taking her virginity, oblivious to her objections.

When he was spent, he threw her from him, tears streaming down her face.

"Wash yourself well and me quickly." He waited, smoking a cigarette.

Her hands were small and tentative. She'd been an innocent, but trainable. He would arrange for her to be his alone. No one else would touch her. He would buy her tonight, and here she would stay for his pleasure. His duty with a female accomplished, he said, "Leave now," banishing her from the room.

Time for dessert, what he had waited for, truly desired.

His gaze traveled across the room to a shrouded divan and the creature lounging naked there. Mirdad studied the tall, powerfully built young man with gorgeous green eyes awaiting him. He gestured him over, watching his graceful movements. "Your name?"

"I'm called Emil, Excellency." His lush lips curved in a modest smile.

"Take me in your mouth, gorgeous Emil. Show me your talent."

Emil kneeled at Mirdad's feet. Warm hands slid up Mirdad's thighs. One hand slid under his sac, caressing ever so gently. "Oh, good," Mirdad groaned. An even warmer mouth, soft and wet, eased over his erection, sucking until Mirdad knew paradise. In his mind he had Anthony on his knees, servicing him.

Regaining his strength, Mirdad rose with Emil, shoving him to face a wall, drawing Emil's buttocks toward him. Emil's arms raised, hands placed high on the flocked wallpaper. Mirdad stroked his way down those arms, over the supple ridges of Emil's spine to grasp his round, firm ass. Mirdad slipped a latex condom over his erection, then slathered sex-salve over its bulging head. He found the crack between Emil's pale twin moons and plunged inside. He plumbed Emil's depths, then retracted to plunge again and again, varying his rhythm until he could hold back no longer, exploding at last in a powerful rage-filled orgasm.

Emil did all Mirdad asked. He begged to do more, pleaded with Mirdad to take him, telling Mirdad he needed him, needed to be fucked like the whore he was. Emil thanked Mirdad, even when it got rough, insisting he deserved the brutality inflicted upon him. As dawn crept near, they lay in bed, the curtains billowing. Mirdad had Emil on his knees once more. "Suck me. Suck me," he moaned, well pleased with this party.

CHAPTER EIGHT

Oblivious to the late hour, Mirdad, sated but restless, needing to relax, slammed into his darkened house in Tehran, heading for the bottle of Absolut tucked away in the refrigerator. He opened the fridge and soothing cool air hit his face. A platter with lamb kabobs and mint-infused rice was waiting for him. His mother had become a good cook of late, but he had no need for food at this hour. He poured himself a stiff drink standing at the sink, his emotions roiling as always after sex.

In truth, old feelings of love had surfaced in his private sanctuary at Madame Shala's. His love-hate relationship with Anthony had been suspended in fantasy for hours of indulgence. After taking Houdin's gift—a young, virginal girl—his duty was discharged for tonight by having a female.

There were no homosexuals in Iran. Homosexuality was punished by slow death. Iranian men married, had children, and perhaps in some clandestine tryst, exercised other passions. He would find a wife soon. It was time.

Mirdad downed his Absolut and went out onto the small courtyard patio where his mother waited up for him as always. She sat alone, lit by the wavering glow of a kerosene lamp at the edge of an old rattan table; her chair, once upholstered silk, now sagged in sun-stripped tatters. She glanced through a worn European fashion magazine. Her still graceful fingers flipped through crinkled pages with an eagerness that confounded him; crackled images she had seen again and again still held her interest.

"You're up early, Mother. Or is it you haven't been to bed yet?" He smelled lilies and jasmine, their scent awakening on the breeze.

"I'm not ready to sleep yet."

She didn't look up at him, but remained turned away, her posture erect under a drab formless dress and veil, a sobering contrast to the magnificently gowned women who had swirled past him at the palace mere hours ago. Mirdad took notice of his mother's appearance, and his stomach twisted.

The once regal Rena Ajani, whose lush, exotic beauty had turned heads, now declined under the weight of poverty and grief. Even with her recent surgery he had yet to see a difference in her, for she refused to unveil the results. He sat next to her. "It's getting cold, Mother. Won't you come inside?"

"Tell me about the ball, Mirdad. Was it grand? Who was there, and what did they wear?" Her countenance softened with her words.

Though weary, Mirdad smiled. "Many ladies wore French gowns. The men as formal as penguins."

She chuckled.

"And Farah Diba dressed in shimmering green like spring leaves kissed with dew. Her crown of emeralds and baroque pearls outshone all other jewels."

His mother leaned forward, attentive.

"The orchestra started off with a waltz. We danced, a rainbow of color swirling under glittering chandeliers. Then a rumba and Ambassador Aman, cinched in his burgundy waistcoat, danced with his niece until bright gold buttons popped off, flying about the room, smacking a colonel on the nose, skittering under Madame Touraj's silk pumps until she teetered like a drunken sailor."

His mother laughed loudly and so did Mirdad, until they both wiped at their eyes.

"Such whimsy, my son," she said, still tittering. Then, head tilted, she asked, "And did a young lady catch your eye tonight?"

"Perhaps."

She clapped her hands joyfully.

"Soon, Mother, you'll accompany me to the marble palace in any gown of your choice."

Her look became doubtful.

"I'm rising in our society. It's time for you to enjoy yourself again."

"And your cousin Anthony, was he there, too?"

"Yes." Mirdad's mood shifted from light to shade.

"He is up to something—I know it." Her fist struck the table.

Mirdad sighed. He would not get into this with her now.

"It's late. Come inside."

"Why else would my illustrious nephew stay in this godforsaken place?"

"Don't make a scene, Mother. Our lives are changing. Your behavior mustn't threaten us."

"You can't let him take my jewels out of the country!"

"When the moment is right he'll be dealt with! Patience, Mother, patience a while longer." He stood, shaking from the strange ache in his stomach. Exhaustion. "I'm going in, Mother. I suggest you do the same."

She put her hands up. "Very well, *pesar*, my son."

Mirdad dragged himself into his room and removed his tie and cufflinks, dropping them in a bureau drawer. His glance fell on the old mahogany furniture, desk chairs, cupboards, and worn Persian carpets. He might never replace them. It all reminded him of a past he couldn't forsake. He scanned the bookcase full of precious history books then peered into the adjacent room cast in shadows: a two-story library annexed to the back of the house, a gift built by his father's four pious brothers when Mirdad had won a scholarship to Iran's finest university, the University of Iran. The twenty thousand books sheltered there were Mirdad's precious legacy, his father's rare library smuggled from his old home to this shabby house. He ran his fingers along worn leather spines for comfort.

With sagging fatigue, he tore off his new clothes, discarding them haphazardly on the floor, forgoing his usual meticulous order. He grabbed a book, *History of the Babylonian Empire*, and fell into his bed and slept, the book cradled in his arms.

Less than an hour later when Rena Ajani answered the phone, she heard Omar Houdin's voice and hope burned.

"Rena, my love."

"What can I do for you, Omar? I'm busy."

"What else is more important?"

"My *Vogue*. I get more satisfaction from a Cartier advertisement than from your empty promises."

A dead silence. So he'd learned to control his anger. She waited.

"Let me see you, touch you."

"Not yet, Omar."

"You have ruined me. I'm not able to marry another woman. I'm obsessed with you."

She said nothing.

"All those years back when you finally told me Mirdad was my own son, my life changed, gained true meaning."

"Now you tell me this."

"Every time you let me speak to you, I tell you this, praying one day you'll hear me, Rena. You deprive me of your body, even the sight of you."

"You could have married me."

"I couldn't. We would have been ruined by Valik's disgrace, lived like peasants, had nothing. A life not fit for you, my beauty. Don't you see? I've been able to bring Mirdad into my plans. I've molded him, done everything to groom him for a future to bring great wealth and power to him."

"When, Omar?"

"Soon, Rena, very soon. And then the truth can be told to my son."

"You've been careful not to let anyone suspect your true relationship, haven't you, Omar?"

"Naturally. My enemies are many. You think I'd jeopardize my only son? We would both be vulnerable."

"And now?"

"Nothing worries me now but you, Rena. You're the only woman who ever affected me. The power you have over me—you dominate my feelings. Your lust, like no other I've ever known."

"Is that what you think about? I thought you were leading a revolution."

"Everything I do is with you in mind, Rena. You and my son."

"Perhaps you won't want me. I am no longer the young woman you knew."

"Make no mistake: I want you."

She heard him lighting his cigarette, and in her mind she could see him without his shirt, his powerful shoulders hunching slightly as he lit it. He inhaled deeply, and she pictured the rise of his chest covered in thick, dark hair, warm, soft, the smell of him still intensely present in her hungry senses. She knew he was thinking of the promises he had made to her, promises of wealth, calling the Persian Glories her own, and above all restoring her honor. Would he marry her?

"Let me be with you and my son, and I'll give you what you want."

"So you always say."

"I'm now in a position to give you everything.

"I want my sister's child gone from this world."

"I can arrange it," he said.

"Why have you called me this time?"

"The money you requested, Rena. It'll be there tonight."

CHAPTER NINE

Anthony rushed into his offices at the Ministry of Culture in Tehran, showered but barely refreshed, his latest run-in with Jamal still biting at him. He had to find out who ratted him out to SAVAK, who let them know when to expect his return via chopper.

He took a breath and somehow the familiar atmosphere of garish French baroque antiques the Iranians favored comforted him. The unthreatening whir of copy machines and tat-tat-tat of IBM typewriters eased his spirit. As he was the Shah's court photographer and friend, the Ministry of Culture had always provided him with a suite of offices. In return, he occasionally acted as ministry liaison for film dignitaries who worked in Iran. And yet, whoever had betrayed him could very well work right here at the ministry.

"Sorry I'm late, Nina. I overslept."

"But not in your own bed, I'll wager," said Nina, his

young office assistant, her soft brown eyes smiling over a pert nose. Nina had emigrated to Iran from South America; she was young and quietly Jewish. Anthony shrugged, comfortable with her warm easy manner. She made his impossible schedule achievable.

"The Americans, the film group?" he asked.

She followed him into his own office. "Our best driver, Habib Ozar, was busy."

"Habib is a terrible driver, Nina."

"Don't worry. I sent Ali."

"Alright, good. I appreciate you taking care of it." He set his briefcase on the desk, thinking of the Boeing stills he'd agreed to shoot for the Americans.

"But I'm sure," Nina went on, "it wasn't the reception they expected. There was some trouble at the airport."

He looked up from his desk.

"Ali took care of it."

"*Pishkesh*, no doubt. That boy learns fast."

"You really should've been there, Anthony."

"You're right, of course. No red carpet. I'll make it up to them." He needed to stay on good terms with the Americans for the week he'd be with them at Persepolis. Without knowing it, they gave him a reason to photograph in a remote region where his activities wouldn't be closely watched. They would provide the perfect alibi for him. What could be more innocuous, more fitting for his image?

He organized a leather portfolio with royal photographs. "Make a dinner reservation for tomorrow night at Kayam's Paradise Club, and send a welcome basket to each of them."

"I've sent them already. What time for dinner?"

He sorted through his thoughts. "Nine o'clock. No, make it eight. They'll have an early call the next day."

"Where shall I say you'll be this afternoon?" Nina asked.

"The palace. I'm dropping off photographs for the empress with her secretary." He hoped Oriana had a message from the empress, now that this murderous group was on to him.

"I'm off," he gathered his things. "Oh, and get Mirdad to handle the bank. And I almost forgot, he's to give the bank manager this letter." He handed her a sealed envelope with instructions to have the Persian Glories removed from display at the bank. "I'll fly to Shiraz after I leave the palace and meet the Americans tomorrow." He opened the door. "Oh, and cancel lunch. I'll eat when I get to Shiraz."

"Got it."

"And Nina. Thank you." She smiled, and he turned to go. The telephone rang and she answered it. "Wait!"

He lifted his hands in protest.

"It's England, Lord Charles."

"Right." Never failed. It seemed his grandfather called whenever Anthony was pressed for time. But he smiled in spite of his hurry.

"Grandfather," he said.

"Anthony, how are you, dear boy?"

"Fine, fine. What can I do for you, Grandfather?"

"I need you to come to England immediately!"

"What?"

"Your gallery would like you in England to review your photographs. They are most insistent." They both knew Anthony's phone was tapped by the SAVAK, a common occurrence these days for anyone on their radar. Anthony evaluated his grandfather's words. He and his family had always built their private or urgent messages around art or photography.

"My work for the exhibition isn't complete yet. Besides, I'm leaving within six weeks. You know that."

"I don't think that will do." The older man's voice grew soft.

Anthony sighed, perhaps because he knew the old man simply cared about him, wanted him safe.

"I'm working on the last photos they requested." Anthony was cautious. They both knew he was referring to the SAVAK death list. Some people on the ever-expanding list were his friends, people he'd known all his life. Naturally, once they were on the list, their exit visas were void, which meant one had to act swiftly and creatively to save their lives.

"We agreed—"

"No, Anthony."

How irritating! He wouldn't leave Iran, now in its worst hour. He'd been using his connections with the Foreign Office and his father's old affiliations with MI-6 to help those he could to escape before the SAVAK drained the country of its finest citizens and their fortunes.

"Leave now."

"I can't."

"Oh, by the way, Anthony, regarding the London Art Critics award list," Lord Charles sighed, "we've heard. You're on it. Congratulations."

Anthony was silent, caught completely off guard. He'd thought himself impervious both to SAVAK and the Black

Glove as a British subject and an unofficial ambassador of the Shah. "You're certain?"

"Yes. But we're not certain when this award will be bestowed." His grandfather cleared his voice. "And by the way, I plan to reopen Blythe Castle this winter. So if you could ship the family paintings, furniture, and what-not back to England to fill up the old place—it's empty as a new nest—I'd appreciate it."

Anthony listened, a sinking feeling in his gut. How could there be another death list? He was supposed to be privy to the most pertinent SAVAK information. What was happening to the heretofore secure and thorough line of communication between his highly placed contacts and those who sought to terminate him?

"How have I not heard of this?"

"It's the inner art circle, Anthony. They have their own rules for judging merit. You know this. And your dedication to your work has received notice."

"Fine. We'll see what . . . I'll do what I can." Anthony felt sickened.

"Pray, do it now! The art world won't wait while you fiddle around with your silly women and fast cars. You could miss this opportunity."

"All right, all right." Anthony ran his fingers through his still damp hair. He'd pushed his luck further than usual this last time. Suddenly the realities of the political climate, the murders, the demonstrations against the Shah, the riots—all of it crashed in on him. His suspicions were correct. Not Sabeti. Not SAVAK. But someone clever enough to use both against the other for their own gain. He needed to find the bastards before they found him.

"I almost forgot to tell you," said Lord Charles. "Philippe arrives in Shiraz tomorrow night to help with the family shipment."

Unanticipated joy surged through Anthony. "Philippe! Here tomorrow night? What good news!" He pictured Philippe Kahlil, his best friend since his childhood, the one who had practically saved him during those first horrible months at Eton.

Lord Charles' husky old voice bellowed, "What you see in that art dealing, camel trading rascal, I'll never know."

"Come now, Grandfather, you're as fond of Philippe as I am." Anthony smiled. "I'll wager he's sitting right there at this very moment in the leather chair by a cozy fire with his feet upon your favorite afghan, smoking one of your finest cigars."

"Utter nonsense. I haven't seen the young devil since God knows when."

Anthony laughed.

"Take care, my boy. And do come home as soon as you can."

Anthony hung up the phone in a much better mood than before. His loneliness lifted. His best friend would soon be there. But would Philippe's arrival put his old friend in danger as well?

TEHRAN, MEHRABAD AIRPORT

On the way to the Bank of Tehran, Kathryn and Peter jumped out of Ali's car, barely waiting for it to screech to a stop at the airport. She had to find Buzz fast.

She was dressed for success in a navy and white linen

business dress. Her spectator pumps clicked along the sidewalk. She rushed past armed soldiers at the terminal entrance to meet Buzz Anderson, senior creative director for the ad agency BBDO and account executive for Boeing. Buzz, her Uncle Buzz, the connection she had used to get a meeting to present her concept, The Birth of Flight, for their Super Bowl spots with Boeing.

As Brett, her ex, had often said, connections are a good thing.

Ali parked the car and caught up with her. Over the heads of countless passengers in the customs area, Kathryn caught a glimpse of her Uncle Buzz, the quintessential media executive dressed in a Cerruti blazer, emerging from the comfort of his luxurious first class Air India flight from the Rome location where Brett was shooting.

Buzz's athletic build stood out as he was herded toward the customs counters, a blast of hot, muggy air wafting into the terminal. He loosened his tie and the collar of his fancy Turnbull and Asser shirt, shrugging out of his jacket, and folding it over his right arm. She saw that he carried the clarinet case that she'd never seen him without. He lifted back his salt-and-pepper gray hair and blotted his forehead with his shirtsleeve. Amid the crowd, Buzz searched for her with an unhappy look on his face. Dark, brooding men heavily armed with assault rifles circled around the ugly, low-ceilinged lobby.

She gestured to Ali. "Let's get him out of here." She needed Buzz to approve their location.

"Done." Ali approached a customs official and did whatever was necessary to free Buzz from red tape.

Kathryn rushed to her client's side.

"Buzz, I'm so glad to see you!" She gave him a warm embrace. Her mom's younger brother had become her surrogate big brother, her savior, making her difficult childhood bearable through sports.

"It's a relief to see you!"

Buzz looked at the tall, young Iranian.

"May I present Ali Zahidi, from the Ministry of Culture."

"Your driver, at your service," said Ali, inclining his head graciously.

"A pleasure," said Buzz, shaking hands. "Thanks for getting me past customs."

"*Pishkesh*," she rubbed her fingers together. "It works wonders! You'll find he's invaluable."

"I'll remember that," he said. "I'm eternally grateful!"

"Wait till you see the charm of this place," Kathryn went on. "You're in Persia, land of magic carpets, camels, gypsies, incredible bazaars, exotic music, and the most spectacular ruins anywhere. They're everything we dreamed of."

"There she goes," he said to Ali. "She's captivating me again." He hugged her back. "But Kathryn, seriously, look at those soldiers. Their AK47s are Russian made, you know."

"They're a bit menacing, aren't they? But it's the same in Rome and Madrid. Come on, I've got things to show you."

"Seriously, Kathryn, what have you gotten me into? Haven't you been reading the newspapers? This place is a powder keg waiting to go off!"

Kathryn watched him glance around. The squalid, hostile-feeling airport truly reeked of neglect. The pungent odor seemed a blend of sheep dung and cheap cigar smoke that hung stale and fetid among the throngs of people standing, leaning, meandering, and sitting on the filthy floors, for there seemed to be no seats anywhere. Many layers of paint were peeling off the walls down to where the worn linoleum had curled up away from the floor back into itself. It was definitely the before picture prior to Mr. Clean's arrival.

"I feel like Khadafi's troops are going to bust through those doors on a pack of camels crying death to anyone without a beard," Buzz said so only she could hear.

"Wrong neck of the woods for Khadafi, Buzz. I hear you but I think we're alright. We rely for safety and protocol on Ali. His boss at the Ministry of Culture will come by to meet us on location tomorrow."

He didn't look convinced. "Brett has no idea how lucky he is, getting the Rome location," Buzz said. "The cagey bastard probably knew that. How could I have let you talk me into this location? Right now a limo and a Jack Daniels is what I need."

"Coming right up," she said, suppressing a chuckle, guiding him toward the exit. *Not exactly a limo, though.*

Ali gathered up the luggage and signaled to some ragged soul who bowed and scurried to assist. With their arms loaded, they led the way out of the airport to a rickety, not-too-old-but-very-abused gray Volvo station wagon where Peter and Teddy waited. They jumped out.

"Hey, Buzz," Teddy said.

"Good to see you, man," said Peter.

"My limo?" Buzz said.

Kathryn laughed. "Only the finest!"

They lurched out of the parking spot and sped out of the airport hurrying to her appointment with the bank manager.

Impatient inside the ornate Bank of Tehran, Kathryn waited beside Mr. Rashid's desk for a letter of credit to secure the film equipment she needed now. She took in the high, plastered ceiling, marble walls, columns, and floors, formal and austere. She had only twenty minutes before the equipment rental house would close. She composed herself, tamping down her assertive L.A. demeanor and frustration over traffic delays and detours into the city from the airport. Her driver and crew still waited in the car, chatting and catching up.

The bank manager adjusted his horn-rimmed glasses and smoothed his sedate tie then extended his hand, holding an envelope. "This document with our seal is all you will need for the duration of your stay with us here in Iran, Ms. Whitney," he said with extreme courtesy. "And if there is anything else, anything at all, please feel free to contact us."

"I'll be certain to remember you, Mr. Rashid. You've been most helpful." The bank atmosphere had changed from foreboding to welcoming.

Kathryn turned, expecting to see Peter following her in, tapping his watch. But instead she noticed a handsome man in his early thirties standing near the entrance, watching her.

Taller than average and impeccably dressed, he had the air of an Islamic prince; and he seemed startled when he realized she had caught him staring at her. Their gazes locked for a moment, but the man looked away quickly. *He's shyer than I am.* It was then she finally spotted Peter across the room, tall and lanky, long brown hair in a ponytail, beckoning her to join him. He was enmeshed in a group of people surrounding a display of some kind.

She moved into the space Peter made for her beside the display.

"Just for a minute, Kat, you gotta see this."

Armed guards in white dress uniforms stood behind a long viewing case that spanned nearly the length of one end of the bank. Inside the case lay a staggering array of jewels. The crown jewels of Persia were arranged side by side with other magnificent gems Iran had acquired throughout the ages. All the jewels were so lavish they looked like studio props.

And there among the extravagant display, she saw a tiny gold and enamel version of her winged lion, its delicate detail and coloring recalling Persian miniatures she had seen in museums.

Suddenly, a woman draped in black pushed her way through the crowd and stood, breathless, across the case from Kathryn. The woman, the lower half of her face veiled, peered into the glass, her hand pressed against it. Kathryn heard someone say, "the Persian Glories," and her glance swerved to the objects demanding such serious attention.

From the velvet bed inside the case glowed a dazzling parure of flawless canary diamonds, as pure in color as any she had ever seen. Kathryn knew at once how good they were. Her mother had taught her about jewelry from the age of seven, and she knew the jewelers' term for the highest grade of canary diamonds: fancy-intense, pure lemon in color, as bright as spring sunshine, the very best quality. The design of each piece of these Persian Glories had an elegant beauty.

The twenty-inch necklace drew her attention first. It was extraordinary, each brilliant diamond perfect. Many stones were over eighty carats, graduating to a 107.2 carat yellow diamond in the center, she learned from the plaque inside the case.

The woman in black made a small sound of distress, capturing Kathryn's attention. It was as if she wore a mask of stone, which, as she stood there, changed: her large, agate-colored eyes were frenzied, awash with anger, flickering with what appeared to be fathomless despair before they reverted with a frightening witch-like resolve back to stone.

Kathryn shuddered, then heard a man say, "Mother, we have to go." The man she'd noticed staring at her earlier tugged the woman's sleeve.

"But they are mine," the woman in black said.

"Come, Mother."

The woman grimaced with apparent reluctance but spun away from the gems and dashed out.

Kathryn nudged Peter. "Let's go." Outside in the daylight, she watched the princely man hold open the door of an official state car for his mother.

He looked up. This time he'd caught her looking, and for one more moment, their gaze held. She caught a little smile before he nodded then folded himself into the car.

Kathryn hurried to her waiting crew, marveling at the unexpected frisson of attraction she felt for the young Islamic prince. But she was disturbed by his mother, the foreboding woman in black.

CHAPTER TEN

NIAVIRAN PALACE, IRAN
September 1942

It was a night of great celebration, the "Night of a Thousand Stars," an annual ball given by the crown prince of Iran, Mohamed Reza Pahlavi, the future Shah. High on the gentle northern slopes of Tehran, Niaviran Palace, solid and resplendent, stretched toward a deepening indigo sky, its immense curved marble brow softening the vivid purple horizon.

Inside, the brilliantly lit palace glowed with festivity, smothering any hint of discord felt by a people shaken from invasion and domination by their supposed allies, the British and the Russians. More than half the world was wrenched apart by war, and all the powers involved continued to vie for Iran's black gold: oil. But tonight on the road leading to the palace, as the stars came out and the moon rose into a golden orb over Tehran, a procession of limousines and foreign state cars snaked up the royal thoroughfare through the palace gates, and the war was far away from Rena Ajani's mind. Rena took Valik's hand and climbed out of the black 1939 Rolls Royce Phantom III, then tossed back her head and looked up at the sky over Niavaran Palace, breathing in the wonder of the night, letting herself be filled with the royal ambience. This would be her night to shine.

Bursts of fireworks exploded overhead in cascades of starry radiance, like a cosmos newly born to the heavens to announce her. At eighteen, she was a bride of four months, and this was her first palace ball, a night she had craved throughout a seeming eternity of dullness.

Many nights she had seen her family—her father, mother, and older sister Ilyia—seeking favor from their monarch, the Shah. Many nights she had jealously watched them sweep off to the palace, dressed in their finest silks, brocades, and tails, while she, three years younger, had been forbidden to leave the house.

She hated the sense of imprisonment she'd felt being left alone—and most of all she hated that it was always Ilyia first. Ilyia, delicate, lissome, and beautiful as a spring willow, whose graceful shape sharply contrasted Rena's own voluptuous curves, exotic face, and more energetic nature.

Rena knew she was beautiful because of her sensuality.

Ilyia, she admitted, was simply beautiful.

Rena was too young, her father had insisted, to go to parties, dances, or with friends, though not too young to be married off. But then, Valik's proposal had surprised even her father. She didn't mind. Being wed to a powerful man had opened the world to her at last.

"You are ravishing, Rena, my love." Her husband's lips caressed her fingertips, and she brought her gaze back to the man at her side. "This is your night to shine," he said.

Valik Ajani was only twenty years her senior and the prime minister of Iran, she thought proudly. With a shiver of excitement she watched courtiers and dignitaries approach and greet him with deference.

Valik was tall and lean, with a keen intelligence reflected in his intense, dark features. He commanded respect from everyone as they crossed the palace courtyard, and the feel of this veneration brought a new kind of thrill to her, a thrill that assuaged a hunger for acclaim long starved.

And now I will share his power, his wealth, and his place in the sun. I will have all that I desire, this man will see to it, I am certain, because of my fervor in the marriage bed.

When they made love on their honeymoon in Egypt, it had been an entirely new and wondrous adventure for her. As for Valik, he seemed overcome with ecstasy. Instinctively her hand moved to her throat, where she touched with pride his finest gift, an astonishing Burmese ruby necklace.

Yes, the honeymoon trip had been a good beginning. Tonight she would greet her family from a new vantage point—that of power. She smiled inwardly, relishing the glow of triumph she felt. And for once not even Ilyia could ruin the moment.

"Shall we go in, my love?" her husband asked. Then in a sexy voice, he whispered, "I have a surprise for you."

Confidently, she smoothed her red Coco Chanel ball gown and gave him a coy glance. "What surprise?"

Valik smiled. "The prince has arranged for the Persian Glories to be removed from the vaults of the Bank of Iran and put on display tonight in the reception hall. I know you'll want to be the first to see."

"The Persian Glories! Yes!" Since she was a girl of seven, she had been captivated by the romantic story surrounding these famous jewels, as were so many Persian girls.

Years ago, a lovestruck Russian prince, overcome by his passion for a young Persian beauty—a girl he was forbidden to marry—commissioned Carl Fabergé, the great Russian artisan, to select flawless diamonds from anywhere in the world to design an astounding gift for the beloved he would be denied. Fabergé fashioned perfect stones into a glorious collection finer than any in the czar's own coffers: yellow diamonds rivaling the brilliance of the sun, pure white diamonds like glinting stars.

It was said the Persian Glories possessed a great legacy and when unselfishly given to one you cared for, brought great love. Great love indeed! Those jewels were price-less—they could bring fortune and power! Rena felt the cool stones of her own magnificent necklace against her skin. Could the famous Persian Glories possibly be as beautiful as her rubies?

"Sir?" A barrel-chested man in an elaborate tux inter-rupted her reverie, touching her husband's arm.

"Go in and see the jewels, my dear. Take your time."

Palace guards in dress whites guided Rena along a marble hall flanked by niches filled with precious Eu-ropean art. Her excitement was great; she could barely acknowledge all the greetings and nods of respect from elite Persian guests.

Rena stepped inside a lavish salon lined with satiny walls of exquisite wood paneling and carved Louis Quinze gilt furniture. A massive chunk crystal chandelier dangled from the towering ceiling like a colossal bauble.

A figure came forward from the shadows; a lieutenant in formal attire melted toward her. Lieutenant Omar Houdin. She had not seen him in months. Shocked, she tamped down the last of her attraction to him.

"Rena. I've longed to see you. I missed you."

"Omar! What are you doing here?"

"I'm now part of the prince's guard. I waited to catch a glimpse of you."

"You must stay away from me, Omar. I'm a married woman. I can never see you again."

He reached for her.

Quickly she pulled away. "It was not meant to be, you and me. Stay away." He looked young, handsome, virile. But she should not even remember the small dalliance she'd had with him in her father's garden before she had any idea Valik was interested in her.

She had teased Omar, led him on out of a young girl's boredom. That was all! "Please go now."

His smile, almost lethal, stunned her.

Fists clenched, Omar said, "For now, Rena, for now." He bowed and faded away.

Rena shook off the meeting, gathering her wits.

Then she saw them.

She stood transfixed before the glass-enclosed display housing the astonishing Persian Glories. The tiara, bracelet, necklace, brooch, earrings, and ring all glinted up at her with a power to light the sun. Never had she seen anything like these. Something extraordinary emanated from these diamonds. A force she felt to her bones took hold, filling her with energy, potent and erotic. Entranced, she wanted to touch them—she wanted to own them. Her fingers lightly gliding over the case, she quelled her hunger and compelled her hands away.

All at once she was conscious of being observed. Valik had come quietly into the salon and moved to her side, his gaze probing, as if he perceived her arousal by the diamonds.

"Enthralled, my love?" He gathered her hands and pressed her fingers to his knowing smile. "Oh, I feel your craving, Rena." His words were eager; his breath felt hot on her skin. "How I would love to cover your naked body with the Persian Glories if they were but mine."

Her body tingled from the encounter with the gems. She breathed deeply, barely able to let Valik guide her to the ballroom. Within seconds friends and courtiers surrounded them, welcoming them back from their trip.

"How wonderful you look, Rena," she heard.

"Such an extravagant ruby necklace! Valik knows how to spoil his bride."

Taking the arm of her husband, her chin tilted, she pushed the Persian Glories for the moment from her mind and basked in the praise.

Then she heard a familiar voice of welcome. "Good evening, Madame Ajani." She looked up into the radiant face of Prince Mohamed Reza Pahlavi, only twenty-two and imbued with the regal self-assurance of a future monarch.

The prince was resplendent in his official dark jacket and trousers trimmed in gold braid and epaulets. He took her hand, his large dark eyes flashing. "You look lovely this evening, Rena." His smile she remembered well from the brief time she had visited the court before he had married

Princess Fawzia of Egypt. The Shah's wife was not with him but in Egypt, visiting her brother, King Farouk.

"Your Majesty," she said.

"You've chosen an incomparable beauty, Prime Minister," the prince said, glancing at her husband and then at her. "I would like the first dance with her."

"But of course, Your Highness." Valik beamed his agreement.

Prince Mohamed guided Rena onto the dance floor. With natural grace he waltzed her around the ballroom for all eyes to see, and her spirit soared above the heavens. With this honor she had outshone every woman there. Her status was secure.

She felt as if she were spinning through stars when the waltz ended. Then, from the edge of her vision, she noticed a group of guests whose entrance was causing a flurry of interest.

The prince's warm gaze left hers and traveled across the room. "Ahhhh . . . the guests of honor."

Guests of honor? What guests of honor? Rena strained to see.

Before she knew what was happening, the prince had escorted her back to her husband. "A pleasure, Rena," he said and promptly turned away.

Rena searched the entrance. She took Valik's arm, and they moved to get a better look.

A party of couples entered, led by a tall, blond infidel— blindingly handsome with emerald eyes and an enticingly warm smile—dressed in British military dress uniform. He and the prince embraced affectionately.

Rena was stunned. His majesty embracing an infidel!

"Reza, *insha allah*," she heard the infidel say to her prince.

"Evans, you devil, you've snatched the prima flower in our Persian garden."

Evans chuckled at the prince's remark.

The room buzzed with speculation. From behind the infidel stepped a vision in white chiffon, more beautiful than anyone had a right to be. Rena staggered, gulping down a fierce need to shriek out in rage, every part of her quivering with hate. It was Ilyia.

Rena grabbed her husband's arm. "The infidel, who is he?" she asked. Her voice sounded harsher than she intended.

"British. Lord Richard Evans, the next Earl of Edyton. He is the prince's close friend from Le Rosey School in Switzerland. But don't you know this, Rena? It is your sister to whom he is betrothed."

The infidel close to the future Shah?

"How could I know any of this? We've been away for four months."

"But there was a cable from your family telling us the news, don't you remember?"

"Cable? What cable?" But she did remember. There had been one in Egypt announcing Ilyia's engagement to some Englishman. Ha! *English*, a mere infidel! Skimming the telegram, she had tossed it aside, not wanting anything from home to spoil the best time of her life. A slow, bitter grimace sliced across her mouth. She had been right to not dwell on the cable, because the news turned out to be devastating. Her sister was going to marry into English aristocracy and be close to the highest-ranking member of Iranian society, in the inner circle.

Rena blanched, holding down irritation.

"Richard Evans," the prince continued, "will protect our peace and keep Iran's wealth in our country."

The prince then turned to a steward and lifted a black cloth from a velvet-lined tray. Instantly, the room was bathed in beams of refracted light emanating from the Persian Glories.

"The legend of the Persian Glories speaks of selfless giving and the flourishing of love. I bestow these jewels upon you, Lord Richard Evans, with love and friendship, cementing our countries' bond for our lifetime."

Rena gasped and took in the reactions of the crowd. Those closest to the prince registered surprise. From the back of the room she heard excited muttering.

The prince gazed at Ilyia, and Rena thought she saw longing in the look. "It is as it should be."

Lord Evans nodded to the monarch and said, "For my bride, a symbol of Persian grace, who will stand beside me and our future children to protect Iran."

Rena watched in horror as the brilliant necklace was lifted from the tray and placed lovingly around Ilyia's slender neck. Then the bracelet was circled about Ilyia's delicate wrist, the earrings put in her ears, the tiara put in her gleaming hair, and the perfect twenty-carat ring handed to her betrothed. The infidel's gaze, fixed on Ilyia, burned as powerfully as the extravagant ring he slipped on her finger.

No! Rena shrieked silently, her mind swirling with hatred. *The Persian Glories should be mine! I saw the prince first—he loved me first!* But the Persian Glories now belonged to her sister.

Everyone watched in silent awe as the prince raised his glass in a toast to the glorious couple. The room cheered. Ilyia stood there in her splendor, as radiant as the sun. Rena's sister had outshone her once again, for their entire world to see.

At that precise moment, something snapped inside Rena, and the world changed color, washed in a grotesque dead gray like the skin of a decaying rat. She stood apart, shaking with envy, cursing her sister, wanting to rip everything away from her: her betrothed, their future heirs, and especially the Persian Glories. Then, as if Ilyia could read her mind, she looked over at Rena with a smile of compassion and extended her hand. Ilyia was urging Rena to share the spotlight.

Rena shot her sister a withering look. *Don't you dare pity me, you slut!* she screamed inside. Involuntarily she backed away. Excited guests quickly filled in the space, edging her back, back, until she was forced into the shadows at the far end of the ballroom. There she stood, shuddering in disbelief, consumed with rage.

This would be the last time, the very last time, that bitch would ever shine.

CHAPTER ELEVEN

The day after his latest completed mission, Anthony feigned an aloof departure from his Shiraz house at dusk. He leaned against the balustrade on his front terrace, his hand shuddering like the flame he brought to his cigarette. He knew he was being watched, but that was not why rage burned through him so hot he felt as if his bones could melt.

The family he'd set to fly out of Iran tonight had disappeared, every last one gone: twin five-year-old boys, their mother and father, aunt and uncle—another massacre. Where the Black Glove threatened, hope grew dim.

The thought of this happening to so many families stoked his fury.

He ground out his cigarette. A gut feeling warned him a family he knew well, the Fahides, owners of the Hotel Persepolis, were next on the death list. This maddening premonition drove him out into the night. A meeting at the hotel with his MI-6 contact and Philippe would give him the perfect opportunity to urge his friends to leave Iran.

The Fahides had been his parents' closest friends in Persia, a genteel family who maintained their hotel, a jewel of a place and the pride of their heritage. He prayed they'd listen. Memories rushed forward of being at the hotel, running through the orchards with the Fahides' sons, playing tag in the gardens, sharing wonderful Persian meals, his parents' laughter with the family.

He pulled out of his driveway and zoomed the 275 GTS Ferrari through the curving streets of Shiraz up into the mountains, his foot to the floor, haunted by the unbearable knowledge that those he knew and loved were being butchered right and left. He ascended the mountain pass and made the broad, banked turn north where the earth seemed to stretch endlessly in front of him.

From behind the furthest rim of darkness, the golden moon rose, spreading light across a blackened terrain and soothing this harsh night into a series of soft-rimmed curves, smiles over the desert that lifted his mood. It was then he thought of her. The woman, bathed in the first rays of morning at Persepolis. She had come to him like a vision and had vanished as quickly. But somehow she had touched him.

As Anthony sped on the mountain roads of highest Shiraz, Kathryn had finally found a moment to relax, the evening warm and sultry in the small Hotel Persepolis lounge. She had survived the first day of her shoot prep and could take a moment now to relax.

Uncle Buzz was on the phone to New York, arguing that today's staggering news headlines of a massacre in Tehran wouldn't affect them. They were hundreds of miles away in Shiraz. But if her Boeing shoot failed, her ex-husband would make sure she would never work again. Her career would be truly dead. He couldn't touch her now. She shook her head, swallowing her fear.

After selecting a volume of poetry from a bookcase in the lounge, she leaned back into a Victorian sofa covered in soft woven fabric and sipped from a tall glass of mint iced tea. She read words from the ancient poet Firdawsi, written over a millennium ago, allowing them to sail her away on the faint breeze created by the churning brass fan above, away into a magical Persian garden thousands of years in the past.

Still thinking about the mysterious woman, Anthony roared into the parking lot of the Hotel Persepolis and let another mood take hold. He jumped out and stood for a moment under the sparkling night, feeling very alive with a passionate thirst for something rare and magical. It would have to be a very strong drink, indeed.

He took long strides, cleared the entrance to the lobby, and stood for a moment, seeking the striking good looks of his friend Philippe. Instead, however, he stared with unbelieving eyes.

The woman from his dreams stood in a group not twenty feet away at a bookcase. He smiled, suddenly understanding why the gods had urged him to get here so quickly. It was to see her.

Anthony forced himself to the front desk to inquire about the men he sought. He learned that Philippe and Jess had been delayed. He should not have felt so elated. The Fahides were expected back from dinner in less than an hour, he was reassured, even as he let his gaze play over the woman.

"Can you tell me about these guests of yours standing by the bookcase?"

"Ah, yes, professors. American, from Princeton University, I believe."

Anthony looked back. The woman he sought walked to a sofa and sat.

She was even more exquisite in person, dressed in a pale aqua dress of fine cotton, the neck cut low, accentuating luscious curves. He admired how the skirt flared with tiny buttons, a few left undone at the hem, exposing shapely calves. She wore sandals with a strap encircling her slim ankles, ending in a small serpent's head. He couldn't have posed her better.

But it was her face, with that look, as if she were miles away and knew something he didn't. Her hair, a flowing blonde mass, brushed her shoulders and cascaded down her back. He couldn't tear his eyes away, his heart pounding.

She looked up at him and her sensuality challenged him. Her hazel eyes, flecked with amber and green, met his.

And although he had never met her, he had known her forever.

Kathryn looked up as if from a dream at an incredibly handsome man, a complete stranger, standing across the room. His gaze landed gently upon her and lingered. *This handsome stranger is touching me as if he were a close friend*, she thought. Instinctively, she welcomed his touch, and the book in her lap slipped from her hands, the movement startling her. She clasped onto it and looked away from him, her face tingling.

She had been swept away quickly, but now she carefully gathered in the reins and shifted her attention back upon the page and read: ". . . garden of delight . . ."

"I must have come here to meet you."

She heard his voice, deep and cultured, and looked up into his vibrant green eyes. His hair was dark, his skin beautifully sun-bronzed. He was casually but impeccably dressed in a taupe linen suit and white shirt. She noticed a gold Patek Philippe watch, oddly on his right arm. A left-handed, green-eyed man, she mused. What could she do but smile back?

He sat down next to her, not too close, but close enough for her to catch his clean scent. He leaned forward, his elbows resting on his knees. He had beautiful hands. His gaze reached for her. "Would you allow me to show you something beautiful?"

"Such as?" Kathryn was mystified.

"A garden, a rare garden."

"Like this one?"

He leaned toward her book as she held it up to show him the cover.

He took it from her, their skin touching for an instant. He read a few lines in English and repeated it in Farsi, his eyes brightening.

"Much like this one, yes." He stood. "Come with me." He held out his hand.

She put down the book, tingling with excitement. It was as if she were watching herself in disbelief when she clasped his fingers and followed him out of the hotel lobby, down a winding torch-lit path, under a velvet blanket of darkness, until they came to a hedged wall of nearly six feet.

The gate was locked, but he reached over the top and opened it. They entered and he turned a switch on the inside of the wall. Instantly the garden was bathed in soft light. She followed him in.

"This pleases you?" he asked, still playful yet heartfelt.

She gazed out at the expanse. "Thoroughly. Incredibly." She would never have guessed.

"It belongs to the couple who own this hotel."

Before them lay an oasis of beauty and repose, fragrant with roses, geraniums, pomegranates, orange trees, and myriad flowers stretching ahead like a magic carpet. Not like gardens at home or anywhere she'd seen before, this was Technicolor with textures, silky, veined, transparent, and vivid.

The garden had perfect symmetry: geometric waterways, lined with blue-glazed, gold and mirrored tile inlays deepening the color of the pools. Dense, shaded areas along either side from the date and orange trees threw off the blossoms' scent and that of narcissus and jasmine. A light breeze lifted her skirt, fragrant air caressed her skin, and her hair billowed off her face. Intoxicated with sensual wonder, Kathryn reached out, touching his arm.

He clasped her hand and held it there.

She raised her gaze and found his expression of pleasure echoed her own.

At the end of the garden stood a columned townhouse with fine crescents of tile-work on its curved brow.

"It was built about a hundred years ago. It's not ancient but . . ."

"You read my mind. The book could have been written in this garden. It's enchanting."

"You're enchanting me."

A current of excitement zipped through her.

Together they strolled through the garden, her senses enraptured. "Listen," she said, stirred by the sound of the nightingale, of gurgling water.

"Breathe deeply," he said. "I can never get over the bouquet here."

She inhaled, scent filling her head.

He turned to her and his eyes held a message. *I want you.* He brought her fingers to his lips. "May I?" He turned her hand in his, kissing her sensitive wrist.

Sparks ignited in her, unleashing a sudden need. He eased her into an embrace.

Too much. She pulled back with a gasp, startled, dizzy with pleasure.

He laughed and whirled her around, then gathered her close, almost protectively. "I want to know everything about you. Until there are no longer secrets between us." He bent close again. "Is it too much to ask?"

"Secrets take time to give up."

He smiled a nervy smile, and all of a sudden it was raining! His shoulder had set off the switch for the sprinkler system, covering them with water droplets, sending them both into gales of laughter before he managed to turn it off.

An aging houseboy came out of the townhouse onto the porch, trying not to laugh as he offered each of them a towel.

"Wow. How was that for first impressions?" he asked, smiling with mischief, drying her face then his.

"You look so happy," she said. "Did you do that on purpose?"

"I couldn't find that switch again if I tried, but it was worth it." His gaze traveled over her.

She looked down. He was taking in the clinging cotton jersey of her dress, her erect nipples and the skirt, melting over her hips.

Kathryn was too embarrassed to laugh. The water had done what she couldn't—cooled her desire. She'd better not press her luck here. Another moment and she'd have a hard time keeping her hands off this man, and a man wasn't what she needed right now. "Thank you for the amazing garden."

"Yes, amazing." His look was intense but not intrusive.

He looked too confident to have to try with women. "Exactly like the one I read about, but I must go."

"No."

He had an endearingly crooked smile that she liked in all its boyishness. She was ridiculously attracted to him.

"When will I see you again?" He leaned closer.

On impulse, she squeezed his arm. "Surprise me." She

made her way to the gate and left him standing there, alone in a puddle of sprinkler water.

Anthony was stunned by his own stupidity. He still didn't know her name.

The houseboy peeked around the doorway. "Mr. Kahlil awaits you in the dining room, Sir Anthony."

"Thank you, Mahmud." Anthony finished drying himself in a turbulence of joy, hope, and need, and went to meet his friend, the noted art dealer and infamous gambler Philippe Kahlil, and the contact he had hoped to avoid from MI-6. He must remember to ask the maître d' who the woman was.

Leaving the attractive Persian Prince Charming behind, Kathryn whisked through the lobby toward the stairway, her sandals squishing with each step, her right hand laid protectively across her damp chest. She couldn't help smiling. She paused by the open double doorway of the beautiful Raj restaurant, glancing inside to see if anyone watched. The maître d' stood inside the entrance, his back to her.

A businessman moved past. "Anthony Evans?"

"This way," said the maître d'.

Her mouth flew open. She couldn't believe it. The elusive Mr. Evans? Here? She scanned the crowd and saw across the room a tall blond man dressed immaculately. His look was very Saville Row; he was wearing a pale gray suit, ivory and blue striped shirt, ruby and crème silk tie. He looked up at his approaching guest, the businessman, then turned his blond head and a gorgeous turquoise gaze to her startled face.

A half smile on his lips, he nodded to her and put on tortoise-rimmed glasses. *Oh!* Evans with a guest, but he had yet to meet the obligation to his client—her. What a flake! If she weren't dripping wet she would confront him now. Boiling with indignation, she went to her room to change.

CHAPTER TWELVE

Mirdad gazed absently at an apple tree heavy with fruit, dappled by early morning sunlight outside his bedroom window. He knew he was obligated to do Anthony's bidding today and meet up with the American film people in Shiraz. Anthony was a pompous ass not worth consideration, and it annoyed him to be the *padar soubhteh*, a son of a bitch's errand boy. But Houdin wanted Anthony watched.

On the way to the airport he'd make a stop somewhere he was eager to go, the orphanage. He was bursting with ideas to build something good, to change lives, to take away degradation, bringing knowledge, confidence, and smiles. He knew he could do it.

A limo screeched to a halt in front of his house. Through the curtain, Mirdad saw that it was Ali who jumped out and was racing to Mirdad's front door.

Mirdad went to the door and yanked it open. "What in God's name has happened?"

"We have to leave Tehran!" Ali rasped. "People are rioting. It's crazy!"

Mirdad dragged Ali to the sofa, nudging him down. "Breathe."

"I've come from the mosque. The news blew through like wildfire." He bent forward, coughing. "The Shah accused Khomeini of being a fag, front page of the *Tehran Gazette* and on National Radio."

Mirdad shook his head. "That's old news. Khomeini accused the Shah of being homosexual and a communist two years ago. They toss insults back and forth like hot potatoes."

"Demonstrators are right now surging through the city!" Ali stood, fighting for breath. "We must go or it won't be safe to drive."

"Where's your inhaler, Ali?"

"The limo," he gasped. "Mirdad, let's go."

"Let me get my suitcase.

The limo bumped along an ill-kept street, half blacktop, half rubble, in a poor section of South Tehran. Mirdad put up his window, waving the dust away.

Ali, keen on leaving the city, drove too fast, pumping on his inhaler. Dust swirls attacked, leaving mosquitoes and wasps stuck to the windshield.

"There," Mirdad touched Ali's shoulder, eager to be at the orphanage.

Ali grumbled. "We shouldn't be stopping."

Battered bicycles leaned against a crumbling wall surrounding a hovel. Boys of all ages kicked stones around a dirt yard. A sign hanging from a rafter announced, EVENING STAR BOYS' ORPHANAGE. Mirdad remembered how close he'd come to being one of those kids.

Ali had barely parked when several young boys caught sight of the car. They cheered, charging the limo.

Mirdad got out, feeling his smile all the way down to his toes. He took a deep breath. "Ali, bring out the sweets."

Ali obeyed, smiling for once, dispensing bags of candy, oranges, and persimmons to groping hands, smaller boys hugging his legs in gratitude.

Sullen construction workers leaned on a grimy bulldozer. Mirdad's hard gaze fixed on repairs the building needed; a new wall to surround the yard squatted unfinished. All had come to a standstill. He had arrived in time. His smile deepened. He could finish this and bring this crumbling haven for lost children up to modern standards. It was his secret project.

A relaxed distance away stood the person Mirdad had come to meet: the orphanage director, Tashi, once a boy who had demanded his attention years back.

"Shitface!" Tashi grinned. "You're here!" He held out his hand.

Mirdad took it.

"You didn't think I'd come?" Trust had always been an issue with Tashi.

Tashi, who was somewhere around Mirdad's age and shorter but strong as an ox, merely grinned. His teeth were uneven, his eyes drooping at the corners and separated by a wide nose—a face that despite those features drew you to its intelligence and hard-won warmth. "You're right. I didn't."

Mirdad laughed. "Come." He gestured toward the car.

Ali popped the trunk with a grin. He lifted a box containing soccer balls. Tashi hefted another with equipment: goal nets, knee pads, shin guards, and jerseys.

Boys rushed over, shouting, laughing, joyously taking the goods.

Mirdad handed Tashi a thick envelope. "There's enough here to finish the walls and gates."

Tashi took the envelope, stuffed it into his worn brown shirt, and shook hands with Mirdad. "You've become the dream maker to these kids, Shitface."

Mirdad smothered a powerful sentiment, a little spilling over with his smile. "And those rags had better be gone when I return—new uniforms for every boy—even you, Camel-Breath."

Tashi pounded Mirdad's back. "Take care of yourself. I'll be here when you get back."

Mirdad almost choked on good feelings whenever he visited the orphanage. He would see these kids through to a better life or die trying. He knew too well what could happen to kids who fell through society's cracks. Tashi had been an exception.

An image of little Siri cowering beneath him crept through his mind and fled as fast. Siri, another orphan.

Minutes later Ali was speeding to Golestan Airport.

"Stop at the tobacco shop in Jaleh Square. I need a gift for a friend," Mirdad said.

Ali pounded the steering wheel. "Are you crazy? With my asthma do you—"

"Wait outside." Good cigars were Houdin's favorite smoke. Mirdad would see him in Shiraz. He couldn't arrive empty handed.

"Disgusting habit," muttered Ali, driving to Jaleh Square as requested. He parked on a side street, for the square was known for its congestion.

The square combined buildings of a unique blend in architecture. The east side of the square housed two-story shops set ten feet back from tall, carved arches and columns flowing for three blocks. Skyscrapers flanked the west side, glass reflecting the noon sun.

Mirdad looked up at a commotion at the far end of the square, demonstrators wearing mostly dark pants and white shirts, some fully robed, all shouting and holding signs.

"Down with the monarchy," came the shouts.

"Long live Ayatollah Khomeini!"

Placards waved overhead: OUT WITH THE SHAH. FREE KHOMEINI!

Ali looked on. "Hey, there are my friends! Sorgi, Achmed!" Ali shouted and bolted from the car. "Be back in a moment," Ali called out, already at a run to greet his friends. "Buy your tobacco. Meet you at the shop."

"Ali, come back!" Mirdad growled in frustration then swore in Farsi. "*An!* Shit! Fucking fools." He watched Ali greet his friends: Achmed tall, Sorgi a little pudgy, both clean-cut in crisp white shirts and pressed slacks, faces glowing with excitement rather than apprehension from this noisy, surging crowd.

Mirdad had warned Ali to keep a lid on his hotheaded instincts. Ali knew better. This Jaleh Square demonstration had already grown to an enormous size. Three blocks away artillery tanks and army trucks boxed in the crowds at the south end. He'd better hurry. This was not a good place to be caught. Mirdad ducked into the tobacco shop at the quiet northeastern corner.

A heady aroma of fine tobacco floated over him. Walls lined with delicate wooden boxes, jars of hand-made pipes near taller inlaid pipes. Small round tables where men could sit and sample the goods hugged the far wall. A long wooden counter stacked with wares from various mid-eastern countries and a carafe of cool mint tea took up most of the wall near the door. Hookahs here and there stood near sofa chairs. He would enjoy some tea if not for the riot in the square.

"*Allu Akbar*, Excellency," a small bearded man said from behind the counter.

"And to you, sir."

"I have the cigars you ordered," said the tobacconist. "The finest in—"

Gunfire blasted outside. Plate glass shattered across the cobblestoned square.

The tobacconist rushed to his glass door, slamming it shut. He looked up forlornly at windows overhead that were far too high to close.

Mirdad ran to the door, cracked it open, and stuck out his head, searching for Ali. Bullets flew as screams and shouts filled the air. The smell of cordite, smoke, and scorched flesh quickly smothered the aroma of fine tobacco from inside the store. Ali and his two friends ran toward the tobacco shop.

Mirdad ran outside, waving wildly at the boys. More

gunfire blasted. The tallest boy jerked, blood spreading across his white shirt where the bullet had exited. Mirdad weaved through panicked rioters to grab the slumped boy.

"Inside!" he yelled.

Tanks and trucks roared toward the square. The pandemonium increased in action and volume. Artillery blasted through the square as if no one stood in the way, as if there were no bloody bodies sprawled, screaming in terror under their treads.

Mirdad burst into the shop. Ali and the plump boy, Sorgi, carried a moaning Achmed.

"Get in here!" the tobacconist called out, slamming the door after them. Gunfire followed. "Get down!" The man pulled the boys behind the counter.

Mirdad stood mesmerized at the glass door. Troops in trucks and tanks closed in over the wide three-block area, shooting everyone in sight. Bodies were strewn in the square like bleeding rag dolls. Horror filled Mirdad's eyes as helicopter gunships circled overhead. There was no escape for those left in the square.

"Quickly!" the tobacconist called Mirdad to hide with them.

Mirdad crouched beside the others, hiding behind the long counter, breathing hard, now out of the line of fire. But how to help Ali's bleeding friend?

Ali, his face stark with fear and disbelief, looked up. "I'm going to be sick." The tobacconist shoved a spittoon under his face. Ali tuned away, vomiting violently.

Mirdad recalled the carafe of tea on the counter and rose up, grabbing it. Scattered shots were fired into the shop but missed him.

The tobacconist handed Mirdad a folded cloth from a stack on a shelf behind the counter.

"Rip open his sleeve," Mirdad said. The young man whimpered, but Mirdad sloshed tea on the cloth, cleaning away the blood as thoroughly as possible. He handed Sorgi another clean cloth. "Press your friend's wound. Hard. We'll get out of here soon." He looked the boys over. Sorgi supported his wounded friend. Ali had cleaned off his own face and swallowed some tea the tobacconist gave him, but his breathing came hard.

"Where's your inhaler?"

"In the limo."

"Naturally." Mirdad exhaled and leaned against the counter, waiting to escape or be killed.

THUMP, THUMP, THUMP. Pounding at the rear door of the tobacco shop grew louder. The tobacconist flashed Mirdad a worried look. The boys cowered against the counter. Ali peered up at Mirdad.

"It could be help." Ali's voice was hopeful.

"Maybe." Gunfire was sporadic now, but harsh voices and screams were getting closer and louder. Mirdad crawled to edge of the counter, looking to see how dangerous it was out front. Maybe they could make it out.

Troops ran under the easement toward the shop, ramming rifle butts through storefront windows. Mirdad threw himself back behind his barrier.

THUMP, THUMP. "Open up. Now!"

Mirdad shuffled like a crab to the back door. "Who's there?" he bellowed.

"Open up, you fool!"

Mirdad struggled with the old-fashioned lock then jerked the door open and gasped, scooting back.

Anthony rushed in. "What took you so long?" He slid the door closed and crouched. "Military is arresting everyone in the area. The Rover's out back, motor running." Anthony looked Mirdad over then leaned forward, spotting the others behind the counter. He looked furious.

"Too bad you didn't follow my orders today and get your dumb ass to Shiraz, cousin." Anthony crouched by the wounded boy. "Come on! Let's get him out of here."

Mirdad, caught in his own folly by the one person he loathed, felt chilled. A hero again, saving the day. *Allah*, how Anthony rankled him.

Once they were all stuffed into the Rover, Anthony drove the wounded student to the hospital and arranged for his care. Sorgi, his plump friend, waited with him. Ali, a nervous wreck, drove the limo behind them. They dropped the tobacconist and the boys at their homes, receiving much gratitude and three boxes of cigars, then they escaped the city and pulled up to the outskirts of Tehran. Combative emotions about the massacre still prodded at him when Anthony stepped into Mirdad's modest house. It had been five years since his last visit, and he was shocked, taking in how shabby, how small it seemed. It hurt him to see his family downtrodden. But at least they were alive.

Had he been more scared or angry with Mirdad and Ali having almost been killed in such a foolish way? They had not been demonstrators, but fools. Anger pulsed through

Anthony. Then relief somewhat softened his nerves. The day was shrinking. Anthony had other fish to fry.

Ali went to call his father, the inhaler pressed to his pale face. A shaky looking Mirdad guided Anthony into the dining room. He stood by the long mahogany table drinking a sweaty glass of iced tea Mirdad had brought him then set his glass down.

Before Mirdad could go, Anthony grabbed his arm. "All those impetuous young men in that square are now corpses. What were you thinking, dragging Ali into that foray?"

Mirdad's features hardened. "As you say—impetuous."

Anthony ran his fingers through his hair, then reached out and hugged Mirdad. "I'm so relieved you're okay, cousin," he said stepping back. Mirdad's eyes had widened. Anthony felt him freeze under the show of affection. It had been a long time since they were as close as brothers.

"I'll get my mother," Mirdad said tonelessly.

Anthony heard rapid muttering from the next room and the rustling of fabric.

Rena walked toward him, looking as if she was about to go out. "My illustrious nephew, what brings you to my home?" She took his hands in hers.

"Do I need a reason to visit my favorite aunt?" She was covered from head to ankle in black chador. "It's been a while, though."

"Hasn't it," she said in the same toneless manner as her son.

"I didn't realize you were so religious, Aunt."

An odd smile slanted her mouth. "And you are not? But then you haven't lived in Iran all your life, have you?"

Was she challenging his spiritualism? "I have a strong faith in Allah from my grandfather." He smiled. "Although, as I see it, a rival vies for power. So much suffering in the world, another evil deity must be in play."

"Interesting philosophy." She glanced from Anthony to Mirdad to Ali. "My son, you and your friends must be famished. Be seated. I'll serve you at the table."

"I'll help you, Mother."

Rena held up her hand. "You must sit with our guests, Mirdad, and allow me the pleasure of presenting a meal." She headed for the kitchen.

Ali downed the rest of his tea. "I'm glad I called my father. He'd already heard of the massacre and was worried." He shrugged. "So many relatives in Iran had already informed my father what is happening."

Rena brought in a platter of flatbread stuffed with minced lamb, mint infused rice, a bowl of fresh figs, grapes, and sliced blood oranges following. Plates and silverware were placed all around, the aroma of steaming lamb encircling the table.

Anthony spooned food and yogurt sauce onto his plate. He was actually ravenous. More tea was poured. Anthony drank slowly, looking around, taking in the poor condition of the furnishings and drapes. What had Rena done with all the money he'd sent her every month for the last fourteen years?

"This looks delicious." He picked up his fork.

Ali and Mirdad joined in.

Like old times, Anthony mused sadly.

Mirdad looked to Anthony then at his mother. "But you shouldn't have gone out, Mother. I warned you to stay inside while I was gone because of the riots. You could've been hurt."

Anthony took pity on Mirdad's obvious humiliation at his mother's willfulness. "Women," he joked. "What can you do?"

"She's safe at least." Mirdad gulped down his tea, annoyance spreading across his handsome face.

"Ali will fly home to Shiraz with me," Anthony said. "You can rest, Mirdad, and fly in tomorrow, early. The American filmmakers will wait another day."

Ali's head bowed over his plate as he shoveled in lamb and flatbread. Hungry and ashamed of behaving irresponsibly, Anthony surmised.

"Mirdad, these Boeing clients are important to the ministry. Do your best, please." Anthony smiled.

"I will, Anthony. I will."

Anthony wiped the napkin across his mouth and stood. "Thank you, Aunt Rena, Mirdad. It's good to be with family again. I've missed this." He gestured to Ali. "Time to go."

Ali bowed, hands together. "Many thanks, Madame Ajani, for the delectable meal."

"You are welcome as always, Ali," Rena said.

"Come," Anthony said, heading for the door, Ali in his wake.

Anthony drew Mirdad aside. "You need to be more careful, Mirdad. Decide where your loyalties lie."

Mirdad was still, eyes wide.

"*Inshah Allah*," Anthony said and strode out to his car. As Ali drove, Anthony worried. What else could he do for his family? Something did not feel right in that household.

CHAPTER THIRTEEN

As soon as that devil Anthony was gone from her home, Rena drew the *chador* about her and rushed into the streets toward the souk, seething. The afternoon sounds and smells of the streets bothered her. The poverty, the stench of the average man disgusted her. She drew her veil around her and ducked into the bazaar, getting closer to Dr. Mosek's blue door and her fate.

She turned the corner, sailing past the smoke where once she had seen Omar come for cigars, where men sat and smoked from their beautiful turquoise inlaid pipes. She passed, stealing a glance inside, hoping to find Omar there again. But no, he wasn't there.

Anthony had thought her religious. No. She wore the veil because of shame. Once beautiful, in poverty she had let herself go, turning fifty and fat. Six months ago she'd begun to work on her body, had slaved to change it with

strenuous dieting and rigorous exercise, until she couldn't
endure another day. She had lost forty-three pounds and
once flaccid muscles were now tight. But her face! She
despaired at never again being beautiful. Then she discovered a fine clinic where top plastic surgeons offered a
woman more than nature ever had. But she lacked funds.
So putting aside her pride, she returned one of Omar's
phone calls.

"Rena, I want to be part of your life. I must see you."

"Fine," she said. "Send me twenty thousand. Then I'll
see you in three months."

"Done," he'd replied. The money arrived without question.

For an enormous fee, Dr. Mosek performed the procedure; now weeks later, she returned to the doctor's office,
terrified to see the results. Since the procedure, she had
covered every house mirror and worn chador, waiting till
the day Dr. Mosek said would constitute her final recovery.
Today she would see her face again.

Turning up a well-kept alley, she stopped in front of
the blue door and froze. She closed her eyes, dripping with
sweat all over, soaking her clothes.

Omar must again desire her, need her like she needed
him, if only to help her eliminate the weasel who continued to blackmail her every month, bleeding her dry. How
could she have known the mechanic she'd paid to plant a
bomb on her sister's airplane would survive the explosion?

She reached toward her covered face, not daring to touch
it. Dear Allah, the results had better be transformative. She
straightened her shoulders and blotted her brow on her
veil, the envelope of money, her last payment, clutched

in her fist. She shuddered with excitement, then fear and finally opened the blue door.

Mirdad kicked off his shoes and slumped over the battered mahogany desk in his room, flicking on a lamp against the failing dusk. His mother napped in her room. He would read to wipe out persisting thoughts of the bloodshed he had witnessed today at Jaleh Square. He pushed aside books on classic Hollywood films of the 1960s and entranced himself in an unpublished manuscript, written by his father, concerning the history of the U.S. and Russia's competition over oil in the Persian Gulf in 1948. Would the lust for black gold ever abate?

The doorknocker clanked. Mirdad looked around for his mother and remembered she was napping. He slipped on his loafers and answered the insistent noise, curious who would be calling.

As the door swung open, Mirdad stepped back.

General Omar Houdin, dressed in full uniform, nodded once and strolled into Mirdad's home as if he'd done so many times.

"Good evening, Mirdad. I've come alone."

Mirdad almost staggered at this surprise but managed to gesture toward the sitting room.

Houdin strode past him, his right-hand pocket bulging. Mirdad had never seen Houdin packing before. Did the older man consider this impoverished neighborhood dangerous? The notion amused Mirdad.

"To what do I owe this privilege, sir?"

Omar Houdin looked around, his expression impassive.

"Come, let's sit." They took worn, overstuffed chairs adjacent to one another. "I bring good news. You've been promoted to colonel in the SAVAK, young man." Houdin handed Mirdad a laminated I.D. card. "You'll need this tomorrow when we go before the Council General."

Speechless, Mirdad cleared his throat, alarm clanging in his head. He was not even a member of SAVAK. How had this "promotion" magically occurred? Suddenly he was entrenched in Iran's merciless secret police? How would he ever get out alive? He gulped down his reaction and said, "You do me great honor, sir."

"Forget formality here," Houdin smiled. "Our relationship will be a long one, no doubt." Houdin reached into his breast pocket and pulled out a fat envelope. "For you. You've earned it with your loyalty."

Mirdad took the envelope and bowed his head.

"Many thanks!" he said, searching for a comfortable way to seem less formal with General Houdin. He stuffed the envelope into his back pocket and rose from the chair, going to the sideboard. He pulled out a bottle from the cabinet. "Shall we toast to the success of our mission, General?" Mirdad held up a bottle of Lanvul single malt, knowing the general's preference.

"Excellent."

Mirdad poured two fingers of liquor into each tumbler, handing Houdin one. They raised their glasses and threw back the scotch. Mirdad's throat burned, his eyes watering, but he poured another for them to sip. He pondered what distasteful task awaited him. The general had not come to share a drink.

Rena tossed and turned in her bed, afraid. She struggled to awaken, but Orpheus drew her deep into the abyss of her dreams.

The room was cold, but it was not her bedroom. She sat in a surgical chair. Thick bandages covered her eyes. Steel scissors clicked, cutting away gauze. The doctor hovered, his body too close, his odor antiseptic, the latex of his protective gloves stinking of sterility. He cut more. She sat still. The rigid chair dug into her back.

"In a moment, my dear. Be patient," he said.

His breath, like icicles on her neck, made her tense. So much pain! Something was wrong.

"The last bandage, doctor," the nurse said. "You've done our best work."

The nurse's voice, Rena knew that voice. Was she dreaming?

Rena opened her eyes, focusing on the mirror. What was that? Not her? "NO!" she screamed. She stared at the face of a gargoyle, slipping still deeper into the abyss.

"You were meant to look like this," the nurse scolded. "It is the real you."

Rena spun around. "Ilyia!" The nurse was her sister, Ilyia. "You're dead! *I killed you*!" Rena's mind reeled, her head splitting.

Rena peered at the mirror in disbelief. She touched her ruined face. "That's not me!"

Laughter rocked the room, the surgeon and her sister mocking her, satisfied smirks distorting their perfect faces.

Rena jumped from the chair as Ilyia moved toward

her, scissors clutched in her left hand. Before they could prevent her, Rena lunged for the scissors, grabbing them from her sister.

The doctor grabbed her arm. "Stop!"

She shoved the doctor off, swung around, and buried the scissors into Ilyia's chest . . . again and again and again. Ilyia's face contorted, her blood gushing over Rena's hands, like human lava, the pungent smell metallic. Rena gasped, wiping at the dark and sticky mess with bare hands. She must get it off—now! *Allah*, let me wake from this!

Mirdad shifted in his chair. Then he heard tortured screams emanating from his mother's bedroom. He bolted for the door, Houdin behind him. It was locked. He pounded on it.

"Mother, open the door. Mother!" He turned to Houdin. "Keep trying." He ran for the key and heard Houdin thumping madly on the wood.

"Rena!" Houdin called out.

Mirdad stuffed the key in the lock.

They entered. Rena, dressed in a pale cotton shift, her hair wild about her shoulders, stood at the foot of her bed, staring at her hands.

"Mother, what is it? What's frightened you?" Mirdad had not seen her without a veil in months.

And he was shocked at what he saw. She was more beautiful than ever, skin flawless, her features lush like those of a 1940s movie star, maybe Heddy Lamar, but more beautiful. Mirdad grabbed her silk robe from the end of the bed to cover her.

"I'll take that." Houdin held out his beefy hand.

Mirdad pulled back and looked from his mother to Houdin, reluctantly handing him the robe.

Gently, Houdin helped her put it on, murmuring soft words. "Rena, my beauty, I'll take care of you." His gaze slid to her breasts as he tied the belt.

Mirdad wanted to smash his face in.

His mother looked toward the mirror, regarding herself, touching her face, then looking up at Houdin. Tears glistened on her long lashes. Mirdad couldn't think of a time his mother had cried before.

His mother reached up to caress Houdin's face.

"Leave us, Mirdad," said Houdin gruffly.

Mirdad's heart pounded, his beautiful mother touching this ruthless swine.

"But, sir . . ."

"She is safe with me. I swear it. Now go."

Incredulous, Mirdad backed away from this grim scene. His mind flashed on images of messengers coming to his house at all hours, his mother's operations, the phone calls late at night.

Most of all, he recalled Houdin's words: "And remember me to your lovely mother." *So this is how it was.* He walked away, his stomach on fire. He had been so blind. His mother and the butcher of Tehran.

He couldn't leave them in her bedroom. He turned back to her room, the door ajar, and quietly looked in.

Houdin, on his knee before his mother, held her hand. "Rena, love of my life, marry me?" The general pulled a ring with a massive diamond from his pocket.

His mother's eyes gleamed.

Mirdad staggered back, back. *No! Never!* He wouldn't bear to hear her answer to Houdin, but raced out onto the patio, the cool night biting his skin, crickets screeching in annoying cadences. Confusion and revulsion attacked him. *His mother with this vile man.* Mirdad couldn't stay there; suddenly it felt unsafe for him. He grabbed his jacket and stumbled through the gate, slouching down the long, dark road.

CHAPTER FOURTEEN

Mirdad slumped in the back of the limo, unsettled, his stomach still on fire. At least he was out of Tehran.

He had barely spoken to Ali since arriving in Shiraz. Yesterday, the massacre, then Anthony in his home had caused a tumult of feeling, comparing Anthony's mansion to his modest home, feeding his anger and jealousy over the disparity. Yet oddly, he felt a longing for what had once been. His adoration for Anthony had withered into hatred.

But Houdin and his mother alone in her bedroom! This shocking development had turned his world inside out. Mirdad shuddered. A relationship between his mother and Houdin was unthinkable. And marriage? A nightmare. Mirdad had fled before she could reveal her decision.

He understood her long fall from the wife of the prime minister of Iran to a poor nobody had forced her into seclusion. But to choose Houdin, the butcher of Tehran? Mirdad could never accept Houdin into their home. True, she needed protection and a better life, and she had guessed, probably correctly, that General Houdin held all the right cards.

Mirdad pondered the situation again as he had last night while walking his neighborhood streets. Always he returned to the same conclusion: Anthony. Why hadn't he taken care of his family, ended his mother's only sister's lowly lifestyle?

Anthony had basked in his unshared wealth, while Mirdad had to cope with the most treacherous bastard in Iran to elevate his and his mother's existence.

Mirdad closed his eyes and let his mind wander, groping for a solution. Somehow he must keep his mother and Houdin apart. He must acquire enough money to better their lifestyle. She would stay with him in Iran and regain her social position as the new and rightful owner of the Persian Glories. This was his goal. Somehow he would make it happen.

"We're approaching Persepolis," Ali said.

Mirdad opened his eyes. He looked out at the tent city of the "Celebrations" that had marked Persia's 2,500th birthday.

They drove by slowly. Mirdad recalled the grand gala six years before, cursing under his breath. He'd been excluded from the splendor and pageantry, having not yet attained a sufficiently high position to be invited. He had watched from afar with the masses.

The pavilions had glittered in Persian blue and gold in a decadent display of outrageous wealth written about by the press around the world. And the French, not the Iranians, had made everything for the event, including the food. The French!

He believed this act had sealed the Shah's fate. Most Iranian people hated this Shah, watching him surrounded by splendor while his country lay wracked by poverty.

The empress had worn a crown with emeralds the size of tangerines. Anthony, who had attended the functions, had shown off the Persian Glories around the throat of some delicious slut. Times, however, were changing, and the Shah would never again have the last word. The Ayatollah Khomeini's Muslim Mullahs would gain control. They were worse; they would disempower the people, wipe out education and women's rights until all friends to the Shah were properly destroyed. Mirdad was no friend to the Shah, but the Shah's brother-in-law, the Minister of Culture, was his boss. Perhaps, Mirdad thought, his dreams of prominence in Iran were merely dreams. Regardless of his future prospects, he needed money now.

The late afternoon sun sent bronze rays over the ruins of Persepolis, energizing Kathryn as she worked with her Iranian crew. "The wide expanse from the south side will be our caravan's approach," she said.

They had spent hours mapping out every production setup for tomorrow's shoot, but the costumes hadn't yet arrived. What was she supposed to do with two hundred extras and no duds? Damn it. Why the hell hadn't their ministry liaison shown up? She'd caught a glimpse of Anthony Evans last night in the Raj, dining sumptuously with well-heeled guests. Anger flared. Screw him. She would handle her own shoot, costumes and all.

As it turned out, her Iranian crew was skilled and easy to work with. Habib, their patient interpreter, explained in Farsi how they would lay hundreds of feet of dolly track, a route for her Ariflex to follow the approaching two hundred extras in procession as they paid homage to the winged creatures. Habib translated for their foreign crew as Kathryn spoke.

She looked at her watch then excused the crew for the day, staying true to her newly strict budget.

"Break time!" Peter shouted, and she looked over her shoulder.

A football arced toward her. She ran out for the pass beneath a soaring column. Stretching, she snatched the ball from the air.

"Nice throw, Petey!" she yelled, turning, setting her feet into a wide stance, and hurling the football in a long, perfect spiral.

Peter broke into a sprint to catch it. She knew he'd make her work for the next one. He caught it and brought his arm back to launch a long, high pass.

She sped across the open terrain, jumped up, and caught the football. "Yes!"

Peter jogged toward her. "See? You needed a break. You go in circles when you don't get exercise, and you drive me nuts." He put his arm around her shoulder.

"Thanks, Petey. I do feel better." Work and exercise were her life. *Not bad, but maybe not enough?*

"Peter, we need the Iranian crew at four-thirty in the morning to get the sunrise tomorrow," she said, pulling herself back to decisions they needed to make.

"Habib says it's not a problem," Peter replied.

They jogged over to the ancient steps and Kathryn, clear-headed and confident, raised her face to the sun. Perhaps her internal crisis of self-doubt after the customs debacle was over. She basked in positive feelings.

"Kathryn. You listening to me?" Peter looked at her. "No, I can see you're not."

"Sorry, Peter. This place bewitches me."

"Well, pay attention. Check out the official-looking limo by the stairs." He pulled her ponytail, nodding toward the steps. "So act like the boss even though you look like a teenager in that getup."

She squirmed out of his reach and pulled her baseball cap on tightly. "Oh, this must be our hotshot photographer finally gracing us with his famous presence."

"Right, Anthony Evans." Peter looked at her askance. "Glad he could make it."

"So he's a little late." Kathryn shrugged. "What's a day or two among professionals, eh?"

Peter laughed. "Go get 'em, lady."

"Okay, smarty. I'll handle this bloke."

The limo stopped at the Persepolis film location. "We're here." Ali turned, looking back. "Are you excited, Mirdad? Your first film assignment from the ministry."

Mirdad could always trust Ali to go straight for the truth. "I am."

"How different do you think your life would've been had you gone to the States?" Ali asked.

"Maybe I wouldn't have come back."

"Humph. You'd not have left me here in Iran, or your mother."

Mirdad leaned forward and ruffled Ali's hair.

Ali batted him off. "This lady director," he said, "she won awards for documentaries in Hollywood. And I hear she's very attractive." Ali wiggled his eyebrows.

"I heard."

Ali jumped out and opened the limo door. It was hot and dusty. "Take off your jacket, Mirdad. You're too . . . neat. They're from Hollywood!"

Mirdad removed his jacket and with the encouragement of Ali's yank on his tie, he took it off, too. He unbuttoned the first button of his collar and rolled up his sleeves two turns. Ali handed him his sunglasses with a thumbs up.

Five people in casual American clothes conversed on the stairway to the Royal Audience Hall. He couldn't tell from this distance which one was the supposed knockout Ali had been touting.

Climbing the stairway, Mirdad was approached by a young girl in an American outfit: jeans, a baggy T-shirt, and hiking boots. He could tell it was a girl by what he could see of her shapely figure. Her face was obscured by a hat and sunglasses.

"Good afternoon," offered Mirdad, "I am—"

"You're not Anthony Evans!" she interrupted. "Oh, I'll bet he couldn't tear himself away from the polo field again last night because he's too tired."

"I don't understand . . ."

"Polo. You know, jodhpurs, mallet, horse . . ."

"Pardon me?"

"Pardon you? Of course, but where is our exalted photographer? You know, SIR Anthony, the Ninth Earl of Tardy."

Mirdad could hardly believe his ears. This little minx was taking Anthony to task. It made Mirdad's day; he couldn't help laughing.

"I fail to see what's so funny," she said. "He sends others in his place. Does the man ever come out in daylight? Maybe he's a vampire."

Mirdad almost choked suppressing his amusement. "Allow me to introduce myself. I am Mirdad Ajani from the ministry of Culture. I'm looking for Kathryn Whitney. I assure you the ministry wishes to satisfy all concerns."

Her face fell, her mouth opened. A longhaired American man walked up behind her.

"You've done it again, Kat," he said.

Her chin raised, her voice subdued, she said, "I'm Kathryn Whitney. We're all pleased to see someone from the ministry. We start shooting tomorrow."

Now it was his turn to be astonished. He looked at her large sunglasses and plain, soap washed face. "You? I was expecting someone . . . older."

The man behind her stepped forward. "Mr. Ajani, it's a pleasure. I'm Peter Shuman, the assistant director."

"Please, call me Mirdad, Peter."

"Mirdad, excuse the little mix-up." He gave the woman a sideways glance. "It's that we're concerned about Mr. Evans not showing up."

"Of course, I can't blame you." Mirdad smoothed his hair off his forehead and removed his sunglasses. "However . . ."

"I know you . . ." Kathryn Whitney stepped forward, lifting her sunglasses and cap, "from the bank in Tehran where the royal jewels are displayed."

Mirdad's brow pinched in concentration. He took a closer look at this female.

"You probably don't recognize me, but I saw you there earlier this week."

Peter turned away, a hand to his forehead.

Kathryn Whitney smiled and then Mirdad remembered. She was the beauty with the guileless smile, warm hazel eyes flecked with amber. "I do recall our . . . meeting, Ka-, uh, Miss Whitney."

"Kathryn."

He cleared his throat. "I'm here to smooth your stay and see to your production needs." He shook hands with Peter, then Kathryn. "Tonight you'll dine with me and Mr. Evans at the Paradise Club. I don't think you've experienced our elegant nightlife."

"Thank you, Mirdad, how nice." She turned to her associate. "Peter, tell Buzz the polo punk was a no-show. Again."

Chuckling, Mirdad took a closer look at her baggy shirt and then Peter's. "UCLA. Did you attend that university?" he asked.

"Film school, Peter and I."

"I almost went to USC film school, a scholarship." Mirdad surveyed Persepolis. A vast assortment of film gear spread across the plateau where crewmembers added the setup. Energy pulsed around him, revving his nerves. A jolt of longing, as acute as ever, hit Mirdad. *A full scholarship to heaven. Water under the bridge.*

"Almost? What happened?"

"Family objections."

"Too bad. You still interested in film?" she asked.

He smiled. "Devoutly."

"Have you seen *Deer Hunter* yet?"

Mirdad shook his head; he had really wanted to see it. "Michael Cimino's epic of war and friendship. I've read about it. DeNiro . . ."

"And Christopher Walken, amazing. Oscar buzz is all over it." She looked at him with those warm eyes. "If it doesn't play here, I'll ship you a copy."

He chuckled. "I don't think that'll happen."

She looked perplexed.

"Censorship is tightening in Iran."

"Oh, sorry." She grabbed a football from Peter's hand and tossed it to Mirdad. To his surprise, he caught it.

"Here, Mirdad!" Peter yelled, sprinting off.

Mirdad looked at the foreign American object in his hand, not knowing what to do.

"This way," said Kathryn. "Hand over the stitching, arm straight back—" she guided his arm. "Now, eye on your target and let her sail."

Relaxed, he followed her lead, and the ball sailed to Peter. Mirdad had no idea what he was doing, but he was definitely entertained.

CHAPTER FIFTEEN

Dressed in his St. Laurent tux that evening, Mirdad paced the small lobby in the Hotel Persepolis, curious about the enchanting Kathryn Whitney. Two days ago he had been bowled over by the sight of the blonde from the bank of Tehran, fantasizing about her since. Would he encounter the feisty tomboy from Persepolis today or the lovely blonde from the bank? Both personas captivated him.

She embodied what he missed in his life: humor, beauty, the film world, and freedom. So constrained by events, forced daily into dangerous entanglements, he was edging perilously close to losing control over his life. Bile rose in his throat when he thought of General Houdin and his mother.

But not this night. Tonight he relished plans to get to know Kathryn, a woman he genuinely liked. And she seemed to like him. *So screw you, Anthony, you missed out. I got here first.* He smoothed his satin bowtie, turning to the sound of high heels clicking on the terrazzo entry, a sound he'd always enjoyed.

She stepped up to him in a shimmering gold gown, offering her hand. "Hello again."

His mouth opened then closed with a smile. She was stunning.

"Kathryn Whitney," she said as if he'd forgotten her name.

He recovered and took her hand. "I remember. It's . . ." He cleared his throat. "You look lovely." He led her outside to the limo.

"Thought I'd try to repair my image tonight." She looked at him sideways with a little grin. "After this afternoon's misunderstanding."

As the limo door closed, Mirdad grinned back, recalling her snide remarks about Anthony. "Well, I'm assured your photographer will join us tonight. He'll probably be at the bar."

"You mean Little Lord Evans? Whoops!" She placed her fingers over her lips.

Mirdad tried to be serious but couldn't. "I liked Polo Punk best." She laughed, and he did, too.

"I apologize," she said. "He's your colleague and . . ."

"No apologies, please." He reached into the door pocket and handed her a book. "Obscure French films of the 1960s," he said. "I'm not sure you even like French . . ."

"Oh, thank you, I love them! Film noir, vérité, and those ridiculous Gerard Oury farces." She turned a page. "Look," she inched closer, "remember, Oury's *Les*

Adventures de Rabbi Jacob?" She pointed to an evocative scene photo, laughter bubbling from her. Mirdad recognized the moment and laughed, not wanting this spontaneous joy to end.

Huddled together, Mirdad and Kathryn discussed various other directors as the limo sped down the highway into the night. They descended a hill and a brilliantly lit oasis came into view.

Kathryn sat forward. "You underestimated the impact of the Paradise Club, Mirdad. It's palatial." She turned to him. "Like a Hollywood set."

"Glamorous," he said, quite charmed, planning for later that night when he could have her to himself.

Anthony rocked with laughter inside the Paradise Club bar, jammed into a plush velvet booth with the American film crew: Buzz Anderson, Peter Shuman, and Teddy Wright, the cinematographer. They traded raucous location stories, enjoying the camaraderie of those who share a profession as well as the revelry encouraged by a bit of drink. And yet, he felt on edge, knowing he would have to slip away later for another mission.

He had saved a seat next to him for Philippe, who—bless him for coming tonight—sauntered up and placed three drinks on the table, his inscrutable poker face intact as he set down two Perriers and a martini next to Anthony.

"Scotch, wasn't it?" Philippe asked Buzz.

"Jack Daniels," said Buzz.

"Right." Philippe sorted out the drinks and returned to the bar for the rest, his stride certain, ever one to play host.

Anthony watched Buzz glance around, lips pursed, nodding appreciatively at the dark-green marble columns rising to the high ceiling and at the elaborate Art Deco grillwork over the windows.

"Philippe did the interior design for this club," Anthony said.

"I'm impressed," said Buzz.

"Yes, four years ago."

Thank God Anthony had arranged that as a way for Philippe to pay off yet another gambling debt.

"Nice aerial shots in *National Geographic* this summer," Buzz said. "Tribal horsemen in formation with dust billowing under galloping hooves over the dunes—strangely abstract, exciting. We're looking for something worth capturing for eternity on this shoot."

Teddy nudged Anthony. "Work beside me in the chopper over the Palace of Darius. I've got an extra camera harness."

"It's difficult, very difficult, getting a permit to fly even close to Persepolis, but Mirdad saw to it." Anthony took a sip of his martini, the Chopin burning his stomach. He needed food. He leaned into the group. "I did aerial footage this summer of—"

"We're an early crew," Peter interrupted. "Five in the morning sound okay with you, Anthony?"

"Five sounds great to me." This group, so unaware of chaos brewing around them, actually offered Anthony a break from his constant stress. "If you'll excuse me," he said, "I'll make a call and rearrange plans for the morning."

Anthony made his way to a bank of telephones along a wall far from the bar. He had managed to grab every moment possible for photography, his way of staying sane in uncertain times. Ironically, since the death squads took over the country, his work had become his cover. The Boeing flights near Persepolis would also yield invaluable information on scattered rebel troops in the area.

He looked at his watch. He planned to get through this business dinner with grace, his alibi for tonight, then excuse himself in time to join his pilot, the prospect of facing violence ever present. Tonight would be no different from other missions. But he was growing edgy as they all waited for Kathryn Whitney and Mirdad to show. He dialed the phone.

"My God," Kathryn said, entering the Paradise Club. "This place is right out of a dream. Magnificent."

"You fit right in," Mirdad said, his look at her appreciative.

She smiled, exhilarated and somehow anxious to confront Sir Unprofessional Evans with a sit-down and a toast to his cleaning up his act before her shoot.

She scanned a fabulous sunken bar to the left, but the enormous, circular, open-air dance floor where couples glided to Cole Porter's "Night and Day," played by a full orchestra in white dinner jackets and black satin bow ties drew her attention. It was from another era—sophisticated, slightly dangerous, elegant—and she loved it. Walking around the edge of the dance floor, she noted the round tables draped in white with ornate silver candelabras dotting the room, candlelight flickering under a starlit sky.

A few stone steps beyond the dining room led to

sweeping lawns below. "I feel like I've stepped into a 1940s movie set."

Mirdad offered his arm. "I agree."

"I'll be Rita Hayworth in *Gilda*."

His eyes brightened. "Then of course, consider me your Glenn Ford."

Conspiratorially she squeezed his arm, while below at the sunken bar it seemed all faces had turned to watch their entrance.

She heard Buzz say, "Here's my director."

Taking the arm Mirdad offered, Kathryn stepped forward. She ignored Mirdad's perceptive smile as she went down the curving staircase.

Buzz came to meet her at the foot of the stairs.

"Sorry we're late, Buzz." She turned to her escort. "I don't believe you've met Mirdad Ajani from the minister's office. He visited the site today, offering his assistance while you were making calls. Naturally, I took advantage of his offer."

While Buzz and Mirdad said hello, Kathryn glanced toward the bar at the tall, blond man she remembered form the Raj Restaurant at the hotel. Mr. Anthony Evans at last. He removed his glasses, his alluring azure eyes twinkling at her, his elegant Saville Row tux, superbly tailored, silhouetted a tall body, strong shoulders. He moved toward her, about to come over, when *pop*—she felt the garter on her right thigh spring loose.

She hesitated, feeling the gold stocking slip along her skin. *Drat.* If the back garter went she'd make a really glamorous entrance with her stocking bagging around her ankle. She smiled coolly and turned away. "Excuse me for a moment?" She looked at Mirdad with a much warmer smile than she felt and let go of his arm.

Mirdad leaned close. "The lounge is at the top of the dance floor stairs."

For a man so handsome he appeared to thrive on her attention. Part of his charm no doubt. "Back in a flash." She did not wait to be introduced to Mr. Evans. Why should she? He had made her wait for three days; he could wait a few minutes.

In the ladies' room, she fixed the garter hook in place, applied lipstick she didn't need, and absently fluffed her hair. She stared at herself in the mirror. God, she was touchy lately. This wasn't like her to act so peevishly over some playboy who'd probably overbooked himself and was doing the best he could to make it all work out.

You know, cut the guy some slack, Kat, she said to herself, realizing it was not only his notoriety as a playboy, but more likely his prominence as a photographer that intimidated her. *Yes, that's it.* Then she noticed an elderly attendant in the corner smiling at her muttering with herself in the mirror. She smiled, placed a tip on the counter, and turned to go.

At the far end of the dimly lit second floor hall, she viewed an enormous pair of brass doors glinting in the shadows. Flanking the doors were heavyset men in dark suits. They watched her, their cold faces menacing.

Shivering with a sense of alarm, Kathryn turned away, anxious to get back to the sounds of music, people, life. For an instant more she wondered what lay behind the foreboding doors, then suppressed her curiosity and headed for the stairs.

Anthony stretched his neck from side to side, growing tense as he listened on the phone from the edge of the dance floor at the Paradise Club.

"Hans," Anthony said after a moment, "these guys won't survive the night. We can't wait." Some highly placed Iranian government officials who had learned it was time to leave—or die—were fleeing Iran tonight over the Iraqi border with their help. As the route he and Hans had used to get out of Tehran had been discovered, so had the one in Shiraz. The Black Glove had tightened its stranglehold on the borders.

"Can we use the Bag?" Hans asked.

"We're thinking alike," Anthony said. "Source says it's clear." The missing Bagazaran family's private helicopter pad, the "Bag," was their option tonight.

"Look," said Hans, "I don't give a fuck what you're doing tonight. But get to the chopper by midnight and not a second later." Hans sounded strained to his limit.

Anthony checked his watch: almost 10:00 P.M. He would need to leave the club by eleven-thirty. "I'll be there."

"You've got an alibi, right?"

"I'm covered."

"Yeah, well, I got the word . . . someone was asking questions about you today."

This last bit of information brought up his grandfather's repeated warnings. Both he and Philippe were down Anthony's throat about getting out of Iran immediately. Now even Hans was on his case. A soon as the shipment was packed, he and Hans would fly to Turkey with the last group he could help escape from the country.

"Don't worry, friend. I'll put out a check on it in the morning." Anthony hung up the phone, fists clenching and unclenching. He walked to the edge of the dance floor, lit a cigarette, and stood watching the Iranian glamour-set move by, wondering sadly which of their families was next on the death list.

He was about to return to his guests when he saw a goddess in gold at the top of the wide marble stairway. His mystery lady. For a moment he was not sure if he was imagining her. Today he had thought of her, their chance meeting in the hotel garden, wet from the sprinklers and images of her crowded his mind. She was bright and fun, and that body—an irresistible package.

He watched her as she surveyed the room. Who was she with? He felt a jealous twinge and stabbed out his cigarette in a nearby ashtray, then moved toward her. *The third time is a charm*. It didn't matter who she was with. This time he would not let her get away.

Kathryn had almost reached the landing when she noticed him, the Persian Prince Charming from the garden. Was it really him? It was! Her heart fluttered. Thank God she hadn't seen him at the top of the stairs, she might have tripped. She stood still, breathing shallowly.

He walked over, his smile warming her. He gathered her fingertips to his lips then turned her hand over, kissing her palm. Without a word, he guided her onto the dance floor where in his arms she felt at ease, gliding as if through clouds, apart from everyone. There was everything to say . . . and nothing to say.

She gazed at him, about to speak.

He pressed her closer. "Don't leave me again."

"But how can I stay?"

"Because we both want you to stay."

With the intensity she saw in his green eyes, she knew her own must be as revealing. "There isn't anywhere I'd rather be," she said, caught in his spell, wondering if she was insane.

She would probably never see this man again, so absorbed was she in her film project. Then she and her crew would leave immediately for London. *Why not let go right now, have fun?* And as she looked up at him, feeling so perfect in his arms, she chose. *One night of romance, Kat.* Her desire for this man overwhelmed her. She wanted him as she'd never wanted anyone else.

"Perhaps caution should rule."

He shook his head. "Caution? Highly overrated."

"Rules are meant to be broken?" she teased.

"Certainly now."

"Are you married?"

"No," he chuckled. "You?"

"Not for three years." She pushed old sadness away. Neither the time nor the place.

"Good," he said, his gaze narrowing.

"What is it?"

"Your expression."

"Sorry," she murmured.

"Don't be." He pushed a strand of hair off her face. "It's a first for me, wanting you but holding back."

Electricity sizzled between them. She relaxed deeper into his embrace.

He whirled her around the open-air dance floor, a full orchestra playing "All the Things You Are." Smiling, she remembered their moments in the private garden and started to laugh. As if reading her mind, he joined in.

His face close, she heard him breathe in, then felt the warmth of his palm on her back, pressing her yearning body to his. She felt his arousal, and gently he released his grip.

"How lucky can one man be?"

"Or one woman." She looked up through the open ceiling. A galaxy of stars seemed to glint with mischief. She hoped the joke wasn't on her.

"Come," he said.

"Where?"

"A garden, naturally," he grinned. "It's secret, no one will find us."

"Promise it won't rain?"

"I know where the sprinkler switch is."

"You wouldn't!" Her eyes blazed.

"No, tonight I've no desire to cool off." Hunger filled his powerful gaze.

She nodded, cautious but eager.

He led her off the dance floor, down a path to a garden lined with ginger and gardenias where other couples strolled. The scent of her favorite flowers intensified her desire. Peacocks strutted the lawns beyond a moonlit pool.

"So far, so good?"

"So far," she grinned, "it's gorgeous."

He whisked her behind the far side of a waterfall, and they were alone in a hidden grotto. Orchestra music filtered through a sheet of cascading water. Wisps of fragrant tuberose, jasmine, and orchids hung from the shell-incrusted ceiling.

A single lantern lit a doorway. He ushered her through, struck a match, and lit a branch of candles on a ledge.

"We're in a private pool house. I'm a friend of the owner."

She scanned the unusual room strewn with soft surfaces, carpets and chaises, enormous pillows in hues of dense burgundy, purple, and teal, brass tables glinting under yet more candles.

He turned a key in the lock and handed it to her.

"You've been here before?"

"Not for years."

She looked away, out of her comfort zone.

He turned her into him. "Tell me your name."

"No," she whispered. "It's better this way."

"Why is that?"

"No expectations. I can be what I want and so can you."

"An interesting approach . . ."

"Yes, we can tell each other anything, because we aren't bound by the past or the future."

"Tell me a secret then," he said.

She took a breath and set the key on a low table. "I eat ice cream in the bathtub."

"I can't sleep with the closet door open."

"Last night I dreamt of you." She looked away.

"Okay." His emerald gaze met hers as she regained her courage. "Then let the fantasy begin." He raised her face to his, lightly kissing her brow, her cheek, her eyelids.

She drank in his woody citrus scent, Lagerfeld, she guessed, and the pulsating sound of the waterfall hiding them.

He sought her mouth, drawing her near, his lips full yet firm, his tongue lightly exploring her mouth. She wanted more. *There's danger here because I don't want him to stop.* Kathryn pulled away.

He stepped closer, his smile disappeared, and a look of tenderness replaced it.

"Stay. Don't leave me."

"I'm . . ."

"Shhh, you're safe." A half grin tilted his beautiful mouth. "I'm the one in danger here." They stood in the middle of the room gazing at one another.

"This feels magical between us," he said. "Or am I living in my own dream?"

"Yes, magic, and I'm in it with you." She kissed him, barely restraining her need for him. It had been so long.

"So lovely," he whispered. His mouth roamed her neck, shoulder, and collarbone, his voice husky. "I want to know you, your wants, desires, spend days and nights exploring each others' lives." He chuckled. "Have I said enough? Should I shut up and kiss you?"

"Um hmm." She was beginning to adore him.

He did. His luscious mouth consumed hers. He ran his hands over her bare shoulders. His thumb skimmed the swell of her breasts over the strapless gown, pushing it down, then his mouth was there, at her nipples, teasing with his tongue and teeth, one then the other. She couldn't think nor did she want to. But when he reached behind her and unzipped her gold dress and it fell to the floor, she froze.

Motionless, she watched his gaze travel upward from her shimmering gold stockings, the garter belt, bikini thong, rising to her breasts. His invisible touch devoured her with heat. She inched back.

His eyes met hers and there was the recognition of her panic. "Too fast." His lips compressed.

He shrugged and knelt before her, retrieving her dress, standing close.

She squared her shoulders. *You're a grown woman, Kat. Take what you want. It's right in front of you.* "No. Just right," she whispered.

"I'm an idiot." He ran a hand through his dark glossy hair. "I'm ruining this." He looked away.

"It's me. I'm the idiot." *Now or never.* She let her dress slide to the floor again, kicking it away. She held out her arms, her gaze locked on his. "Come here."

The yearning in his glance intensified, his irises turning a dark forest shade. He removed his dinner jacket and tossed it on a banquette and drew her close. "Your skin, as I imagined, like velvet," he murmured, running his hands up her body.

She let him pull her down on a satin chaise, her hair spilling over the edge.

He knelt beside her on the carpet, unbuttoning his crisp white shirt and discarded it. "Wherever your fantasy leads, I'm there."

She reached up, her hands molding over his powerful chest, tapering to his stomach. "You feel wonderful," she said, her fingers gliding over his candlelit body.

He pulled her hands away, up over her head. He skimmed her body with his fingertips, moving lower, between her legs, gently spreading them apart.

Kathryn, filled with moist, burning heat, moved in

a slow rhythm to his touch. "My God," she murmured.

He lowered his body over hers, his warm chest brushing her nipples.

She grabbed his dark head and pulled him to her mouth, the kiss powerful.

"Don't ever forget my touch," he said, his mouth traveling down her throat to her breast, cupping it, stroking, bringing her pebbled nipple to his lips.

His skillful fingers played between her legs. She ached with desire.

She moved beneath his warmth, and he brushed her hands aside and went lower, kissing the inside of her thighs, escalating her need.

"Open your legs, for me," he said.

She did, her knees trembling, and his large hands gently opened her wider, exploring with his tongue, lips, and fingers, in a way she had never felt, never knew existed until the world behind her eyes lit in a kaleidoscope of refracted light, her pleasure swelling. She'd never been to this place before, careening through sensation, erupting over the edge. She grabbed his hand, the one covering her mouth, screaming her release.

"I want you now!" she cried out.

He stopped and pulled away.

She sat up. "I have to have every inch of you." She knew she was rushing but she couldn't hold back, opening his belt buckle, undoing his pants, pulling them down, releasing all of him. "Gorgeous," she said, stroking him until he grabbed her to him, crushing her breasts against his chest.

"Hope you don't mind the carpet," she said, pushing him over onto his back.

He laughed and kicked off the rest of his clothes, pulling her with him. "Your wish is my command."

She held his shoulders down, straddling him, and lifted herself, easing him inside her. They locked gazes, faces flushed, her hands traveling over his body, his caressing hers. She set a gentle rhythm, riding him, friction building with her need. His mouth, the feel of his hands on her, his movements possessed her, keeping her on the brink for endless moments.

Then he pulled her over beneath him and thrust deep inside her. She encircled her legs around him, moaning with each thrust, again, again, higher and higher. He brought her along with his abandonment until they both shattered into wild orgasm.

He held her, their chests rising and falling together, their warm breath mingled.

She nestled into his slick warmth, studying his handsome face, flushed in afterglow.

"That was . . ."

They both smiled.

". . . spectacular." Kathryn's body tingled all over; every part of her seemed to smile.

He kissed the inside of her arms, sweet kisses.

"Shall I go on?" he teased.

"Where else could we go?"

He looked into her eyes, saying softly, "I'd go anywhere with you." He sat up with her in his embrace. "But let's save something for next time. And I vow there *will* be a next time."

She looked away.

"Won't you tell me your name, Cinderella?"

"If I did it wouldn't be a fairy tale."

"Then I'd better get you dressed and back to the ball." They dressed quickly, he zipped up her dress, she slipped on her shoes, and together they blew out the candles.

He guided her back to the edge of the terrace and pressed her fingers to his lips.

"Goodbye, Prince Charming," she said.

"No, not goodbye." He took her hand and held it. "Not goodbye."

She blew him kiss and forced herself to walk away.

As Anthony watched her cross the dance floor, his friend Philippe came toward him scowling. "I thought you'd left without telling me." Philippe said. "Is everything all right?"

Philippe followed his gaze up to the landing at the top of the stairs. "That's Kathryn Whitney going into the ladies' lounge. How could you let Mirdad escort her on your behalf? You've given your cousin quite a gift."

"*She's* the lady director?"

"The same."

Anthony paused. "My," he said almost to himself, determination flaring. "Well, I'm taking her back." He brushed himself off. "Philippe, I have to go now. Hans expects me."

"Can't it wait? You haven't eaten."

"I'm not hungry. Send my regrets to the table and sign my name to the tab." He hesitated. "And do me a favor. Make sure the lady gets home safely."

"For God's sake, Anthony, make this your last trip."

Anthony squeezed Philippe's shoulder. "I'll be okay."

When Mirdad spotted Anthony glide Kathryn onto the dance floor, he burned with anger, pulverizing the breadstick in his hand. Crumbs spilled on the table. *Anthony, you'll never stick your greedy fist into my plate again—you can't have her, bastard.*

Memories flooded Mirdad's mind, all the things that had painfully eluded him and flown to Anthony's door: a respected family, wealth, fame. Next to Anthony, Mirdad always felt diminished.

A waiter carrying a small silver tray with an envelope approached Mirdad.

"A message, Excellency."

Mirdad, lost in hate, whirled around in his chair, almost knocking the man off his feet.

"What is it, fool?" Mirdad snarled in Farsi.

"Sorry, Excellency, a million pardons." The man obsequiously extended the tray.

Mirdad snatched the envelope, ripping it open. He regained his composure as he read the message. He stuck it in his pocket and glanced around to see who had noticed him lose control. No, the Americans were lost in their drinks. Only Philippe Kahlil turned to him.

"I do hope it's from a lady, old man," Philippe slurred, clearly in his cups as well.

Mirdad relaxed a little. "A lady, yes. Will you excuse me? I must tend to her needs."

They both chuckled as he got up.

Mirdad walked through the dining room, glancing at the occupants to see if any watched him. They were too interested in their own decadence. He ascended the marble staircase, steeling himself for his first Black Glove inner sanctum meeting. He headed for the ominous brass doors, facing his future with dread.

CHAPTER SIXTEEN

SHIRAZ, PARADISE CLUB

Upstairs at the end of the hall, Mirdad passed three leaders of the Shiite Revolutionary Council on their way out, heads high, shoulders back, looking confident. Mirdad executed a polite bow in their direction, his stomach squirming.

"*Allah-u Akbar*! God is great!" he said. How he dreaded this meeting.

A guard opened a polished brass door, and Mirdad strode into a palatial cream-colored salon. Six men lounged on overstuffed sofas around a large glass table, the only color in the room coming from the multitude of vivid carpets, swept like a garden of paradise beneath their feet. Mirdad could not dispel his foul mood. He was as consumed with fear and loathing as the room was consumed with smoke and the pungent odor of greed.

He looked around at men of conspicuous wealth wearing

gold Rolex watches, oversized star sapphire and ruby rings, and handmade Italian shoes peeking out under their pants or the hem of their robes. They smoked Turkish cigarettes and Cuban cigars and sipped sweet mint tea from gold goblets. They were all leaders of the Shiite Revolutionary Council, all familiar with one another. But Mirdad possessed a deeper knowledge of their quest and how low these supposed devout Muslims would go to achieve greater wealth and power, all in the name of Allah.

Two of the men were dressed in fine business suits, well-groomed down to their freshly manicured nails. No one would guess they had recently tortured a wealthy doctor's three children while their father, bound to the grill of his Rolls Royce, had looked on crying, pleading. When they began mutilating the face of his four-year-old daughter, Dr. Farami howled, relenting, and handed over access to his staggering assets. Black Glove methods were efficient. They were practiced often lately.

What the hell was he doing here? *Poverty brought out his basest traits.*

Someone stepped in front of him, smiling.

"Touraj." Mirdad was surprised but glad to see a friendly face.

"It's been a while," said Touraj.

It had been thirteen years since Touraj had gone off to Boston and Harvard, the same year Mirdad reluctantly accepted a history scholarship to the University of Shiraz when he had longed only for America.

"Good to see you." Mirdad clasped his friend's hand.

Sensing a dark look, Mirdad looked over Touraj's shoulder, into the face of Hafiz, Touraj's father. The bulky man with large, square hands sat on cushions, his droopy eyes menacing, so different from his slim, good-looking son.

Mirdad leaned closer to his friend, whispering. "Do you miss the States?"

"Now more than ever," Touraj murmured without moving his lips.

Mirdad nodded. *Me, too. He would take his mother to America, to safe harbor.* The remaining two men barely grunted from their respective sofas. It was then he noticed the buzz around the room.

These six men spoke in subdued Farsi, but their words were clear. Out of Tehran's mosques a fanatical revolutionary committee had developed, a new militia: the Komiteh, or Green Bands.

"They grow in strength and numbers daily," said the man next to him. Others around him joined in, pride sounding in their voices.

"Soon they'll be fully armed and thousands of revolutionary *komitehs*, all over the countryside, will serve us well." He was referring to the committees of angry, fired up young fighters who would fight or die in the name of their precious Allah.

Hafiz spoke up. "Already they've intimidated thousands once loyal to the Shah. They're upholding strict moral behavior." A murmur of agreement surrounded Mirdad who sat quietly among them.

Touraj leaned closer. "I saw Green Bands prowling city streets last night. They grabbed a woman and beat her because she showed a bit of ankle." Touraj shuddered.

Mirdad said, "When they have weapons we'll all have to run for cover."

Hafiz narrowed his eyes at his son, and Touraj returned to his father's side.

Mirdad then realized the Green Band *komitehs* would become worse than SAVAK, if only because they were younger and more energized, with a fresh sense of purpose and immediacy. He sat on the nearest seat, leaned back and lit a cigarette, his knee jerking as he waited. He needed a lot of money to get the hell out of Iran.

The formidable General Omar Houdin entered the adjoining room, and every man stood as a ripple of greeting circled the space. Nodding to the other men, Houdin then came over to Mirdad. They shook hands warmly. Affection from the general was an elixir in this tension filled room. The Black Glove was his. It was ironic the Black Glove terrorists had spawned from SAVAK, yet worked in concert with Khomeini's *komiteh*, inflaming the zealot's rebellion, all for greed. How long would Houdin be able to pull this off?

Houdin circled the splendid Boulle desk and sat, indicating for Mirdad to sit near him in a Louis XV chair upholstered in tiger skin.

Major Demetrius Nassiri, Houdin's adjutant, followed behind Houdin with pantherlike movements. He was rumored to have lethal martial arts abilities. Demitrius stood like a sentinel behind the general and shot Mirdad a confrontational look.

Mirdad instantly disliked this man.

This major's unscrupulous ambition was well known; he had ascended military ranks from the lowly position as corporal in only six years. Recently the major never seemed to be far from General Houdin's side, a fact that annoyed

Mirdad. This man stood in the way of Mirdad's plans to make enough money to escape Iran.

When Mirdad realized the general's eyes were on him, he flushed. The look bore through him and the smile vanished.

Houdin leaned forward over his desk. "At least tonight, Mirdad, we know where your treacherous cousin Anthony Evans is."

Mirdad nodded, not grasping where this conversation was headed, but tasting the edge of humiliation with reference to Anthony's family connection to him.

"Tonight, he is with you . . . but today he was with the empress again. Did you know this?"

Mirdad did not flinch.

"A very confidential meeting," the general went on. "She agreed to place something of great value in his hands for safekeeping. And do you know what it is?" Houdin's voice resonated, filling the room. "The crown jewels of Persia." Houdin leaned back. "She, a woman, has no right to them, but nonetheless she plans to take them as her own." Houdin shifted in his chair, asking in a quieter tone, "Now, tell me Mirdad, whose responsibility is it to know everything Evans does?"

Apprehension jangled Mirdad, but he refused to feel humiliated in front of these hypocritical cutthroats.

"We know Farah Diba's plans," Houdin went on, not waiting for an answer. "But our informer must make certain the stones the empress gave Evans are authentic, not decoys she's put in our way." He scanned the room. "You see, the French company Van Cleef and Arpels was the jeweler who created the crown jewels of Iran, and Arpels made twenty-five versions of her coronation crown *alone*.

Some of the decoys are so similar, only an expert would know the difference."

Muttering filled the room. One of the other men stared at Mirdad demanding, "Where is this man's loyalty?"

The general held up his hand for silence. "I know of your intense dislike for your infidel cousin," he said to Mirdad. "And your loyalty to me is faultless." He paused. "Therefore, we place the responsibility back in your hands, Mirdad."

Touraj's father, Hafiz, called out, "You must not let this dog, Evans, out of your sight again."

Iraj, in his fine suit, stood, wiping down the expensive fabric of his trousers with his palms. "Use as many men as you need. He has snatched from under our noses the wealth of half the infidels on our list."

"Half *our* wealth!" others shouted.

Houdin stood, his eyes narrowing. "Once these jewels reach Evans' hands, you, Mirdad, will take them and make certain Evans bothers us no further, *Insha Allah*."

He placed a hand on Mirdad's shoulder. "Is my meaning clear, dear Mirdad?"

"Crystal clear." A claw gripped at Mirdad's heart. He was in hell. Anthony had risked his own life to save him two days ago in Jaleh Square, but Mirdad looked at the faces of these ruthless men and stuffed down his guilty thoughts. "I'll be only too glad to fulfill this task." He crossed to the window overlooking the gardens to hide the conflict he could feel on his face.

"Sir," Demitrius spoke up, "Evans is an international figure, nobility in the English realm. This must be done thoughtfully or Iran will swarm with even more MI-6 and CIA agents."

"Naturally," Mirdad snapped, whirling around. "It must appear an accident."

"And must not be linked to any of us," Touraj added.

Demitrius crossed to stand next to Mirdad at the window. "Isn't that your cousin now?"

Mirdad looked from Demitrius' face to the garden below where Anthony and the beautiful Kathryn walked along the winding path, disappearing onto the terrace dance floor. Grim determination engulfed Mirdad.

"First," he said without turning, "I will get my hands on the jewels. And then I'll get my hands on Evans' throat." He felt empowered hearing his own words.

"Mirdad, before you go," General Houdin said, as the others left the room. Once the doors closed and the sentries were in place again on the other side, the general opened his wall safe.

Mirdad waited. Was he being replaced with Demitrius Nassiri? *How much would this problem with Anthony cost him? His fortune? His life?*

"There's something I want to give you." Houdin closed the safe. "Something you deserve."

Mirdad froze.

"Sit down, sit down."

Mirdad did not want to sit. He wanted to leave. He heaved an anxious breath and sat once again on the tiger skin chair.

The general poured two tumblers of Lanvul. "I was rough on you earlier, but I'm grooming you for leadership. These terrorists must see you as strong." He handed Mirdad a glass.

"Never let anything slip past you," he gestured with his

Cuban cigar. "Never give anyone an opportunity to seize your power or make a fool of you." He raised his glass. "Tonight, you did well."

Mirdad raised his glass and drank. A rain of fire drenched his esophagus, pooling in his gut.

"Give me your left arm."

Wary, Mirdad held out his arm.

Houdin removed Mirdad's watch, tossing it to the floor like a used bone. He opened the box in his fist and took out an eighteen-carat gold and diamond Vacheron Constantin watch of unequaled taste. Mirdad had seen one other, the one Philippe Kahlil had owned and Mirdad had coveted, only to see Kahlil casually toss it onto a roulette table to cover a bet.

Houdin clasped the watch onto Mirdad's wrist.

Mirdad exhaled, stunned. He had never owned a watch of any value. He flushed with pride, deeply flattered the general would think him worthy of this expensive reward. "I'm overwhelmed, sir."

"Think nothing of it. The first of many rewards." The general walked around his desk and sat behind it. "There is something I purposely left unsaid here tonight so those grasping thieves would not know of it. Your mother's Persian Glories will accompany the crown jewels when they are moved," the general said. "Exactly what the empress and your cousin have in mind, I don't know."

Mirdad knew his duty. He looked at his gleaming gold and diamond watch. *Quid pro quo.* "Rest assured, I'll find out."

The general came over, clasping Mirdad in a quick, awkward embrace. "Your mother has consented to be my wife." He stood taller. "I've waited a long time to marry. This is a proud day for me."

Mirdad's emotions spun, his brain whirling toward a dark, horrifying place. With a monumental effort, he seized control of himself and choked out, "May you both find every happiness, sir."

Mirdad grabbed the elegant watch box and left, his mood fouler than when he'd entered this evil den.

Colonel Demitrius Nassiri was leaning against the bar when Mirdad came downstairs from Houdin's office. His mood seemed as dark as Mirdad's, his face almost as young.

"The Americans have gone," Nassiri said, shrugging.

"I need to fly to Tehran tonight, return tomorrow," Mirdad said, regretting his missed opportunity to be with Kathryn.

Nassiri looked him over coolly and finished his drink. "Follow me."

Mirdad was led out a side exit into a waiting SAVAK Mercedes and driven to a nearby airstrip without a word from Nassiri.

Mirdad thanked the colonel and boarded a small plane. His insides roiled, for he knew his life was surging into uncharted waters. But if he was soon to be related to Houdin, he intended to take advantage of every perk. Yet again, he felt conflicted, for when he arrived home in a cab, he wanted to wake his mother and shout, "Maman, how could you?"

But she was awake, waiting for him.

He stared at her, forming his words.

"You've heard?" she said. "I wanted to be the one to tell you the good news." Tears welled in her eyes. "At last. I'm so tired of being isolated from the social groups I long to entertain." She fell into Mirdad's arms. "My son, my son, we're saved."

"Saved?" He backed away from her. "From a hard life maybe, but there are worse things."

"Such as?" She dried her eyes.

"I know you long for the rich pleasures, and I don't blame you. But thinking of you with Houdin sickens me!"

"Mirdad, you mustn't—"

"You should be with a statesman, a man of business and knowledge, like my father. Not Houdin. He's a peasant."

"A generous peasant. A powerful peasant! General Houdin is governor of Tehran, with a legendary military record. And he will be my husband—and your father!"

"Never!" Mirdad spun to leave, but turned back to her. "As soon as I have enough money, I'm leaving for the U.S., New York or California. It's time for me to live *my* dreams. I wanted you to come with me."

"But my Glories!"

Mirdad sighed. "You'll have them."

"And your cousin?"

"I'll take care of him."

"And Raymond, the murderer, Ali's traitor of a father who serves Anthony like a slave. Don't forget Raymond."

Mirdad's stomach tightened. "Him, too. Then I go!"

At eight the next morning, Mirdad stepped out of a cab at the orphanage in Tehran. "Wait," he ordered the driver.

The new concrete wall surrounded the property. The roof had been replaced, and a freshly painted sign painted in bold script hung from the eaves: EVENING STAR HOME FOR BOYS.

Tashi, the headmaster, met him and brought him through the gate. "Take tea with me, Mirdad."

Mirdad joined him at a scarred wooden table under the only tree in the yard. Boys of all ages bobbed around them, playing with sticks and a black and red striped ball.

"I'm spending time in Shiraz on business." Mirdad sipped savory mint tea. "I won't get here as often."

Tashi nodded, looking disappointed.

"But I'll send Ali when I can. He's a good man."

"Man? He barely grows a beard." Tashi liked to tease.

Mirdad set a paper bag on the table. "I want you to buy the two vacant lots next door."

"They're huge."

"We're adding a soccer field and a gym with a trampoline, rings, bars, and mats. These boys will be strong and disciplined. They'll use their energy wisely."

"A big endeavor," Tashi said.

"There will be a locker room with showers and an attendant to supervise and care for the equipment."

"You have big dreams, my brother. Do you suddenly have big pockets, too?" Tashi grinned but only briefly; orphanage business was serious.

Mirdad took an elegant box out of the bag and opened it. The Vacheron Constantin watch gleamed in the sunlight. "This should get you going."

Tashi picked up the watch. "This will bring a small fortune."

"Ali will bring more funds soon."

Tashi clasped Mirdad's hand, his voice tighter. "You do well by us, shitface."

Mirdad smiled, a few pieces of his soul reaching for light. The surrounding snow-capped Elburz Mountains gleamed white, reaching for the fall sky, and for one fragile moment, Mirdad felt blessed.

Tashi handed Mirdad a folded paper. Mirdad knew what he'd find there. He stuck it in his pocket and got back into the waiting cab. He patted his pocket. Another downtrodden orphan's home he was being asked to rescue in Shiraz. A few hundred thousand less ill-gotten gains for Houdin's rich cutthroats would help countless children in need. The swine would never guess their riches helped forward a good cause.

CHAPTER SEVENTEEN

It was 5:00 A.M. when Kathryn gently opened her eyes in her hotel room and stretched her limbs, awakening her body even before her alarm went off. Today her new life began, her first day's shoot. She darted out of bed.

A shaft of pale sunlight melted shadows and spread like creamy butter over the walls. Then an image of last night sprang into her mind. It was impossible for it not to—she had made love with a perfect stranger. Perfect yes, and she had been naughty. Thoughts of her sensual night took hold. She skimmed her fingers over her arms, the skin sensitive, recalling the mysterious green-eyed man's touch. She shivered, eyes closed, imprinting images of their time together to last. Impulsive lovemaking was out of character for her, yet had felt natural.

Drawing on her robe, she threw open the French doors and swept out onto the balcony. A breeze, redolent with jasmine, caressed her skin, welcoming her, and the day became her friend. Peter had known what he was talking about. This interlude had reawakened her, brought her to life. All the heaviness inside her had lifted. The bond with Brett was broken. She was free of his grasp.

Inside her room the phone rang. She rushed back in to answer. Before she could say hello, a voice jolted her. "You're in trouble!"

Wouldn't you know? Brett.

A half hour later—showered and dressed in khaki slacks, a UCLA tank, and a white shirt with sleeves rolled up—Kathryn grabbed her notes, briefcase, and baseball cap and hurried downstairs.

She burst out of the Hotel Persepolis where Buzz stood frowning by an idling Jeep. He took one irritated look at her, hands dug deep into his Levis pockets, and kicked a stone with his leather topsiders.

"Get in."

"Good morning, to you, too," she said.

"Collect your thoughts, kid." He jumped in and shoved the Jeep in gear, screeching away from the hotel.

Kathryn looked over. "I see you've taken driving lessons from Habib."

"That remark will cost you a thousand Rials. *Piskeesh,*" he said. The Jeep tore down the road, Kathryn gathering her notes to her chest.

She laughed, but frustration surfaced. Was she still a pawn in Brett's game?

"Christ! Been on the phone since the crack of dawn with the agency. I overheard your call from Brett, the hotel walls are pretty thin. Thought maybe you'd heard mine."

He glanced at her, his eyes angry sapphires. "What's got me is, why is he interfering?" Buzz bashed his palm against the steering wheel. "The nervy son of a bitch went over my head to *my* agency," he shouted. "Am I blind? There are no problems here except what Brett's making for us." He shook his head.

She knew only too well. "It's all about control."

Buzz's mouth twisted. "He's determined to make this shoot impossible for you to finish!" Buzz turned to her and smirked. "Probably worried about ya', huh?"

She responded with a dirty look. They hit a pothole, the Jeep lurched, and Kathryn's notes slid off her lap. She again pulled them together, cramming them into her briefcase.

"Life on the road," he chuckled.

A cool breeze brushed their faces, clearing their mood. The dashboard temperature read 25 degrees Celsius—about 70 degrees Fahrenheit—and would probably go up another twenty degrees if the weather held.

In the distance, imposing columns of the Palace of Darius stretched upward to blue sky, no cloud in sight.

The crew had set up a giant condor crane looming above the location. Lights, reflectors, camera mounts, and dollies were in place. Exhilarated, Kathryn stood up in the Jeep and held onto the top edge of the windshield, her energy humming. She barely waited for Buzz to stop before jumping out and grabbing her briefcase.

Smooth convex stones under her feet echoed the approach of the thousands who'd walked on them over two centuries before her. A sense of timelessness buoyed her. She waved to Peter.

He jogged over, a whistle bobbed around his neck,

clipboard in hand. "It's all great, Kat. We've rechecked the equipment, and we're ready to roll."

"Everyone's here? The pilot?" she asked.

"Right on schedule."

"Even that jackass photographer?"

Peter cringed, screwing his eyes up. "Uh . . ."

A deep and familiar voice said, "The jackass photographer is right here."

Kathryn whirled around to the sound.

He leaned against a camera mount, his gaze hard.

She was speechless, incredulous. An avalanche of feelings let loose and buried her.

He looked at her, and his smile ripped apart her remains.

Oh, you idiot! She grabbed onto the Jeep. *Fool! The playboy. How could she have let herself . . . ?*

"Would you like me to begin with shots of the Immortals, or perhaps the lion itself?" He pushed away from the equipment and came toward her. "Yes, I think the lion first, don't you? And, possibly, we'll talk later."

"You . . . !"

"Yes." His smile was cool. "Anthony Evans. I'm delighted to finally meet you. Kathryn Whitney, isn't it?"

Kathryn tried to smile, but her lips stuck to her teeth. She could barely look at him. She was so embarrassed. *Quick, quick, who wouldn't be embarrassed?* Barbara Stanwick, *Double Indemnity.* No! Anthony Perkins, *Psycho!* And how she wished she had that knife.

Peter stepped back abruptly, his face showing alarm, looking from one to the other. "Hey, I'll come back later," he said and took off.

"You're angry with me," Anthony said, "but believe me,

when we came upon each other last night, I thought you were a professor from Princeton. Foolish of me."

"Oh? When did your head clear?"

"Afterwards."

Her face flushed.

"Why didn't you say who you were?" He tried to take her hand.

She retracted it as if it had been singed. He was turning this back on her. "Would it have made any difference?"

He hesitated. "I'm glad I didn't know," he said quietly. "It might have stopped me."

Teddy came running up. "Are you ready?" he asked Anthony, then turned to Kathryn. "Anthony wants to go up with us to shoot aerial stills. We cleared it with Buzz. You okay with it, Kat?"

"That'll mean extra weight for our take," she said. "Doesn't sound like a good idea." Her shot at Anthony didn't seem to faze him.

"Why don't we clear it with the pilot?" Anthony suggested.

"Fine." *The arrogance.* She whipped around to go and her briefcase fell open, the contents spilling on the ground between them.

He knelt to retrieve the mess the moment she did.

She gasped, strewn in front of them, were the many clippings from Peter's folder, photographs from magazines and newspapers—of Anthony! On the polo pony, the yacht with the two brunette cupcakes, at parties, skiing on the Alps, half nude on the Riviera along with a stack of his stills from *National Geographic*. Had she bothered to look at the damn things earlier she would have known. She cursed herself. This was her fault.

Her eyes darted from one shot to the next as his gorgeous smile mocked her. She wanted to scream. Kneeling face to face, they both rushed to grab the clippings, and their hands collided.

"How interesting!" His gaze not six inches away, pierced her with inquiry. Then he laughed, holding the photograph from *Paris Match* of him on the topless beach at San Tropez. "It seems one of us did know."

Kathryn snatched the clipping from him and crammed it in the briefcase with the rest. "I never saw those," she said with futility.

"You're amazing." He grabbed her wrist, scanning her body. "Every last inch of you." He stood, taking her with him.

She shook loose of his grasp, but his burning gaze held her. What did she care what he thought? He was an arrogant playboy, a one-night stand. He meant nothing to her.

"Let's go speak to the pilot." She turned on her heel and tromped across the wide plain to the helicopter.

The pilot walked straight past her and shook hands with Anthony like they were old friends.

"A new 206 Jet Ranger?" Anthony said. "Only the best for you, eh, Duncan?"

"You bet, your lordship. The Shah knows who his best pilots are."

Kathryn stood beside them, completely ignored and growing increasingly annoyed.

"Ms. Whitney," Anthony said, "this wiry Scot is Duncan MacShane. I can say firsthand you've chosen the best pilot I've ever come across."

"I'll reserve judgment until I see what he can do." Kathryn winked secretly at MacShane.

Duncan covered his smile.

"Seems the lady means business, Duncan."

"Aye, 'tis reasonable, m'lord. She's the boss."

She shook hands with him. "Call me Kathryn."

Teddy meandered over and greeted Duncan and Anthony.

Kathryn put two fingers in her mouth and gave an ear-splitting whistle, waving across for Peter and Buzz to join them by the video monitor.

"Listen up, folks. Our schedule has tightened to five days," she said.

"Five days?" Peter grumbled. "Where'd that come from?"

Tight lipped, she looked at him, not wanting to admit Brett had bullied her.

"Never mind." Peter shrugged. "I can guess."

"So it's a push," Kathryn said. "Stay focused, and we'll finish on time." She paused, getting their full attention. "I want to open on the face of the lion from a dead stop in front of it. From there," she backed up a foot, "we pull back. Buzz and I'll watch the shots on the monitor."

"Revealing the lion?" Duncan asked.

"Exactly. We have to show how huge this fella really is." Kathryn couldn't stop herself from glancing over at Anthony, who stood with his arms folded across his chest, maybe listening, maybe not. She yanked her gaze away.

"Duncan, you'll circle around the right wing, around the back, and when you get to the opposite wing, lift off." She looked over at Teddy for confirmation.

They nodded all around.

"With a swoop, we soar over the Palace of Darius, as if the camera is the lion. A slow sweep around the entire palace, Duncan and you glide to the front gates and the carved Ten Thousand Immortals."

"Close up?" Teddy asked.

"As close as possible. Then we're off again, up high. Dive down at our two hundred extras in full costume. They should be entranced with the flight of the winged lion—awed. Peter, I want lots of reaction here."

"Ali and Habib and I can do it," Peter said, confidence radiating from his tone.

"Good. Here, as before, we have to be close. I want to see their authentic tribal costumes."

"We better see 'em," Buzz said. "Those replacement threads cost a mint."

"Right," Kat laughed. "We'll play a little with the extras. Do some of your fancy footwork, Duncan, and when the lion flies off into space, we'll have our first shot of the day."

Duncan and Teddy looked at each other uncertainly.

"Don't worry. You'll have on headsets. Down here, Buzz, Peter, and I will as well." She looked around at her crew. "Teddy, do you have anything to add?"

"Yeah. Not too fancy, Duncan. I want to hold down my breakfast."

"Is everybody with me, so far?" Kathryn said.

Buzz grabbed the inch-thick binder of full-color storyboards. "These are first class, Kat," he said. "Anthony, take a look at these."

Anthony moved over, studying the boards.

"Okay folks." Kathryn said. "We've set a fast pace for the day, and I know you can do it."

By 7:00 A.M. the Jet Ranger approached the winged lion in soft light, and Anthony, harnessed in next to Teddy, was hooked. He had quickly studied Kathryn's boards, curious after watching her expression as she clarified a shot while they sorted through the images. As many times as he'd been there, it had never occurred to him that every carved creature, man or beast, even the Ten Thousand Immortal Soldiers, had wings. Man's ancient desire for flight. Her vision was exquisite.

He reached for his motorized Nikon, mounted the lens, adjusted, and started shooting, riveted on the changing light, wind whipping his face, he was soon lost in his own work. He would use these aerial stills as part of his Persian suite of photographs for London.

They did another pass around the lion and turned toward the Tomb of King Darius. Storm clouds pressed in from the east, still far off. The sun would not crest the Zargos Mountains for at least four hours. Anthony realized when the sun blasted over the mountain crest, the Tomb of Darius would be hit with startling light, dazzling. What an incredible shot with two hundred mounted extras cantering in front of it.

Would he dare suggest it to the testy Ms. Whitney? He smirked. She was furious with him. And glorious. What did he expect? She hadn't wished to reveal her identity. But had she really thought she would not see him again? That infuriated *him*; he was unable to recall a woman willing to let him go so easily. It was a first, in fact. He had wanted her the instant she had appeared at dawn on that ledge.

The Ranger ascended the lion's face. "Hold that." He

heard Kathryn's voice over the radio. "You've established your first mark."

They rehearsed the shot four times, around the statue and over the palace. But each time Kathryn stopped them before reaching the extras. "I don't like what I'm seeing, Teddy. We're too removed from the shot for what I want."

Hours passed too quickly and the chopper had to come down after every couple of passes. Although Anthony heard her frustration over the headset, he hadn't paid much attention. The hundred-millimeter lens had been a perfect choice. He glanced over at Teddy's Arri with the fifty millimeter.

"What about a seventy-five, Teddy?" Anthony blurted out.

Teddy gave him a dirty look.

"Sorry." Anthony went back to his camera. But Kathryn had picked it up.

"Yeah, what about it, Teddy?" Her voice came over the headset.

"It won't work for the whole shot, but . . ." Teddy balked. "I could try the sixty. We'll compromise a little on the lion's wing, but we might get what you want for the rest."

Anthony liked Teddy's deft maneuvers capturing many angles of the troops rearing back in awe of the lion's presence.

"Good moves, Teddy. It's working well." Her voice crackled over the radio.

When they came down with the first shot complete, Teddy gave Anthony a nod. "Going after my job, eh?"

"No thanks. From the look of those boards, I'll leave it to you." He paused. "But I do have an idea." Teddy listened then called Kathryn over.

"Let's do it." Kathryn was going for Anthony's notion of parading the extras in front of the massive ten-story tomb, light exploding over them, vivid, otherworldly when the sun crested the ridge. The fact that enormous black clouds were moving from beyond the ridge could add shadow, deepening the colors or she could lose a half day to weather and go over on the largest budget day of Boeing's shoot. A budget she had pledged to shrink. She considered her options. She wanted the shot. "Load up!"

Crewmembers scurried, organizing and shouting as trucks were crammed with equipment and gaffers, and electricians tore across the plain up a winding road, skidding to a stop and unloading in record time. Teddy used the documentary Bolex to shoot the crew while they set up for Boeing's next shot.

"Peter," she said, "have the crew grab thirty tarps and space stacks about eight horses apart under the rocks. If the storm breaks loose, choose a point guy for each group and cover up. If we're lucky, the downpour won't last. Beyond ten minutes we've blown it, day over."

"Got it." Peter charged off.

At the new position, the Tomb of Darius, Anthony, Habib, Ali, and their crew guided extras and mounts into position. Anthony shot film of the extras, the Tomb, crew, and backdrop during the set up. Kathryn watched him from the sidelines. Kathryn, Duncan and Teddy set up the shot plan. The sun crept higher. Anthony stayed behind with the extras. He threw on a tribal robe and mounted the lead horse to guide them to the palace. He shot from his horse, sometimes facing backward. Iranian cameramen shot from the ground.

Duncan took off with Teddy. The Iranian crew had laid dolly track in tight along the trail. Kathryn used two handheld cameras for coverage. Time ticked on.

"In position, Kat." She heard Duncan's voice on her headset.

"Ready, Kat." Teddy was set.

"Rolling," she said. "Peter, cue extras." The clouds hovered beyond the mountain. "Ali, cue your camera people. Stay on your marks." Before she finished her thought, the sun burst over the ridge. "Holy Mother of God!"

"Damn, that's pretty!" Duncan said.

"Glide Duncan! Move in slow," she radioed. "Great, Teddy,"

Prickles of awe crept up Kathryn's spine. She handed her Bolex to an Iranian assistant cameraman, the one who had watched her, Peter, and Teddy switch off shooting bootleg whenever they got a chance. "Go for it!" she told him. "Let's get our own footage."

The documentary project was to be a three-way deal between Kathryn, Peter, and Teddy. Buzz kindly looked the other way, knowing some of it would be for Boeing. How they would be able to use the rest would depend on what footage they wound up with at the end of the shoot. The assistant smiled, focused, shooting as he moved, steady as a rock.

Teddy's camera on the monitor absorbed the full regalia, recreating a twice-yearly festival from two and a half centuries past.

Lightning crackled on the horizon.

Deep shadows crowded the monitor table, light disappearing across the plain, a ceiling of storm clouds covered them. "Peter, the tarps!"

CRASH!

Peter looked up. "Thunder," he called out. "Move, people!" She heard Anthony and Habib shouting signals. Their point men leapt off horses, tarps flared, covering costumed riders. Apprehension shot through her. She couldn't lose the rest of this day! *No way.*

The sky opened, a deluge falling, wind gusting. "Yipes." Kathryn pulled up her hooded sweatshirt.

Buzz crammed close, his Harrods umbrella billowing overhead. He looked dour.

"Don't panic," she said, covering her video monitor, huddling in with him. "We'll wait it out."

"You hope so!" he said.

Ten minutes, she had assured Peter, but the drenching continued. No way they could last much longer without a flash flood sweeping through the valley. Sheets of water coming at a diagonal thoroughly drenched them. She wiped her Timex on her sweatshirt, checked the time. Six minutes, then eight. She feared they were finished. *Damn.*

Wind howled across the plain, clouds rumbled by, changing color. By the time she turned to face Buzz, the rain had suddenly dwindled to a mere drizzle then stopped completely. Scents of sage, juniper, wet earth, and fresh rain filled her senses. She waited, holding her breath.

The sun flared. *Yes!* She pulled up canvas and flipped on the monitor, then grabbed Buzz and hugged him, wet sweatshirt and all.

"I knew it, I knew it." She danced around, switching on the headset, watching tarps fly off the mounted riders, crewmembers quickly folding and stashing them under rocks or sodden foliage. "Peter, you okay?"

"Yeah."

"First mark," she called out.

"We're there, waiting for cue," Peter said.

"Duncan?"

"We started her up!" The light shifted. "Would ya look at that!"

Vivid and enormous, a rainbow arched over the face of the Tombs to Persepolis.

"Lift off, Duncan," she said. "First position. We're going again. You're pulled back enough for Teddy to get God's incredible gift for posterity. Does the color read, Teddy?" She heard him laugh.

"Look for yerself," he said.

Kathryn watched on the monitor, blown away by what she saw: the storm, the amazing rainbow, the extras galloping through startling light and shadow like in a blockbuster Technicolor movie—gorgeous. It grabbed her. She stepped back, breathing hard.

The chopper landed. Anthony had sacrificed his own shots to help with the extras.

When the chopper came down again, lunch had been set up, tarps covering the wet ground.

Kathryn rushed over to greet the crew with Peter and Buzz.

"You guys did a great job." Teddy undid his harness, and she hugged him.

"Where's mine?" Duncan said.

"You *are* the best!" She hugged Duncan out of sheer joy. "Those sweeps were falcon-like."

She turned around and faced Anthony.

"And mine?" he whispered, leaning in.

She held back a beat, then nodded and hugged him briefly before traitorous desire took over.

Needing some space to breathe, she walked away, back toward the ruins looking out over the Great Hall, picturing the camera sweep through the palace like a low flying glider.

"I imagine this room adorned in ancient elegance. Do you?"

His deep voice came from behind as he walked up beside her and put his hand on her back. "We'll capture that image this afternoon."

Her gaze shifted warmly to his amazing face. "Good choice today," she said. "It went well." He had been a real asset on set, and her narrow opinions of him were crumbling.

"Do you think we've been here before?" His voice was soft.

"In my dreams." She recalled her private visit to the lion.

His mouth was tilted in that half-grin of his. He took her hand. "You hungry?"

She couldn't help her gaze being drawn to his lips, and then he kissed her, and all the anger melted away.

Hours later Kathryn yelled, "That's a wrap!" It was 5:30 P.M. "Load up, we're outta here!"

"Listen up, everyone!" Peter yelled. "Same call tomorrow. five-thirty—sharp."

"We've been at it for twelve exhilarating hours, Peter, and I'm eager for tomorrow." Kathryn put her notes in her briefcase.

"Speak for yourself, woman," he said. "After twelve hours on set, the rest of us are zonked."

It had gone well. Making up part of the lost time with

the storm using Anthony's suggestion with the cresting sun over the extras was key. Tomorrow she had to make up more time. "Peter, have you got the video system loaded in the Jeep? I'll review everything tonight in sequence."

"Yeah, sure, but don't expect to see me. Anthony's arranged for a Persian barbeque at some special place nearby. He invited everyone, and I'm going."

She looked up. "Oh."

Anthony jogged over. His hair was mussed, his chambray work shirt still damp and wrinkled. His jeans clung to his thighs, his smile brilliant. "Ready?" He held out his hand. "They're loading the Jeeps. Shall we join them?"

"Okay." She looked back at Peter.

"This stuff will be in your hotel room," Peter said.

She smiled hugely and winked, then they ran off to Anthony's Jeep where Ali was honking away in celebratory cacophony. She climbed in the back with Buzz and the Bolex, the perfect opportunity to capture B-roll footage of regular Persian people living their regular lives.

Anthony jumped in the front seat. "Takht-e Tavoos, driver, on the double!"

The Jeep lurched away, and Ali's driving for once had them laughing like kids. Buzz smirked behind sunglasses, grabbing Ali's prayer beads from the rearview mirror, solemnly fingering them.

From behind, moving in a cloud of dust, a pack of horsemen galloped toward them, shouting and waving swords. Kathryn gasped, aiming the Bolex at the spectacular sight of the charging warriors.

Anthony stood, holding onto the roll bar. "Tabriz!" he shouted, waving back. He looked back at Kathryn, filming the galloping pack through the dust. These guys were authentic nomadic horsemen.

"They're Kash Kai tribesmen, my friends." Anthony waved again.

She wondered where these amazing looking men would fit as Persia changed. She steadied the Bolex. She'd ponder the bigger questions later. Right now she was going to capture every ounce of authenticity she came across.

The open-air restaurant at Takht-i-Tavoos, with its lapping pond surrounded by willow trees and towering date palms, bustled with activity. Enticing aromas of roasting lamb, chicken, herbed rice, and freshly baked bread drifted around them as soon as the Jeep stopped.

Anthony jumped out to greet friends, pulling Kathryn along.

On the far side, brick open pit barbeques bordered the eating area filled with wide planked tables and benches. A hut served as an open bar, its countertop stacked with tubs of ice, soda, and jars of mint tea. Kathryn thought she saw some kegs.

"Beer?"

"I had some trucked in." Anthony shrugged. "My English pub roots showing."

Three Persian musicians and a singer stood by with string instruments Kathryn could not identify. But he sang a song she knew, one she'd played on her stereo at home while preparing for this trip. "That's a song by Sattar."

"And he's singing," Anthony said. "So you know the Pahlavi's favorite singer?"

Suddenly she got chills. "I've never heard him in person before." It didn't get more real than this.

They listened then Anthony said, "There's a place I want to show you before dark."

The nomadic horsemen had reigned in. Some watered the horses at the pool, others came over to greet Anthony, their deep colored robes billowing around them in shades of cranberry, eggplant, indigo, and bronze, some trimmed in braid or embroidery, all made of woven cotton. Their heads were covered, and they all wore beards. This was so much better than her mother's equestrian club. These men rode bareback, as if born on horses.

"Kathryn, meet my good friend Tabriz. He taught me to ride in his village when I was a boy."

The man had an elegant face and held the reins of a gorgeous black Arabian and a sixteen-hand perfectly tan bay. She looked from the horses back to the man. She would have cast him in Omar Sharif's role in *Lawrence of Arabia*, the leader of his people. His dark eyes inscrutable, he nodded a greeting at her, then said, "We waited before selecting the lady's horse." His smile had transformed his face from mysterious to friendly, his eyes now sparkling. "Would you like to choose?" he said to her.

Choose a horse? "Why do I need a horse?"

"I'm taking you to see something lovely," Anthony replied.

"I need a horse to get there?"

"You don't want to go?"

"Actually, I'm hungry," she said, turning away before he saw she was upset. "A nosh first, okay? Then we can go. Don't want me fainting off one of those beasts of a horse now, do you?" But then she really wanted to go. Her hunger was gone. How did she get herself into this? She took a deep breath and exhaled. *Get a grip, Kathryn. Your life is changing. New risks, new experiences.*

"You'd better choose one for me," Kathryn managed to say, wanting to add, the oldest, slowest, most gentle, most decrepit . . .

"I'll bring one right over."

"Can't wait," she said resignedly. And as she stood there, a miracle occurred. Someone brought her food unbidden. She devoured a lamb kabob wrapped in flatbread and rice with ravenous abandon, never one to apologize for her appetite. She followed it with a beer and, finally sated, smiled up at Anthony. "That was good. Let's do it."

Not far from ancient Persepolis, across the wide plain from Takht-e Tavoos, a road spiraled up an enormous mountain. Anthony and Kathryn rode along the trail, their horses at an even gait. He had been intrigued with her since he first saw her on the lion. Who was this woman inside? Had he made her up in his mind? For him, her sensuality had no match, but with her he wanted more than a superficial toss. He needed more.

Rounding another bend, Anthony felt Kathryn's tension ebb, saw her shoulders almost relax, her nervousness obvious. It disturbed him. She wasn't the nervous type. He heard she held a double license to fly planes and helicopters. He simply couldn't imagine anyone afraid of a horse.

Kathryn peered over the edge. "I can picture driving up here in my old Porsche with this heart-stopping curve."

"Are you calculating each angle?"

"And wondering how fast I could take it." A gust rifled the air.

"Don't look so worried," he said. "We're safe."

"Of course we are!" She sounded less than convinced.

"Would I kid you? Look out there." He pointed below to the Valley of Tombs, the face of King Darius' tomb carved into a sheet of rock. Ebbing sun and shadows played across the surface, making it shimmer as if it were animate.

They ascended the mountain, and the world below became tiny.

"A staggering sight." Kathryn's beautiful eyes flared to his.

Anthony guided her horse around the gaping cliff line.

The arid wind rose, whirling, thrashing the mountain. "Stay close to me," he called out. "We'll be safe beyond the point."

The point, a cliff protruding in a stubborn chin of granite, defied the flat earth that lay thousands of feet below.

"We're almost there." Ripping wind muffled his voice. The last gusts propelled them around the point.

Within seconds the wind vanished and before them, as if they had entered another world, lay a meadow sheltered by trees and giant boulders, carpeted in mountain moss of various greens and chestnut browns, circling a glistening pool of clear water.

"In the rainy season, this pond spills over the mountain. From Takht-e Tavoos you can see the waterfall cascading over the cliffs." He lifted her off the horse, easing her to the ground, but didn't let go.

She looked up and he recognized an expression from last night's intimacy lighting her eyes. She laughed low in her throat.

Bedroom laughter. Arousing.

With that smile his body remembered her touch, her taste. The veil of professionalism he had maintained through the years blurred. His body stirred, his senses quivered. He wanted this woman with more heat than last night, if that was even possible. He needed to touch her, anywhere. His gaze steadied on hers.

She blushed. Laughter again.

His hands smoothed up from her waist until the weight of her breasts lay against his thumbs. With her sharp intake of breath he eased his hands away. He stomped on his lust, which did not obey, did not abate. Privacy was what he needed.

Hot wind roared through the clearing in a tornado of dust.

"Stay close."

Arms protecting their eyes from debris, breath held, they fled across the meadow, Anthony guiding her to an enclave in the granite boulder by the pool. "We're safe here."

Sheltered, Kathryn gasped for a clean breath and coughed. They knelt over the pool cleansing their faces and drinking deep swallows. "This is good," she said through great gulps.

"Slow down, you'll choke." He brushed water from her damp windblown hair, her eyebrows, then her full lower lip.

Her hot gaze met his. "Will the wind stop soon?"

"Are you worried?" He moved toward her.

"Not at all." She pulled back.

The raspy timbre of her voice went through him like heat. He cleared his throat and pulled the horses in behind them. Why did she resist him?

The horses stomped and whinnied, shaking off dust and bending their heads to water as they settled.

"Then let's make ourselves comfortable."

She flashed a speculative look at his bulging saddlebag.

"I sleep under the stars sometimes." He unbuckled the saddlebag and pulled out a tartan blanket, spreading it over the cushiony moss near the boulder.

"You know the most amazing places. Little treasures of nature." She dropped onto the blanket next to him, watching the horses drink. "Inconceivable," she said. "I can't believe I made it up here."

He stretched out, resting on his elbow. "Still in one piece."

"You knew it." She sat up grinning. "You knew I was terrified getting on that horse and you didn't say anything."

"So tell me why," he said. "You can trust me."

"You make it easy to be open about embarrassing incidents in my life."

"Um hmm."

The wind howled beyond the cave.

She told Anthony about her mother's unrelenting pressure for riding lessons since Kathryn was five, being thrown off and forced back on each time. "I had no rapport with horses. In fact, I could stand still in a serene pasture, and they'd stampede. Why did my mom continue the dance? Later at boarding school," she said, shrugging, "my dubious relationship with horses was confirmed. I was hopeless, embarrassed time after time." When she'd finished, she sat up, face flushed.

He felt wrenched with tenderness, the emotions surprising him. This was not going like he had planned. He pulled her into his arms. "Five is young, and yet your mother kept pushing," he held her close. "I pushed you. I'm sorry."

He bent to kiss her, but she put her hand on his cheek and said, "No, you must have me under a spell." She sat up. "A good spell because I rode up here and it gave me a chance to move past unpleasant memories. That ride was nearly—well, not completely—painless."

He flinched. "Wait till tomorrow. You may not thank me then." He fiddled with a tiny wildflower tucked between the rocks. "I've wanted to show you this place since I first saw you."

She leaned against the boulder, her hands behind her head. "Up here, cares of my world are receding like morning mist." She turned to him. "Tell me about yourself, Anthony."

Whoa.

"Mysterious green-eyed man."

He took her hand. "I can't think of a more uninteresting topic."

"Not to me."

Resistance reared as always when it came to revealing anything personal.

"I know little about you," she said. "Although I'll admit I had your name listed under dilettantes. I should apologize."

"You needn't. The apology should come from me. I let you down, wasn't at the airport or the location when I agreed to be." He exhaled, letting go a little. "My life is more demanding than I'd ever anticipated. Yet on a personal level, infinitely pallid . . . until I found you."

Kathryn stiffened.

"You're thinking," he said, "'this guy's not real,' aren't you?"

She blanched.

"A notorious player."

"From your press clippings, your life glitters."

"A role I've played." He gazed beyond the trees. "One I'd like to be rid of."

"Really?" she whispered.

He handed her a miniature bouquet and scooted over, laying his head on her lap. She stroked his hair while he closed his eyes, resigned.

"I was born in Iran," he said. "My mother was Persian. Mirdad Ajani is my cousin."

"Mirdad? He's great. But Sir Anthony Evans . . . aren't you British?"

He grinned. "I am. My father was in the diplomatic corps stationed in Iran during World War II."

He spoke of his fun growing up in Persia, his horses and polo, the Shah, his father and beautiful mother. Anthony suddenly found he had much to say, was compelled to bring her into his world. Strange, telling her buried things, dormant inside him for so long, like aging cargo. He sat up and crossed his legs.

"One day at school in Tehran, when I was fourteen, we were on the soccer field halfway through the game. The score was tied. I was led by a beautiful pass down center field, free to go in on goal with only one man to beat."

"Go on." She scooted up against the tree.

"I'd never been the best ball handler, but faked one way and went the other. As I fired my shot, the one defender fell on his back. The ball flew past the goalie into the up-per corner."

"Good shot!"

"My teammates swarmed, lifting me in the air. It was a good moment. But the referee blew his whistle. Everyone went quiet. Storming right up to my face, he yelled, 'NO GOAL, NO GOAL, NO GOAL!' waving a yellow flag, signifying I'd fouled the defender."

"No way." She leaned forward.

He slumped, remembering. "I hadn't touched him. I was stunned. My frenzied teammates yelled their protests. The referee shooed them away." Anthony straightened and looked at her. "After the commotion, I approached the ref. Before I could speak, he put his mouth to my ear, 'Go back to your position, half-breed. And don't ever dispute me again.'"

Kathryn's mouth opened slightly, but she didn't speak.

"The rest of the game, I couldn't concentrate. I let good passes from my teammates slip away. When I did get the ball, I'd lose it."

She took his hand. Warmth.

"I would've rebounded, but right then my father's limousine pulled up next to the field. The driver leaped out of the car toward me." Anthony moved beside her, on the moss. "You must understand this was horribly humiliating. My father and I'd agreed no official car with British flags would be sent to pick me up at school—I wasn't of pure Persian descent—and it would call atten-tion to that fact. Persians are *very* clannish. Classmates snickered as the driver raced up to me.

"Adolescent rage got the best of me. I yelled the worst obscenities I could think of at the poor man. I wanted to make him look like a fool, an imbecile. But I must have known . . . I must have sensed something, because I found myself crying through my rage. Then the driver broke into tears."

Anthony smirked ironically. "I had to lead the distraught man back to the limo. We drove to the embassy, and there I was told both my parents had been killed in a plane crash."

For the first time, he looked up and saw tears in Kathryn's eyes.

"This was a bad idea." He took out his handkerchief and dried her eyes.

"No. You got me." She gazed off. "My dad was killed in a plane crash when I was nine."

Anthony pulled her into his arms and they watched the sun, huge and low, a great Golden Buddha belly, descending.

He spoke of many things. Words tumbled out with thoughts and feelings, describing dreams, past and present. They traded stories from their careers, back through school, and finally childhood.

Not surprising, the same year she had been sent to boarding school, he had been sent to England, his grandfather and Eton. Through miserable winter nights, so lonely, he had gaped out windows, wondering if anyone, anywhere, felt as lost as he.

Her smile melted his loneliness.

He felt a gate open, as if he had walked into a pasture their minds were sharing. Something invisible touched him and lit up feelings tucked inside.

He turned her to him and kissed her. Passion sparked, then roared.

Behind a gauzy veil of clouds, the moon crept into the night. The clouds raised their curtain and offered a brilliant spray of gems across the sky. Stars.

We're dreamers, he thought and held her close. "I'm sure you're hungry again," he teased. "We'll miss more dinner if I don't get you back. You'll like Persian barbeque." He took her hand, pulling her up.

CRACK! CRACK! Gunshot ricocheted off the boulder.

"What's that?" Kathryn crouched, the noise frightening.

CRACK!

Anthony ducked, pulling Kathryn to the ground, covering her with his body.

"Oh my God!" she gasped.

"Don't move." Her body trembled beneath him. His trembled with rage. He was the target and that left her vulnerable. A level of protectiveness for this woman surged. "Hunters," he said, excusing the inexcusable. "Overeager for a kill."

"Are they gone?"

They waited. Darkness covered them. A moment of silence. He listened, in the distance horses hooves clomping down rock, faded in the distance. The shooters were leaving, for now.

"We'll go," he said. Under moonlight they made their way to the horses. The wind had disappeared with the marksman. Anthony grabbed a wide flashlight, handing it to Kathryn and saying, "Ride with me. It's a little more difficult going down. Use the flashlight for the trail while I sing you the song of a Persian hunter."

He helped her onto his horse, Kismet, and jumped up behind her. He held the reins of the other horse, which followed behind them.

He began singing of the hunter who bumbled into a field at dusk to catch a rabbit and caught a wife instead.

Kathryn chuckled.

They headed down the mountain, Anthony recited poetry in Farsi then translated for her, using a very bad Farsi accent.

Ah, moon of my delight, who know'st no wane,
The moon of Heav'n is rising once again:
How oft hereafter rising shall she look
Through this same garden after me—in vain!

He recited until they both laughed so hard he could hardly speak, all in an effort to take her mind off the danger and his away from the reminder of his stupidity for putting her at risk.

It was time to accelerate his exit plan from Iran.

CHAPTER EIGHTEEN

Kathryn stirred, asleep slumped against Anthony's chest as he reined in Kismet at the Takht-e Tavoos hitching post under a wooden overhang. A single lantern swayed against the breeze. Trees and shrubs abundant on the mountain were sparse here, except for the restaurant's owner's wired off vegetable and herb garden. Anthony brushed a tangled strand of hair off her face and kissed her temple.

"We've arrived," he said, glancing about. "And the place looks dead. Jeeps and crew are gone—chopper, too." He peered beyond into the open-air restaurant. The night was dark, and tension hummed in the air around him. "I don't see Buzz, either."

It was Tabriz he needed to see. His heartbeat accelerated; he was concerned about the sniper fire on the mountain.

She sat up. "What time is it?"

"Early. Eight-thirty. We've only been gone about two and half hours, and the place folded." He helped her off Kismet.

"Well, they all have an early morning." She suppressed a yawn and gazed up at him.

Her sleepy smile was one he could wake up to again and again, not a usual feeling for him. He looked around for Tabriz, for some reason feeling leery.

"Riding down together was nice." She put her hand in his.

"Hmmm," he said, his emotions warring, already missing her in his arms. They had definitely bonded tonight, pulling up intimate recollections he had never planned to share. He wanted to kiss her but spotted a tribesman coming over. And Anthony knew the man had stayed behind for them.

With a toothy grin he took the horses.

"Tabriz?" Anthony asked softly, hoping his friends watching out for him had not been hurt.

"Waiting." The tribesman motioned toward the field. "I will join him. All is well."

"Thank you, brother."

With an appreciative look from under bushy brows, the man took the horses.

Relieved, Anthony turned to Kathryn. "Right, and now I'm hungry."

The tribesman had heard. Looking back he said, "On the brick oven, the cook left food. It is wrapped for you."

"Bless him." He took Kathryn inside, recalling how festive the Takht-e Tavoos's barbeque had been earlier, now lit only by a string of lights tinkling with the breeze.

The wonderful music lingered in his mind. The restaurant looked deserted with the kitchen help gone.

He heard an engine rev and looked up. The musicians with their van loaded slammed the car doors, the sitar player waving out an open window as they drove off.

Peter sat on a bench under the lights, drinking a beer, waiting for Kathryn. "Have a nice time?" he asked her. Before she could answer he continued, "We heard shots fired on the mountain where you guys went."

"Hunters," Kathryn said. "We're okay." She hugged Peter and motioned toward the kitchen. "I'll bring food. Back in a sec."

Peter stood and leaned against a post, arms folded over his chest, his biceps flexing.

"Thanks for waiting," Anthony said. "We were gone longer than I planned."

"Hunters?"

"Well, that's my guess."

"Bullshit!" Peter stepped forward, his voice low, and his tone hard. "Militia passed by in a Jeep. Armed soldiers." His fists clenched at his sides. "You want to tell me what the fuck's goin' on down here?"

Anthony's shoulders straightened. "A revolution." He kept his voice low. "Escalating faster than anyone thought." He returned Peter's hard look. "You want to tell me how the hell your State Department gave you visas to Iran? Little risky, no?"

"State Department's in the dark. They obviously don't know shit, or believe me, we wouldn't be here."

Anthony shook his head. "Peter, I'm sorry. If I'd known Green Bands were this far from the city I'd have—"

In a swirl of dust, Tabriz swept out from the shadows on horseback and pulled Anthony away, his Farsi low. "Militia is coming back—two Jeeps. We go now. You, too."

Anthony squeezed his arm. "Tabriz, thank you for saving our lives tonight."

"*Allah Akbar*. We live another day to fight Houdin." They hugged. "Get lady Kathryn away—fast." He disappeared into the night, pounding hoof beats fading in the rising then settling of dust.

Anthony's ears rang with alarm. He rushed back. Kathryn had returned with food set on the table, but she ignored it and was now in a heated discussion with Peter.

Anthony grabbed her shoulders. "Listen. There's no time. Peter, help me move this table quickly." He lifted one end.

Kathryn and Peter shot each other a look then moved into action.

Anthony and Peter hefted the table off the rug while Kathryn moved the bench away. The roar of vehicles and headlights coming their way spurred them to move faster yet. Anthony kicked aside the rug where earlier musicians had played and threw open a trap door, pointing down at the root cellar.

"There's a ladder. Get in." Kathryn looked into the black hole and back at Anthony. "I know it's dark," he said, "but . . . don't make a sound."

"Seriously?" Kathryn said.

"Move!"

Kathryn and Peter clamored down the narrow ladder.

Anthony shoved the rug back in place, dragged a bench over it, grabbed the food off the table, and then dove behind the wooden bar across the room. He grabbed the owner's hidden rifle and cocked it, drawing a dark tablecloth over his head. He pressed his face next to the bar's wooden slats and watched.

Militia Jeeps skidded to a halt in the dirt, engines running, dust swirling. Riled up soldiers spoke in harsh whispers, wearing telltale mismatched camouflage khakis of the Green Band militia. "Find the shooter—or anyone. Keep them alive. We will interrogate." They jumped out.

Not a good sign.

One man remained in the Jeep, cradling a dead soldier, rocking and praying over the body.

A sergeant crouched low, his AK-47 steady, waving for his eight men to fan out. "Remember, torture will open any mouth," he said.

His men, weapons ready, spread through the restaurant, their heads turning, searching, tipping over chairs, benches, grimy combat boots scraping the floor next to Anthony's hiding place.

"Where are they?" the sergeant grumbled, kicking the bar inches from Anthony's face.

The rifle he clutched couldn't stop all eight men, but he might save Kathryn.

An owl hooted in the distance. The breeze picked up, taking tumbleweeds bouncing and rushing with it down the roadway.

A militiaman examined Cook's food on the table. It had turned cold. He swept it onto the floor. So far they had found no one.

"We go. We will capture this shooter along the road to Shiraz, whoever he is.

They headed for the Jeeps.

"Look!" A soldier still inside shouted, holding up a half-empty beer bottle.

The sergeant stood up in the Jeep. "Search!"

Three soldiers ran back inside, grumbling. Still they found no one.

Anthony heard a soldier mention a Colonel Agani—an uncle of Mirdad's?

"Infidels!" shouted the sergeant. "We torch this place."

They hopped back in the Jeep.

One of his men remained, emptying a gasoline can around Takht-e Tavoos—splashing tables, chairs, benches and then struck a match. He ran back to his vehicle, his comrades shouting, "Go!" They fishtailed down the road out of sight.

Anthony leapt from behind the bar into a rising inferno, fearing for Kathryn's life. There would soon be no oxygen down below. He yanked up the rug and beat back flames then grabbed the hatch with the edge of his jacket and flung it open. "Hurry!"

He pulled Kathryn out, stumbling, coughing, Peter following through thickening smoke. "This way. Grab hands!" He took Kathryn's and they all ran, dodging furniture and flames, out through a side exit, gasping for air.

The breeze rose, fueling the fire. The smell of the flames was suffocating. Kathryn stumbled, but Anthony caught her.

She wrenched away furiously. Tears and soot smudged her face. "For God's sake, what's going on here?" Her chest heaved with emotion. "There were no goat hunters, were there, Anthony?"

He read fear and confusion in her eyes, and his mind raced for excuses.

"It's chaos after one spectacular day of shooting." She was sobbing now. "And last night . . . was perfect." The last came out in a whisper.

Peter's eyes widened.

Anthony reached for her.

"No!" she hissed, straightening. "It's all falling apart."

Peter broke in. "Some guys left us a Jeep in back."

"Friends," Anthony said. "Let's go. I'll explain when we're out of here." He tugged Kathryn to him.

They sped away in the Jeep, Peter in the backseat leaning forward to hear Anthony, all shivering against both the chill and the terror. Anthony drove and spoke, Iran's troubles spilling out.

They reached the Hotel Persepolis in minutes. Anthony climbed with Kathryn and Peter up the wooden staircase off the balcony to Kathryn's room, feeling keyed up. He opened the French doors wide, filmy curtains billowing into the room. He checked the area outside. He needed to get going, but not before Peter and Kathryn felt more settled.

She turned on small lamps, and he glanced around her room: clean, simple Middle Eastern style with whitewashed walls, modestly carved mahogany furniture including a bed, nightstands, a dresser, and a round corner table with four chairs encircling it. The one stunning feature was the art, vividly colored framed posters of Iranian arts festivals.

They all spoke at once, still agitated.

"Let's clean up first," she insisted, tossing them warm, wet washcloths and towels. They needed to find out what damage lay underneath all the soot.

Anthony washed his face and hands, discovering burns. "I feel like hell about tonight, these anarchists." He reached to caress Kathryn's sooty cheek, but she stopped him, pulling back and shaking her head. "Your face is burned?"

"No. Well, not badly." He winced. "You shouldn't be here. No one is safe. The situation is incendiary."

"Bad pun, Anthony."

"We Iranians are famous for our bad puns." He tried a smile then shook his head. "Seriously, all hell can break loose anytime now. Nobody holds the reins here." Anthony trembled in anger. He walked to the balcony railing, the breeze wafting over him, calming him. He checked below for unwanted visitors. He looked up as helicopters circled overhead, looking for what? He could not guess, but hoped it wasn't them. The sound faded in the distance, Anthony still staring unseeing into the darkness. He ducked back inside. "Nobody in the government, except the traitors, ever knows anything about what's going on or who's in control," he continued.

"That's crazy." Peter waved his burned hand in the air, wincing.

"Absolutely," Anthony said. "The Shah speaks to no one, not even his closest advisors." He paced, voicing plaguing thoughts, his sense of helplessness, leaving out the part about his rescue flights. "Thank God the Shah confides in the empress."

"Your friend?" Kathryn said.

"Yes, she is. But the Shah looks only to the West, to the U.S. for guidance, and they refuse to give him any."

Kathryn shook her head. "But our own State Department—why would they give us the okay if it's not really safe to be filming here, much less be in the country?"

"They obviously don't know shit, either," Peter said.

"Both our governments are denying the truth."

"Okay, I get it now," she said. "We're basically on our own here." She grabbed the dirty washcloths and tossed them into the bathroom sink, shaking her head. Her burned wrist aching with a sharp pain whenever she moved the joint under the skin.

Peter threw up his hands. "I'm gonna take a shower," he said, looking from Anthony to Kathryn. "I'll be back to go over tomorrow's shooting schedule afterwards, Kat." He headed for the door. "Later, you two."

Anthony nodded as Peter closed the door. "I'm flying to Rome tomorrow," he said. "Call the ministry and demand help. You need to finish up this commercial and get out of the country. And while you're here, please be extremely careful."

"I'm always careful on a shoot." She stepped in close to him. "You're not telling me everything about your involvement in all this, are you?"

He pulled back. "Against all reason, I've been flying illegal missions, trying to save some innocent lives that have been targeted through no fault of their own."

"Saving them from the radicals. . . ?"

"That's more than I should have said."

"So you're in deep. That's why all the no-shows, your secretive conversations with Philippe and Mirdad?"

"No. Not Mirdad. He knows nothing of this, and I don't want him to. The fewer people who have even an inkling the better. That includes Peter. Knowledge puts people in jeopardy, where I've placed you by telling you this."

"What do we do now?" she said, almost to herself.

"Get as much as possible shot tomorrow because you're out of time. You probably have a day here—two at best." He sighed, whispering. "You must leave Iran soon. Can you do it?"

Kathryn brushed her hair off her still smudged face, her left cheek red and chafed. She ignored the pain. "I need more time. I need more of you. . . ."

"I'll be home by evening." He bent his head, longing to hold her. "Have dinner with me tomorrow night. I'll send a car at seven." He started to kiss her but thought better of it in front of the open French doors. "We'll speak then."

She offered a tight smile. "Your word."

He nodded. Clearly they needed to talk. "Good night then."

Kathryn felt her world careening out of orbit, spinning beyond her control. Her big comeback shoot, so perfect today, was now atop a revolutionary powder keg. No wonder there had been so many weapons at the airport, so many articles crowding newspapers' front pages, reporting violence, people gunned down, missing, or kidnapped in plain sight. What the hell had she done, coming to Iran with even a skeleton crew? Brett had warned her. She had to figure out contingencies. A director always had to be ready for Plan B.

She showered and shampooed her hair, trimming the singed parts the best she could, letting it dry. Sooty towels cluttered the bathroom corner. Uncomfortable blisters had formed on her left hand, her arm, and her cheek. She applied an antibiotic salve, adding some Benadryl ointment to stop the burning. A knock at the door interrupted her ablutions.

"I've showered. Felt good." Peter slouched in Kathryn's doorway.

"You shaved off your Fu Manchu." She hadn't seen his bare face since her first year at UCLA in the middle sixties when two unlikely rebels had come together in a sea of political and sexual revolution.

Longhaired Peter with his smiling soulful eyes had definitely been part of the in-group at film school. A New Wave foreign film aficionado, Peter had espoused the methodology and vision of directors like Antonioni, Goddard, and Truffaut, always dressing in the hippest bell-bottoms and paisley shirts open practically to the navel. Kathryn had been a classic American film buff, venerating directors like John Ford, William Wyler, and John Houston. She expressed herself by wearing only beatnik black.

"Peter . . . ?"

"I know I'm irresistible, but you're staring."

She stepped back, opening the door wider, and he wheeled in the video monitor.

"Trimmed the burnt part first but couldn't get rid of the ashy smell." He shrugged, looking so much younger without the mustache.

"Okay, let's go to work," she said, ignoring her throbbing hand.

Peter started the video feed.

They sat in the same chairs where an hour ago Anthony

had explained what it seemed no U.S. official had figured out: The Iranian revolution was not some wild, futuristic notion; its reality had already exploded onto the streets. She tried to focus on their amazing footage. "Could this have been shot today?"

"It's friggin' beautiful, exotic." Peter's eyes were open wide, his head shaking at the marvelous reel. "That sweep around the lion's wing—Teddy's work is incredible."

She nodded watching. "Okay, we see the parade of extras, horses, camels, closer . . . spectacular! Those costumes and the rainbow. Wow! Even I'm impressed." They both laughed and then caught the irony, looking over at each other's scorched flesh. What was going on in this country wasn't that bad, she told herself, if they could generate this kind of footage.

She knew Peter read her anxiety.

"Some barbeque tonight, huh? Cool music before they tried roasting us."

"We can finish this shoot."

"Yeah," he said. "Those crazy militia don't know our crew was at Takht-e Tavoos tonight when the soldier was killed, do they?"

She shrugged, more concerned than she let on. "Who do you think killed him and why?"

Peter raised an eyebrow. "Tabriz's guys were patrolling. Could be them. Some powerful shit is going down here that neither one of us understands, Kat."

She paced the room. A horrible thought occurred to her. "You know Brett warned me again and again not to come to Iran."

"So?"

"Maybe he wasn't trying to sabotage me. Maybe I should have listened to him. Look at the danger we're facing. I'm responsible for all you guys."

Peter grinned. "Nah. It was Brett, not some humble dude speaking."

"Right. I almost forgot myself."

Peter leaned back, stretching out his lanky legs, Adidas replaced by moccasins. "And Anthony?" His tone was casual. "It's obvious you two got together."

"Got together? More like I fell off a cliff." With a comb in hand, she motioned him to sit at her table.

"Geez . . ."

"I'm not going there tonight." She combed out Peter's dark, wavy hair and picked up her small scissors. "Got to trim this mess. You're all singed." She snipped at his hair. *Anthony.* "With his loyalty to the Shah, I know Anthony's already deeply involved in this revolution. I can feel it." She was probing Peter to see the extent of his knowledge. *I need answers.* He didn't bite.

They both looked at the clock. Peter stood. "Thanks for the trim. Get some sleep." He dabbed some ointment onto his burns. "People count on your flawless work." He kissed her unburned cheek. "No pressure."

"Of course not," she smiled wryly. "Sleep well." She closed the door and looked at the bed. Fat chance.

Two days left to shoot, the finish line in sight. She had nothing to go back to—this was it for her. She had not traveled this far to blow her dream by caving in to danger. She sat, reviewing her options. An idea formed.

First thing in the morning she would call Mirdad. He could use Ministry influence and place Iranian military guards, loyal to the Shah, around the location to keep her crew safe from the radical Komiteh.

Teddy, Peter, and Buzz were her closest friends, and she had sold them on how perfect Iran was for this shoot. Her crew was her responsibility. She had to secure their safety, the safety of an American guest from Boeing. And she had to fight like hell to finish her unannounced documentary, *Faces of Iran*, her ace in the hole in the event that Boeing did not come through as planned. A documentary could open up even more doors than a commercial. And it would be especially timely if it took place in an inaccessible country under siege by its own people.

Kathryn had worked on the *Faces* theme all along, but not until tonight had the concept really come together. Now it was crystal clear what she had to do to move forward with that project simultaneously.

She would start with the amazing faces her team had filmed already of the people they had come into contact with, people simply living their lives, going about their rituals of everyday living. These faces would then have a layover by those of the Islamic revolution, and the modern looking people would dissolve, shoved back into a time of tyranny and black shrouds, a time when the mosques and their leaders ruled, when women were chattel, when secular education was reserved for only the sons of the wealthy, and religious teachings were considered law. Kathryn shivered. Could Iran, such a cosmopolitan, civilized country, ever fall back into the Middle Ages like that? Was her vision for the documentary actually a premonition of what was coming for the Iranians? No. She was bone tired.

Once back in L.A. she planned to gather AP footage

for the effects, photos of uprisings in Jaleh Square, the Abadan Cinema, and other odious events she had read about in the newspapers but had not borne witness to. She tapped her folder of newspaper clippings guiltily. She had not mentioned these to Buzz. But he read the papers, too. He knew.

On top of it all she had broken a promise to herself and fallen in love. Tomorrow night she would have her answers or forget him. Never again would she be involved with a deceitful man. Staggering to bed, Kathryn finally collapsed. A deep sigh slipped from her. Sleep overtook her.

CHAPTER NINETEEN

Anthony arrived at his home in Shiraz late that night, treading lightly across the marble floors, anxious to develop the Boeing stills promised for tomorrow, eager for Kathryn to see them.

What had he been thinking, taking Kathryn up on the mountain alone? They could've been killed. Damn near were. Philippe was right, his grandfather was right. He was an ass.

No flights were scheduled for tonight, and yet he still had to meet Philippe at the transport house. Much was left to complete before this, their last shipment, could sail for London on the morning tide. Anthony had to work efficiently and fast.

The families he had helped flee Iran depended on him to transport their belongings, their treasures. They would be sold to finance new lives for all these refugees. Without proceeds from a sale, they would be destitute. Anthony's own penthouse in Tehran had been stripped and added to the same shipment as his grandfather had requested. This Shiraz house was next.

In his darkroom, he flipped on infrared lights, and got to work.

Proof sheets from three rolls now hung on the rack, showing the light cresting the Elburz Mountains, better than he had imagined after the storm, the extras gathered under the rainbow.

Alongside was a page of candid shots of Kathryn and her crew interacting, unaware he had captured them. Regardless of his lack of sleep and days of physical exertion, creative energy pulsed through his body. The missing sensation was that of Kathryn in his arms, riding together down the mountain on Kismet, the moon their beacon under a starlit sky. That sense of timelessness had banished his nagging concerns about death. She warmed his spirit, made him certain he could continue missions and face ordeals ahead—as long as his enemies were not aware he cared about her until he was free, back in London. He had to stop seeing her after work. He would have to stop wanting her. For her sake, he would say goodbye.

Tomorrow he would fly to Rome and shoot stills for Brett Whitney. *What was he like, this man Kathryn had married?*

"Sorry I'm late." Anthony slipped through the heavy doors of warehouse number fifty-seven on the outskirts of Shiraz at midnight. An armed guard slid the door shut, nodding in recognition, his eyes steady.

Anthony whipped off his jacket and glanced up at the high windows darkened and sealed in tarpaper. Crates ready to leave the country, aligned in neat rows, hugged the walls, nearly clogging the brightly lit warehouse. It was enough to fill a freighter's hold.

And there, bent over a carton and wrapping a Daum vase, was Philippe. He looked up. His blond hair messed, glasses slipping forward on a nose glazed with sweat. It was a completely slovenly look for his usually dapper friend. He looked as tired and anxious as Anthony felt, needing to keep his friends safe from escalating violence. *It was too close tonight.*

Down a long row of crates, Ali waved his inventory clipboard.

Philippe raised an eyebrow, shadowing tension. "You look like hell," he said, glancing at his watch. "We expected you back by seven at Takht-e Tavoos." Philippe shoved down the lid on a crate he finished packing, his shirtsleeves rolled up, his manicured hands now filthy and scraped.

"I'm a rat." Anthony picked up a hammer, ready to seal the crate Philippe had finished packing.

"Buzz and I left early, back to the hotel for a drink." Philippe huffed. "That's twice I've played host for your Americans. Next time, you do the honors, and I'll go off with the beautiful lady."

"You're asking too much."

"I told them she was in safe hands. Now I wonder."

Anthony glanced up blandly, masking his guilt. "I wonder myself, but we were fine," he lied. Tonight's incident must not reach his grandfather's ears or MI-6 would extract him by first light, leaving the Black Glove free reign. He shook off the thought and took the wrapped vase from Philippe and put it in the box, nailed it shut, and faced his friend.

Philippe's poker face didn't fool Anthony. He had more to say. "And may I ask, how do you explain the gunshots we heard?"

Anthony shrugged. "Goat hunters?"

"Ahhh, perfectly implausible." Philippe glanced over the soiled shirt and soot-stained jeans Anthony wore and winced. "You look like the bottom of the barrel." He moved closer. "Your hands are burnt."

"Darkroom chemicals that's all. They'll be fine."

Philippe tossed him a pair of jersey work gloves. "Did you misplace your razor, too?"

Anthony exhaled, tossing the hammer down on a crate. "What the hell is chafing at you?"

Outside the rumble of slow moving trucks was heard. The guard dimmed the lights.

CRACK! CRACK!

The sound of gunfire ricocheted throughout the room.

Anthony and Philippe each ducked behind a crate, holding their breath. They waited, alert.

Ali soon poked his head around a stack of cartons at the end of the row. "Truck backfired. It's okay." He disappeared back behind boxes. The lights brightened once more.

Philippe squared his shoulders, his voice raised. "Godammit! How do you live like this? Jumping at every noise!"

The images of Green Bands and gunshots, the fire, Kathryn in danger—all of these thoughts swirled in his mind. His missions teetered on the edge of discovery. Time to amp them up. Anthony squashed apprehension. "Take it easy, Philippe."

Philippe glared at him. "We need at least six more men here, Anthony. We won't finish in time."

"You'll have them tomorrow."

"Not good enough."

"Impossible to get them past the patrols unseen tonight anyway," Anthony said. "I was pulled over by a car full of Green Band Militia."

"Khomeini's group? Like the truck bumping along past Takht-e Tavoos after Tabriz and his men melted into the desert?"

"The government won't stop them."

"That's another reason to leave," Philippe said. "If we get all this ready by tomorrow night, you can return to England with me."

Anthony banged the last nail into a crate and set the hammer down. He leaned back against the wood.

"Men are packing your apartment in Tehran," Philippe said. "Raymond and the servants should hurry in Shiraz." Philippe looked hopeful.

"You're right. I'm getting Raymond and my household away. But I'm not going with you."

"You can't mean it!" Frustration rang through Philippe's voice. "You have a death warrant on your head. They almost got you tonight."

Anthony picked the hammer back up. "How do they fucking know what I'm doing?" He slammed another nail into the heavy box.

Philippe leaned against the crate. "Have you ever for one moment considered Mirdad may've caught on?"

"Philippe, don't."

"Don't! So I despise the little shit. Forget that." He nudged Anthony's arm. "At the Paradise Bar last night, I overheard two Iranian officers mention Mirdad's name with yours in the same breath."

Anthony started to walk away.

"Wait a minute! One of those men was that general you pointed out to me, the one you said was the Scourge of Iran, Houdin. He was with some young major, a short, powerfully built bloke."

"Nassiri, Demetrius Nassiri. He's Houdin's adjutant."

"Evidently Mirdad is close to this Houdin, because the major was pissed, complaining about authority the general had given Mirdad Ajani!"

"Your Farsi is not that good," Anthony said. "You're mistaken."

Philippe fumed. "Pay attention!"

Anthony shook his head. "You really have it in for Mirdad, don't you? Thought your wounds had healed."

"This has nothing to do with old times!" Philippe shouted. "They spoke of an informant watching you."

Anthony frowned, remembering a face in the photo he developed earlier.

"Do you think they're stupid enough to use someone you'd suspect? They're the secret police. The SAVAK, for fuck's sake!" Philippe looked exasperated. "Oh, why do I bother?"

"I hear you. I . . . though can't believe it."

"Mirdad doesn't know you sent money all these years. Or that you got him his job." Philippe stepped forward. "He thinks you're a selfish prick."

"Stop it!"

Philippe pulled back as if acknowledging the anguish Anthony felt. Mirdad's suffering from his father's murder conviction had been a topic they had gone around and around on.

"Must you take on the weight of the world?" Philippe said. "You can't do it all."

Anthony stared at his hands. "That's enough, Philippe," he said quietly. "No more."

Philippe's shoulders sank. "I'll never understand you."

"My friends are murdered in their homes. Can I simply fly off to my peaceful estate in the Cotswolds and go fox hunting? What do you think I am?"

"I think you're the best friend I've ever had. Please come with me. It'll kill your grandfather if anything happens to you. Doesn't that count?"

Anthony leaned his forehead on his hand. "I'm so tired, Philippe."

"I can see that."

"I fly to Rome tomorrow to shoot stills with Brett Whitney for Boeing."

"Kathryn's ex?"

"Right. And I'm taking eighteen top-of-the-list dissidents out with me on a Palhavi jet. A rare opportunity—no customs, no one will be questioned."

"They'll pose as crewmembers, flight attendants, mechanics, or some such?"

Anthony nodded. "I'll be home by evening."

Philippe sighed.

Anthony grabbed his shoulder. "And I'll return to England in a week."

"Is that a promise?"

"It is."

"Then I only partially failed."

"Actually, you did well," Anthony said, a tired smile crossing his face.

Philippe grinned. "But Anthony, watch out for Mirdad. Don't be a blind fool."

Anthony pictured Mirdad and heard an echo of gunfire. Now he knew who the rat might be, and the mere thought was killing him.

CHAPTER TWENTY

Kathyrn looked up at a spectacular sky over Persepolis, not a cloud in sight as she set a swift pace for the day, determined to land ahead of schedule on the commercial. She started to dig her hands into her jean pockets and winced, extracting her burned left hand. It hurt like hell.

"Get the Condor closer, Peter, and make sure all the cameras on the hill are on their marks, ready to cue." Kathryn sounded strident, even to herself.

Peter put a calming hand on her shoulder.

She took in a big breath and looked around.

Armed men in black, the Shah's men, guarded the perimeters of her set from Komiteh rebels, the Green Bands, providing her a safety net and protection. Tension drained from her, energy replacing it. Mirdad had been true to his word. He had sent a hand written note with Ali:

Sorry I can't be there today.
It is my mother's wedding day.
Be safe.
Best Regards, Mirdad

"How wonderful, Ali. Who is his mother marrying?"

Ali looked down, blinking. "She marries the governor of Tehran, General Omar Houdin, Madame Kathryn."

"Oh, my sincerest congratulations to them all."

"Just so," Ali said and muttered, "*Insha Allah*," and he ran back to his assistant cameraman duties, the black clad guards alert to his movements.

These were serious men. She wondered if they were with SAVAK. Her questions about this volatile revolution bludgeoned her mind. Anthony. She shook her head and buried her questions for later. She suppressed her fear of the Green Band militia interfering on her shoot, convinced last night had nothing to do with her or Boeing and glanced over at Buzz, his nose buried in the *London Times* world section.

The news of Khomeini escalating his efforts to take power riddled her with anxiety. She peered over Buzz's shoulder, reading the same news. He looked up, shook his head, handed her the paper, and walked away. She read the headlines:

Khomeini rants against the Shah of Iran, influences French bias.

Mullah's broadcasts from Paris rumored to gain favor in Tehran.

Resistance to Iranian government escalating in bloody clashes.

Two days left to shoot in Iran. She had to make it three.

Kathryn unclenched her fists and crumbled the annoying article and joined her crew. No tension there, just excitement to finish.

Peter, slathered in Benadryl and sunscreen as she was, dodged comments from Buzz and the crew about his missing mustache and burns, making jokes instead.

"You'd think Malibu beach bums could handle one little butane tank for the patio fire pit." Peter's eyebrows pinched together. "Losing my touch."

Buzz chuckled. "You and Kathryn'll never barbeque at my place. Tough luck. Takeout Chinese is all you get."

"Amen to that," Teddy said walking up.

Even Duncan, strapping into his flight seat, laughed.

But Ali, standing beside Teddy, smiled. *How much did he know?* Kathryn wondered.

Gravel crunched under a purring engine, and all heads turned as Anthony's limo pulled up. Philippe stepped out, dressed all Saville Row with Lanvin sunglasses. He glanced from her to Peter, taking in what he saw without reaction. He removed his shades and smiled.

"Jolly good morning, isn't it?" Philippe said. "Had to stop by and say goodbye." He air-kissed Kathryn, gingerly glancing past her face, and shook hands with Peter and Buzz.

Did he know about last night's fire?

"Brought stills from Anthony," Philippe said.

"Did you know I mistook you for Anthony twice before we met?"

"How so?" He smirked.

"I guess I thought he would look more like you."

He raised a quizzical eyebrow.

"You know, tall blond, very English." She chuckled.

"Yes, and I'm French Lebanese." They both laughed, walking over to the podium-style table by her video monitor and had a look. Astounding photos, naturally.

"He's a talent," Buzz said. "My recommendation, of course," he preened.

Philippe leaned in close to Kathryn whispering, "You're about out of time here, my dear. Get your crew out while you can." He pulled out his business card, which read: MAISON PHILIPPE, FINE ANTIQUE COLLECTORS GALLERY, FULHAM ROAD, KNIGHTSBRIDGE. "I'll do anything I can to help you."

She stepped forward to question him, but he'd already turned back to the group.

"You lot'll be in London in a day or so, and I'm inviting you all to dine with me at Annabelle's," he said.

"London nightlife is tops," Buzz said. "Look forward to it, Philippe."

"Stay safe." Philippe looked sharply at Kathryn. "Too bad my best friend saw you first or I would've tried." He winked and looked at his watch. "Must go." He climbed into the car. "It's rough going at the airport now—and all about timing if you want to board for London." He closed the door. "We can't all travel to Europe on the Shah's jet like some people."

The limo disappeared down the road, and Kathryn thought of Anthony and Brett together in Rome. Ironic.

She refocused on her work, once again exhilarated, her competitive spirit kicking in.

The roaring engines of the Pahlavi Gulfstream wound down. The plane taxied to a private terminal after a four-and-a-half-hour flight from Tehran to Rome that had passed in a blur for Anthony. The Shah's SAVAK pilots were well trained. He had slept for two hours in the private cabin, a dreamless sleep, his first in forty-eight hours.

Thoughts swirled around his mind, bouncing off his triple involvement in Rome: his high profile Boeing shoot, his very personal need to find out what Kathryn's involvement was with her ex, and more immediately the eighteen illegals on board with forged diplomatic passports, his most precarious move yet.

He showered quickly, skipped the shave, dressed for a day of work in jeans, T-shirt, and V-neck cashmere, and pulled on lightweight Italian work boots. From the main cabin he heard laughing. If he kept his incognito eighteen in a light mood, they might pass through customs and immigration easily, even with tighter scrutiny of Iranian passports of late.

He rubbed his scruffy jaw and answered a knock at the door. A male flight attendant handed him a steaming double espresso.

"Two sugars and lemon peel, correct, sir?"

"*Si, Gio. Mille grazi.*" Anthony smiled. "You'll do fine in Rome," he said to his favorite Tahkt-e Tavoos waiter.

"*Prego.*" Gio handed him his leather safari jacket.

Nerves buzzed around the main cabin as Anthony entered. The group of eighteen newly appointed "diplomats" were dressed in business suits except for his two Armenian camera assistants, casually clad as he was. The men fidgeted, anticipating, he suspected, Italian customs and immigration. Dari, his friend and copilot, filled a plate with pastries and looked up. "Captain's hungry."

Anthony grabbed one and popped it in his mouth. "Mmm."

Dari shook his head and went back into the flight cabin. The captain was speaking to the tower as the door closed. All SAVAK were fierce, but not all were despicable like the Black Glove thugs.

Anthony, assured the door was shut, hissed, "Listen up!" He kept his voice low, though loud enough to cover the idling jet engine.

"You know the drill," he said. "Be polite and dignified." He made eye contact with them all, except for an attorney who somehow had sparked concern among the others in the crowd. No time to think about it right now. "Gio, start with the jokes. Save the mother-in-law story for immigration officials. They'll love it. Remember you have diplomatic immunity as part of the royal court. You'll casually show your Iranian embassy passports, and keep walking."

Hopeful faces turned his way; only the attorney wore a grim expression until Gio nudged his ribs.

"You heard, lighten up," Gio said.

What was it about this guy? Something teased at Anthony's recollection.

"In an hour you'll be absorbed by a new life," Anthony said. "So let's go!"

Some of these men's eagerness to join families he had previously relocated shone in their faces, others headed for jobs lined up for them. The two Armenian photographers had worked on minor Pahlavi events, and Anthony planned to hook them up with someone he knew from Brett Whitney's Italian crew.

The engine stopped, and the plane's door opened. Four serious customs officials in dark uniforms waited on the tarmac. *Why? His group had diplomatic immunity.*

Anthony's mind raced, his adrenalin spiking as he searched for a reason for their presence. How could they know? A trap, a bust. Only his ministry knew about this flight: Mirdad knew. *Baradar Koochooloo*, beloved little one. A chill coursed through him. It could only have been Mirdad—Mirdad the Rat. Anthony felt a part of his soul shrivel. *You finally got me, cousin.*

Philippe's warnings replayed in his mind as he watched several of his diplomats deplane, passports in hand.

But the waiting Italian customs officers didn't stop them. No. The eighteen were not the target. They were there for *him*. Patiently they waited below.

So it's come down to this. I have a quick choice. He looked below at the tarmac. Thirty feet away an Italian prison awaited him. His glance shot back into the cabin. SAVAK torture and the Quaar prison were but ten feet away in the flight cabin with unwitting SAVAK agents.

His choice.

In that moment something clicked in his brain, a clear revelation. He spun around to block passage for the man hurrying to get off the plane, the man posing as an attorney.

Anthony's hand shot out, edging the man back and smashing him against a bulkhead, fuming. "Where is it? Now!"

The attorney stunned at first, sneered, his eyes beady obsidians. "You're finished, infidel."

"How different you look out of camouflage fatigues,

Green Band. You even saw a barber—no beard. Jaleh Square, wasn't it? Gunning down innocent students."

Swift as a hawk, the guy pulled a switchblade, driving it to Anthony's throat.

With an elbow jab, Anthony knocked the knife away. "Filthy spy." He spun him around, pinning the traitor to the wall. "About to sell out your Iranian brothers, were you?"

"Infidel! Swine," he hissed. "Help!" He tried to shout but it came out a gurgle.

"Shut your stinking face, murderer." Anthony jabbed his kidney. He couldn't let this guy speak out in front of SAVAK pilots.

"What's going on here?" The copilot shot out of the flight cabin.

"This man, he deceives—"

Anthony smashed his arm across the spy's windpipe, cutting off his air.

"He's militia, Dari," Anthony said. "Didn't they raid your sister's schoolroom last week?"

Anthony gripped his captive's jacket lapels and jerked his head toward the copilot. "Get this spy's wallet."

"Traitor!" the spy yelled. "Those men outside will arrest—"

Anthony banged the spy hard against the bulkhead, knocking the wind out of him.

The copilot grabbed the man's inner breast pocket and ripped it open. He found what he was looking for concealed in the lining. Dari held up a Komiteh Council I.D. card then shoved it into the spy's face.

"Piece of shit!" Dari's fist plowed into the Green Band's gut again and again.

"What the hell?" The plane's captain leaned out.

"Komiteh dog! My sister . . ." Dari's fist pummeled the militia's face.

"Dari, stop! I'll handle this." The Shah's captain pulled out his SAVAK badge. "Traitor, you're under arrest." His foot shot out, kicking the Komiteh's groin.

Howling, the grim man doubled over.

The copilot reached inside the flight cabin and grabbed duct tape. He covered his captive's mouth and bound his hands and ankles, finally stuffing him into a storage bin, clamping down the lid, and sliding the lock closed.

Dari breathed heavily, pain and humiliation etched on his face. Two days before Komiteh Green Bands had stormed his sister's Shiraz school, soldiers defiling many young girls. Anthony hadn't the heart to ask if Dari's sister had been one of them. It didn't matter, because this traitor would be dumped in shark-infested Gulf waters on the return trip, of that Anthony was certain.

He signaled his flabbergasted assistants to keep quiet. "You two, off the plane. Now."

The captain straightened his tie and made a call from the cockpit. "The situation has been handled. Yes, SAVAK."

Anthony heard this and to his astonishment, the four customs officials lurking outside melted away.

Anthony straightened his clothing, flexed trembling hands, then went to the kitchen to plunge his bleeding right knuckles into a bucket of melting ice. He dried his hand on a monogrammed Pahlavi napkin, regained composure by steadying his breath, and then leaned into the flight cabin as if nothing had happened. "Captain, thanks for the ride. See you guys at four o'clock."

"Don't be late—unless she's gorgeous," the captain called out. Anthony saluted and joined the eighteen in the terminal. The diplomats, once out of the confines of the tarmac, went on their way to freedom.

It had been close.

A car waited for Anthony and crew outside the bustling terminal. The smell of belching Italian diesel taxis reminded him he was in Rome. But the revolution seemed to follow him everywhere.

A few kilometers outside of the city, a northerly wind blew in crisply off Lake Bracciano. From the village taxi stand nestled below Odescalchi Castle, Anthony hiked up the winding cobblestone road, reminding himself he was here to shoot spectacular stills for Boeing. And on a personal level, he needed to know what remained, if anything, between Kathryn and her ex.

He watched a blustery tableau unfold on Brett Whitney's Boeing location, the wind causing havoc with reflectors, light stands, actors, and crew. Clouds shifted, light and shadows played over the fifteenth-century montage. Gaffers and electricians chased reflectors and light stands, sandbagged what they could hang on to. Grips angled cable out of the crew's path. And in charge in the center of the scene a tall blond man gestured, most definitely the director, Brett Whitney.

The feudal stronghold that had withstood an assault by natural sons of Pope Allessandro Borgia VI, now cast shadows across ruffled waters of the deepest sapphire. Brett looked up as Anthony's long shadow crept over him. Film people were ever conscious of even a subtle light change.

Anthony nodded, sizing him up as both a professional and as the man still entrenched in Kathryn's life.

Brett stared, windblown, his expression oozing natural confidence bordering on arrogance. The air grew still.

Anthony returned the look, heading over to introduce himself, wondering if Brett was really a decent sort or a self-absorbed egomaniac. Could he be trusted to aid Kathryn's departure from Tehran before the revolution found her? And then the thought niggling Anthony: What chemistry still lingered between Brett and Kathryn? Regardless, he had to shoot spectacular stills for this guy, for Boeing, for Kathryn.

Brett said something to his assistant director next to him, and Enzo, an A.D. Bernardo Bertolucci had used, jogged up to Anthony.

"Ciao, Anthony." They shook hands. "Two years, like yesterday."

"Monte Carlo, my yacht." A moment of fond memories passed between the old friends.

"Come. Whitney wants to meet you."

"On my way."

"So far he's not the prick I've heard he can be."

They shared a wry smile.

"This should be interesting," Anthony said.

"You've been working with his ex-wife, no?" Enzo muttered. "With your reputation, eh?" he shrugged. "A man doesn't let go of a beautiful woman easily, my friend, even when he has others."

"You know Kathryn Whitney?" Anthony asked, adjusting a camera lens as he walked.

Enzo grinned. "We shot a Pepsi commercial together in Paris. *Bellissima.*" He nodded. "*Buon directore.*"

A sense of pride filled him with the mention of Kathryn's talent.

They joined Brett. Enzo introduced them.

"Heard amazing things about your work, Brett."

"You, too, Evans." His smile was cold. "Glad you could get away from Tehran. No problems, I trust?"

Anthony squashed images of his nearly fatal mission and smiled back. "None whatsoever."

He and Brett faced off, two pros, and Anthony felt the air tighten around him as if Brett in some manner felt threatened by him. Was this some industry bias or a male dominance issue? He looked to Enzo, who shrugged. He would definitely have to mask his relationship with Kathryn.

Brett put a heavy hand on Anthony's shoulder. "I want an old-world canvas feel to the lighting," he said, sounding so American, direct with no pleasant preambles. He pointed up to a long turreted balcony curving around the southern side of the castle. "Got it?"

Anthony couldn't hold back a smirk.

Brett went on. "Here we've jumped a few centuries to the early fifteen hundreds . . ."

He nodded, barely keeping the peace. "Ah, I see." Anthony interrupted. He knew the Boeing storyboards cold. "Master Leonardo da Vinci on his balcony, contemplating man's continued quest for flight, testing his invention." Anthony lifted his Nikon, focusing and clicked off a few shots of the costumed actor da Vinci on his turret balcony, then shots of the crew setting up. "This feudal castle is exquisitely preserved."

Brett's eyes narrowed. "You'll be going airborne next." He gestured to the far side of the lake. "I assume you're not squeamish shooting over water."

On the lake's east bank sat an Allouette helicopter, one he was familiar with. "Whenever you're ready."

By the time they broke for lunch, Anthony had finished. Two passes in the Allouette, long shots, mid-range, and zooming in for close shots on the Renaissance set-up, a gorgeous location, one he would love to visit with Kathryn.

His peripheral scan took in Brett's coverage. Top work, a little showy, but hey, why not? He was from Hollywood.

Anthony was packing up when Brett walked over.

"Thought we could grab lunch together, find out how my other crew fares in Iran."

"Sure," Anthony said. *No clean getaway, too bad.*

Huddled in conversation after plates of pasta and branzino, they munched almond biscotti and sipped espresso, Brett going on about himself, his films, awards. But when he mentioned formula racing Anthony's ears perked up.

"And Kathryn raced as well, I take it?"

Brett leaned back. "She was never cut out for it really."

"How so?" Anthony managed to ask blandly.

"Well, she crashed. We had to peel her off a wall after she hit an oil slick going about one-eighty." He shook his head. "Terrible."

Anthony's gut tightened, anguished at the thought of anything hurting her. "She must have been badly injured?"

Brett was still a moment. "It was pretty bad. And she lost our baby." He looked up darkly.

Stunned by this revelation, Anthony mumbled, "I'm sorry, man."

"I admit I didn't really want kids. But she did." Brett sat up. "And she's fine now, even flies planes."

Anthony had had enough of Brett's sidestepping. "So what is it you want to ask me, Brett?"

Brett leaned in. "Are you fucking my wife, Evans?"

Anthony stood. "You're an arrogant prick, you know?" He peeled off a stack of lira and jammed it under his espresso cup. "It's on me."

"So you are!" Brett snarled.

"But you, Whitney, not anymore, are you? Is that your problem?" He walked away before he flattened the sod.

Plagued by bleak misgivings about mortality, Anthony boarded the Pahlavi Gulfstream in Rome, heading back to Iran, back to Kathryn. He hadn't reckoned with mortality before, but as the cargo hatch opened over Mediterranean waters, he knew the body being dumped had nearly been his. Philippe was right. He had been a fool about Mirdad.

It was time to move on his last missions.

Kathryn would join him for a special dinner tonight. To insure her safety Tabriz would station guards around his home, silent and invisible, but deadly if need be.

His mind lifted away from dark thoughts of enemies and turned to his last night with Kathryn in Iran.

CHAPTER TWENTY-ONE

Darkness fell like a heavy veil, Kathryn observed, slumped in the back seat of the car Anthony had sent, the driver unknown to her. Older, his face was softened by kindness when he said politely, "We will soon be there."

They wound through narrow city streets, scenery blurring in a dim haze. Her day had not gone well, and she roiled in frustration. Two days left to shoot in Iran. She had to finish or her career would be thoroughly tanked. She knew how to save her shoot. She had made copious notes, a rapid shooting schedule, and would work everyone's tail off to complete it. But that was tomorrow.

One hurdle at a time.

She sank into the deep leather seat, relishing the warm glow of her healing skin, freshly bathed and scented under a soft ivory cashmere dress, on her way to dinner at Anthony's.

This evening was vastly different territory for her because tonight, mysteries about this Islamic war and Anthony's activities would unravel, questions would be answered, no matter how painful, or she would say goodbye before her heart was trampled to dust. She wouldn't let any man hurt her again.

A sense of intrigue crept over her as they wound through the city streets, where everything in this neighborhood was locked behind high walls and heavy gates all hidden from view, mysterious. Like Anthony.

She closed her eyes and pictured Anthony working today at the lake by Odescalchi Castle outside of Rome, his wide sun-bronzed shoulders lifting heavy camera gear. A fluttering sensation swept through her.

The car hit a bump in the road, and her mind took hold of reality. Sun-bronzed body! Was she sun-stroked? What had gotten into her? She had half a mind to tell the driver to turn around and take her back, if she weren't so damned hungry. There wasn't even a candy bar in this dumb purse, it was so small. Or maybe this uncomfortable feeling in the pit of her stomach wasn't a need for food at all. She tapped her foot.

Who was she kidding? She was falling for this man and was plain afraid of getting hurt.

She sensed Anthony held back from her. But behind his intense moods she wanted to know what his troubling secrets were. *Well, we all have our mysteries*, she tried to tell herself. Another woman? Or could it be his involvement against the Shah's insurgences? Or the vicious Black Glove the newspaper said terrorized the country, murdering entire families one by one in front of each other? She shuddered at the thought. Had they indeed shared more than a tryst? Or was she an alibi for his rescue flights? *Flights.*

What was he really about? But until the moment of inquiry she had promised to enjoy the feast Anthony planned.

"You have my word I'll explain after we dine."

"Yes. Yes, we'll take at least that," she had replied.

The car stopped in front of a large iron gate. The driver honked twice. The entry slid open. This was it.

They swept up a long driveway, passing orange trees and date palms to pass a beautifully manicured, expansive property dramatically lit for acres, illuminating an immaculate formal garden and a fruit orchard beyond.

At the top of the driveway they pulled into a courtyard lined with topiary where lights circled an enormous Roman fountain, sparkling water cascading over ancient stone layers into a pool lit from below. The car stopped beside a stone porch flanked by carved balustrades, leading up to the front doors.

The driver helped her out of the limo. This tall, distinguished man wore long robes she hadn't noticed before at the hotel, his face sober.

"Miss Whitney, I am Raymond, Sir Anthony's butler.

"You're Ali's father?"

The man's eyes widened. "Why, yes. My son."

"Ali is terrific, such a boon to us on location. A fine young man."

A flicker of pride lit Raymond's dark eyes. "Please come in. Sir Anthony waits on the terrace."

Raymond turned and led her into a large octagonal-shaped foyer with a patterned marble floor. Mirrored walls and doors stretched to twenty feet high, reflecting her image in the cashmere dress on all sides.

Everywhere she looked her image was reflected as each panel created an optical illusion obscuring any doorway, disorienting her. The ceiling, encrusted with myriad seashells in an elaborate design, was replicated around the room. Luscious blooming orchids: Vanda, Phalaenopsis, and Cattleya spilled from massive porcelain pots, lending the space a magical effect. Double mirrored doors opened with a flourish, and Kathryn followed Raymond through, her heels faintly clicking on taupe marble.

They entered a grand salon, and her jaw dropped at its beauty. This was no bachelor pad; this was a home where every vase and stunning piece of ancient art had been chosen and placed with care.

Several tufted sofas in sea foam green moiré were arranged around antique mirrored and carved gilt tables. Her feet sank into a thick carpet that swept across the floor, reminding her of an illustrated page from the Rubaiyat, an intricate Persian miniature translated into silk tapestry in brilliant jewel-like colors. She wanted to stop and look at it more closely, to run her hands over it.

Hearing the tinkling of crystal, she looked up into three sparkling Baccarat chandeliers. The tall curved French doors that made up the outer wall of this room were open, a gentle evening breeze wafting through the glorious setting. So this was Anthony's home, his lifestyle: lush, warm, and tastefully magnificent.

She wondered whose hand had so expertly placed all these artistic elements, because this was paradise. And when strains of a Miles Davis ballad, "It Never Entered My

Mind," played softly from speakers above her, she could have pinched herself to make sure she wasn't dreaming.

Through the French doors on the terrace stood Anthony, elegantly dressed for evening, looking like he'd walked right off a movie screen, too delicious to resist.

He saw her and beamed.

Don't let go of why you're here, Kat, she reminded herself.

Leaning into his terrace doorway, Anthony shifted his weight, feeling himself grow hard at the sight of Kathryn. She was lovelier each time they met. Her smile was the sunlight he'd craved all day. He wanted her badly, but knew she wanted disclosure, and maybe something else. This was the last night he would spend in his home, and he intended to enjoy every aspect of being here with her.

"At last. *Khosh amadid, ziba banu,*" he said in Persian and translated. "Welcome to my home, beautiful lady." He took her hands and gently kissed her wrists. He felt her shiver and drew her closer, looking her over, soaking in the pleasure of what he saw.

"Your home is spectacular."

Her voice sounded tight. He wanted her at ease.

"Now that you're in it."

He offered her champagne in fluted stemware, the chill refreshing. "I've missed you," he said and her look softened. "Cheers," they clinked glasses and drank. "How was your day?" He guided her to a sofa where they sat, obviously both wanting the other to speak.

She hesitated for a second. "Perfect. Mirdad sent armed guards to protect the location. I've only got two more days. The Ranger was grounded with a fuel leak. It took all day to fix."

"Poor darling."

"But we shot documentary footage." She sipped her champagne. "I'm more curious to hear about your day in Rome, the shoot."

Secrets. She wanted his, and he hers. He guessed they both had them. And Brett with all his insensitivity had unveiled perhaps Kathryn's most painful secret: losing a baby, a hard turn for anyone, except it seemed, for Brett.

His gaze caressed her. "Nothing exceptional."

A corner of her mouth slid up. "I'll bet otherwise since you're incredibly talented." They scooted closer to each other and energy charged the air around him. She nuzzled into him.

"You mean you thought I was just talk?"

"Well, not in all things," she said coolly, but he sensed cool was not what she was feeling.

He raised his glass. "Here's to our next moonlit garden," he said, but his smile faded when he sensed her resistance.

Sighing, he shook his head. "Rome was beautiful, but I wanted you there."

She raised an eyebrow.

"And your ex. He's a bit full of himself." He shook his head, his voice light. "Really, what did you see in him?"

Kathryn's chin came up sharply, her lips quivered into a smile. "Ah, but when I slipped into a seat in the front row of his UCLA film seminar at age nineteen, to me he was God, a film god." She looked up. "But we're here to talk about you."

"Right." He stroked her cheek and pulled her closer, inhaling her fragrance.

"Unless," she said, her eyes turning a forest hazel, "there is another woman to discuss? Now would be the moment to disclose that little morsel."

He knew better than to be evasive. "Kathryn, there's only one woman I want." He swallowed champagne, cooling his irritating apprehension regarding invasion of privacy, and then bent to her mouth, a sigh escaping.

The kiss was gentle at first, but his desire was hot and the kiss deepened with his need. "Ummm, love touching you," he murmured, and they sat up before Raymond appeared with a tray of hors d'oeuvres.

"Over here please, Raymond," Anthony beckoned. "No, I have a better idea. Would you mind bringing it into my studio? Thank you." He took her hand. "Come with me. I have something to show you."

He guided her down a portrait-lined hallway into a spacious photographic studio and living area. Plush Italian leather sofas flanked a black granite coffee table where Raymond placed the wide silver tray heaped with delicacies: beluga caviar, homemade blinis, mounds of sour cream, minced egg, smoked Norwegian salmon on thinly sliced French bread.

"Will there be anything else, sir?"

"No, that will be fine. Thank you, Raymond."

He watched Kathryn gaze about his studio, his worktable with packed cartons stacked beneath.

"My darkroom is down the hall, and through there is my bedroom and bath." As she turned, her lips curved.

With a look of amazement, she set her glass down and

walked to the end of the room, staring above the ancient limestone fireplace at an enormous photograph of her at the winged lion. Dressed in white, her arms reached above her head and an expression of ecstatic joy.

"My God. How . . . ?" She turned and gaped at him. "You were there! The first time I saw the lion."

"In that moment I knew I had to find you." He was beside her. "My favorite photograph."

She ran her hand over the black and white surface, exploring the light and shadows he had captured.

"I've had a love affair with this lion since I was five," she said. "My father would drink cocoa with me in his study and make up stories about magic flights the lion and I would take, our adventures." Her gaze met his. "We're old friends."

Anthony brushed his hand across her cheek, recalling the intensity of his reaction to her that first morning, the same desire he felt now. "Amazing to find you by your ancient friend. You're a lovely gift. More than I imagined." He caressed her shoulders, bringing her close, and when his mouth covered hers, raw memories from his rotten day dissolved.

"So good," she moaned, her soft warm body against his. But she pulled back, her breathing quickened already. "Anthony, I need to know what you're up to, why you're so secretive. I'm largely in the dark, and I don't like it."

He looked away, not wanting to face questions, but her gaze followed his. "Okay." He sat, pulling her down next to him on the leather sofa. "Comfortable?"

"Yes." She handed him a blini with caviar and capers. "Fortification."

He popped it in his mouth, marveling at how famished he was. Anthony wiped his fingers on a napkin, emptied his champagne glass, and then offered the tray of appetizers to Kathryn.

She nodded, took two blinis heaped with caviar, egg, capers, and a dollop of sour cream. He looked at her, amused.

She wrinkled her nose. "Long day," she said, "and I'm all riled up about Khomeini." She plopped a towering blini in her mouth, eyes closed; he thought he heard her moan. He knew then—she wanted to trust him. He wanted the same.

Sitting next to her, he brought her hand to his mouth, licking a drop of sour cream off her finger, taking that finger in his mouth, sucking it. Her gaze met his.

"More champagne?" Anthony asked.

"Please, sir," she said demurely.

He poured; she drank, then lit into her second tower of blini.

Anthony turned away, chuckling to himself. She was no celery nibbler like the others he had dated.

Her chest expanded with a deep breath, and she slipped off her shoes, curling her legs under her on the sofa. Lovely ankles he noticed. When he looked up she had a knowing smile on her lips.

She reached for her drink, breaking the moment. For now, he mused, but not for long. "I read Khomeini's religious rantings in *Paris Match*," she said. "He defiles the Shah." She swallowed. "Please tell me what's going on."

"Remember, you asked." Anthony stood and paced. "The Shah's ultimate mistake was allowing Khomeini to leave his exile in Iraq and seek asylum in France, where he has access to media. Soon the Shah's reign will end, and Iran's revolution will drag Persian culture back into the dark ages. Women will be back under the veil."

"That's ridiculous. Iranian women are doctors, hold cabinet posts—"

"That will all end. Khomeini is no righteous leader, believe me. He's a tyrant who draws sympathy from western intellectuals. They see him as a saintly old man, wrongly deposed by a ruthless Shah. You met his cutthroat followers at Takht-e Tavoos."

She shivered. "Green Bands."

"Shiite radicals at their worst." Anthony sighed. "Trust me, this is only the beginning. They won't stop with Iran."

"Why doesn't the Shah stop this guy?"

"The Shah has cancer."

"That's terrible! Will he survive?"

Anthony shrugged. "He's weak, out of touch with his people, even with his own SAVAK. And he ignored advice to execute Khomeini. Now it's too late. Khomeini's influence is too strong."

"And the Black Glove murders?" she said.

He pulled back, shaking his head. "How do you know about these terrorists?"

"How deeply are you involved in this, Anthony?"

He leaned back. "There's a death list. I'm privy to it. This gives me a window to fly Black Glove targets to safety, covertly, over the Iranian border, Kuwait, Iraq, sometimes in sea planes to boats on the Caspian."

"Sounds dangerous."

"Sometimes. Often."

"How often are these flights?

"None tonight," he smiled. "This night is ours." He moved closer. The outline of her breasts in the soft ivory dress enticed him, her nipples pebbling under his scrutiny. He reacted, hardening. "I've wanted you all day."

She nodded and pulled his mouth to hers. The kiss deepened, their arms tangling, her leg reached around his, her dress slid up her thigh.

"Over here," he said and drew her to her bare feet then over to the fur rug by the fireplace, tossing throw pillows to the floor. "Dinner can wait."

Smiling she unbuttoned his shirt. "I'm so relieved."

"That I'm risking my life?" He tossed the shirt away and smoothed a wisp of hair off her forehead.

"That you told me." She ran her hands over his abs.

"I can't lose you. I won't." Slowly he turned her bare back to his chest, and reached around her torso, caressing her breasts, his eyes closing for a moment with the pleasure. And then he felt her restrained passion flare, the cue he wanted.

"It's hard for me to trust," she said, pushing against his erection. "You men . . . leave."

"Not me." He ran his tongue along her neck, her earlobe.

"What are you doing to me?" she breathed heavily.

"I'm loving you, Kathryn, all of you."

"Good."

He slid the dress from her shoulders, and it dropped to the rug. Kneeling behind her, he slid a lace bikini over her rear, down her calves, her ankles.

She stepped out of them and turned to face him.

"Your scent excites me," he murmured, licking her stomach, tasting her. "God." He scooped her down to the rug alongside him. She reached for him, sliding her hand along his erection.

"I need you. Now," she said and opened her legs.

"Too good to resist." He swung over between her legs and drove into her slick heat. *Heaven*. Again, again.

She grabbed on to him, her legs circling his hips, her rhythm matching his until she cried out her release, and he bent his head, groaning.

They lay spent and happily entwined on the soft rug, the fireplace crackling until Kathryn pecked his nose and stood gathering her things. "Better get it together."

She headed for his bathroom, her incredible derriere glowing in the firelight and his randy cock stood alert again. What she did to him.

The intercom buzzed twice, announcing dinner in ten minutes, and Anthony sprang up. "I'm falling. Hard. Unbelievable . . ." he muttered, and then went to dress.

Kathryn took Anthony's hand and he led her into a splendid dining room. But as her focus fell to the sideboard and the sumptuous feast before them, the beauty surrounding her vanished from view.

"You weren't kidding," she said.

Anthony dismissed the servants. "I want to serve you myself," he said, bowing, and pulled out the chair for her.

She lifted a shoulder and fluttered her eyelashes, recalling how playful he'd been at the Paradise Club garden, how charming. His captivating smile was back.

He brought her course after course, leading up to the rack of lamb cooked to perfection, served with herbed roasted potatoes, then saffron rice with grilled lobster and a steaming array of vegetables.

"If I may assist you, Madame." He made a show of coming around the table to select the largest lobster bits from the platter, spooning beurre blanc, sorrel, and delicate tarragon sauces beside her asparagus and *haricot verre*.

"Ah, musn't forget Tali's fresh baked bread." He placed a small plate to the side and buttered her bread.

Only at first did he look astonished when she finished every bite and looked up at him for more. Between courses he teased her. "Won't you have another helping? Don't be shy! I love a woman with a healthy appetite." He poured her wine, delicate white Bordeaux with the fish and heady Chateau Margaux with the lamb.

When at last she finished, she dabbed her napkin to her lips, and as if on cue, Tali, his cook, appeared.

"My compliments to the chef," Kathryn said. "That was truly superb."

A round, apple-cheeked woman in a blue uniform, Tali folded her hands in front of her, blushing. "Thank you, Madame."

Kathryn lifted her hand toward Anthony. "And the service—excellent."

Two pretty teenage girls peeking into the room giggled.

Anthony pretended he hadn't seen them. "We aim to please."

With a nod to Anthony, Tali shooed her girls along and left.

Anthony had shown her his family: Ali, Raymond, Tali, and those sweet girls. "How difficult for you to leave this household," she said.

"Difficult times, Kathryn." He came around to her chair and led her into the drawing room. "You're probably stuffed, but we can't ignore Tali's dessert. Not tonight."

There on the coffee table before them was set a tray with a glorious tarte tartan, and a steaming Grand Marnier soufflé with a frothy vanilla sauce, chocolate hazelnut torte, fresh fruit, and several international cheeses. Kathryn laughed. "I've never seen so much delicious food. Who else is coming?"

"My staff will dine well tonight." He kissed her cheek. She squeezed his hand.

Kathryn allowed Anthony to feed her two small desserts and then sat back with a double espresso, noticing the portrait of a woman, bejeweled, wearing a chiffon gown, looking down at them. "Such a beautiful smile, and she wears an astonishing collection of canary diamonds."

Kathryn stood, drawn to the portrait. "Your mother?"

He nodded. "It was painted in 1943, right after I was born."

She gazed at the painting. "She's lovely. You have her beautiful mouth, and her dark hair, but not her eyes."

"My father's eyes." He came to her side, encircling her with his arms.

She leaned back, gazing at the portrait. "I've seen those jewels before, but where? Ah. I remember, the bank in Tehran with the Crown Jewels."

"On display until yesterday."

"The most perfect yellow diamonds I've ever seen, like glittering chunks of sunlight. Fancy intense, I believe."

He looked at her. "You know diamonds?"

"Not as well as my mother had hoped. But there is

something extraordinary about those diamonds, mesmerizing." She shifted her weight.

He laughed quietly. "These diamonds have a legacy. Come here," he said, "I'll tell you a story."

They kicked off their shoes and lay down side by side on the deep sofa.

"My father used to turn the tales of art treasures into bedtime stories," she said.

"With this tale, you must pay close attention, because these diamonds carry a curse."

"Are you cursed?" she asked.

"Far from it. Long ago, the czar of Russia fell in love with a Persian princess whom he could never marry. But he wanted her to remember him with a gift as pure and exquisite as his love for her. So he commissioned Carl Fabergé to choose the finest stones in all Russia and create a treasure for his Persian love. Faberge went to immeasurable lengths to capture flawless yellow diamonds of unequaled quality in the world. From those stones, he created what became known as the Persian Glories."

Kathryn watched his face with rapt interest, feeling as safe as she had as a child in her father's arms.

"But," Anthony continued, "Fabergé warned that because of their uniqueness they would attract great love, but could never be sold or used for material gain. There lays the curse. They must only be given away in one's lifetime or the possessor risked never having love.

"In time, the diamonds came to the Shah, who had been in love with Ilyia Razim, a Persian beauty he, too, could never marry. It was the night of the Thousand Stars Ball, and the Shah gave Ilyia these diamonds at a grand party at the palace—a betrothal gift when she was to marry another man, his close friend, my father. It was a night spoken about for years.

"One evening when I was fourteen, my mother came to my room after an embassy ball with my father. She looked especially lovely in her ball gown and wearing the Persian Glories. She sat next to me holding the box."

He shifted, and Kathryn leaned closer.

"I didn't take much notice, I was so glad to see her.

"She said, 'I give these to you, my son. They were meant for you one day, and I choose this day. And I'll wear them only when you want me to.'

"I was astounded! 'Mother,' I said, 'why're you doing this?' She bent to me, whispering, 'Because it's my wish to do so.' Bewildered, I said, 'I'm honored, Mother. But will you teach me when a lady should wear them?'

"'Of course, my love.' She smiled. 'It will be my pleasure.' She held me for a moment. A sad look crossed her face for an instant, and then she left my room. The following week she and my father were killed. I always wondered why she chose that moment. Did she have a premonition? Did she know something she'd not told me, or was she afraid? I'll never know."

It took a moment for him to return from the place this memory resided. Kathryn held him. The memory of her own father's death constricted her chest.

"Come, let's get some air." Anthony walked her out onto the softly lit terrace overlooking the gardens. The air was fragrant with night blooming jasmine. "Before you must go . . ." He reached into his pocket and drew out a flat, black satin box, handing it to her. "For you," he said. She opened it slowly. Lying in a bed of white satin, a spectacular diamond gardenia gleamed. It was the size of a real gardenia. *Her favorite flower.* Each petal had been sculpted out of platinum; every stone was set seamlessly against the next, with petals layered one over the other. The center was an enormous, perfect pearl. Surrounding the flower were three emerald leaves.

Astonished and seeking words to respond, she lifted the brooch from the Van Cleef & Arpels box. "I'm speechless. Funny, I can only think of my mother's words, 'When a man speaks of love and hands you a gift, look him in the eye, smile, and say thank you.'" Her voice quivered. "Thank you." Her fingers trembled. "I'm stunned. I've never held a piece of jewelry of this importance, this unique."

"It was my mother's," he said, "I want you to have it."

"Your mother's . . ." She touched his face, bringing it to hers, kissing him. "I'm very happy."

"So am I."

"You're whispering."

"So the gods don't hear," he said.

From inside the house, she heard muffled voices, agitated. Raymond argued with a man, someone very distraught.

Anthony's look of tenderness dissolved, replaced by one of uneasiness.

"Too much to ask. Wait here," he said, pushing her from him, his gestures tense. "I won't be long."

Chilled, she forced away speculations of danger. She wouldn't ruin this moment. She turned her gaze to the garden. From there she saw a floating deck. It was a style she'd known from photographs of Persian homes she'd seen in her father's books.

A wooden platform suspended by cables over a garden, a place where tea was served with polite conversation or to be enjoyed alone, in reverie. She crossed a narrow wooden bridge to a little island suspended over a lit pond where lily pads floated and tiny frogs chased insects among the vegetation. The pond was edged with dense ferns and slender bamboo grown tall beyond the height of the deck. The deck was adorned with tapestry covered cushions and layers of lovely rugs.

Kathryn sank down into the luscious banquette and gazed at the silvery moon, waning slightly but still luminous. Bright like her reflections of this glorious night, the magnitude of Anthony's gift, and her feelings floating with the deck. The powerful draw between them was one she had never imagined possible.

All at once, voices from inside intruded on her peace. Sounds of an ugly argument swept out to the garden. She shuddered and sat up. The night's energy shifted. Something was wrong.

"Kathryn! Where are you? Kathryn!"

Anthony's voice rang through the bamboo.

"Up here!" She waved, her smile fading with his irritation, wanting it to go away.

She rushed out to where he stood. "It's lovely out here. I had to experience this." Even in the shadows she felt his anxiety. Trouble brewing.

Anthony climbed up to meet Kathryn, but stood back, vibrating with rage, keeping a distance between them, fearing his anxiety was contagious.

She smiled and moved toward him, her expression trusting. Giving in, he swept her into his arms, crushing her to him, burying his face against her neck. "You're so warm."

"What's wrong, darling?"

He moved away, disturbed by the circumstances. "Tonight's not safe for the civilized," he said. "Only the ruthless survive on nights like this." His voice choked. "I'll get you back to the hotel."

"Damn it, Anthony, what's happened?"

He walked to the railing and stared into the unknowable darkness, so like his future. "My good friend, Madame Renudi, owner and chief editor of the *Tehran Global Press*, was murdered tonight in her own home." He bowed his head, sadness and revulsion warring inside. "Her servants, her household—all of them—found dead. Mutilated . . ."

Kathryn gasped, her posture rigid. "Are . . . are you . . . ?"

He turned to her. "I'm next, Kathryn."

"You can't be certain." Her face etched with concern.

"These men seized her assets . . . and laid the blame at the Shah's door. Now others are threatened. I have to act swiftly." This information buzzed through his head. "My life's a colossal disaster." He broke away, sorrow burrowing in his gut. "Only two people in Iran know what I'm doing. They're the only ones who even know I'm a pilot." He smoothed a strand from her forehead. "Kathryn. . . I can't stay. People who can must get out of Iran—tonight."

"I'm going with you."

"No! You don't want to be linked with me. Not at all."

Her mouth set firm. "Let me help."

"You need to get the hell out. Now. No joke."

She glared at him, determination written across her

face—part of why he loved her. "I won't leave without you. I want to help." Her voice was steady.

"Damn it! You simply don't get it. I need you to drive with me to the airstrip." He looked her over and grabbed her hand. "We can talk on the way."

CHAPTER TWENTY-TWO

Forty minutes later, racing the Ferrari to a private airstrip on the outskirts of Shiraz, Anthony explained tonight's mission. The other pilots couldn't make the run. Kathryn's nerves hummed; she was awed that Anthony trusted her for this assignment. She aimed a pin light at a topographical map of the region, studying the mountain range they would soon cross over.

With no time to go back to the hotel and change, she dressed in Anthony's clothes, belted jeans bagging on her and tucked into warm socks, a black cashmere sweater, and gardening sneakers offered by Tali's youngest daughters, both little eavesdroppers. Clearly his household knew more than they let on, their loyalty notwithstanding.

"You'll need to fly in a close pattern to me." He glanced over. "Can you?"

"You bet." She did not look up.

"Good. So if we get separated here's what you do . . ."

He finished filling her in and swerved the Ferrari onto a narrow paved road. Lights dimmed, he drove about a half mile then slowed and flashed his lights three times at an airplane hangar she had not seen in the dark. "Hans will be under surveillance at another airstrip, our decoy 'waiting' for me to show up."

The large door slid open. Foot off the brake, Anthony idled the car into the hangar. The door slid shut behind them. As they got out, figures emerged from shadows. At least fifteen men came forward, then four women, holding two small children. All wore dark clothing.

A man in black-rimmed glasses and a stocking cap stepped up, hand extended to Anthony.

"*Insha Allah*," he said, pulling Anthony forward into a hug.

"Hassan. Good to see you. We can do this thing," Anthony said. Then he introduced Kathryn.

Hassan gave Kathryn a questioning glance.

"What happened to the other pilot?"

"He was picked up at his house."

Anthony inhaled. "Did they arrest him?"

"No. For questioning, they say." Hassan leaned closer. "He thinks these Black Glove traitors wait for you to show up. They have sniper rifles."

Avenues for escape were closing. There was no time for delays. Anthony knew Hans would sit tight at the other airstrip, playing his part, pacing, glancing at his watch. He looked over at Kathryn as she helped Hassan load all the passengers onto the two waiting planes. Even with two, it was a tight squeeze.

"Several of those here," he said under his breath to Kathryn, "are extremely wealthy, all their assets in Iran seized." He motioned around the group. "Those three are filmmakers, one a writer and the—"

"I recognize that man from Takht-e Tavoos. He's the sitar player."

"Yes. Two of the women are prominent heiresses, highly involved in business. Another is director of the National Arts Council, and the lovely young woman over there is wife to the musician." The young mother clutched her two small children to her, her eyes wide with trepidation.

All were dissidents who had spoken out against human rights violations of both the Shah's SAVAK and Khomeini's fanatics who hid behind the Koran while imposing stricter and stricter religious dictates upon the citizens.

"But what has sealed their fate," Anthony said, "is the attention drawn by a worse foe. The Black Glove's death squads."

Kathryn kept her expression bland but her pulse pounded in an adrenalin rush. She was no stranger to physical danger, but these stakes were higher than a racing trophy. This was real, and she had signed on. She looked into the face of the young mother, her sleepy kids, and others in the group whose keen eyes shone with a fierce desire for life. Her heart melted.

The enormity of their need wrestled with her own— and won. The clear drive she had before a race kicked in. Thoughts of her show-biz life in L.A. diminished in importance. Yes, some things loomed larger than a Hollywood career. This situation eclipsed her shoot, her deal with Wally, and her professional yearnings. Kathryn's resolve set firm.

If she could save one life she would.

VILLA KISMET, KISH ISLAND
THE PERSIAN GULF, IRAN

It was her wedding day, and the ceremony in this glorious villa had choked Rena to joyful tears and relief. Select guests, sixty or so dignitaries emblazoned with gold braids and countless metals, were an impressive statement to her own re-instated social standing. Their wives, elegant and curious, paled, she thought, in comparison to herself.

Rena, Iran's fallen first lady, vanished from the public eye for years, had snagged the illustrious General Omar Houdin, governor of Tehran, a man of ever soaring power. Her stature had risen once again.

She strode along the upstairs villa hall smiling, soaking in her new environment: high corniced ceilings, limestone walls adorned with hammered gold sconces whispering of ancient times. Elaborate furniture, huge vases of red and white roses, the scent tickling her nose: everything she saw was glittering and golden.

Rena's fingertips quivered, brushing against the rich crimson silk of her wedding dress, and she breathed in affluence, her husband's and—finally, her soaring spirit whispered—hers. She was about to find out how much he respected her when she would behold this suite where he had installed her. And when he joined her, she must set the tone of this marriage, how they would go on. She would never allow another man in the driver's seat with her again.

Towering double doors swung open before her; flanking footmen bowed and soundlessly closed the doors behind her.

Her Christian Dior stilettos sank into an aqua and beige Kayseri silk carpet, Persia's finest. She observed the massive salon of the sumptuous suite, passing emerald green velvet sofas before an ornate malachite fireplace. She peered into the bedroom, her gaze drawn to a great domed ceiling hung with a filigreed gold chandelier.

She hurried into the bedroom. Kicking off her pumps, arms wide she spun around, taking in the pale paneling carved with rosebuds and hydrangeas, peau de soie covered chairs, gilt mirrors, and clustered French perfume bottles. There was a massive blue-canopied bed with embroidered satin pillows and bed coverings. All of it swirled and twirled before her. The sound of her own laughter reverberated through the space, trailing out through open terrace doors, and then she staggered to an armchair, plopping down on powder blue goose feather cushions to regain her breath. *She had done it. She had done it. She was saved.*

Drawn to the dressing table, she rose and moved closer, staring into the mirror. Her likeness was that of a stunning thirty-five-year old whom no one would guess was in her fifties. She touched the face reflected there, her breath hitching at her own beauty.

There was a knock at the door.

She smoothed her dress, slipping on her shoes. "Enter," she said, her voice lilting.

A steward in cutaways, a towel over his arm, carried a tray laden with a beading silver champagne bucket, Dom Perignon, and two fluted glasses rimmed with gold. "Where would you like this, Madame?" He bowed.

Rena indicated a marble topped table near the terrace. "Open it," she said.

His hesitation, though infinitesimal, she caught. He was probably expecting her to wait patiently for her husband's arrival. Her lip curled, her gaze imperious.

"At o-once," he stammered.

Pop.

Chilled wine vapors rose from the green bottle, and her mouth watered. She nodded, and he poured pale bubbles into a frosted Baccarat flute. With a wave of her hand she dismissed him.

Breathless, she took her glass onto the terrace overlooking cerulean waters surrounding Kish Island. Was this real?

She clutched the bronze balcony railing as the sun hovered on the horizon, blasting the sky with hot color, crimson, coral, cerise, as if shrieking, "You'll not forget me," and then sank into waves of cool sapphire.

This day. I will remember this day always.

A flash image of her marriage to her son Mirdad's once powerful father intruded into her mind. What had started out gloriously had warped into utter disaster, haunting her still. She squelched vile memories, and held up her glass in salute.

Blessed Allah, she was rich! How long had it been since she had savored good champagne? The first sip was like liquid gold, delectable. The second even better, and she drank the rest down and went to refill her glass. Her dress fluttered against her legs. She had been married in red. She lifted her chin proudly and laughed.

The suite's double doors burst open, and she pivoted to greet her impressive husband and his entourage, his adjutant, Demetrius Nassiri, at the lead. Mirdad, looking splendid in his new suit, hung back.

She held her regal posture. For over thirty years she had wanted Omar, and now he was hers. She wanted to melt into his arms.

"Ah, my dear," the general beamed, his chest puffing against a white dress uniform blazing with metals from the Iraq war and who knew what other conquests. He said in a low tone, "We should have privacy." He stepped closer, his intense look pinning her.

She stood back. "Omar."

His fellows by the doors, Colonel Demetrius Nassiri at the lead, saluted. "Congratulations, General, Madame Houdin," Nassiri said. The general shooed the men out but before leaving, Mirdad stepped forward and came to his mother's side, kissing her cheek. "Much happiness, Mother." He swiveled to her husband and clicked his heels. "And to you, sir."

The general tugged Mirdad into a quick squeeze. "Thank you, Mirdad," he said, his voice raspy with emotion.

Mirdad left and the door swung shut. They were alone at last.

She glowed inside. Omar cared for Mirdad; that was evident. Both she and Mirdad would have the life she had dreamed of for years. She set down her glass and sank into a deep curtsy, one eyebrow raised. "Husband?"

He watched closely, taking in her breasts against the crimson bodice, her wicked smile making her eyes sparkle.

Desire for Omar, but a whisper at age seventeen, was now an opus to passion, singing through her body.

He took her hands and pulled her to him. "Rena, my

vixen." His powerful arms engulfed her; his mouth took hers, warm and firm, his body pressed into her. He was fully aroused, as was she. She had him. And the best part of all of this, she vowed, was yet to come.

The night was humid. Rena, sated and languid, strolled beside Omar through Villa Kismet's well-guarded gardens. A half-mile pool rippled beneath columns from the reign of King Xerxes in 350 B.C.E., carved bulls topping the capitals. Mirdad, the history student, had droned on about this when they had arrived this morning. She savored her sublime mood, wanting it to last forever. Omar squeezed her hand and bent toward her, but then inexplicably stopped.

From the shadows a maroon liveried footman approached holding a silver tray with a white envelope.

"So sorry, Excellency, but an urgent message has arrived."

Omar reached out.

"It is for madam, sir." He bowed.

Omar grabbed the note and read aloud:

Many congratulations on your
Fortuitous Marriage.

Who would dare interrupt her honeymoon with General Houdin?

On edge, Rena asked, "And who is it from?"

"It is signed: Azi." His look questioned her, jealousy barely hidden.

"Mirdad's uncle, a pesky brother of Valik's. Always checking up on me. Horrid man, really."

"I should never have allowed that fool messenger to find you on this glorious day."

She touched his cheek. "It's nothing, my love. Nothing should ruin this moment." But she was suddenly nerve racked, gulping down fear. Her past had followed her to Kish. Azi, the ancient word for snake, her dirty blackmailer. How should she proceed? She crushed his vile message against her palm and looked up at Omar with a brittle smile.

Omar, the governor of Tehran, was in position to take the wealth and power he had always coveted. He had been reluctant to marry her all those years ago before her son was born. He would never want a bride who was a liability.

Omar gazed down at her. "My dear, have you received bad news?" His eyes shadowed against lowered lids.

"Of course not. I'm so happy with you."

He gave her an inscrutable look. "Of course." He kissed her palm, and they resumed their stroll.

"Did you know," Omar said, "that the Shah once planned Kish to be the Monte Carlo of the Mideast, an extravagant gambling resort? Hundreds of millions of dollars were invested and the building began, then all was lost by the Shah and the SAVAK leader, Sabeti."

"But why? It's magnificent here."

"The Shah caved to clergy pressure. Mullahs used all their forces to shut down 'houses of sin.'" He shrugged. "Naturally, with no financial gain to them they felt they had to quash them. So the Shah's investment was as ill-fated as his reign. And Sabeti's beautiful Villa Kismet has changed hands."

"This villa belonged to Sabeti? Head of SAVAK?" She cringed inside.

"Not anymore." He smirked. "He became reckless with success, and tides turn. The Shah crumbles, and Sabeti looks to me for a way out." He laughed and hugged her close. "I hold Sabeti's markers."

What would this mean for her? Instinct said she could speak to him of her dilemma, for he was even more devious than she. "How brilliant you are, Omar. How I admire your skills."

He laughed deeply, the rumble echoing from his gut and through his chest. "What is it you want, my beauty? Tell me and it is yours."

She almost gagged, her relief was so great. "Later, my love." She stroked his chest, gazing at him. "Make love to me first."

His eyes widened before he bent forward to kiss her smiling lips.

By the ornate mantle clock it was almost 10:00 P.M. Mirdad had flown back to Shiraz after his mother's wedding. He slammed down the phone in the general's Paradise Club salon and sloshed back the last of the champagne in a fluted Lalique glass. He flung it into the fireplace.

"Having a tantrum, are we?" Major Demetrius Nassiri swaggered across the room to the sofa opposite Mirdad, sinking into it. He was dressed in a gi, for his martial arts practice, some barbaric, deadly ritual that Mirdad never could understand.

"Over some woman, no doubt?" Demi added.

"And why not?" Mirdad said. "She's desirable."

He had called her hotel a dozen times and "Ms. Whitney isn't in," was all he got. She should've been back by now. He had looked forward to taking her to dinner alone without her crew. Away from Anthony. And he wanted his mother to see her on his arm, so lovely, so blond, so American. He smiled, visualizing the moment.

He stood and moved to the long, brass-railed, cherry wood bar at the end of the room, selecting another glass. He pulled the champagne bottle from the gold ice bucket. It was empty. He yanked open the refrigerator under the bar, pulled out another bottle of 1957 Dom Perignon and uncorked it, the golden bubbles spilling over his thumb. He filled his glass and slugged down a gulp, then sipped.

Across the room, Demi stared at him.

So far Anthony had eluded every trap he had set. Those idiot Green Band Militia were amateurs. He needed professionals. He needed the Black Glove.

"Your body is too soft, Mirdad. You should let me train you. Then you could fight your own battles for your woman and win."

Mirdad looked over at Demi, wondering. Could he actually train for that barbaric combat ritual? "Perhaps I will do it." But his thoughts slid back to Anthony, who had not been out at Persepolis today and was nowhere in sight, Mirdad's man had said. Why hadn't the fool found out where Anthony had gone? These Green Bands were no match for Black Glove officers. So BGOs must be the ones to carry out Houdin's orders. Mirdad's livelihood depended on their success.

And then there was his obsessive desire for Kathryn.

He wanted the Americans out of the way before he took care of Anthony. But perhaps he wouldn't wait. In fact, tonight would be a perfect night. "Anthony will have to fly out of Shiraz tonight, of that I'm certain." He turned to Demi. "Hans Eber and his helicopter are under surveillance?"

"Who?" Demi looked up.

"Anthony's pilot!"

Demi smirked. "They'll never make it off the ground tonight."

"Make certain Evans shows first. No mistakes." Mirdad dialed the Hotel Persepolis, watching as Demetrius put his feet on the coffee table and picked at a pomegranate.

"Connect me with Buzz Anderson's room." A click. "Hello? Buzz, this is Mirdad Ajani."

"Mirdad, hello."

"I'm looking for Kathryn."

"I don't think she's here now. She's having dinner with Anthony. Shall I give her a message?"

Mirdad wanted to spit and throw the phone through the wall at the same time. "Yes. Tell her I'll join you out at the set tomorrow."

"Sure thing."

"How's it going?"

There was silence, and then, "We had problems today. Put us behind."

"Sorry to hear that. We want you to be satisfied."

"We're out of time. We've only got one more day, but we'll do our best."

So she was with Anthony! "Thank you, Buzz. See you tomorrow."

"Look forward to it, Mirdad."

Mirdad hung up the phone. "Tell me, Demetrius, which officer is the best marksman?"

CHAPTER TWENTY-THREE

The danger should have scared Kathryn, flying the Cessna in hostile skies, weather growing heavy, avoiding radio contact and radar. She was tight in formation with the plane on her left wing, but something about space between brilliant stars and dense earth and the tilting horizon heightened awareness of Kathryn's connection to Anthony and his purpose. Saving lives.

Packed beyond capacity, the plane's pressurized cabin was filled with the smell of bodies pressed too closely to one another. Two men, Anthony's friend, Hassan, and Raj the musician, were forced to lay along the aisle, their heads resting on backpacks, the young mother behind Kathryn's cabin crooning to her children.

The Zargos Mountain peaks rimmed with September snow loomed ahead like sleeping giants against a stellar horizon, cloud formations moving in. Kathryn adjusted to turbulence, sudden and unpredictable, focused and now feeling a trickle of that absent fear. She held formation with Anthony's aircraft and remembered his instructions:

"Get above any clouds or you'll lose me." He had told her. *"Crossing the highest Zargos peak, the turbulence gets nasty."*

The cabin's chill grew colder, but adrenaline kept her warm. Ten passengers shivered behind her.

The plane bumped through heavy chop then dropped, rattling everyone on board. Passengers screamed, the small girl wailed, her brother snuffling against his mother's lap. From the aisle, Hassan calmed the group with prayer. *"Allah Akbar . . ."* In that moment Kathryn fought a jolt of apprehension, unused to the sounds and smells of frantic passengers on her own daredevil exploits.

The sitar player, Raj, knelt behind her pilot's chair, soothing his daughter, singing softly. Soon others joined in, and a Persian lullaby floated through cabin noise as the plane battered turbulence. Snow flurries gathered ahead. The coordinates were locked in her brain but her wing partner was missing, off course. Or was *she?*

Buffeting the snow blitz, Kathryn nosed the plane up. Her chilled fingers itched to break radio silence, to speak with Anthony, but stealth was key. If she didn't spot him in another minute she'd be flying blind. Okay, so maybe she was a little scared, but at this point she was still exhilarated, too. She held on to her coordinates through filmy clouds.

With a break in the atmosphere, she spotted Anthony there on the left and exhaled, reclaiming her confidence. She leveled; the crags disappeared below like magic.

Finally over the mountains, they dropped altitude,

heading south between Kowiss and Kharg. She considered Anthony's instructions.

"*The 414 has an eight passenger capacity. We'll carry ten each. With our heavy cargo we can't outrun Iranian fighters, it's dangerous to even try. So we'll avoid raking Abadan Airbase tonight and wind through Iran's oil fields, our only option.*"

"*Won't those rigs be guarded?*" she said.

"*Yes. And they could be armed. But it's only thirty miles across at top speed, then we'll be over the Gulf, Kuwait a few miles ahead.*"

"*You're in charge.*" She shrugged, first time jitters settling in. She tamped them down.

"*Mostly Russians work the fields and are heavy drinkers,*" Anthony told her. "*Let's hope they're soused.*"

The Cessna cabin warmed a bit over the temperate desert. Teeth rattling ceased. Kathryn searched ahead, spotting oil derricks scattered across a scrubby terrain in all directions. *The wealth of a nation.* She held position on Anthony's right wing and caught sight of manned gun turrets around the field perimeter.

Both Cessnas increased speed, soaring across the oil field. Not a glimmer of activity below.

A turret light blipped on. *No, not a light—gunfire, blasting at them. Holy saints!* Anthony's plane veered left, Kathryn's to the right, dodging bullets with twenty miles of oil fields to go. Like scurrying insects, the ground came alive. Long-range weapons tracking, mortars blasting, the Russian oil workers below definitely weren't too soused for target practice on the Cessnas.

Abruptly she angled away. Someone, she feared, would be sick with her flying—better than dead. She swerved hard to her left and kept up evasive maneuvers, gaining altitude and speed. The plane had a top range of 270 and she would hit that soon.

Cessna One flashed his green wing light three times, and she banked to regain formation. A rocket zoomed past on her left. The plane shook. So did Kathryn, realizing if she had been in formation there would be nothing left of her Cessna but particles.

She squashed down an enormous wave of anxiety. So cocksure, she hadn't fathomed the enormous peril everyone on this plane faced or the raging adrenaline kicking in. This was no raceway. This was war.

Riveted on escape, she shut out the trauma in the cabin behind her, pursuing her wingman. Lights blinked on ahead.

Soon they skimmed gulf waters and she noted her instructions: *"The next land you spot will be Kuwait. Three minutes over land lights will indicate the airstrip."*

Okay, almost three minutes. She caught Anthony's signal, a short series of blinking lights, then again. She waited. Her breath stuck in her chest. Nothing appeared below. What now?

She glimpsed a dim ground glow. An airstrip. *Dear God.*

Gratitude swelled in her heart at the sight. She exhaled a deep breath and concentrated on landing.

Anthony's plane circled the airstrip on approach.

Kathryn tailed him and came around again. But glancing out the window she spotted a truck full of men and two black cars speeding across the desert toward the airstrip. Shiite rebels had crossed into Kuwait, ruthless and filled with hatred. She recalled her sense of helplessness as rebels had torched the lovely restaurant at Takht-e Tavoos and she hit the radio call button. "Cess One, Cess One, militia dusting up the road. You've got ten minutes max. Do you read?"

"Damn! Cess Two, abort landing, no time, you won't make it. Do you copy? Abort landing! Head west. I'll find you."

"Hell no. Get out of my way. I'm coming in. Out." Kathryn tightened the circle, a steeper landing, but so be it. "Brace yourselves—this could get rough!" Kathryn shouted and went in steep. *Come on, Anthony; get that plane out of my way.* She let out a shuddered breath as landing lights brightened. *May as well, they were no longer a secret.*

Anthony landed and taxied his plane behind the shed, cut engines, and jumped out.

Two gray vans and a Land Rover parked by a storage shed were hopefully part of the plan. Jogging over to the Land Rover, Anthony greeted the driver, passing him an envelope. His group of ten clamored into a gray van and took off, headlights dimmed. *Friends.*

"Hassan, Raj!" she yelled over engine noise. "When I brake, get 'em off the plane fast, into the vans. Forget the bags, run for it."

She was coming in too fast, the end of the runway too close. She needed 5,000 feet to land, but had less than 4,500. They would come down hard.

Hassan shouted orders behind her to his colleagues. This group knew what getting caught would mean. They'd be ready to move out. She adjusted, centering over the runway. Wings teetered against strong wind currents. She wrestled to steady the aircraft, clutching her controls, dropping lower, lower, not enough room . . .

Once again, back on the racetrack at Laguna Seca doing a hundred and sixty, heading into the first curve of the northern S-turn. Car twenty-three, just ahead of her, lost oil. She saw it too late, hitting his slick. Her car spun. Her mind screamed. She felt her rear tires go.

"No!" she shrieked. A full 360. She fought the spin, adjusting every millisecond against centrifugal force but the car spun, grinding the guardrail and crashing into the embankment. The engine shoved back toward her; she was trapped—screaming. Men from the pit crew sprinted onto the track and pulled her out as the car caught fire. The baby she had not known existed didn't survive. Her marriage, her career died, too. She had only barely survived.

The same heightened terror she'd had that day at the track bore into her now, but with eleven lives on her shoulders. With all her might she pounded the brakes, holding course, her muscles rigid. The plane scrunched against the ground, weaving, the tricycle landing gear squealing, wheels skidding. Smoking tires screeched, biting into the blacktop, speeding toward a high metal fence, and ground to a halt, buckling the fence.

Gasping for air, Kathryn set the emergency brake and let her head fall forward, relief flooding into her. Pent-up emotions of fear and doubt she'd unconsciously suppressed now surfaced, and her hands shook. The turmoil behind her grabbed her attention. She turned off the engines and gathered her wits. Out on the tarmac, gunmen in ski masks carrying M16s closed in around the plane. *Get out now!* Kathryn clicked off her seat belt and jumped up.

"Hurry!" yelled Raj, grabbing his son up in his arms, nudging his wife along. The others, clamoring down retractable stairs, ran for the second idling van. As soon as the doorway cleared she moved to go, but a gunman climbed on board and faced her.

Startled, Kathryn froze, shaking. "Uh-oh," she groaned, dread sweeping her body. A zillion thoughts of escape competed in her mind. She backed up.

He moved toward her. Pulling off the ski mask, his bushy hair fell forward, his mouth split in a grin of crooked teeth. "We go now," he said.

Cautiously she stepped forward, but he held up his hand. "No. We fly."

Was he kidding? There was barely any fuel. "No gasoline," she said, pointing at the instrument panel.

"We fix," he said.

Before he swung the plane's door shut, the truck of militia she had spotted from the air swerved onto the airstrip road.

Quickly she strapped in, started the engine, and maneuvered the plane around, catching sight of Anthony's plane taxiing out from behind the shed onto the runway right behind her. She throttled forward, increasing speed and took off—to where, she had no idea. They couldn't go far with a bouncing fuel gauge, that was certain.

She glanced at the man with the gun in the copilot's seat, and a sinking feeling deepened. She was afraid of who he was, of his intentions.

He yelled at her in Farsi and then jumped as rapid gunfire pinged around them. Bullets strafed the Cessna undercarriage and Kathryn banked right, climbing to escape the barrage.

Red hot panic shot through her, but she couldn't give

in to it. She trounced it and clung to the hope that her group had gotten away, even if she hadn't. *Well, she had known, if not fully appreciated, the risk.*

"Cess Two," she heard Anthony's scratchy voice from the radio. "Get going. The sergeant, my friend, will escort you. I won't be far behind."

"Friend?" she yelled.

"Friend, yes, yes!" The man's head bobbed.

"Now he tells me."

The "friend" pointed ahead, gesturing toward distant foothills, indicating she should go over them and land.

Gunfire diminished behind the hills.

The engines sputtered. This could be it.

Beyond low mountains a barren valley floor swept for miles. She scanned the space. Landing lights flickered about ten miles out. Could she make it? *Was this it?* She had a moment to suck in the beauty around her, the desert silhouetted against a shimmering sky, the tilted moon, determined to again survive. The sound of his voice on the radio made her heart swell with hope.

"Should I expect gunfire?"

"No guns here. We re-fuel and take off together.

Together. She liked that. "Okay." She checked her sputtering fuel gauge, her stomach clenching. *I've got to do this.*

"Sweetheart . . ."

"Yes?"

"Our twenty. They made it."

"Oh . . . good." Her voice broke.

"And we'll be fine. We're going back." Then silence.

"You still there?" she said.

"Yeah."

"Fuel's about gone."

"Mine, too."

"So . . . we go in on fumes?"

"Keep the faith, my love. Out."

Ahead landing lights switched on, the airfield in plain sight.

This baby'll bounce hard. But please don't let it skid.

Within minutes a tailwind picked up, a good push, but bumpy. She was going in wobbly and getting close when the engine sputtered out. "Hang on!" she shouted.

She jolted onto the tarmac and bounced, nose scraping, sparks flying, sliding. "No, you don't, damn it." She held on, until screeching brakes ground the plane to a sideways halt.

She looked over, her breath catching. "You okay, friend?"

He nodded, sweating, his eyes wide.

"Let's go." They unbuckled their belts, shot out of the plane, and stood watching it get towed away to refuel.

Anthony's aircraft neared approach in a swift descent, the engine gasping. Her breath caught as the nose dropped and the wings teetered unsteadily like a playground toy, fighting wind currents. The engine cut out.

Silence.

No. *Come on, start!*

The engine sputtered, popped, and started again, smoking badly, almost down. *Had he been hit?* Her fists clenched, her jaw tightened.

Wheels crunching down, Anthony's aircraft skidded and tilted, fighting not to flip over and finally slid to a stop. Kathryn was hyperventilating, struggling to slow her breath. *Shhh, shhh. He made it.*

The ground crew ran toward the Cessna, and Anthony appeared through the smoke, dirty and smudged, walking toward her. Kathryn ran to him and stopped in front of him, breathing hard. She pulled off her baseball cap, wiped her forehead with her sleeve, and gaped at him like the first time she had seen him at the Hotel Persepolis, a stranger then, now the man she loved. Wind rustled through her hair, cooling her skin.

"Hi," she said.

He grinned his gorgeous lopsided grin, a little like the tilted moon tonight. She knew this moment would stay with her forever.

"Hi, yourself," he said and folded her into his arms. "Don't ask me to let go. I never want to let go of you, my brave wing mate."

She melted against him, her tightly gripped emotions dissolving in tears and a few gulpy sobs. She felt him chuckling quietly against her.

Pulling back, she looked up at him. "You laughing at me, dude?"

He shook his head. "No, I'm enjoying you. More than I can say."

"Good." She nestled back into his embrace.

After the flight back to Shiraz in Cessna Two, Anthony drove Kathryn back to her hotel, the top down on the Ferrari. He parked under her balcony and leaned back. "I won't be in touch tomorrow," he said. "It's the third day of your shoot, I know, and . . ." He wouldn't nag her again to be cautious, but his concern was epic. There was so much he wanted to discuss with her later about a future together.

"I'll miss you every minute," he said and grinned at how soppy he sounded. "I think you might have a few hours to sleep if you hurry."

She looked over, pensive exhaustion registering on her lovely face. "How many airstrips do you have?"

"We've had to build them," he said. "It was critical. The families of a lot of people who made it out safely funded construction and camouflage costs."

"Helping others escape," she said. "You've been doing these missions for eight months?"

"Or more," he said. "The more frequent the missions, the worse things get. The oppression, threats, the . . . *deaths*, I . . ."

"You can't do it all." She took his hand. "And if what you say is true, you're next up." She reached for him. "Oh, Anthony, get out. Fly your last group somewhere and keep going. Please."

He pulled her to him, knowing she was right, but not ready to tell her his plan yet.

She pulled back, slipping off the borrowed sneakers. "The strife here was difficult for me to grasp until tonight. My only run-ins with authorities are speeding tickets on Pacific Coast Highway." She ran a finger over his bottom lip, her gaze fixed there.

"I'm almost out, Kathryn. A few more days and I'll leave."

He read hope and strength in her expression and then fear flashed briefly. She leaned in with a quick, sexy kiss, and was gone. He remembered her at the top of the Paradise Club stairs glamorous in a shimmering gold gown and stiletto sandals. Now he watched her climb stairs to her balcony in baggy pants and stocking feet, her parcel tucked under her arm, and he smiled, thinking her allure at this moment as profound.

He pulled back onto the road for home. Tomorrow he would finish his business with the empress. But he needed to tie up loose ends before he could go. *Mirdad.*

CHAPTER TWENTY-FOUR

Mirdad stepped from the limo into a scene of chaos at the Persepolis location, where tempers were running high for Kathryn and her crew. The day was hot, the mood hotter. *Why?*

He swirled around, wary that Green Bands might have shown up, the fools, but spotted instead the armed guards in black uniforms he had ordered to protect the location perimeter. He nodded to the sergeant in charge, Demetrius Nassiri's man.

Mirdad found Kathryn looking tired but beautiful in a discussion with an agitated Iranian crew who looked mutinous. He listened to Habib, the interpreter vigorously translating her words.

"Don't worry, we're fixing the equipment. So now you must set up the next shot," Habib translated. "We're behind schedule. We must catch up. Understand?"

The clamor finally quieted.

"Okay, let's move, people!" Peter shouted. The crew dispersed to do their jobs. Kathryn headed over to greet Mirdad.

"A friendly face in the crowd, how nice," she said.

Before he could respond, Duncan scampered out from the undercarriage of the Jet Ranger, wrench in hand, splattered with oil.

Duncan cursed under his breath as Teddy crawled out behind him coated in grease. "It's a bloody fuel line all right. A damn good thing 'tis that Teddy spotted it. Eagle eye," Duncan said, glaring up at Mirdad as if he had some grasp of how to repair the line, which he didn't. Nor did he care, really.

"Can't be too difficult," Mirdad said.

"Yeah, imagine if we'd gone up in that thing?" Teddy said in a nasty tone, wiping at oil stains covering his arms and face.

Ali ran over with towels and turpentine. "We will fix it. You're not to worry."

"Go clean up, Teddy," Kathryn said. "You'll feel better."

Grumbling, he took the towels and went off.

"Dammit," Peter swore. "Me, Teddy, and Ali checked and rechecked all the equipment ourselves before we left the location last night. It was perfect."

"Bolt's missing on the camera mount, and the chopper's down," Kathryn said. "It doesn't add up, Peter. Somebody's been at them. Whatever the cause, it's all about setbacks now, one after another. We're half a day behind. I'd counted on shooting double setups today!" Kathryn turned to Mirdad. "Our shooting schedule is tight."

Even angry, she was lovely. Her gaze stayed with him, her expression softened into a smile. Mirdad held out his hand, and she took it.

"Welcome to the Whitney farrago," she said. "This morning we've managed to break the equipment, even the new helicopter. Batting a thousand in the failure league today."

Mirdad stepped closer to her. "Now, it's not all bad, Kathryn," he said. "Ali and Duncan assure me your Jet Ranger will be repaired by the time I get you back from lunch. I've arranged something special. I will not accept no for an answer."

"Lunch?" she looked at him as if he were mad. "Ridiculous! We're behind, I'm too concerned about—"

"Go on, Kat," Buzz said, "Duncan swears the chopper repairs will take a few hours at least. He and Ali don't need you hovering while they do their job, so . . ."

Kathryn grumbled but finally relented, conceding the point. She shrugged. "Okay, I get the drift." Turning to Mirdad, she said, "Looks like I'm yours, Mirdad." Her hazel eyes sparkled. "On one condition."

He didn't want conditions. The man planted on her crew had done well causing minor mischief, creating an opportunity for him to be with her. Nothing serious, time enough for a beginning since she had refused his previous invitations to lunch or dinner. He swallowed, "And what would that be?"

Moments later Mirdad had Kathryn, Teddy, Peter, and Buzz pile into his limo, and they whisked away to the old bazaar in Shiraz. He was annoyed; he hadn't counted on others being with them.

Once out of the limo, they walked a twisting, turning, maze-like alleyway into the heart of the Shiraz marketplace. Trapped sunlight splayed in uneven patterns along the winding passage. The noise of workers clanging brass and rolling open carpets while they haggled over the price of wares met the smells of tobacco, mint, and food to set the stage as Mirdad intended. He led them to a charming outdoor café where well known dignitaries and other businessmen came to eat authentic Persian food: lamb and chicken kabobs with aromatic blends of rice and herbs savoring on the grill, chicken koubideh with jasmine rice and whole grilled tomatoes, an entire onion sliced in half to munch on, and lemon wrapped in a cloth to squeeze over the meat. Fish, heads intact, nestled in a bed of cranberry rice, the grains tinted pink from the berries, with a side of pureed zucchini. Delectable, all of it.

"Unlike in other parts of the world," Mirdad explained, "one does not talk business during the noon meal." They were seated at a table, and the owner clapped his hands in the air. Servers bustled, bringing trays of hot chicken and lamb, fish, several kinds of herbed rice, and salads. Glasses of cool mint tea were set next to each of them.

He was amused when his guests kept filming during the meal, him, other café diners, waiters, and the crowds below in the bazaar. Soon he realized Kathryn had a plan, that this was not random tourist footage.

"In Iran," he said, "we hold discussions of political views, and correct responses we're expected to uphold as dictated by our Muslim faith." Mirdad added this last for the camera while they all enjoyed the meal. "The Ayatollah Khomeini, our new leader, believes religion should govern politics in every way. This is a doctrine of the Koran, and so it shall be."

Kathryn raised an eyebrow behind her camera lens.

He smiled back, knowing he had slathered the religious bit on a bit thick.

After the meal, Mirdad took the group back within the bazaar, the narrow street, flanked by masses of stalls, bustled with merchants hocking wares: fake and authentic artifacts, woven goods, brass fixtures, furniture, and some glorious carpets. Mirdad knew this bazaar well, having come here often as a boy with his Aunt Ilyia and Uncle Richard. And Anthony.

"Look at these stalls, five feet off the ground," Peter said. "It's like standing next to mini-theater stages, the entrances are up to my shoulders. You need a ladder."

"A custom in this section of the marketplace," Mirdad said. "Unwanted persons are dissuaded while serious bartering is in session."

"Hey!" Teddy said. "Ya won't catch me makin' a hasty departure with a rug under my arm. A guy could fall and break his thieving neck."

Steadily they crept deeper inside the bazaar. The filmmakers hoisted equipment, Teddy with a 16mm Arri SR, Kathryn with her Bolex, and Peter with a Nagra sound recorder and clapper to sync sound with footage. The noises of haggling merchants conducting commerce in and out of these stalls, laughter, and children playing among themselves filled the fragrant air. Smells of coriander, pepper, wool, metals, grain and fruit mingled in their nostrils as Mirdad, keenly aware of Kathryn and Teddy, concentrated on helping them get the footage for *Faces of Iran*, the documentary Kathryn still hoped to produce.

Mirdad watched children who played among themselves, spending their days in this cavernous environment.

His fingers tingled when Kathryn handed him the Bolex. "Go for it," she said.

He was exhilarated.

"Have fun." She nodded toward a crowd of onlookers who surreptitiously watched. "We want the faces of Iran, Persian culture."

Mirdad's instincts took over. He fell under the film spell, focused, and was riveted to what he was shooting. He cajoled merchants into conversation on the state of Iran, on their personal lives, continuing down the extended aisle until he felt Kathryn shudder.

She'd noticed people staring.

"I feel claustrophobic," she said.

Mirdad tried to make the experience agreeable, but it was a rare occasion for "foreign devils" to be seen in this inner market area. Men, openly leering at Kathryn, called out obscenities in Farsi.

"Your beautiful hair, the color of sunlight, it provokes them," Mirdad explained apologetically. "These peasants say it's Satan's invitation to sin and fornication."

"I thought the Shah lifted the veil and liberated women from those restrictions," she said.

"True," he said, "but our ways change slowly, and a resurgence of religious thinking is pushing us backward, not forward."

"They'd have a tough time on Malibu beach," Peter said.

Quickly, Kathryn took her cap out of her bag and tucked her hair under it. Mirdad smiled approvingly.

Buzz aimed a reflector at her and Teddy laughed. "Get behind us, woman! Ten paces!"

"Where I can kick you both in the rear?" she said as they walked ahead.

Mirdad diplomatically held out his arm and guided her in a safe direction, telling the others to meet them at the car later.

"You must know the best shops here," Kathryn said as he led her through the labyrinth of the bazaar.

"What would you like?"

"Persian miniatures. Not the ones meant for tourists. The real deal."

"A fine old one?"

"Exactly."

"I know the place."

They turned down a narrow passage to a little shop tucked under an eave away from the main bazaar. Inside the shop, Kathryn browsed among the usual tourist bait, the commercial ivories, brass, and imitation antiquities.

Mirdad explained to the frail, little man what she wanted. He nodded politely and disappeared behind a curtain.

"These miniatures are very fine, Kathryn, as you will see. I happen to know that the man is desperate to sell them, and he is not asking much. He's trying to get his family out of the country."

"Oh," she turned away. For an instant Mirdad wondered if she knew about Anthony's night flights over the Iranian border with people like this shopkeeper, but he switched his attention to the store owner, who returned with a small bundle wrapped in black cloth, setting it on the counter.

The man's hands trembled slightly and unfolded the fabric, revealing a set of three exquisitely framed ivory miniatures, each about eight by eleven inches, the detail breathtaking. Mirdad held one up to the light. "The scene here depicts pages from Firdwasi's book on paradise." Each transparent miniature was elaborately carved into the ivory and delicately tinted with muted colors.

"These are beautiful, Mirdad." She smiled at the man. "Ask him how much he'll take."

Kathryn browsed as Mirdad bargained with the man. "He'll take the equivalent of three hundred dollars, a hundred dollars each. It's an incredible bargain. They're worth far more than that. Probably about six hundred each."

"Then he deserves more. I can't take advantage of his misfortune."

"He'll be happy to get that much."

"Will he take U.S. currency?"

"Gladly."

She opened in her wallet. "I have five hundred dollars." She pulled it out, but Mirdad stopped her.

"That's too much."

"No, it's not. They're worth far more than this, but it's all I have with me. I didn't come here to cheat this man." She offered it to him, along with the remaining Rials in her bag. "And I'll take those beads, as well." She pointed to amber beads priced at twenty dollars. "I don't want to embarrass him," she whispered.

"Remind me not to go into business with you," Mirdad

said, leading her out of the shop. The little man followed, thanking her profusely and handing her a black silk tribal scarf banded with red, yellow, and blue. "*Insha Allah*," he said, bowing.

"Thank you," she said in halting Farsi.

Before making their way back to meet the others, Mirdad guided Kathryn into a small empty corner stall and ordered two Turkish coffees, rich and aromatic. Kathryn removed her baseball cap and shook out her gleaming hair, then took a sip of the dark, sweet coffee.

Mirdad couldn't pull his gaze from her. Thoughts and questions whipped around his mind, disturbing thoughts. Had she been with Anthony, let him make love to her? Did she care about him? How much did she know of him? Finally, the intensity of his desire to have Anthony out of the way jolted him, bringing him back to the moment. He reached across the table and touched her hand. "Kathryn, I want very much to spend time with you, I . . ."

She put her cup down and touched his shoulder briefly. "You're my friend, Mirdad. I value that. I mean it. True friends are rare, aren't they?" she asked. "I'm too busy for anything else now."

Mirdad felt surprise and confusion cross his face before he masked his reaction. He wanted to yell at her: "*What were you doing with Anthony? You manage enough time with that bastard!*" Instead he threw some money on the table and reinstated his diplomatic posture. "Let's go find those film rats of yours and get back to the location." Stinging disappointment tightened his features as his limo with her crew pulled up. But he wouldn't give up.

Disturbing news awaited Kathryn when Mirdad returned them to Persepolis.

"Sorry, Kathryn," Duncan shrugged. "Chopper won't be repaired before four o'clock." He looked at his feet. "Doin' the best I can."

"Don't worry, Duncan, we'll be okay."

Kathryn buried her disappointment and gathered her crew around her. No chopper, no aerial footage. If the crew moved quickly, she could get at least one shot. "Peter, call the crew together for the next setup. We'll use the dolly track."

Teddy and Buzz came over, conferring on the setup.

So while Duncan continued to mutter over his ailing bird, they got the first shot of the day. But something seemed different with her crew. They were somehow off kilter. The mutinous looks this morning, the equipment failure and . . . She glanced over their faces and wondered who the troublemaker was. Ali was the best person to ask.

She and Teddy climbed the hill overlooking the valley, unobtrusively shooting footage of the black uniformed SAVAK guards Mirdad had provided. Pete, Buzz, and Ali joined her and they struck up a somewhat stilted conversation with two of the SAVAK officers who spoke fairly good English, admiring their uniforms and emblems of half-man, half-winged creatures.

They filmed close-ups and asked questions about which province they were from, who their families were. She even organized a baseball game with everyone, including Buzz, Ali, and the Iranian crew to keep up the morale. She refused to let anything bring her down. Not the delays, the chopper, not the polite but unwelcome come-on from Mirdad, not the sweltering heat. For one brief moment she longed for her mother and female comfort. Then the moment was gone, and she thought of Anthony, his secrets, his life helping endangered families. She missed him, was blown away by the danger he faced nightly.

His life made hers feel ridiculous.

She stepped up at bat.

He faced life and death situations to help others, and her biggest concerns were how her thirty- and sixty-second spots for the U.S. Super Bowl would play. And right now they were a big concern. She'd lost a full day of shooting today. Her adrenalin shot up.

She hit Peter's fastball and ran.

Later Kathryn joined the others for dinner, a beer, and poker in Buzz's room, determined to relax and be ready for a heavy day of work tomorrow.

"I'll raise you ten," she said, looking across at Buzz, daring him to discuss the mess their shoot was in. He didn't take the bait.

"Showdown time," said Teddy.

"Yeah, Buzz, show the woman who's boss around here," Peter grinned.

"You guys are really asking for it," Kat said.

"She'll be sorry," Buzz vowed. "I call, and raise you twenty."

"Okay." Kathryn held on to her stoic expression and laid out her hand: eight, nine, ten, Jack, and Queen, all hearts, a straight flush, beating Buzz's full house of three aces and a pair of eights. "Yes!" She'd won over fifty bucks on that hand.

By ten o'clock, she clomped upstairs to her room, seventy-five bucks richer, singing the Beatles' "Yellow Submarine" to herself, her arms filled with baseball equipment from this afternoon's game. She nudged open the door to her darkened room.

The sound of someone breathing heavily in her bed made her check to see if she had the right room. She did! Gripping hold of the baseball bat she clicked on the light.

Anthony bolted off her bed, looking startled and dazed. He must've been sound asleep.

"How'd you get in here?" she said.

"Balcony," he rubbed his face.

"I thought I wouldn't see you for days . . ." She let equipment crash to the floor and lunged for him, knocking him backward onto the bed. She climbed on top and held him down. "What a nice surprise!"

"Kathryn, you're drunk!"

"Nah! I'm not drunk! I'm just happy to see you."

He flopped her over on her back and held her there. "You are pure temptation," he said. "But I've been delayed too long. Where the hell've you been?"

"Buzz's room. We played poker. I won."

"I'll bet you did." He kissed her nose and let her up. "I need a favor. Need to borrow your chopper for a few hours. Now."

"I lost a day with that chopper. Just got it fixed!"

"Kathryn, my love, I seriously need that chopper."

"That's too bad. Forget it." She shook her head. "Not unless I'm flying, *my love*." Whoops! She'd offered to fly another mission. But upon closer consideration, she found she actually wanted to. It had been well worth it. But that's not what she said. "I've had enough of your orders."

He hesitated.

"I'm firm on this." Her lips were pressed tight, unrelenting.

"You win again. Okay? But keep your mouth shut, or I won't be around anymore."

She sat up straight.

"The family we'll be flying out tonight has been in hiding for five months, switching from place to place, eluding the Black Glove. There's a newborn. His mother was ill at the end of her pregnancy, and she has since died." He swiped a hand through his dark hair. "One would have hoped my friend's wife might have been saved." Grief flashed across his face. "I guess fate had other plans." He cleared his throat. "These are personal friends, childhood friends."

"I'm so sorry, Anthony. I don't mean to hassle you, really." She straightened. "What do you need?"

"My aircraft is down east of the Tomb of Kings. I'm not cleared to fly helicopters. I need Duncan to pilot as well. Reason enough?"

She took a moment, knowing he'd balk at what she would say. "Okay, Duncan can work on your chopper, but I mean it. I'll be flying mine."

"You're nuts!"

"We could be here all night, Anthony."

"Understand this! We can easily be shot down by Iranian military. What I'm doing is illegal."

"I was there two nights ago. Have you forgotten? Besides, my chopper, my rules."

He let out an exasperated sigh. "Tonight could get rough. This is no movie set, Kathryn."

"I've flown worse," she said.

"Stubborn brat."

Duncan met them at her Jet Ranger location to check the 'copter out. He looked at Anthony long and hard. "I'll help, but I won't fly. I have a bit of night blindness to tell you the truth, sir. But the lady's not a bad pilot, sir. I reckon she's a wee bit gifted if you want the truth."

It was decided that the 'copter was good to go and that Kathryn could handle it. She flew low along the desert floor, over sweeping shadows and rolling terrain. Shrub and scrub brush bent under the rotor's force, tumbling, bouncing like toys in the sand. There was nothing else around for miles.

As it was landing past the Tomb of Kings, the lights from their chopper picked up the shadowy hulk of another helicopter with a man lying beside it. Kathryn landed nearby, and they got out. Anthony ran to the powerfully built Hans, Duncan following. He gave him fresh water, then a brandy flask.

"Hans, my partner and pilot. My friend," Anthony said.

Even flat on his back Kathryn recognized the demeanor of a U.S. Marine on the white-blond headed Swedish American. His look at her was direct, straight in the eye, and she liked him immediately.

After Kathryn met Hans, Anthony led her to a clump of rocks nearby. A somber man in a heavy pea coat stood up. The widower who had lost his wife in childbirth. His aging mother cradled a baby. A four-year-old girl ran over to Anthony and hugged him. He picked her up. "Mira, we're taking you to a new home. Come."

Leaving Hans and Duncan there to attempt the repairs on Anthony's chopper, they climbed into the Jet Ranger, and Kathryn took over, swinging them out into the darkness over the desert. Beside her Anthony looked over maps with a pin light.

"I've got a new route for us," he cautioned.

The father sat behind them, comforting his ailing mother, the sleeping baby cradled on her lap. Four-year-old Mira sat beside her, restless.

The belly of the chopper grew bitterly cold during the long flight. Anthony lifted Mira onto his lap and wrapped her in a blanket.

He gestured to the man behind, gently reassuring, making faces that had the man smiling, then looked at Kathryn, his eyes a mixture of warmth and sadness. His country was disintegrating more each day.

"We're close to Abadan air base," he said. "Keep a look out." Anthony shifted the now sleeping child. "If we're going to have trouble, this'll be the spot."

They flew as low as possible to avoid detection, and thinking they were clear, Anthony handed the child back to her father.

"We've been spotted. Military choppers, coming in from the south."

"Got it," Kathryn said. "We'll leave these guys in our trail." She veered north, gaining altitude quickly.

"Abadan's a training base," Anthony said. "They're probably running on one cylinder." He hefted an M-16 rifle. "They haven't received parts in months," he said over the headset.

Kathryn grimaced, wondering if that were true, shivering but alert, understanding this challenge for the second time. She knew what to do.

She veered off, nose down, hot-dogging it out of the tailing aircraft's sight.

The Iranian choppers followed like angry hornets. But her determination was locked in, and her skill took over, gauging her altitude and the need to avoid attracting more enemy aircraft. A bit terrified by her own maneuvers, her stomach lurching, Kathryn dove through a desert fog bank, rotors whipping the mist, and kept low, her sense of purpose keen.

Checking coordinates, she changed course and swept out over the sea, avoiding tricky wind currents too dangerous to navigate. Her attention strictly on flying, she tuned out the passengers' distress, checking her instrument panel, listening only to her instincts and Anthony's voice on the headset as he interpreted Farsi radio control.

At last she had lost their pursuers, but was way off course for the rendezvous point Anthony insisted was crucial.

"We can't circle back now," he said. "So follow the coastline south for three miles. I'll guide you."

It took only seven minutes to make their rendezvous. She landed in a sandy terrain and took off her headset. Sounds of whimpering passengers filled the cabin.

Across the desert terrain Tabriz and his tribesmen appeared from the shadows. Kathryn recognized them from Takht-e Tavoos, a night she would never forget. She saluted him from the cockpit, and Tabriz nodded back, quickly taking charge of the shaking Iranian family.

Tabriz, his men, and the family disappeared back into shadow, en route to a safe haven, Kathryn hoped with all her heart. This mission's risks were daunting. She hadn't considered the more sinister aspects, such as being charged with treason against Islam, or being shot by a firing squad as a spy. But she agreed with Anthony. Sitting by complacently was out of the question. No question, her mother was right. Her daredevil tendencies were scary. She had assimilated all Anthony had said last night; Iran was a dangerous place where life was fragile. She'd had another close-up view and was choked with concern for the people here. Could she help others before she left Iran?

By the time they returned to the place where Anthony's helicopter was being repaired, Duncan had finished fixing Hans' chopper. Duncan refused payment for his work.

"I'm happy to fix 'er up for you," he said, "but don't ask me to fly missions, your lordship."

Kathryn smiled to herself. She'd flown well, as well as Duncan on any given day. Even with all the risks, she would fly again in an instant.

Never had she guessed what this trip would bring her.

"I'm proud of you," Anthony whispered.

"Proud of you, too," Kathryn whispered back. "You got your way." She kissed him passionately and headed back to the hotel with Duncan.

She ignored the hint of dawn breaking when she finally fell into bed, an hour and a half before her wake-up call.

CHAPTER TWENTY-FIVE

On the fourth day of her shoot, Kathryn breathed a relieved sigh. Her luck changed on set. They were back to work and everything was moving forward smoothly.

Duncan and Teddy lifted off and rehearsed their chopper moves for the day's first shot.

Kathryn and Buzz, with Habib's help, directed the Iranian crew, laying out the path for the dolly track. Working feverishly, everyone helped to make up for the delays. Ali, the clown, kept their mood up by juggling oranges near the props truck. A group of children surrounded him, laughing at his antics.

She checked the track position. "We're good," she told Buzz. "Ready to move." They high-fived.

Mr. Kasadi, curator of the little museum next to the Palace of Darius, rushed up to Kathryn. "I am so sorry, so sorry, madame."

"What is it?" Kathryn dreaded his answer.

"There's a misunderstanding, you must go!" He panted, trying to catch his breath. "Soldiers, they're on their way here! I want no trouble!"

"Soldiers? What soldiers? You mean our armed guards?" But she looked around, realizing there were no armed guards, not today.

"Militia, Khomeini militia, the revolutionary Green Bands, rebels. You must go!"

"Go!" she said. "Go where?" Was he nuts? But she was getting the picture. Memories of Takht-e Tavoos screamed in her brain. Shots, fire, young faces distorted with hate, visions of it all surged before her. "I need to use your phone, sir. Now!" she headed for the small museum office.

"I was afraid this would happen." The curator followed on her heels. "Please, understand." He rushed ahead, shooing her away with nervous gestures.

"Green Band, barbarians, they hate Americans, not like most Iranians, you understand. Extremists, happy to destroy what's left of Persepolis." He spoke so fast spittle sprayed his chin.

"Buzz," she yelled over her shoulder, "talk to this guy. We have to reach Mirdad." Kathryn ran for the curator's office.

Mr. Kasadi wiped at his brow, following. "Priceless art relics, surviving for centuries, but they would destroy them all." He shielded his desk form her. "You must go!"

Controlling her anger, she said, "I need your phone—now."

The little man sweated. He kept switching from English to Farsi.

She sent one of the Iranian crew to bring Ali.

Ali came through the door and tried to calm the ruffled curator. They spoke in rapid Farsi. Ali looked frightened. "He says the Green Bands are soon here. We have to leave— immediately."

"Please, Madame Whitney," Mr. Kasadi implored.

"We'll see about that. Your ministry will object." She dialed Mirdad. Busy. She dialed again.

Mirdad slammed down his office phone and paced wildly in front of his desk. He flung his arm wide, flipping papers to the floor, kicking at them, picturing Anthony's head. The slime was missing. Once again nobody knew where he was.

Mirdad's gaze flew to the window, out to the city street choked with traffic in dull morning haze, heat already rising from the black top. Yesterday he had been with Kathryn's crew, and all he could get out of Ali was that Anthony had gone off on business to Rome. *Rome?* But he had returned that evening. Where was Anthony now?

For two nights Mirdad had been at Madame Shala's thinking, *tonight Anthony will die.* But he had evaded sharpshooters two nights running. How? Now the morons had lost him again. He was only one man and still somewhere in Iran or Mirdad's office would've been alerted by customs officials. Praise Allah, every exit route was covered.

Mirdad slumped into his chair, wishing to break everything in sight, his fury growing, getting the better of him.

His mother had called, wanting to hear that Anthony was dead.

"These things take time," he had told her.

"You've had enough time. Do it!" She ranted at his incompetence. He bent his head forward, bracing his brow with shaking fingers, craving shelter from her demands. He could not face another of her calls. He had jumped again and again to please her and failed.

The phone jangled. Mirdad jumped back as if it were a tarantula.

"Ajani here," he said reluctantly, but the voice on the other end pleased his spirit. "Kathryn. What?" He leapt up. "Outrageous! Where's Kasadi? They've made a mistake. I'll handle this," he hung up the phone, bolting out of his office.

Kathryn's eyes widened on seeing an open truck filled with soldiers speeding up the road toward them. Instinctively she grabbed Teddy's Arriflex sixteen SR and focused the long lens, filming. Even from a distance Kathryn could see rifles held by men with stern faces.

They screeched to a halt. Soldiers jumped out, pointing guns directly at her and her crew, shouting in Farsi.

Anxiety shot through her as she put the camera down just so on her folding chair.

Very deliberately, an officer got out of the passenger's side and came toward her. The way he glared made her skin crawl.

"I am Captain Nubriand," he said in English. "You're here illegally. You've no right to use our heritage for your Satan country's worship of money. You commit grave sins against Allah."

One side of the man's face was disfigured, a war wound she guessed. He had a terrifying glower, but as usual when officials got in her face, anger rose.

He moved closer. "For this you and your men will suffer consequences."

Kathryn had never heard such bullshit, but before she could open her mouth Buzz put his hand out.

"I understand your concern, Captain," he said calmly, "However, we do have permission from your government to be here."

"Give me your papers."

Peter pulled the documents from his briefcase.

The captain continued to leer at Kathryn like the men in the marketplace had. She grew increasingly prickly under his scrutiny. He stepped up to her, pressing his marred face close to hers, his voice low and deliberate.

"Foreign harlot, you can be stoned in the street for temptation of my men. I should let them all take you right here, slut."

"Wait a fucking minute, slime bag, you're out of line!" Buzz shouted. "Back your filthy ass . . ." Kathryn grabbed Buzz's arm but too late.

Nubriand clutched his gun, shoving it hard against Buzz's temple. An evil grin spread across his face. "You think so, American?"

Buzz wobbled, dropping his gaze, clutching his bloody head.

A gleam of sadistic pleasure flashed in Nubriand's eyes. Then he caught Kathryn staring at his scars. "Shall he be the first to die, golden bitch?" he goaded.

The other soldiers laughed, holding back Peter and Teddy.

"Or shall I let him watch what I do to you first?"

Unable to tear her eyes away from the gun barrel pressed to Buzz's head, Kathryn's fear rose like a cresting tidal wave. The expression on Buzz's ashen face ripped her apart. She barely noticed the sleek black limousine slamming to a dead stop next to the truck.

The door flew open, and Mirdad in an elegant suit leaped out. "What is the meaning of this?" he roared, coming face to face with the officer. "No need for violence is there, Captain?" Mirdad's features hardened, steel over that smooth skin. "Allow me to straighten this matter out for you," he said.

Nubriand's face darkened with fury looking at Mirdad. His constrained voice enunciated, "I have my orders, Minister. You're not needed here. Go!"

Mirdad sighed. "I understand you have orders, Captain, but perhaps we'd better discuss them. Join me in the curator's office—please."

Nubriand stood his ground. Kathryn saw he was not about to give in.

"There is something you should know, Captain Nubriand, so if you'll be so kind as to come with me? Or I can call your superior, Colonel Nassiri, if you'd rather?"

Jaw clenched, Nubriand yelled for his sergeant, a young, gleaming-eyed zealot, to take over and his men to stand down. He begrudgingly followed Mirdad into the office, outmaneuvered.

Anger and frustration overrode fear, and tears filled Kathryn's eyes, stinging her cheeks, emotions whipping inside her. Nothing was worth shoving people near this kind of danger. *I've done this. Brett was right, my God.* Her brain flooded with self-doubt. *She had been wrong all along. Brett had only been protective, not suppressive. Why hadn't she seen the danger?*

Well, she did now. She choked back sobs, fighting for composure. She was not going to cow under to this dog. She edged closer to Buzz. Peter and Teddy and Duncan scooted closer, forced to sit in the dirt.

"That rotten sonofabitch," she muttered under her breath.

"Neanderthal," Peter said. "Where's his goddamn club?"

Buzz chuckled in spite of himself.

"Silence!" the young sergeant yelled. "No speak!"

Kathryn put her arm around Buzz and his slipped around her waist and held on. They stood looking at the automatic weapons pointed at them. She felt Buzz shake.

The afternoon heat was stifling in the small museum office when Mirdad entered. He had to put a stop to the intimidation. This had gone too far.

Cowering at his desk, a terrified Mr. Kasadi quickly jumped to his feet upon seeing Mirdad and the captain. Mirdad held out his hand to the frightened man, who took it in a weak gesture, smiling obsequiously.

"Deputy Minister, it is an honor to have you in my humble office. Welcome, and you too, Captain."

"If you could be so kind, Mr. Kasadi, to lend us your office for a few moments, sir." Mirdad spoke gently and ushered Kasadi out the door.

He then turned to the captain and looked into his steely, dark eyes, repulsed by the lust he had seen on his damaged face, wanting to crush the man's skull with his bare hands. He looked away, suppressing the feeling. Who could know what the peasant bastard was capable of?

"Excellent. Captain Nubriand, I see you're punctual as always. I commend you for that. However . . ." he circled the captain. "Were you not told to be prudent? Well, weren't you?"

"Yes, Excellency, but I thought . . ."

"You thought putting a gun to the American's head was prudent, is that it?" His temper threatened. Slowly he continued circling the soldier, smelling his reeking camel's breath.

"Certainly not, Excellency," Nubriand said. "Perhaps I did go too far, but . . ."

"But nothing! And where could you've gone from that point? You would've killed that man. Your orders were to disrupt this production, not to create an international incident. Understand?"

The captain bowed his head in agreement, but Mirdad wasn't fooled. He saw the white knuckled fists Nubriand clenched at his sides. He could never turn his back with this one. "Very well, you and your men may leave." Mirdad's smile was cold. "Don't worry, Captain, you'll get your chance to curb foreign devils soon enough. Now, here is what I want of you . . ."

Aghast at this horrible turn of events, Kathryn surveyed her somber crew. Guilt overwhelmed her. She had put them in this place by denying to herself and everyone else the escalating violence in Iran, even out here so far into the countryside. She had flown strangers to safety but not her own crew. Time to get them all the hell out of danger. She thought again of Brett's warnings.

Peter, Teddy, and Duncan huddled together on the ground; their facial expressions ranging from helpless indignation to suppressed fury. Soldiers stood over them, weapons drawn. Ali hung close to the Iranian crew, who spoke quietly among themselves. For a fleeting moment Kathryn thought of Anthony and swallowed her yearning.

The captain came out of the office, a hard look on his odious face. He yelled to his men. They lifted their rifles, whining and snarling like the mad dogs they were, then piled into the truck as it turned around, sending up dirt as it tore back down the dusty road.

Kathryn and Buzz turned their backs to the dirt cloud and exhaled sharply.

"Damn. I haven't felt that kind of fear since Korea," Buzz said. "Swore never to face combat again in my life, but guess I was wrong." He looked shaken down to his shoelaces.

"You okay, Buzz?" Teddy, the worrier, got Buzz to sit in one of the folding chairs.

"Hey, I dare you to think with the cold steel of a 9mm Beretta next to your brain. I'm still in shock. Hell! Maybe I'm dead."

Kathryn watched Mirdad come from the office, blotting his brow with a linen handkerchief, all the while consoling the little curator, appearing to give the man back some of his stripped dignity.

Another side of Mirdad had surfaced from under his diplomatic stance: relaxed, in charge. He had saved their lives. Approaching Kathryn, his eyes met hers with a reassuring smile.

Dust settled around Kathryn at Persepolis with the departure of the Green Bands. A breeze chilled her face, plastered with sweat-dampened strands of hair. She shuddered, regaining equilibrium against the surreal and horrible encounter. She had figured out what she must do. Now she had to make it happen.

"They'll not bother you again. They're gone," Mirdad said. "I'm so sorry you had to endure this, but it's over." He took her hand. "Please feel better." He turned to Buzz. "And what about you, my friend? Are you all right?"

"Yeah, I'm okay, thanks to you. But what the hell is going on, Mirdad? Those guys are monsters."

"Come." Mirdad motioned to the limo, Anthony's limo. "Perhaps we should talk."

Kathryn dropped into the deep seat drained but thinking. She breathed deeply, looking into Mirdad's smiling eyes and seeing comfort, comfort she needed.

"Those Green Bands are not from our government. Those hotheads are anti-Shah and vehemently anti-U.S. But don't worry, you're safe now."

"You could've had an international incident on your hands, ya know?" Buzz said, the color returning to his face. "Your government has to control terrorists."

"Believe me, I agree."

"Okay." Buzz threw his hands up. "I'm sure you know your stuff, Mirdad."

Kathryn tried for a smile. "We're grateful, Mirdad."

"Let's push this incident aside." His smile warmed her. "Oh, I almost forgot," Mirdad said, handing her the morning's English-language newspaper from Tehran. "You see, we do honor our visiting celebrities."

She accepted the paper and, along with Buzz, scanned several photos of themselves on their first day's shoot, which to Kathryn seemed an eternity ago. Another photo, however, leaped off the page at her—a photo of Anthony with a raving dark-haired beauty. The copy read:

"Sir Anthony Evans, one of the Shah's top advisors, attended the annual 'Night of 1000 Stars Ball' with his constant companion, Miss Alexandria Badiyi. Rumors of impending wedding circulate."

Kathryn's focus riveted on the photo of Anthony and this gorgeous creature, so much like that of the portrait of his mother in his home. She felt blood drain from her face. "This can't be true."

"What the hell?" Buzz took the paper from. "Kathryn," he said sympathetically, "take a deep breath."

She managed a slow intake of air, her eyes meeting his.

Mirdad took her hand. "I thought you knew."

It's you who doesn't know, Mirdad, she thought. She remembered every minute spent with Anthony and everything they had shared. The missions they flew, the way they played, made love. Anthony had given her that beautiful brooch, a family heirloom. "*Don't ever return my gifts! Can't you see I love you?*" No, it was a mistake. She didn't believe this stupid article.

"Anthony's betrothal arrangement with Miss Badiyi has never been secret," Mirdad said gently.

Betrothal? Kathryn's already shaky spirit plummeted like a skyscraper elevator, plunging out of control to her soul's basement. Shivers ran through her, then a wave of heat burned her cheeks and as quickly left her cold. First, Brett's demands, and today those stupid soldiers had stopped her shoot and threatened her life and now, Anthony had betrayed her. Something inside her slammed shut. The last nail. Never again would she let a man get the best of her. She looked out the window, the winged lion basking bright in sunlight. This was what had brought her here and she knew what she had to do. A plan formulated.

"Buzz, get Samuelsson in London on the phone before they close. Here's what we need . . ."

Still clutching the Tehran café newspaper, Kathryn, overwhelmed by the devastating news, shoved the limo door open, escaping back to work.

"Please wait," Mirdad's voice, low and calm, pleaded. He handed Kathryn an invitation to a party for the following night in Tehran at the Marble Palace, honoring his mother's marriage to General Omar Houdin. "Please come," he said. "My mother will be intrigued by you."

Numb, eviscerated, Kathryn gazed blankly at the invitation and looked over at Mirdad's beaming face. She remembered his kindness. So she lied. "It'll be a pleasure, Mirdad."

She stepped out of the limo and took a deep breath, shielding her eyes from slanting sunrays as the car disappeared down the road to Shiraz. Already the morning was gone. Frowning, Ali waited for her. His gaze didn't disguise the compassion she saw there, as if there was more to say, but he wouldn't. "It'll be okay, Ali. Go ahead and rally the crew."

Peter ran up, his face still pale, his brows pinched. "You all right, Kat?"

"I'm fine." Fine wasn't exactly what she was, more like furious, fuming . . . and motivated. She stuffed the newspaper article into Peter's hand. He glanced at the page and did a double take.

"What the fuck?" He scrutinized her face. "He fooled me, too."

"Forget it," she said. "The light's still good, so let's get our dolly shot." Work was Kathryn's solace, quelling her whimpering heart.

"Good call," Peter nodded. "Crew's ready, all that pent up aggression. We film types bristle at terrorists."

"Especially with assault rifles aimed at your head."

"Yeah. Hate that." Peter shuddered and jogged across back to the crew.

Buzz sauntered up from Kasadi's office, his nod certain. "Samuelson's scored for us. We're in early. British Museum agreed, too." A faint smile bent his stern lips as they followed Peter over to the ruins. "The agency bought it. We're in." He snickered. "Wally sends his regards."

She stopped. "Our footage better be as great as we think it is."

He flicked dirt off his windbreaker. "Finish it, 'cause I'm not stickin' around here after today. Get what you need now. Tomorrow, we head for London." Buzz leaned into her. "Way I see it, the challenge is getting out of Iran in one piece."

Kathryn ignored Buzz's ominous statement for the most part. The clench in her stomach, the arrhythmic thud of her heart, was stamped to submission. She dashed up the stone stairs to her crew to finish what she'd come here to do.

She glanced over her crew's stricken faces, their sagging posture. Everyone on set needed a mood change. With Ali and Peter's help, she fired them up, out of their dazed sensibilities and got them to finish the wide-angled approach shot, gliding on dolly track through the palace interior.

"They're pros," Buzz puffed out. "They didn't miss a beat, got right back into it, every one of them."

"We're done here," Kathryn said, reviewing footage on the monitor. They high-fived.

After the day's wrap by late afternoon, her exhausted film group packed it in and headed back to the Hotel Persepolis. Kathryn, tired beyond measure, needed to pull herself together. Her insides felt seared, a visceral pain that, if she could rip it from her body, she would. She held fast to work, but the day was over, and soon she would face an endless night. Even reading it in print was hard to accept: "His constant companion . . . wedding plans . . ."

God, she ached. What a fool she'd been.

The temperature had plunged. She threw on her suede jacket and descended the stairs off the balcony of her room, headed toward the ruins, thinking about today's debacle with the Green Bands. Could tomorrow be a repeat if they went for the last chopper at first light? After today's trauma, she would put the decision to a vote.

The late rays of the sun were harsh. She smacked her baseball cap on her head and ran, needing to wipe out a deepening sense of failure and her disappointing attempt to reach Mr. Evans. A chilling wind whipped under her jacket and made it difficult to keep her hair tucked under the baseball cap. She tightened it again and circled around to the side of the ruins, to the spot where Anthony had taken photographs of her first moments at Persepolis.

She stopped to look up at the gigantic stone lion and felt this was the place where Anthony must have stood. Incredible timing had brought him into her life in such an intimate way. *But then, betrayal.*

Shadows deepened around the tall stone structure. She leaned against a heavy boulder, looking out into encroaching dusk. Time to go back. Exhausted and cold, she jogged back, gazing down at the dark earth, the tiny rocks, and little green and yellow plants on the desert floor.

Through the stillness, she heard a truck start up behind the last ridge about a hundred yards away. She recognized the sound.

She ran for her life.

Shouts rang in her ears. The truck drew alongside her. Soldiers shouted in Farsi, but there was no doubting their intent. She veered away from grasping arms; her hat flew off, and her hair tumbled free. The truck screeched to a halt and men jumped out, chasing her on foot.

Terrified, Kathryn ran. Her hair blew in her face.

She stumbled.

From nowhere, a rough hand caught her.

She screamed and was thrown to the ground, the wind knocked out of her. She fought against him, gasping, struggling to get up, but he was on top of her, the captain with the horribly wounded face. He shoved her down again on her back and ripped open her jacket and blouse in one tear.

"Get off me!" she yelled. "Stop!"

His eyes were filled with lust. He grabbed her bra. It held, digging into her back.

No! No! No! In a flash, her fear turned to rage. She rammed her knee into his groin.

He reeled back in agony, howling, his oncoming successors right behind him.

She grabbed a fist full of sand and flung it in the next man's face, blinding him long enough for her to leap up. She zigged around boulders, putting them in the truck's path, and zagged around juniper, snagging her skin, dust in her nose and mouth. The smell of the soldier still with her, she struggled for breath, barely eluding the truckload of jeering men, searching for a way out. Any second, they would be on her like locusts. She ran harder than ever before in her life.

Far away, she saw a Jeep flying across the desert toward her, honking in a pattern—Ali. The soldiers ignored him; they were all out of the truck now, six of them, coming at her, laughing, screaming wildly, reaching for her. Two of them stopped and exposed their engorged organs, waving them at her.

The captain bolted forward, shouting in English, "You beg for it, slut! We'll give it to you! Foreign bitch." He caught up to her and grabbed her hair, tugging her to the ground. "I'll be first to fill your golden pussy!" He reeled her into him and slapped her hard. "Then you kneel. Suck me in your pink mouth."

"Stop!" she yelled. "Disgusting pig!" Her teeth found his ear. She bit down hard into his salty flesh and tasted blood.

He yowled but let go.

She scampered up spitting, making a run for the Jeep. Ali aimed a rifle and fired.

She heard the captain scream behind her, and she picked up speed.

Ali fired again.

She didn't look back, she kept running, hearing the outraged shouts of the soldiers, cursing and wailing in Farsi, as they scrambled back into their truck.

Gunfire blasted around her, the dust kicked up, obscuring her view. A bullet whizzed past her ankle, exploding into the ground. *Just a few more yards.*

The Jeep pounded toward her, screeching up beside her, dirt flying. She clambered partway in. Ali pulled her the rest of the way. She clung to the side of the Jeep as Ali pushed to gain distance from the soldier, hunting for an escape route. He drove farther from the road and safety, desperate to outrun them. The Jeep rushed on in a drunken path, dodging a barrage of bullets ricocheting off the metal body, the noise deafening, the soldiers' aim improving, until Ali cried out. Ali had been shot.

His right arm dropped to his side. Pain distorted his face. "Ali!"

"I'm all right. It's my arm," he croaked.

Kathryn steadied herself. "I'm taking over!"

He looked at her, astonished.

"Slip under me—now! Keep your foot on the gas until I'm over."

In a mad maneuver, they switched positions.

Ali, probably more afraid of her driving than the soldiers, pressed his wound and held on.

Kathryn gripped the wheel, a sense of power replacing her fear. How many times had she vented anger and frustration behind the wheel at raceways, Laguna Secca or Willow Springs?

"Let's show the bastards!" Kathryn yelled, boosting her courage.

Ahead she saw the road she'd climbed with Anthony on horseback to view the king's burial grounds and valley below. She had to get there.

Dodging bullets, she crouched over the wheel and veered left, up the hill in a sharp turn, gaining distance. The Jeep climbed. It wasn't a Porsche but she was in control, not like she had been on the horse with Anthony. A horse had a mind, but a machine would obey hers.

"Let's see what this old crate can do!" she shouted over the roar of the engine. The oncoming turn loomed in front of her. She swept wide and kept to the outside edge, clipping the curve's apex.

They skidded a little too near the edge. The Jeep recovered but engulfed them in a cloud of gravel and dirt, sending back a dark plume, helping them escape the marksman's aim.

Kathryn glanced in the rear view mirror. The more powerful truck was gaining on them. The incline grew steeper, the Valley of Tombs spread out below in failing light.

"They're too close," Ali coughed.

Ferocious jeers and curses broke through the dust. Her solar plexus clenched against images of what they would do to Ali and her if they caught them.

The road grew difficult to see but she didn't dare turn on her lights. She counted on honed instinct to light the trail.

"*Inshah Allah, Allu Akbar,*" Ali prayed, slumped next to her, blood dripping down his arm.

She threw in the clutch and downshifted for a speedier climb, willing the car to reach the spot she wanted. Dimly in the distance, it came into view, a jutting chin of rock, a hairpin turn with a sheer outside drop of several thousand feet to the valley floor below.

She leaned on the horn and raised a fist, challenging her pursuers further. She felt their electric venom and gripped the wheel at ten o'clock, stretching to the rim's outer edge. Ali swiveled around, shouting in Farsi. A barrage of stones and dust pelted the Jeep, bullets ricocheting off metal, wheels almost over the edge.

The truck followed. She braked lightly to further goad them.

On they came.

The sun shrank from sight, deserting her with only a hint of sunset glow. Here it was, the horseshoe at the rim of the world. She could barely see anything. Her timing had better be perfect or they'd be dead. "Pray harder, Ali."

"*Inshah Allah, Allu Akbar . . .*"

Headlights came on behind them, overly bright.

She floored the Jeep into the turn, her arms outstretched on the wheel, gripping tightly, counting the distance, pressing to the apex, her foot pushed against the floorboard, clipping her movements right to the edge.

Time to slice it.

She leaned hard to the right, cutting away from the cliff, away from the straight-drop, straining out of the turn, fishtailing back onto the road, tucking the Jeep close along the mountain and slowing to a stop.

Ali sat upright.

They were alive, panting, covered in dust.

She clung to the wheel, trembling. And like a dream in slow motion, they heard it happen. Skidding, the guardrail snapping, angry shouts morphing into terrified wails as the truck plunged over the cliff, deep into the gorge.

An explosion resonated up through the canyon.

Flames and smoke plumed from the valley floor.

Kathryn inched the Jeep around on the narrow road and turned off the engine.

She sat shaking until the awful sounds of destruction died down and she could climb out.

Ali got out of the Jeep, too, holding his arm.

Darkness descended but the grim, glowing flames, smoke and wreckage flickered far below in the canyon. Kathryn shuddered and turned away. A crisp breeze chilled her skin. Dusky shrubs, barely discernable, swayed against the dim mountain, oblivious to the carnage below. She let the tranquility of it encompass her, and she was filled with gratitude. They were alive. Ali leaned into her, still praying and shaking.

The night air chilled her skin. She looked down at her sheer bra and blushed. Ali went to the Jeep and dug in the back seat, tossing her a work vest. She shrugged into it and tore off the hem of her blouse, wrapping his wound in a swath of blue chambray.

A waning moon blinked into sight, tilted as if shrinking from the view. She remembered happiness here, a few days before. She had basked in moonlight and fallen in love with a man she shouldn't have let get close. Shivering against those emotions, she climbed back into the Jeep, Ali getting into the seat next to her.

Ali touched her hand, a thin smile on his lips.

"*Allah Akbar*," he whispered. "God is mighty."

"Yes," she said, "God is great." She started the engine.

Kathryn, Buzz, Peter, Teddy, and Duncan met that night in Buzz's suite. No prying eyes or ears. Ali had gone off to deal with authorities regarding the soldiers' truck accident. Peter, Buzz, and Teddy hovered around Kathryn, as if not sure how to comfort her. She had called Wally. He was fuming. "Get your asses out of that powder keg, NOW."

She may not have mentioned that to the guys yet.

They had all bathed and were hanging out in sweats; the room service meal had been hauled away. Duncan handed her a cup of tea he'd brewed. They sat around a stone coffee table on carved mahogany sofas and chairs upholstered in deep blue linen, not the kind one could sink into for a good read. It was meant for business meetings, and that's what they were having.

Buzz said. "Geez, kiddo, sure you can cope after what those gorillas tried?" He shook his head. "Hell, I'm shaking, and I wasn't even there."

She sipped her tea and faced Peter's questioning look.

He said, "You better think hard about doing the last chopper shot, Kat."

"We need it. One pass. We'll be gone, on our way back to Tehran before the Komiteh blinks," she glanced at each of them, her team.

"Most of the equipment is already loaded on the trucks, ready to move out," Peter said.

"We can grab what we need for a last go," Teddy said.

"We should have enough to cover with pickup shots in the British Museum," Buzz added.

The concerned looks around Buzz's table almost undid her. She was on an emotional edge, refusing to give in. "I say yes. We go at first light."

By 3:00 A.M. they'd struck a solid decision to go ahead.

By 5:00 A.M. the sound of whirring Jet Ranger propeller blades warming up at the Persepolis site snapped Kathryn out of her funk. Buzz parked the Jeep while she checked her notes. She hadn't been up for driving today. She zipped up her UCLA hoodie, focusing on the Ranger. "Let's go." They hopped out to view the last Boeing shot in Iran. Buzz flipped on the video monitor, his cheeks flushed with the same visceral excitement she felt. At that moment, Duncan soared off, getting in position for the approach.

The chopper came in at a perfect angle with Teddy and the Ari harnessed on the side, his legs dangling. The day was clear with no interfering wind. The Jet Ranger swept smoothly toward the palace, as if slipping on ice.

Gunshots blasted out of nowhere, explosive, fracturing the moment. Everyone ducked for cover behind trucks, boulders, and the monitor podium.

"What the hell? That's an RPG firing." Buzz flashed her a confounded look.

"They're firing on our aircraft!" Kathryn yelled, her gaze locked on the chopper.

Smoked billowed from the Jet Ranger's engine.

"They can't see!" Kathryn screamed and ran.

"Some asshole hit our Ranger!" Peter yelled, running beside her across the plain from the ruins, scanning upward. The rotors whined, the smoking engine sputtered, the chopper teetered and wobbled.

"No!" she yelled, as if her insides were erupting.

"Teddy! Oh, God!" Peter shielded his eyes. "I can't tell what's happening." They both strained to assess the damage.

The chopper descended rapidly. Teddy strapped with the camera mount, clung to the open doorway. "He's scared to death!" she said. It was a long way down, some eighty feet, at least.

The smoke dissipated, and through the windshield they watched Duncan frantically combating to land the aircraft. Buzz squinted toward the $750,000 machine, coughing, spurting, and awkwardly tumbling from the sky.

The chopper hesitated then crunched down, skittering over rough terrain, metal screeching. The body lifted, teetering, as the blades hacked the ground, dust and gravel diffusing the tableau. Kathryn heard the Ranger crunch against a boulder and watched as the Ari, dislodged from its mount, went sailing into the brush. The chopper flopped over on its side, the rotor's whine slowing.

Peter, Buzz, and Kathryn ran like hell to get to them.

"Duncan, Teddy!" she yelled, her stomach clenching.

Duncan flipped off the power and slumped forward, panting.

Teddy struggled to unbuckle his harness; his hands shook, and he was drenched in sweat. Blood seeped from a gash over his eye.

"Quick!" Kathryn said, and Peter yanked the harness off, dragging Teddy away.

Ali shouted toward the hills, "You crazy bunch!" and ran to retrieve the camera.

Buzz yelled to Kathryn, "Let's get 'em out of here before she blows." Together they untangled her pilot. Visions of racetrack flames bombarded Kathryn's brain. She sucked in air and coughed as they dragged Duncan away from the chopper.

From the equipment truck her Iranian crew grabbed fire extinguishers, dousing the chopper.

Duncan clutched his shoulder, trembling. His skill had managed to keep himself and Teddy alive through the crash.

"Who the hell fired on you?" Buzz asked, fists clenched.

"More o' those terrorists from yesterday." He leaned on Buzz. "Holy Christ, they almost killed us."

"We need to get you to a doctor," Kathryn said. Her gaze darted to Buzz's gray face. "Now."

Buzz got Duncan into the Jeep.

Peter helped Teddy then hopped in and started her up.

"Some job that deputy minister did on 'em," Duncan said. "Son of a virgin! Will ye look at the bird? What a mess." Slipping a handkerchief out of his pocket, his hand shook as he removed his cap and tried to mop his brow.

"Come on, let's get you out of here." Kathryn took the cloth from him and wiped his dripping face.

Duncan steadied himself and swiveled toward the smoking bird. "So sorry, Miss," he slurred and collapsed.

"Peter, you and Teddy get him to Shiraz hospital. And take care of Teddy's cut. I'll join you after I secure things here."

"Go now," Buzz said. "Before those fanatics start shooting again."

Peter peeled out.

Ali hurried, lugging the battered Ari over to the truck.

She and Buzz looked at each other, silently speculating on film damage. Crap. Had all this been for nothing? They'd find out in Tehran.

The Iranian crew disengaged the mount and gear, muttering uneasily to themselves. They shoved equipment into the trucks and took off, back to Tehran—a five-hour drive.

Ali waved sadly. He would meet up with them at the equipment rental house later.

Overlooked lamp-stands, silk diffusers, and lights scattered the area.

"Leave that stuff," Kathryn shouted. "Someone will come back for it. Buzz, let's grab everyone else."

Ali said, "I'll leave men down at the museum to guard the chopper until we can make arrangements for it."

"This has gone too far. I'm going to try to reach Anthony." *Even though I don't want to.*

Buzz looked at her. "What the hell can *he* do?"

"Stop these men from killing us. The crew is terrified, an expensive chopper ruined." Kathryn headed to Mr. Kasadi's office. Her muscles tensed, her head throbbed, but she was not backing out of Iran without facing Anthony with his BS. She got through to Nina, his secretary.

"He's not available, Ms. Whitney. I'm sorry."

"But it's an emergency."

"If I could help you I would," the kind voice said. "He simply can't be reached at this time." Polite, but no Anthony. She hung up and walked outside.

Buzz took her arm. "Forget him. Let's book it outta here." *Yes, our flight to Tehran.*

CHAPTER TWENTY-SIX

RAMSAR, IRAN

Anthony stood back from the beautiful people on the Summer Palace lawn, catching his breath, shifting the photo portfolio in his hand. The churning of Hans' chopper rotors faded behind him with images of his last two-day mission. Seventeen children ferried from Iran into Kuwait to begin new lives. *New lives without their murdered parents.*

His thoughts raced forward with the crucial logistics the empress needed to approve before his weekend departure from Iran.

Avoiding usual social formalities required at a festive afternoon picnic, he chose a familiar path to the right of the rose garden and skirted the blue and white striped marquee shading the diners lunching on squab, pheasant, foie gras, and other trademarks of Pahlavi hospitality. He smoothed back his hair, adjusted his shirt-cuffs and nodded to the SAVAK palace guards. He had not told anyone from his office about this palace visit.

Oriana, the empress's personal assistant, greeted him inside the foyer to her royal offices, took his portfolio in hand and stepped into the private office.

"Don't be long, Anthony. I must return her to her guests."

"Of course," he said, "I'll be as quick as possible."

"Will you stay for lunch? The ladies adore you. We all do," she said, her kind eyes glinting.

"Another time, thank you." He nodded and entered the empress's private suite, the door clicking behind him.

Across the room, Farah Diba gazed through half-open French doors onto a courtyard enclosed by stone walls draped with English ivy and trumpet flowers. Splashing water from an ancient patio fountain broke the room's silence.

"Your Majesty," he said softly, reluctantly intruding on her reverie.

Auburn lights reflected in her rich dark hair. She turned, her movement fluid in a dress of deep blues, the full skirt swishing as she approached. One hand casually caressed a sapphire and diamond necklace, the other extended to greet him. "Anthony, I'm pleased you are here, especially as I may not have the pleasure of your company for a while."

"The pleasure is mine, Majesty." He bowed over her hand with a reverent kiss, never reaching her skin.

"Your mission went well?" He heard a tremble in her voice.

"Relatives greeted seventeen excited children happy to be safe."

"I'm relieved."

As their gazes met, he sensed a decade of memories flashing between them: royal sittings, foreign trips, family outings, parties, skiing, and horseback riding. His father had been the Shah's great friend, as was he, but somehow being of a similar age and with shared interests a camaraderie between Anthony and Farah Diba had sparked. She was both monarch and friend. With a passing look both knew this was the end of an era.

"Let's sit," she said, her eyes drawn across the room.

He sank into a sumptuous Italian leather sofa and scanned the space, so different from the rest of the palace, which was filled with formal French furniture with carved, spindly legs, all dwarfed beneath twenty-foot ceilings. Here, however, Farah Diba's worldly taste shone with stunning contemporary decor. The sofas flanked a flat, floor-to-ceiling travertine fireplace; rough marble spanned the wall.

Atop the Knoll chrome and glass coffee table sat a stack of Anthony's portraits of her with her children. With a look of tenderness, she slid her fingers over her children's images. "The expressions you captured on their faces are priceless, Anthony. However did you manage such gaiety? I can't get them to sit for a second with other than sour looks."

"I simply described your last art festival," he said.

Her mouth opened at the mention of the now-banned festivals.

"Remember those noisy chickens escaping their coops?" he asked. "And the clowns squishing through mud, chasing the birds, wings flapping. The garden club ladies were splashed, their hats wilted and muck dripped from their noses, their frocks and soaked shoes."

She covered her face, chortling. And when she looked up, her infectious smile lit her warm brown eyes, a light he'd not seen for ages.

"You rascal, you didn't?"

"And your children howled."

Their own laughter swelled as they recalled shared mischievous mishaps over the last eight years.

"The snowball fight with the children in St. Moritz," she said.

"And I let a packed snowball fly just as you ducked," he shook with laughter.

"It hit the dowager queen square on the rump and she squealed."

Next to him, the empress rocked with glee.

"Naturally, I apologized profusely," he said.

"My husband almost fell over laughing—"

"But I recall making up for the *faux pas*," he chuckled. "Chasing the dowager's tasseled *chapeau* when a gust blew it toward a cliff . . ."

"And you toppled over a SAVAK guard, sprawling in the snow!"

"Clumsy of me, wasn't it?"

"Oh, Anthony, I'll miss you." She stood, wiping her eyes with the handkerchief he'd handed her and said, "Now we must behave." She handed back the linen. "Come."

She led him across the room to an Italian neoclassical demi Lune commode raised on square tapering legs.

"Do you remember this piece?" She ran her fingers lightly over the fine marquetry veneer surface.

Anthony looked closely at the commode with its peach veined marble top. "Christie's on King Street." He drew his eyebrows together. "As I recall it fetched rather a hand-some sum."

An incredulous gasp escaped her lips. "Tease. You know I got a wonderful price with your friend Mr. Kahlil's help." For a second she looked wistful. "How is Philippe?"

"He's fine, back in London."

"Please send him warm regards for such a fun day. I've enjoyed all the pieces we selected," she said. "However, this one is my favorite. It's unique." She opened each of the three shallow drawers, one after the other, and closed them. "When the auctioneer showed me its secret . . ." She reached behind the side panel, and silently the entire front sprang open, revealing a small safe. "I knew at once I would find a purpose for it." She smiled at his surprise. "I have yet to tell anyone else about it."

"You've piqued my interest." He examined the piece.

"This brings me to our goal."

She spoke while opening the safe and removing a beauti-fully ornate gold chest about twelve inches square encrusted with amethysts, garnets, peridots, moonstones, and other semi-precious stones, which she held in the palms of her steady hands.

"This box is unique, as well." She opened the top of the chest, and there lay his Persian Glories, gleaming like yellow starlight on black velvet.

He looked up at her, astonished.

"I thought it best to remove temptation from greedy hands," she said, reading his surprise.

"Thank you. I appreciate your doing so."

She pressed an oval cabochon amethyst on the chest's side, and a tray popped out, revealing a small mass of the world's most precious and priceless gems nested in a tray of velvet according to their size. "No one knows."

Her face was solemn, her look direct.

His smile faded, for it was time to face the real task for which he had been summoned.

He took the chest from her hands, his heart rate accelerating, and examined the incredible stones, recognizing them immediately. The first was the Daria-I-Nour, the second largest diamond known to man, 182 carats. Lying next to it were the Maharani rubies, three huge stones close to 160 carats each, acquired by Persia when they captured India and sacked Delhi in the eighteenth century. And in the next tray below the rubies, the 150-carat emerald that had been the center of the empress's coronation crown shone. A number of enormous pear-shaped pearls and other precious gems, which had made up her crown, each lay in its velvet bed.

"These must not fall into the wrong hands. You understand?" she asked.

He understood perfectly. He was about to smuggle the crown jewels of Persia out of Iran, ensuring they would never fall into her enemies' grasp.

She sat down in the chair beside the window. "Perhaps for the time being your Persian Glories should remain with the other jewels."

"Agreed." He strode to the window, his plan coming together in his mind. "Since we're both being watched, and since I have delivered two portraits of your children . . ."

"I perhaps will have this lovely veneered commode sent to your home as repayment," she said.

"Philippe and I prepared a shipment of furniture bound

for London in two days' time. This piece will be crated separately and delivered to Edyton Manor, my grandfather's estate, where he'll hold this unique commode in his vault until you come for it."

"Dear Charles is well, I trust?"

"As autocratic as ever."

Her smile brightened. "He's a charmer, and you know it."

His mouth twitched with a smile and he handed the chest back to her. For a moment their hands rested together on the bejeweled cache. They exchanged solemn glances as if acknowledging the years he'd been court photographer, confidant and friend had ended. And the new era ahead was a mystery.

The empress turned away and replaced the jewels in their secret dwelling, locking the safe and closing the commode panel.

"Does this plan for shipment meet with your approval, Majesty?" he said.

"Yes, Anthony. I'll consider it done."

"And so it will be."

As Anthony jogged across the palace lawn to the waiting chopper, he weighed his new challenge against a sense of foreboding. Hans lifted off in silence, much appreciated by Anthony. He had promised his grandfather he'd leave Iran immediately. Now he'd taken on another and even more dangerous assignment, his promise now regrettably on hold.

TEHRAN

By 10:40 A.M. Kathryn and her crew had landed back at Mehrebad Airport, where travelers moved frantically through the terminal, and the Iranian military, shouldering assault rifles, haunted the overheated terminal in greater numbers than last week. The potential for violence unnerved her. She'd seen too much already and wanted no more.

She shook it off, her gaze connecting with Teddy's, the master of channeling anxiety into brilliance; she took his cue. They both clung to handheld camera gear: his Arri, her Bolex, keenly aware these were their last hours to get footage. Both were focused, yet wanted to be unobtrusive, hiding behind press passes secured by Ali.

"We go quickly through this place, yes," Ali said, herding them along.

"No screwups, Kat," Buzz said.

"Got it." She focused her lens on the sea of people spread before them. Women sobbed discreetly, children howling, and men, frantic, pleaded with officials. Somehow she'd thought Tehran would be as she'd left it, cosmopolitan people moving confidently through daily life, but the air vibrated with a heightened desperation that was missing eight days ago.

Her team moved swiftly through the terminal. Teddy, in a semi-crouch, steadied the Arri on close-ups, Peter worked with the Nikon zoom lens for stills to be mixed in with moving film. Today she would finish *Faces of Iran*, her documentary, and leave Iran before more trouble found her.

"What lens you using, Teddy?" Peter asked.

"You don't call my shots, man. Back off." Peter stepped up into Teddy's face, towering over him, grabbing his shirtfront. "You don't tell me what to do—ever." They drew the attention of surrounding people.

Buzz broke them apart. "Easy, guys. We work together, dig?"

Peter and Teddy scowled at each other, both breathing hard. Peter said. "I dig. Sorry man, didn't mean shit by it."

Teddy smoothed his shirtfront, looking away. "Me, neither. We're cool." They nodded to each other as if barely holding on to a truce.

People around them turned to glare.

Kathryn whispered, "One more day, guys, and we're outta here." Though she too hid uneasy thoughts, she tried to remain the objective filmmaker.

The crew was tense, exhausted and sickened by their growing sense of powerlessness against aggression. Shaking off complex feelings was easier said than done.

One more day.

She lifted her camera, the red light blinking, and peered through the lens into compelling faces etched with anxiety, eyes filled with fright, so like the death-listed families she'd flown out of Iran. Her own life had been profoundly altered; she recognized despair and for those who sought sanctuary, anguish warring against hope.

Ali stayed close to Kathryn, seeming to share Buzz's apprehension, and said, "Please, you do not speak unless ordered to. I'll handle everything."

"I don't like the sound of that," Buzz said.

"I've had enough," said Teddy, lowering his camera.

"I'm not saying a word."

Hurrying toward the exit, Kathryn accidentally bumped an officious looking man in a crumpled gray suit backed up by two-armed militia, berating a tourist. "Beg your pardon," she muttered, her radar buzzing alarm, vividly recalling her last run-in with airport officials.

Head down, her gaze locked on speckled stone and scurrying feet, she took shallow breaths to avoid the stench of too much fear-soaked humanity.

Peter slid his arm through hers, propelling her through the double exit doors. "We're fine, Kat."

"Oh, shit," Teddy mumbled, shoving his sacred hat low on his head. A breeze lifted the Hemingway relic, and he grabbed for it, clutching it to his chest. He never filmed without the felt hat.

Oblivious, an eager Ali—who, looped on pain meds, favored his wounded arm in a sling—led the way to the terminal exit. He waved to a youth about eighteen outside on the sidewalk, a younger version of himself: tall, thin with large dark eyes and a wide, toothy grin. Ali motioned to the lad, calling out "Come, Davood, my cousin, and meet my friends from the United States of America. Mr. Buzz, Mr. Teddy, Mr. Peter, and my dear Madame Kathryn, to whom I owe my life."

Kathryn filmed the familial greeting and lowered her camera. "Ali, I owe you *my* life," she said. "You were in the right place when I needed you, and I thank you." He beamed, and she adjusted her setting, capturing the respectful gleam in Davood's eyes as she honored his cousin.

The truth was she owed more than her life to Ali. After the truckload of militia crashed over the mountain, Ali had insisted on dealing with the authorities that night and had kept her out of it. He'd reported seeing Captain Nubriand drinking with his squad, "a sin against the Koran," then recklessly driving up the cliff road. Ali had wiped his brow and solemnly added, "Before long, a plume of smoke rose from the canyon floor like a bad omen."

Ali's connections with the Ministry of Culture carried weight with the police, enough for them to accept his story, and who knew how much *pishkesh* he'd paid to ward off questions about his wounded arm.

Kathryn smiled at Ali's cousin. "Davood, it's a pleasure to meet you."

"Yes. Yes." He bowed. "I will do my best, until my cousin recovers from the accident and can once more drive." Davood gestured. "This way, please."

Ali and Kathryn were on the down low about the "accident." She doubted Ali had even divulged the ordeal to his father Raymond. She definitely wasn't ready for further discussion.

Buzz pressed ahead, wasting no time following Davood to his remarkably unscratched metallic blue 1967 Buick Sport Wagon with four sky windows bordering the roof.

Buzz scooted in the middle of the blue vinyl bench between Davood and Kathryn with her Bolex aimed out the window.

Luggage loaded, Ali, Teddy, and Peter jumped in the backseat. The Buick screeched into traffic, where the jammed road grew worse as they jostled over potholes, around cars on Eisenhower Avenue, moving sluggishly into the city. The surprise through it all? Davood was a stellar driver.

As they drove, Kathryn filmed burned out buses, wrecked

cars, smashed storefronts boarded over, and broken wooden signs with painted curlicue letters swinging in a dusty haze, the remnants of violence. They approached the city center and she panned her camera, searching for the landmark Freedom Arch, once gleaming in sunlight, now barely discernable, obscured with smoke and grime.

The confident demeanor of people on the avenues where smartly dressed women had jauntily strolled but a week ago had disappeared, replaced by women shrouded in black, eyes downcast, scurrying along sidewalks as if unsure they would make it back home.

Kathryn remembered Anthony's words, "A revolution punishes everyone." At that peaceful moment in Shiraz an uprising had seemed remote, but a tempest of unrest in Tehran had escalated three fold. She handed her camera back to Peter to check film and exhaled a long breath.

Eisenhower Avenue was a wide highway divided by a manicured lawn in the median running for miles that Kathryn earlier had admired, but now was already brown from neglect. The men she had noticed watering these lawns here were missing. Ali said people were divided. It was dangerous to openly do the Shah's work. As he said this, a group of darkly dressed rabble, men not much older than Davood, rushed onto the highway lawns, grabbing an old man in a crumbling straw hat with a hose, who stubbornly watered the dry lawn.

Shouts were hurled at him.

He waved his hose, squirting them. Scolding, the angry youths charged at him, punching the poor soul.

Kathryn's breath caught. Dark flashes of the violence in Shiraz crashed in on her.

Davood slammed on the brakes, honking, shouting out the window, and backing up the car.

A thug looked up and flipped an obscene gesture at him. Davood responded in Farsi, "Your mother fucks dogs!"

Ali franticly implored, "Cousin, don't! They could have weapons. Please stop." He tugged at Davood's arm. Cars behind veered away to avoid hitting them, horns blasting.

"Look at those bullies!" Peter shouted over the racket.

"My God," Teddy yelled. "They're beating him!"

"Not for long!" Peter jumped out.

"Yeah, screw 'em!" Teddy, close behind, tossed Kathryn his hat, shouting, "Take care of it."

Ali tried to restrain his cousin, but Davood broke away and burst out of the car. "I have to help your American friends, Ali," the boy yelled, darting onto the center divider.

Behind them, drivers went wild. Ali leaned out of the car and shook his fist, swearing at them.

"Stop Ali! Don't make it worse, please!" Kathryn twisted toward Buzz's tight face. He gripped the door handle.

"We've all taken enough bullying," Buzz growled. "Dammit, I'm in!" He threw open the car door.

Kathryn restrained him from jumping out. "Don't, Buzz. I need protection!"

"Ali, protect her," Buzz shouted and leapt from the car into the brawl.

"What's wrong with them?" Kathryn grumbled, sliding to the driver's seat, shoving into gear and screeching around the corner to a side street away from blasting horns. She slammed the car into park and jumped out, her jaw clenching, eyebrows pinched, watching her guys tackle the thugs, probably militia, her panic rising off the charts.

Peter, in the fray, grabbed a guy his own height, and threw a blistering right cross. Startled, the guy staggered before punching Peter back. But Peter was all over him—and the guy next to him, crashing their heads together. Curses in Farsi and English rent the air. Teddy jabbed and kicked, barroom style, until his groaning prey sprawled on the turf.

Teddy had barely noticed the two guys yanking at him from behind until he swung around, his fist crashing into a nose; the guy screamed, and blood splattered. The furious buddy connected, splitting Teddy's lip. Teddy leveled him.

Trucks clattered on the uneven highway behind Kathryn and fright thundered in her chest. She spun toward the sound, fearing the arrival of Komiteh militia and the nightmare of prison.

A European looking couple in a tan Fiat slowed, shouting, "Go! Komiteh trucks, a minute behind us." They sped away.

Time to go.

Frantically, she searched for Buzz and spotted him flipping two guys to the ground with military ju-jitsu.

Kathryn darted over. "Komiteh, on the way. LET'S GO!"

The rabble caught sight of her and gaped.

"Right!" Buzz yelled, pounding a distracted bully.

"NOW!" she shouted to Davood. "And Davood, borrow the man's hose."

Unleashing suppressed fury, Peter and Teddy let loose their last good licks, ending the brawl. The rabble fled with bloody noses, limping, clutching midsections and probably with blackened eyes.

Her guys ripped off their torn, bloodied shirts and quickly hosed down, leaving their old shirts on the ground.

Buzz stuffed the dazed old man's pocket with rials. "Take care, buddy."

Peter, Teddy, Buzz, and Davood darted around the corner to the Buick and clamored in.

Davood peeled out, angling down side streets, beating it to their destination. Ali grabbed give-away Boeing T-shirts from the back, shoving them at the bare-chested crew. The guys wiggled them over damp chests, fairly presentable now.

Kathryn's hands shook as her emboldened crew congratulated each other. The foray, it seemed, had relieved pent-up frustrations from armed militia terrorizing them at Persepolis. Their confidence and camaraderie had resurfaced.

Her team was again tight, eager to roll. She knocked Buzz on the arm. "You took a big chance. We could've been thrown in jail."

He steadied her hands. "Men can take only so much before standing up, kiddo." He pulled her in for a hug. "Women, too, I've noticed," he said, hiding a smirk as they arrived at their last location of the day.

A sign swung on a glossy iron gate, designating the Morning Star Orphanage. Groups of boys peered through the gate, straining to discover who had pulled up. Smaller lads were held in check by muscular arms and the brook-no-nonsense voice of a tough looking character. Tashi, Mirdad's friend.

With Ali beside her, she waved, calling out, "Hello," over the din of excited children.

Tashi opened the gate. "Welcome, please come in." He shooed the boys back and she entered. Scanning beyond the boys still streaming out of a concrete building, she saw an immense field.

The boys quieted, studying her. She shook hands with Tashi and a boy with blue eyes and crooked teeth. "Our custom of greeting in the U.S.," she said. "Or like this." She held her hand up to an older boy who smiled, and they high fived. The other boys laughed and did the same, shaking hands and high fiving with each other.

Buzz and Peter came up and got into the act with the kids. Teddy and Davood emptied the Buick of sports equipment used on the shoot, baseball gear, American footballs, and soccer balls. Ali passed out stacks of T-shirts and hoodies branded with UCLA and Boeing logos. Kathryn's spirit lightened. *This is going to be fun.*

Her crew had but one more shooting location. Tonight. The culmination of *Faces of Iran*. And with all her heart she hoped it would go well.

CHAPTER TWENTY-SEVEN

They arrived at the Tehran Hilton late in the day, dirty from the city and shooting at Mirdad's orphanage. She and Buzz would join Mirdad for the embassy party at 8:00 P.M. Tonight they would shoot the finale for *Faces of Iran* at the Marble Palace. She needed to wrap up the documentary. Wally had quietly funded the project. This footage was all that stood between her ruin and redemption. Boeing's last sabotaged helicopter shot had skyrocketed the Iran Boeing shoot over budget though Wally couldn't have heard about today's disaster yet. Geez, she was tense and exhausted. She had to relax.

"Buzz, I'll meet you in the lounge at seven forty-five. Don't be late."

"I'll be there. I wouldn't miss seeing the Marble Palace for the world." He gave her a quick kiss on the cheek and got into the elevator.

In her room, Kathryn unpacked only one bag and rang for the maid to take her dress to be pressed. She kicked off her shoes, removed her clothes, put on a comfortable hotel robe and belted it. Setting out her makeup and other items—shampoo, hair dryer, electric rollers, and nail polish—she rinsed her face and put on La Prairie moisturizer.

The maid came for her dress and left. And with her sleep-mask secure, Kathryn sprawled on the large bed and closed her eyes to unwind for a moment.

The next thing she knew, the phone was ringing in her dreams. No, it wasn't a dream. She grabbed it.

"Hello?"

"Kat, my love." It was Buzz. "We're waiting for you. It's ten before eight."

"You serious? It can't be!" She jumped out of bed.

"You ready? Mirdad's here. We're waiting."

"Be down soon. Keep him company for a few minutes, will you? I won't be long." Damn! She hadn't even showered yet. This wasn't how she had planned it. She threw off her robe, plugged in her hot rollers, and jumped in the shower.

Thank God she had done all this so many times before.

Her dress hung on the closet door. She raced like a character in an old time slapstick movie: drying herself, her hair, throwing it in rollers, doing her makeup, donning her panties, garter belt, and sheer white stockings, shoving into the dress and her pumps. She took the plastic cylinders out of her hair, shook it out, and ran a brush through it. She looked at herself in the mirror. *Oh, yes.* She had forgotten Anthony's diamond gardenia. She fastened it to the point at her shoulder where the dress came together, then slipped on matching elbow-length evening gloves. She stood back for a moment to look.

"Not bad," she assured herself, "even if it did take only twenty minutes." She smoothed her hand over her Christian Dior gown. Brett had sent it to her from Paris the year before they'd separated. A floor-length, double layer of heavy white silk that hooked over one shoulder where she had placed the gem gardenia. All around the side slit and up the narrow skirt tiny seed pearls and bugle beads shimmered; the same beading glistened on the heels of her white silk pumps. She grabbed her crystal Judith Lieber evening bag and rushed to meet Mirdad and Buzz.

Entering the lobby bar she spotted them seated at a deep green velvet corner booth. As soon as she saw him, Mirdad stood and flashed her a radiant smile. He looked very *G.Q.* in his tux.

"Here she is," Buzz said, looking from Mirdad to Kathryn.

"Ravishing, Kathryn." Mirdad took her hand.

"Hey, you kids have a drink, will you?" Buzz nodded to Mirdad. "I have to make a quick call. Be right back," he said, striding across the lobby to greet Teddy and Peter, both nicely dressed. Their official palace press passes in place, they carried film gear.

"You did it, Mirdad. You got them in," Kathryn said.

"The least I could do. No doubt they'll film us arriving like celebrities as well." They bent heads together, suppressing a chuckle.

"Our film debut," she said.

"Champagne then," Mirdad said, seating her on the plush velour.

A moment later the waiter brought over a bottle of Veuve Cliquot and poured for them.

"Wonderful," she said. "And tonight I'll meet your mother, yes?"

"I've looked forward to introducing you."

They tipped glasses.

"Cheers," they said and sipped the chilled bubbles.

"Are you happy with her marriage?" Kathryn leaned forward and wished she were shooting a close-up on him. A thousand emotions played across his handsome face with stories she bet he'd never tell her.

"She is happy." His eyes met hers. "And that's what counts, is it not?"

"And what of your happiness?" She smiled. "What do you want from this life?"

He laughed gently, a low warm sound. "More moments like this—with you." They sipped champagne, relaxing, and the waiter brought over some delectable spanakopita appetizers, oozing feta and spinach from warm puff pastry.

"We could stay," he said.

"I wouldn't mind," she whispered. "I'm not big on grand parties."

He chuckled and leaned closer. "What a relief, neither am I. And there have been many to attend lately."

They bit into flaky appetizers and both moaned with pleasure, covering their grins. They each drained another glass of champagne and laughed like naughty conspirators. They spoke again of noir films and the boys at the orphanage that afternoon, how those children would fare with the revolution, his friend Tashi, and Tashi's intense devotion to those boys.

"And young orphan girls, Mirdad, who watches over them?" she said.

A muscle flexed in his jaw. "We passed the burnt out girls' orphanage in Shiraz. I intend to see it reopen with a proper staff."

"Mirdad, I recall seeing you with your mother once at the bank, remember? Where the jewels were on display."

"How can I ever forget?" He motioned to the waiter for the bill. "You will find her appearance different tonight."

His mood changed and she wished she hadn't mentioned his mother.

"Happier?" she said.

"Yes." He took her hand and kissed it, his lips lingering. "I regret we must go, Kathryn."

"Of course." She regretted it as well. Troubling people could be there.

Kathryn stepped from Mirdad's limo, her one-shouldered gown shimmying down her legs. Absently she touched the diamond and pearl gardenia cresting her shoulder. Anthony may belong to someone else, but this jewel was hers. She wore it defiantly as she looked up.

She was awed by the splendor surrounding the Marble Palace with its soaring colonnades, the palace where the Shah at age thirty-six had first been installed. Kathryn's gaze steadied on a glimmering hundred foot reflecting pool that flanked the entrance, reminiscent of fine Persian miniatures.

Guests spilled out of grand cars: Daimlers; Rolls Royces; Bentleys; a vintage 1937 Mercedes Cabriolet, the top down; and a 1938 Hispano-Suiza H6 lined the crowded courtyard drive. Flash bulbs for this photo-op splashed through the courtyard. Statesman from select countries escorted glamorous women dressed in couture grandeur, a declaration that peace prevailed and the Shah held control.

On Mirdad's arm and with Buzz at her side, Kathryn climbed the steps to the palace where flashes momentarily blinded her. "Come," Mirdad said, waving to Teddy and Peter filming below. "Your own paparazzi, Kathryn."

She smiled. "Yes, our last location for *Faces*, and you're in it, Minister Ajani."

"My mother will be overjoyed." They chuckled, heads together, all pretense of being dignified obliterated.

They entered a lengthy colonnade topped with intricate tile-worked arches, inlayed bits of cobalt, gold, turquoise, yellow, and orange soaring to an immense groin-vaulted ceiling. Kathryn paused, as if pictures from her father's art books had come to life and she soaked in the dramatically lit palace, eyes wide in wonderment. She touched Mirdad's sleeve and said, "We've stepped into the Rubaiyat."

"Like your ivory miniatures."

"Yes."

"Come this way." Mirdad led them up a grand staircase into the hall of mirrors, splashed with gilt and hung on brocaded walls along corridors where Louis XVI antiques looked perfectly at home, opulence confirming her every image of the wealth associated with the Shah of Iran.

With a peak social protocol performance, Mirdad led them through groups of mingling guests. He ushered them to a large drawing room adjacent to the dazzling ballroom, introducing Kathryn and Buzz to various dignitaries. A charming Frenchman, le Comte Alex Philippe de Marenches, whom, Mirdad explained in a hushed whisper, was the head of the French Secret Service; the British ambassador, Anthony Parsons, looking more like a professor than a diplomat; and a slender, balding American undersecretary of State, George Witzel, were but a few.

From across the room she heard, "There's Mirdad," as an attractive general and a younger officer broke away from a group of official Iranians resplendent in dress uniforms, and came over to Mirdad. On his arm the general escorted a stunning dark-eyed woman dripping in rubies.

"Mother." Mirdad leaned forward, kissing the woman's cheek. "How lovely you look," he said, his eyes a well of affection.

"Mirdad." His mother smiled brightly and put her cheek next to his. As she looked at Kathryn, her glance chilled.

"May I present my friend Kathryn Whitney. Kathryn, my mother Madame . . . Houdin."

"A pleasure, my dear," said Madame Houdin. "You're American. The film director, I'd venture."

Kathryn smiled, not knowing how to interpret the inflection behind the comment from Mirdad's mother.

Rena Ajani Houdin, although she must be at least fifty, had flawless skin over stunning features, her long-lashed eyes much like Mirdad's. And still there seemed to be another reason Kathryn felt she knew this woman.

Mirdad introduced his mother's new husband, General Omar Houdin, governor of Tehran, and his attaché, Major Demetrius Nassiri.

"My compliments, Mirdad," said the general. "There isn't a man in this room who is not taken with your beauty,

Miss Whitney." General Houdin took her hand to his lips. "As I myself am spellbound."

"Kind of you, General." As light conversation coursed through the group, Kathryn caught the dark glare of Madame Houdin next to him.

"The Shah flies to Tabas tomorrow to survey earthquake damage," said Colonel Nassiri. "Tragic, a seven point eight. Over twenty-five thousand dead."

"Our Shah brings hope to our people," said Mirdad, nodding at the others.

Suddenly gunfire tattered in the distance. Four guards hurried through the foyer. Sounds of a vehicle screeching away were barely discernable through the orchestra's crescendo. Faces around them froze for a split second.

A samba floated up to them, and after a pause, conversation continued, filled with the puns Iranians enjoyed in their humor. But Kathryn had picked up an undercurrent, announcing the heat had been turned up under a smoldering political caldron, and was about to boil over.

She wanted to ask Witzel from the U.S. State Department about the U.S. position on revolution in Iran, but that was not why she was here. She admitted to herself she was here to look Anthony in the face and see if it had all been a lie.

Neither her heart nor head was into this adroit banter. She excused herself, leaving Buzz and Mirdad in conversation, and moved to the top of the staircase leading to the ballroom below.

"A glittering array of gaiety, wouldn't you agree, Miss Whitney?"

Kathryn turned to Madame Houdin, standing by her side. "Please call me Kathryn, Madame."

"Rena," the woman said, extending her hand, her nails the exact color of her ruby bracelet. "A pleasure to meet a young lady friend of Mirdad's."

"Mirdad has been very helpful in smoothing the way for our production in Iran," said Kathryn.

"He's quite the diplomat." Rena's eyes focused on Kathryn's shoulder.

Instinctively Kathryn raised her hand to where Rena's gaze held.

"I once knew someone who wore a similar gardenia brooch, equally magnificent," said Rena. "My sister, Illyia."

Kathryn felt her face flush. "It was a gift," she said lamely.

"Ah, from my nephew." Rena patted her hand and walked away, accentuating the hurtful knowledge Kathryn had been but a dalliance to a betrothed Persian man. Tamping down the pain in her heart, she looked over the magnificent room below.

Dancers swayed to the rich sound of the orchestra's samba, while others in animated groups seemed to reach for sanity, laughing and chatting, amusing themselves under the many brilliant chandeliers.

The most dazzling of all the international guests were the Iranians themselves. The beautiful Persian women who, at other times could be considered overdressed, were here intoxicatingly stunning. Their incomparable gowns and jewelry were straight off Paris runways. It had been a while since Kathryn had been close to so much society. With the mesmeric sight, she halted.

Poised on the top step, Kathryn searched for him, fool that she was. She held her head high, picturing the most elegant star she could think of. "Audrey Hepburn," she muttered. *My Fair Lady*.

Fury and longing battled inside her; she missed Anthony, the scoundrel. News of his upcoming wedding to another chafed, no, pummeled her heart. Unbelievable. She had thought herself immune to love by now.

Her foot reached the next step, and she saw him. He turned, as though sensing her. His gaze reached hers and there were no others in the room. For a delicious moment, Anthony, tall and devastatingly handsome in his evening attire, had a smile on his lips, she hoped meant for her alone.

Anthony excused himself from a group of people and made his way toward her. She could not deny her feelings for him. She was lost.

But when he moved from the group he was with, the woman next to him stood out, seeming reluctant to release his arm. He shrugged away. She then looked directly at Kathryn, recognition on her face. The dark-haired siren from the newspaper photo, Alexandria Badiyi, more stunning than anyone had a right to be. Daggers blazed from her black eyes. Her blood-red satin gown, edged in black jet beads, set off alabaster skin. Dark, glossy hair, pulled away from her exotic face, was piled high on her head, displaying her long, slender neck encircled with a Victorian dog collar of diamonds and onyx. Her territory had been invaded, and she looked ready to kill.

Miss Badiyi was the most arrogant-looking creature Kathryn had ever seen. She clutched the diamonds at her throat with the drama of an opera diva. The gesture wasn't lost on Kathryn, who wondered who had given the diva her diamonds.

The summation took no more than seconds, and Kathryn's eyes returned to Anthony. But seeing him with this woman from the newspaper article, remembering the torment of the last few violent days and her desperate calls to him without answer, her warm gaze chilled though she burned inside, fire and ice, like the diamonds at her shoulder.

Anthony reached her and took her hand.

A rush swept over her.

"My God, you're lovely." He drew her hand to his lips. Slowly, he kissed her fingertips. "The hotel in Persepolis said you'd gone and were evasive about an incident." His eyes devoured her. "What incident? Are you all right?" He caressed her cheek, glancing at the cut on her chin.

"More or less." She was torn. Her body said one thing, her mind another, the heat from his lips blanching her icy fingertips. "So, you're engaged to be married."

Instantly his face closed down. He took her arm. "Come with me."

She hesitated, but he moved her back up the stairs, away from the crowds. Alone, she turned to him in fury.

"I'm not engaged," he held her arms.

"But I saw the press . . ."

"Wishful thinking on someone's part—not mine."

She shook her head, uneasy, not sure what to believe.

"Kathryn, tell me what happened."

"Soldiers were breathing down our necks, held a gun to Buzz's head, and chased me through the desert."

"What? Good God, Kathryn! What're you . . . ?"

Her ordeal spilled over—all of it. "I led those men to their deaths. It was the only way to survive." She fought her tears.

"My God. I didn't . . ."

She didn't let him answer. "I see where you were. In fact, Mirdad showed me your news clippings, you and her."

"They were seriously mistaken . . ."

"Please! These things happen. People meet, have flings, say things they don't mean. Besides, I leave tomorrow . . ."

"Tomorrow?"

"Our last day at Persepolis was ruined."

"Mirdad assured me . . ."

"Mirdad was there for part of it. And Ali. We fended for ourselves, sort of." She glanced across the room at Alexandria. "And you took care of yourself, I see."

"You think . . . ? I wasn't with her. That's been over since I met you." He held her wrists. "Why are you doing this? I love you." He didn't let go. "I'd no idea—Mirdad said nothing. Believe me."

"Right. He called you. I called." She struggled in his grip.

"Kathryn, I'd have come if I'd known."

"Don't touch me."

"Kathryn, please . . ."

Mirdad moved their way, along with Buzz. She couldn't speak to any of them.

"*Please*, excuse me." She twisted away, leaving the unfinished phrase on Anthony's lips.

This hadn't gone as she'd wanted. She had opened her mouth but his words confused her more than what she had seen with her own eyes. She needed to think and headed for the ladies' lounge.

Passing a waiter, she grabbed a glass of champagne from his tray and drank it straight down like a shot of Tequila. The icy liquid cooled her temper.

Kathryn faced herself in the lounge mirror. She opened her evening bag and took out a tissue, dabbing her eyes, trying to repair the damage. She extracted her lipstick and fixed her mouth. She hadn't listened to Anthony's words, unwilling to trust him, or any man it seemed. Had she become so jaded from marriage to Brett? Caught up in her anger she'd been eager to believe the worst.

Head lowered, she leaned her hands on the granite counter. She was afraid of emotional risk. She felt a shuddering response to that knowledge. Afraid of . . . being left again, abandoned, unimportant, not worth loving. *Get a grip*. He'd come to her, said, "I love you, Kathryn, please . . ."

Coming into the reflection behind her in the mirror was Alexandria, and she remembered why Anthony's words were so hard to believe. Dark eyes locked into hers. *This should be interesting.* She drew in a breath. *Lana Turner*, she thought to herself, *Green Dolphin Street*, and turned around slowly, eyebrow raised, keeping her cool.

Alexandria set her black Chanel evening bag on the frosted glass counter. "Anthony was intrigued with you, I can see why. You're attractive." She sniffed, returning her gaze to her own reflection. "But Anthony and I have been together for two years. His behavior displeases me, naturally, but such things are expected of Persian men."

"You should know," Kathryn responded casually, swiping a makeup brush across her cheek.

Alexandria replaced her compact into her bag and withdrew a jeweled lipstick case.

Kathryn watched, wanting to put the lipstick on for her—all over her face. "Oh, what a lovely necklace. An heirloom?" Kathryn said, biting her tongue.

Alexandria smiled and touched her throat. "A betrothal gift from Anthony."

"How appropriate! A dog collar!"

Alexandria's eyes widened with fire. Her mouth opened momentarily, then she regained her assured demeanor. "Our wedding takes place in three months." She gave Kathryn a withering look. "Make no mistake, you are not permanent, miss."

"Whitney. Kathryn Whitney. And I couldn't care less about your marital status. Good night." With doubt eating at her resolve, but head high, Kathryn left the lounge.

With murder in his heart, Anthony slammed Mirdad against the alcove wall. The sconce above Mirdad's head rattled.

"Why the hell didn't you tell me?" He shoved Mirdad harder against the wall. "They ripped her clothes! They would've raped her!"

"No!"

"Where the hell were you, then?"

"It didn't happen. I stopped it." He tried to push Anthony away.

"Stopped it like hell." He shoved Mirdad harder against the wall. A table teetered, a vase crashed to the floor. "She was almost killed!" Anthony tightened his grip on Mirdad's collar.

"But I sent them away." Mirdad's hands covered Anthony's, yanking them off.

Buzz had stepped into the alcove with them. "You're

wrong about that, Mirdad. They came back and damn near killed her. If it weren't for Ali, they would have."

Mirdad's face fell. He huffed for breath. "I-I didn't know. The Green Bands." His eyes darted from Buzz to Anthony. "I-I thought . . ."

Reluctantly, hands shaking, Anthony released Mirdad, rage still boiling inside him. "You knew she was in trouble and you didn't try to reach me?"

Mirdad sank back against the wall, rubbing his throat. "Didn't know where you were. Your office . . ."

Anthony moved forward again, menacingly.

Mirdad shrank back. "I thought it was under control, cousin. I didn't see what difference you'd have made."

"That's the woman I love, 'cousin.'" He barked the word back at him.

"And there she goes," Buzz said, touching Anthony's shoulder. "One disgruntled female."

Anthony saw Kathryn rushing toward the foyer—leaving.

"If you'll excuse me . . ."

"Go for it," Buzz said.

Anthony started after Kathryn, but Alexandria caught up to him.

"Anthony darling, there you are. Dance with me? I've missed you." She smiled brightly, too brightly, her hand on his arm. He saw menace in her eye. Her other hand clutched an evening bag, the one carrying the Walther PPK.

"Not now." He brushed her away.

Desolate, not knowing what to do to get Kathryn back, Mirdad listened to Buzz describe Kathryn's ordeal with that pig, Nubriand. The consolation was the bastard burned alive. But he'd almost gotten Kathryn killed with his insane need to punish her. The thought sickened him. Now without a word, she had rushed away. And all his plans for a beautiful evening crumbled. Ironic. What wasn't ripped away from him, he managed to destroy by his own hand.

"Oh, hell, Mirdad," Buzz said, "don't blame yourself for those bastards. They were outta control. You did your best. C'mon. Let's get drunk. It's the only cure when the gal you want walks away."

Mirdad turned, astounded at the empathy in Buzz's face.

"Yeah, I've lost someone myself," Buzz said, reading his mind again. "In fact, she was a lot like Kathryn. Hey, they've got a bottle of Jack Daniels at the Hilton bar with our name on it." He put his arm around Mirdad's shoulders and walked him away. "And I've had my eye on a pair of cute cocktail waitresses there."

"My car awaits." Mirdad sounded calm. He wasn't. He needed that drink.

Kathryn's cool exterior had cracked after encountering Alexandria. She needed an escape from any reminder of Anthony. Loving him was painful. And she might never see him again, but what difference did it make? He was with someone else. She swallowed hard.

She charged down the palace steps and came to a halt; she staggered, seeing a mass of limousines lined up along the driveway, the drivers clustered in animated conversation. Undaunted, she hunted until she spotted the limo driver that had brought them.

"Please take me to my hotel," she said. But as the driver pulled up and opened the door for her, she saw Ali standing across the courtyard, leaning against a Silver Cloud Rolls Royce. "Stay here. I'll be right back."

She marched across the marble courtyard to Ali and unpinned the diamond gardenia from her shoulder. It means nothing anymore, she told herself.

"Ali, please return this to Anthony." She would rather have thrown it in his face, but this would do. "And tell him . . ."

Before she could speak another word, a hand covered her mouth, and she was shoved through the open door into the back seat of the Rolls. As the back door slammed, a shot rang out, glancing off it. "My God!" She jumped but was held firm, her heart racing. A voice growled, "*Ali, vite vite, retourne a chez moi vite. Assurez-vous que nous avons pas survi*, make sure we're not followed." The Rolls skidded from the parking spot, and through the window she saw her.

Alexandria, not twenty feet away, feet planted, taking aim. A large hand shoved Kathryn's head down and the second shot rang out, cracking the rear door window, a third crunched through the door, lodging into the seat in front of her.

Gulping back fear, Kathryn scrambled to be free from her attacker and caught his familiar scent, citrusy—Lagerfeld—Anthony. His arms tightened around her. "Kathryn."

"Anthony?" Breathing hard she said, "She shot at us!"

"She's like that."

"An assassin?"

"Let's say, dangerous, more than she seems. Come here."

She sputtered, "You're not off the hook, buster."

"You're my love, Kathryn, my light," he murmured. And his lips found hers on a sigh. "I won't let you go like this. I'll never let you go."

But now in the arms of the man she unwittingly had fallen in love with against all odds, she heard the words, wrong or right she craved to hear, and softened, her anger teetering.

"Your brunette is pretty determined to have you," she said.

"Too bad," he said. "I have what I want." His kiss deepened.

She caressed his face, reassured he wasn't hurt, that the moment was real.

His gaze fell to the diamond gardenia in her hand.

"I was bringing it to you," she said.

He stiffened. "I meant what I said. Don't ever return my gifts."

She pulled back and he took hold of the brooch and re-pinned it at her shoulder. "Okay? Are we clear?"

She had hurt him. Nodding, she leaned her forehead against his. "Yes." She caressed his face, and Ali drove them through dark streets as Anthony learned about her encounter with Alexandria, and she about his with Mirdad. Then he explained to her about Alexandria's persistence, her unwanted betrothal to an older, very wealthy man, trying to use Anthony as a way out. The air cleared by the time they arrived at a towering Tehran apartment building. The elevator doors opened onto the eighteenth floor penthouse, and they stepped into a cavernously empty apartment.

"Where are we?"

"What's left of my apartment. Almost everything is packed. I'm leaving in a week." This was said almost to himself.

He took her hand and walked her across the spacious, contemporary foyer into an expansive living room, walled in glass, overlooking the city. The pale walls and plush carpets were bare. Empty wires dangled from the twenty-foot ceiling, boxes were stacked to the side. A telephone sat on a lone crate in the middle of the floor. An older model turntable, stacked with long-playing records, sat on another crate. Jazz, classical, and Latin album covers crowded the turntable. He flipped on music, a sultry Miles Davis wafting over bare walls, and held her hand in the dark room, no longer silent. Lights glowed from streets below, his warmth and nearness scalding her emotions.

"I leave tomorrow morning," she said.

It was over.

The realization shattered her. Tears welled over. An audible shudder escaped her lips. She looked away.

Tenderness in his gaze, Anthony drew her to him, folding his arms around her. The mood now charged, he lifted her and carried her to his bedroom.

There was only one piece of furniture in the room, an art deco Jules Leleu bed, and he laid her on the soft duvet.

She watched him undress slowly, his eyes never leaving her face. First, he dropped his jacket and lazily freed himself of his dress tie. His smile deliberate, he removed each gold Boucheron cufflink, placing them in his pants pocket.

Enjoying the show, Kathryn relaxed back against the pillows as he uncovered his masculine form: his contoured chest, the ripple of muscle down his abdomen, fascinated her.

He took one step forward and opened his belt, unzipped his trousers and removed them; turning, playfully displaying his powerful back, and looked over his shoulder at her, grinning in his tailored boxer shorts.

Holding out his hand, he pulled her to her feet and she slid her hands under the waistband of his shorts, reaching around, grabbing him closer.

Chuckling, he rubbed his body into hers, smooth against silk, soft against hard. He slipped his hand into the slit on the side of her gown, massaging between her legs, his gaze intensifying.

Moaning, she reached for him, but he pulled her hands away and unsnapped his shorts, letting them drop to the floor. His playful side was back, like their first encounters.

He undid her gown.

She stepped out of it, and he picked it up, tossing it over the corner of the headboard.

He dropped to his knees and unhooked each garter, skimming her stockings down her legs, his touch sending shivers through her.

She slipped off her shoes, removed the garter belt, and stepped out of her thong.

Leaning close, he kissed the curls between her legs, making her quake with desire, and then he stood before her, his eyes filled with passion, his voice husky, saying, "How can I let you go?" His beautiful smile above her and any animosity she'd harbored melted away. Hunger for his touch pulsed through her.

"I think you need personal attention," he said, and his capable hands covered her breasts, his gaze locked there, caressing less gently than a moment before.

She moaned, her latent reckless nature breaking through old barriers, craving him. "I think you're right. Attention is what I need," she whispered, sculpting her hands over his firm pectorals, moving down to his trim waist and further. "I need everything you've got." She filled both hands with him.

He groaned under her touch and clutched her to him, his kiss incendiary, and the warmth of his body seeping into hers. She never wanted to let go.

He swept her over to the bed and came down, full and hard against her on the lush duvet. "You have my full attention." He brought his mouth to hers, kissing deeply, his hands, shaping over her collarbone, and then his body slid lower, taking her nipple in his mouth.

Aware of his powerful desire, her senses roared, hot and wild with her moans.

Fingers slid along her rib cage, lower, over her stomach. He scooted back, raised her knees and sat back. "Open your legs for me. I want to look at you." Her eyes widened while his eyelids hooded over fiery green, his full mouth intent with desire.

Her body reacted, sizzling and moist. He raised an eyebrow, a sign of command, and she did as he asked.

"Beautiful," he said, opening her further, touching her wetness with his fingers until her need became an obsession.

"I'm burning," she cried out.

"Yes, you are. I've waited for you." He moved his hand

away and his mouth was there, driving sensation higher, higher, until she cried out with an explosive orgasm.

Kissing his way up her body, her stomach, breasts, and throat, he entered her slowly at first; their gazes locked together, their bodies fusing. He thrust deeper, faster, more until *ecstasy*. She felt each powerful stroke, and knew there'd be more coming. Ooh, she was getting better with Persian puns. Moments later, pleasure overtook her again.

"Oh God," she moaned, clutching him to her, her senses soaring out of control.

"You're mine," he roared, coming with her.

At the pinnacle of her vulnerability, every nerve ending aroused, he made love to her again and she him, slowly: tasting, touching, and loving every inch of each other. Breathing heavily, she said, "I'm love-starved." She coyly smiled, realizing how true this was.

"Then I'm your man," he said.

She licked her way down his body, having her way with him again. The force grew more intense. Comets, she thought, colliding in the universe. He barely breathed.

"More," she heard herself say. And he gave her more, until neither had more to give. No doubts, no reservations; they belonged together.

"My God, woman, you're astounding," he said, stroking her arm. "And you glisten."

Sated, Kathryn nuzzled closer.

Hours slid by. They lay together, entwined, slippery with love. Fulfilled and released from her past, she snuggled into him, comforted in blissful lovers' afterglow.

But old wounds resurfaced: this was it. She wouldn't see him. L.A.—London. That was if he even survived his last week in Tehran against the Black Glove. Left again. *The men she loved always left. . . .*

Stop this! She quashed back tears. *Just enjoy him now.*

She stretched her body, straddling him. "I'm famished!"

"Does loving make you hungry?" He laughed, sliding his hands from her shoulders to her waist.

"Yes, and you're delicious." She nibbled his ear, treasuring the taste of him.

"Stop it, you little animal. There'll be nothing left of me."

"Hmm. We can't have that." She pulled him to his feet and patted his taut behind. "I'm ready to feast. Is your cupboard bare, too?"

Naked, he chased her into the chrome and granite kitchen. They rummaged through the refrigerator and cupboards, coming up with a bag of mixed oranges, Brie, a carton of marinated mushrooms, olives and a semi-stale baguette.

Anthony squeezed glasses of fresh orange juice. She watched in wonder, a heavenly moment.

He turned and stared. She felt him drink in the sight, her hair tousled, cascading over her bare body.

He moved close, caressing her shoulder. "For a moment, I was afraid you wouldn't be there. I haven't let anyone get close for some time. I don't want this to end."

"I'm here," she said. "Where I want to be." *More than you know.*

They lounged on the bed, feeding each other crunchy bread dripping with Brie, mushrooms, olives and slices of Mandarin oranges, sweeter than any Persian candy, finishing every bite of food.

Brushing away crumbs he said, "Come, darling, let's get wet." He grabbed two robes and pulled her along. "A bath with lots of bubbles."

"Glorious." She felt like a child at a party awaiting every new treat.

They bathed in the enormous rose and black marble tub, brimming with steamy, scented bubbles, the sound of Dvorak filling the candlelit room. They lay side by side, enveloped in warmth, peering upward through the glass-domed skylight Anthony had opened to reveal a starry Persian sky.

Stroking her skin with a large sponge, he said, "I've waited a long time to share my world . . . with someone I cared for." His green gaze was soft upon her; his thick lashes wet and glistening.

She nibbled his chin, soothed.

"But it's not the right time. In fact, it couldn't be worse." He rubbed his eyebrows and looked away. "I'm sorry. This is difficult for me to say."

She stopped, feeling herself plummet from an ecstatic high into to a cavernous pit in her stomach. *Rejection?*

"I never thought I'd speak these words, unfamiliar turf." He stroked her tense shoulder, kneading it. "I want you—need you in my life," he said, threading his fingers through her wet hair.

She looked up.

"Not just now—always, my love." He reached into the pocket of his robe and turned, taking her hand in his, holding up a ring in his other—a gorgeous, emerald cut diamond ring, maybe fifteen-carats with triangular, two-carat diamonds on either side.

"Kathryn . . . will you marry me?"

Whoa! What kind of magic was this? Was this the magic she'd longed for but could never admit wanting? Yes. This was the sublime moment one never forgets. To look into another's eyes and see your own feelings reflected there.

She'd come a long way and had found the intimacy poets speak of—Rumi, Hafez—the love everyone longs to find at least once. This was hers, and seizing it she said, "Yes. Yes, I'll marry you."

He gulped down unexpected sentiment so intense, he'd never dreamed he could hold a place in his heart, but it consumed him like flames. "This ring, my father gave to my mother." He slid the diamond on her ring finger. "Forever?" he said.

"Yes, forever."

He leaned in and kissed her with a possessiveness that shocked him.

She melted into him. "I'm soaring inside."

He cradled her, speechless. They stared at the brilliant engagement ring bonding their future.

She turned in his embrace, and threw her arms around him. "I love it, I love you." Tears choked her.

She was his, forever. He kissed her face and dried her tears.

"I don't want to lose you—ever."

"But I leave in the morning." She splashed him. "Early."

"I'm not about to let you go—until you're thoroughly clean, that is." He dunked her under the water.

She sputtered up for a breath, and he laughed.

With the soggy sponge, she squished it in his face, squealing.

They played until the room was drenched, and he

chased her from the tub into the sauna. They made love one more delicious time in a clump of towels, massaging jasmine scented oil into each other's skin, before he dried her and tossed her a white silk robe, donning a black one himself. She wrapped up her hair in a dry towel and tied the robe.

Anthony took her into his photography studio to tell her of his plans, moments before resolving his future—their future.

From behind the built-in walnut bookcase, he opened a safe and removed a gold and jewel encrusted chest. Placing it on the low marble table beside the Victorian velvet chaise, he sat down next to her. "Kathryn, my love, I can be in London in less than two weeks. Wait for me there."

"I'll take my film back to L.A. and return."

"Good." He knew she wouldn't like his next words. "But I won't be able to contact you for a while."

She sat up. "Don't frighten me, Anthony."

He took her shoulders, remembering the trouble they'd had over Alexandria. "Never doubt that I love you and I'm coming to be with you. Understand?"

She blushed. "Yes, I understand."

"Great! We'll meet in London in two weeks' time. Philippe will take you to meet my grandfather." He envisioned Lord Charles' gruff manner melting when he met his future countess and granddaughter. "He'll adore you. And will, no doubt, already know all about you. If you have any problems, contact Philippe."

"Anthony, I hate leaving you—the situation is so dangerous. Things are deteriorating fast."

He led her over in front of the long cheval mirror

and touched his finger to her lips, ignoring her words. "I thought I could never bear to see another woman wear them, until you."

He opened the lid of the gold jewel encrusted chest, revealing one of Iran's great treasures, the Persian Glories, and heard her intake of breath.

"Ohhh, Anthony. They're spectacular, but . . ."

"I want you to have them," he said.

"It's too great a gift, Anthony."

"They are mine and . . ." He clasped the canary diamond bracelet on her wrist. "It is my wish." He kissed her fingertips. "You can keep them in my grandfather's vault. I'll handle everything, all the arrangements tomorrow morning. Kathryn, you must carry these stamped documents from the Royal office to pass through customs."

"But . . ."

"Shhh." He clasped the necklace around her throat, his lips on the hollow of her neck.

"These stones radiate warmth, as if they contained an energy of their own I can feel."

"Because I give them with all my love."

"Amazing," she said, her fingers skimming over the glorious canary diamonds.

He untied the white silk robe, and it slid from her shoulders.

She untied his. It fell to the floor. "You, sir, are even more amazing." She reached for him.

THE END

ACKNOWLEDGEMENTS

Writing a book is a journey with guides and supporters along the way. I was fortunate to have many. I am grateful to the following:

Joseph Angard, my love, who said, "Write the book! I'll read the pages." He read countless versions, bless him.

Kudos to my son, Kristian, a tough, clever critic. I listened. My daughters, Kathryn and Summer, whose endless encouragement I value. To my son, Kent, who is always there for me in a major way. And to Papa Bear, Kent Wakeford Sr. who brought me into the world of TV commercials. To Jill Dexter who introduced us after UCLA, Thanks, roomie.

Lisa Rojany, *Editorial Services of Los Angeles*, who's gentle but firm coaxing, and wise edits have been indispensible through each draft. Lisa you are amazing.

My two astute writing mentors, Marjorie Miller, at UCLA who, when I thought I would write a mystery, said, "Choose the most exotic setting you've ever been to and set your story there." The light bulb in my head popped on and I knew what I had to write.

My UCI mentor, Louella Nelson, who taught me how to structure fiction much as I had in writing screenplays, with a clear three-act paradigm where characters could explode off the page as they arced. Lou, your keen insightful direction has shepherded me through many drafts and into the sequel.

Appreciation to Kristin Lindstrom, at *Flying Pig Media*, a lifeline, your riveting attention to detail in editing and continuity has produced this book. Your input is priceless. Thank you.

Sandra Harmon, God love you, your devoted support will never be forgotten. To Owen Laster, your monumental encouragement is remembered.

Writers groups give fuel to the solitary writer when they critique pages. With thanks to fellow writers whose generous, focused insights brought light into my writing: Brad Oatman, Deborah Gaal, Kristen James, Beverly Plass, Herb Williams-Gelbart, David Collins, Debra Garfinkle, Begonia Echeverria, Dennis Copeland, Dennis Phinney, Tim Twombly, Will Hager, Rosie Lewis, Judith Whitmore, Laurie Casey, Michelle Khoury, Sara Winokur, Alan Hunter. And thanks to Bill Markey for his spot-on flying info!

My UCLA cheerleaders for more than five years, Elaine Franklin, Lana Dietrich and Mimi Latt, I thank you.

It takes a special friend to take the time to read and comment on an unpublished manuscript. I treasure you: John Dismukes, Barry Drinkwater and Jo-Anne Redwood first to offer rave reviews. Carol Richmond, a talented writer and mentor who nudged me onto the writer's road. Frank and Lynne Erpelding, who championed the first lengthy draft, saying, "This should go straight to the big screen!" Nancy Hirsch, writer's dream assistant, Carol Stulberg, cherished friend. Other loyal friends whose encouragement never wavered; Arlene Angard, beloved niece, Carole Reed, Sharon Kletzky, Erica Freidman, Diane Carnell, Marlene Macewan, Sue Sanft, and so many more.

To my dear Persian friends, thank you for Farsi phrases with perhaps a few cuss words, you've been indispensible.

AUTHORS NOTE

This book is a work of fiction. Although events depicting historical facts and characters are included in the book, the story is derived solely from this author's imagination. My experiences while in Iran and other incidents recited to me by Iranians with whom I met and filmed with, have influenced this narrative. Countless news articles and documentary films corroborated much of the information I amassed.

Books I specifically referenced were:

Fereydham Hoveyda, *The Fall of the Shah*, Wyndham Books, 1980

William Shawcross, *The Shah's Last Ride,* Simon and Shuster, 1988

Sattareh Farmanfermaian, *Daughters of Persia*, Crown Hardcover, 1992

ABOUT THE AUTHOR

Susan Wakeford Angard graduated high school on the lot of Twentieth Century Fox Studio. During this time she had leading roles in major television shows at Fox Studios, Warner Bros, Paramount, Universal and MGM. Her fascination for Ancient art then led her to study for an art history MFA at UCLA.

After leaving UCLA, Susan joined a family-owned TV Commercial Production Company, shooting consumer product commercials from McDonald's to Budweiser, Purina and Boeing. She traveled much of the world filming on location, including in the Middle East during the last months of the Shah of Iran's regime. Susan became an eye-witness to the Islamic Revolution.

Her attraction to visual arts persisted leading to a career as an architectural interior designer and owner of an award winning Los Angeles design firm and has won competitions on several episodes of *Designer's Challenge*, an HGTV design show.

Susan wrote briefly for CBS episodic television but with a need to tell her own stories, she changed genres to write fiction. She attended the UCLA Writers Program and the advanced writers program at The University of California at Irvine, and is currently involved in a follow up writer's critique group. During this time she raced vintage autos, was director of a prominent Arts Décoratif Collectors Gallery as well as raising four children. Susan lives with her present husband, her love, and is currently finishing her next novel.

susan.angard@me.com